D1714272

THE PRESS PRAISES MARA PURL'S MILFORD-HAVEN NOVELS

Book Two – *Where the Heart Lives*

"[In] the second Milford-Haven novel, award-winning writer Mara Purl deepens the intrigue in this captivating window into the little battles, victories, successes, and failings of ordinary people in [the] complicated world [of] Milford-Haven." – *Midwest Book Review*

Book One – *What the Heart Knows*

"Former *Days of Our Lives* star Purl presents the first novel in her Milford-Haven series, which . . . features a setting of unadulterated beauty—the small coastal town of Milford-Haven, CA in the prosperous mid-'90s—and a cast of successful, sexy, sometimes quirkily independent characters. . . . Readers will find details galore . . . and the novel's many inner monologues reveal scheming, secretly confused, or flawed personalities. . . . Milford-Haven offers depictions of daily life, hints of possible future romance, the threat of scandal, and carefully parsed out mystery. . . . the novel is poised to convince readers to continue with the series." – *Publishers Weekly*

"Former *Days of Our Lives* actress Purl imbues her soap opera finesse into the fictional setting of Milford-Haven, a sleepy California coastal town. This may be Apple Pie, USA, but hearts are on the line, professions are at stake and a possible murder has tainted the landscape. A whirlwind of juicy drama with dangling-carrot closure." – *Kirkus Review*

"*What the Heart Knows* is an upbeat novel . . . the first book of Milford-Haven. The book opens powerfully . . . Purl does not use external paraphernalia to bring her characters to life. Multiple love stories, friendships, crushes. . . . Purl's characters are well-traveled, educated, and street smart." – *ForeWord Magazine*

". . . in Mara Purl's enchanting novel *What the Heart Knows* . . . although the picturesque, seaside setting of Milford-Haven plays an important role in the novel, the cast of interesting and eccentric characters is what really draws the reader into the book. Purl skillfully tackles tough environmental issues such as land development and offshore oil drilling through the lives of her characters and the events that unfold. Detailed descriptions of scenic settings, eccentric characters, and tantalizing storylines combine to make this book one that fans of romance will enjoy." – *BookWire*

"Mara Purl's *What the Heart Knows* is a first class novel by a very talented writer with strong believable characters, a rapid pace delivery of story, and very tight writing that make this novel such a delight to read. I look forward to seeing other titles in this impressive series." – *Gary Roen, Nationally Syndicated Bookreviewer*

Where the

Heart Lives

Also by MARA PURL

Fiction

What the Heart Knows
A Milford-Haven Novel (Book One)

When Hummers Dream
A Milford-Haven Story (Prequel to Book One)

When Whales Watch
A Milford-Haven Story (Prequel to Book Two)

Whose Angel Key Ring
A Milford-Haven Story

Christmas Angels
A Milford-Haven Story Collection

The Milford-Haven Novels
Early Editions

Non-Fiction

Act Right: A Manual
for the On-Camera Actor
(with Erin Gray)

Kenneth Leventhal & Co.:
A History of the Firm

S.T.A.R. –Student Theatre & Radio
High School Curriculum; College Curriculum

Plays
Mary Shelley–
In Her Own Words
(with Sydney Swire)

Dracula's Last Tour

Screenplays &
Teleplays

The Meridian Factor
(with Verne Nobles)

Welcome to
Milford-Haven
(with Katherine
Doughtie Nolan)

Guiding Light

Radio Plays

Milford-Haven, U.S.A.
(100 episodes)

Green Valley

Haven Ten

S.T.A.R.
Teleplay

Only A Test

S.T.A.R.
Radio Plays

(Twenty Trilogies)

Mara Purl

Where the Heart Lives

Book Two
A Milford-Haven Novel

Bellekeep Books

Where the Heart Lives ©2012 by Mara Purl
New Edition
No part of this book may be reproduced or transmitted in any form or by any means, electronic or mechanical, including information storage and retrieval systems, without permission in writing from the publisher, except by a reviewer who may quote brief passages in a review.
For information address: Bellekeep Books
29 Fifth Avenue, New York, NY 10003
www.BellekeepBooks.com
Front Cover – Original Watercolor by Mary Helsaple ©2010
Front, Back Covers and Jacket design by Tara Goff, Bellekeep Books &
Kevin Meyer, Amalgamated Pixels
©2012 by Milford-Haven Enterprises, LLC.
Copy Editor: Vicki Werkley. Proofreader: Jean Laidig.
Author photos: Lesley Bohm.

Milford-Haven PUBLISHING, RECORDING & BROADCASTING HISTORY
This book is based in part upon the original radio drama Milford-Haven ©1987 by Mara Purl, Library of Congress numbers SR188828, SR190790, SR194010; and upon the original radio drama Milford-Haven, U.S.A. ©1992 by Mara Purl, Library of Congress number SR232-483, which was broadcast by the British Broadcasting Company's BBC Radio 5 Network, and which is also currently in release in audio formats as Milford-Haven, U.S.A. ©1992 by Mara Purl. Portions of this material also appear on the Milford-Haven Web Site, http://www.MilfordHaven.com
© by Mara Purl.
All rights reserved.
Portions of this work were published in early editions
Test-Marketing Novelization Edition Copyright © 1998 by Mara Purl
Library of Congress Txu-846-611
Closer Than You Think Early Edition Copyright © 2006 by Mara Purl
Library of Congress TX 6-838-222

The Library of Congress has cataloged this book as follows:
Purl, Mara.
  Where the heart lives / Mara Purl.
  p. ; cm. -- (A Milford-Haven novel ; bk. 2)

  Based in part upon the original radio dramas Milford-Haven and Milford-Haven U.S.A., broadcast by BBC Radio 5 Network.
  Portions also appear on the World Wide Web at
http://www.milfordhaven.com and were published in early editions.
  ISBN: 978-1-936878-02-4

  1. Women painters--California--Fiction. 2. California--Fiction. 3. Mystery fiction. I. Title. II. Title: Milford-Haven U.S.A. (Radio program) III. Title: Milford-Haven (Radio program)

PS3566.U75 W45 2012
813/.6

Published in the U.S. by Bellekeep Books, New York
www.BellekeepBooks.com
Distributed by Midpoint Trade Books, New York
www.MidpointTrade.com
10 9 8 7 6 5 4 3 2 1
Printed in the United States of America

*This book is dedicated
to the Doobie Brothers,
for decades of uplifting music, sensitive lyrics,
great recordings, rousing concerts, and the
greatness of heart to donate generously
of their time and resources.
And to the veterans of wars—
near and far, recent and long past—
who have served, and who have waited.*

Acknowledgments

The New Edition

Thanks to my new publishers: Eric Kampmann and the entire team at Midpoint Trade Books; Margot Atwell, Patrice Samara, Kara Johnson and Tara Goff at Bellekeep Books. Thanks to my gifted editorial team: Vicki Hessel Werkley, editor; Jean Laidig, proofreader. Thanks to Mary Helsaple for exquisite watercolors for my book covers, and to Kevin Meyer and Amalgamated Pixels for superb cover design and graphics.

Thanks to my marketing team: Dianemarie and Doug Collins at DM Productions for PR and marketing; Jonatha King for MH Novels list-building and special events; Wendy Wilkinson for national magazine articles; Amber Ludwig and Sky Esser for Internet design and wizardry; Kelly Johnson for Social Media expertise and creativity.

Thanks to those who provide expertise during my research: to artists Mary Helsaple, Caren Pearson for inspiration and depth of detail; to Dr. Laurance Doyle for astronomical specifics; to Pilulaw Khus for Chumash wisdom and for her book *Earth Wisdom* co-written with Yolanda Broyles-Gonzalez; to Dr. Lou Blanck for Central Coast geology; to Carole Adams and Harrison Gruman for lighthouse history at Piedras Blancas; and to Eric Castrobran and Kim Castrobran of the USCG for lighthouse history at Point Vicente; to Joan and Jeff Stanford of Stanford Inn; to staff at the Feline Conservation Center in Rosamund, California.

Thanks to the Doobie Brothers for appearing in the original radio drama in 1992. Especially I thank dear friends John McFee, the late Keith Knudsen and the late Cornelius Bumpus, whose music will always be a joy, and who first invited me backstage. Thanks to John McFee and Marcy McFee, both of whom were original cast members of *Milford-Haven*; and to John whose musicianship led to the development of the character "Notes."

Thanks to the Doobies and to their manager Bruce Cohn for allowing me to include them in the novel, and for arranging our recent backstage video. The concerts mentioned in this book are fictionalized. They were inspired by the many concerts I've enjoyed and by the first real Doobies reunion concert, organized by Keith Knudsen and Shad Meshad as a benefit for the Vietnam Veterans Aid Foundation (now the National Veterans Foundation). The songs and albums mentioned in the story are real.

Thanks to dear friends in Cambria who've supported Milford-Haven for many years with such enthusiasm, including Elaine Evans, Kathe Tanner, Susan Berry, Simon Wilder, Freedom Barry, and Jim Buckley. Thanks to Verne Nobles for vision and commitment to the Milford-Haven Television project.

Thanks for special events: to dynamic organizations in several parts of the country for working with me to produce the community-based Milford-Haven Socie-Teas® (Possibili-Teas, Generosi-Teas, Hospitali-Teas, Creativi-Teas, and our list continues!) and to Unique Soap Boutique for the wonderful *Days Of Our Lives* events. Thanks in particular to the charities with whom I've worked on special events over the past year: Unity Shoppe (Santa Barbara); Haven House (Los Angeles); Lake Forest Women's Club literacy program (Chicago); Bethany House (Cincinnati); American Heart Association (Colorado Springs).

Thanks for book mentoring: Judith Briles, Marcella Smith, Peggy McColl, and Ellen Reid. Thanks for organization support: WWW (Women Writing the West), CLAS (California Literary Arts Society), IBPA (Independent Book Publishing Association), the Author's Guild and Author U.

Thanks to all at Haven Books for helping to create the original platform. Thanks to my mentor Louis L'Amour, who believed in my project and told me to keep going with it.

And most important of all—thanks to *you*, my readers! I'm thrilled to welcome those of you who are new to my books. And I extend a special heartfelt thanks to the core group of readers who began with the novels' early editions. I appreciate your steadfast support during my publishing journey.

The Radio Drama

Milford-Haven had its first air date in 1987, and my thanks go to KOTR in Cambria, California, our first radio home. In its next incarnation *Milford-Haven, U.S.A.* was broadcast on the BBC, thanks to Ms. Pat Ewing, Director of Radio 5—a maverick network that launched a maverick show, and celebrated with us when we reached 4.5 million listeners.

Before there were any shows to broadcast, there were the cast members, and my thanks go to both the original cast of *Milford-Haven* and to the cast of *Milford-Haven, U.S.A.*, seasoned professionals who brought my characters so vividly to life that their work is inextricably woven into the fabric of the characters themselves.

Before there were cast members to record, there had to be a studio, and my thanks go to Engineer Bill Berkuta whose Afterhours Recording Company became our studio home, a workshop in which we created one hundred episodes of the first show and sixty of the second, and where we now create audio books of the novels.

Thanks to the late great David L. Krebs, our Foley master, a gifted sound artist who created our aural reality. Thanks to Marilyn Harris and Mark Wolfram, who composed the haunting *Milford-Haven* theme and all the music cues that support the emotional ebb and flow of the story. Thanks to Warren Talcott for the intriguing *Milford-Haven* poster, and to Caren Pearson for the compelling *Milford-Haven* logo art—each of which gave our town its visual reality.

Before I created my own soap opera, there was *Days of Our Lives* and my thanks go to the producers, writers, directors and fellow cast members with whom I worked, and from whom I learned so much.

And before there was a *Milford-Haven*, there was a young woman who had always lived in cities—Tokyo, New York, Los Angeles. I spent a summer performing in a play at Jim and Olga Buckley's Pewter Plough Playhouse in Cambria, and became fascinated with the life in and of a small town. With Elaine Traxel Evans's help, I immersed myself in this new culture—admittedly seeing it through the eyes of an environmentalist—and began to realize that it was not only a local drama that was being played out in its quiet streets, but a universal one as well.

Listeners in the U.S. and in the U.K. agreed, writing to me about their own lives, their own towns, and the commonality of the situations we face globally. My thanks go to my listeners everywhere. Several years later the link with listeners was to be vividly demonstrated when the original Milford Haven in Wales embraced me as an honorary citizen and showed me those same streets, those same dramas, uncannily alike in the multi-cultural parallel universes we all inhabit. Thanks to Bruce Henrickson of the Belhaven House Hotel. Special thanks to Jim and Anne Hughes, who shared my vision even before we met, who welcomed me into their home, and with whom I continue to forge a unique town-to-town relationship.

My thanks go to my family and friends—helpful, discerning and, above all, supportive—Ray Purl, Marshie Purl, Linda Purl, Larry Norfleet, Erin Gray, Miranda Kenrick, Vickie and Bob Zoellner.

And finally my thanks go to my characters, among whom are—Jack, Zack, Miranda, Cornelius, Samantha, Rune, Meredith, Kevin, Joseph, Sally, Tony, Zelda, Notes, Susan and Cynthia, who are building, buying, painting, observing, planning, rehearsing, advising, cogitating, dominating, dishing, traveling, conniving, playing, sneaking and seducing, respectively.

Dear Reader,

Welcome back to Milford-Haven! And if this is your first visit—it is my pleasure to introduce you to my favorite little town and to its many residents, all of whom are described in the Cast of Characters at the back of the book.

The first step in plotting your way to a delicious getaway might be opening a map. For pure escape, might you choose a place that would give you a chance to wander through a pristine pine forest or sink your toes into untrodden sand, invite you to browse through shops, tempt you to have a home-cooked meal or enjoy a cup of tea overlooking the ocean?

The second step in choosing your destination might be ignoring where your *head* tells you to go, and listening to where your *heart* guides. What if your intuition could be trusted to navigate as well as your logic does? Milford-Haven is a little town full of as many possibilities as you can fit in your imagination. As you read about its residents, my hope is that you'll resonate with your *own* possibilities.

You may read these books out of sequence, but I think you'll enjoy them most reading them as I wrote them. *Where the Heart Lives* is the second novel, and short stories will continue to augment the story as well, including the prequel to this book, *When Whales Watch.*

Though my series is a saga, each book has a beginning, middle and end. Each Prologue proceeds with the investigation of journalist Chris Christian's disappearance. The heart of the story is seen through the artist-eyes of Miranda Jones. And each novel's themes are concluded by environmentalist Samantha Hugo in her ongoing journals.

In each novel beginning with this one, we leave Milford-Haven to follow Miranda Jones to destinations that fascinate her painter's eye and her restless heart. This novel takes her—and you—to my own home town of Los Angeles: from its western border at the Pacific Ocean, to its towering Angeles Crest mountain range, into the expanse of the adjacent Mojave Desert. And in its heart, we go backstage and on-stage at the Hollywood Bowl with a major rock-and-roll band.

While we're on this external journey across a beautiful stretch of California's map, might we also be on a journey of the heart, mapping goals, desires, and a deepening purpose?

As the story unfolds, follow my footsteps over the inter-connected pathways of those who inhabit Milford-Haven, and come to sense your real home is . . . where the heart lives.

"Home is where the heart is."

– Pliny the Elder

"Wherever you go, go with all your heart."

– Confucius

"Go where he will, the wise man is at home."

– Ralph Waldo Emerson

"When we listen to the soul's desire,
 we find where the heart lives."

– from Samantha Hugo's Journal

Prologue

Senior Deputy Delmar Johnson, startled at a tapping sound, darted a look around his shadowed office.

Just the rain . . . or the wind. There it was again. *Like someone's knocking to get in.* His scalp prickling, he pushed back from his desk. Remaining seated, he interlaced his long fingers and reached overhead to stretch his back.

Still, he couldn't shake his feeling of foreboding. Highway 1 stretched past his window, a slick ribbon of asphalt devoid of traffic. He'd stayed in his office long enough that now it was dark outside. Daylight hours had grown short, and December rains doused the Central Coast much of the day—again.

Television journalist Christine Christian was still listed as a missing person. *Hate to think of anyone stuck out in this weather . . . living . . . or dead. Plenty of people in the "Missing" files. Seven weeks, now, and no one seems to know what's happened to the popular broadcaster.*

According to the satellite station where she had a contract,

Christian had planned to drive north to the Bay Area to do seismic research for a few days. Then she'd been scheduled to fly to Tokyo from the local airport. *That makes sense . . . study earthquakes in San Francisco, and in Japan.* She'd never made her flight, however, and never turned up anywhere else.

When her boss reported her missing, the sheriff's department had checked her Santa Maria condo, but found nothing amiss, and her rent paid for months in advance. Her car wasn't at her residence and hadn't been discovered at the airport.

Though there were no real leads, Del did have a police sketch of an unnamed man who'd visited Sally's Restaurant in Milford-Haven. Owner Sally O'Mally herself had seen and talked to this guy, who'd said at the time he was looking for the journalist. But circulation of both that sketch and Christine's photograph, had yielded nothing further, at which point the case had been filed away. Officially, Del had let it go. Yet something about the case wouldn't let go of *him.*

Why does a successful journalist—on her way to what sounds like an exciting trip—suddenly fall off the radar? According to the DMV, she owned a black Ford Explorer. *If, instead of taking the more usual 101, she drove Highway 1 . . . all those treacherous curves along the coast . . . that black car of hers could be hidden at the bottom of some steep ravine or even submerged in a rocky cove. Might take us months to locate it.*

On the other hand, she wouldn't be the first person who'd decided to slip away from a job—or from a relationship.

There'd been nothing new for weeks. But now the cold case could be warming up. Today's call wasn't a break exactly, but at least it could be a starting point.

Mr. Joseph Calvin—a wealthy icon of Santa Barbara

society—had reported a connection with the journalist, but had asked that Captain Sandoval oversee the matter personally.

Sandoval had assigned Detective Dexter. *And for some reason, Dex wants me in on the interview with him. And he said not to be in uniform.* Apparently, Calvin had called to explain that—though he didn't feel he had any actual information relevant to Ms. Christian's disappearance—he did know her, and thought it likely he'd seen her close to the time she must've gone missing. He'd added that he'd like to keep his cooperation as discreet as possible. Otherwise, the press would probably have their typical field day, which would not only be unpleasant for him, but might also harm their investigation.

Dex had placed the call and discovered that the earliest time Mr. Calvin could be available was this evening. Though he'd be at a charity function, he'd cut it short and return to his residence for a ten p.m. meeting with Dexter and Johnson.

Time to hit the road. Del wondered what it'd be like for a bastion of white society to be questioned in his home late at night, especially with one white officer, and one black. *You never know how someone will feel about race until you get past the first veneer of manners.*

Del pulled on his all-weather jacket and headed outside. Making sure the building was locked, he pressed his vehicle's keyless entry remote, its mechanical chirp still an uncommon sound on the Central Coast. One of the perks of being a member of the Special Problems Unit was access to four-by-four vehicles. The Suburban coughed into activity and, a few moments later, settled into a deep, growling purr as it gathered speed.

For the moment, this stretch of Highway 1 appeared safe

and clear. But the mean streets of his own childhood in South Central L.A. sometimes rose out of the dark to haunt him. If a car backfired, he always first assumed it was a gunshot, his body reflexively tensing, his senses coming to full alert. Even after twenty-six months on the Central Coast, he hadn't yet unlearned those inner-city reactions. *Perhaps,* he thought as the Suburban ate up the miles, *I never will. Indeed, perhaps I never should.*

Though he still had much to learn about his new area, he'd been spending some of his free time browsing local libraries. The San Luis Obispo County Library system turned out to have several branches along the north-south route Del routinely traveled, each with its own distinct character. The hub was in SLO—thanks to a 1905 grant from Andrew Carnegie that established the first library in the county. One of his favorite branches was the Morro Bay, with its colorful murals; another was in the town of Cambria just south of Milford-Haven— far too cozy, now, for its small-but-committed-to-reading population.

His reading varied widely from studies of the local architecture and landscaping to its political history, surprisingly rich in multicultural lore that held a particular appeal for Del. And though Santa Barbara now occupied its own county to the south, the indigenous people who'd lived here first had seen it as one land, nestled against the coastal range. Through the centuries, it seemed new arrivals were always eager to confiscate its assets and claim its spectacular terrain for their own: first the Spanish; then the Mexicans; ultimately, the Americans.

Where I'm heading tonight was in the thick of it at one time. Interesting that's where my meeting is. The story he'd read had resonated powerfully: betrayal and dislocation, if not actual slavery. In the 1880s, the Indian Agent Thomas Hope was put in charge of protecting the Chumash who lived high on the mountains overlooking the ocean in their Kashwa Reservation. Instead, he evicted them. *Today it's known as the Hope Ranch.*

Del rolled his shoulders and blew out an exhalation. He'd kept his radio on low volume. Now, halfway to his destination, he heard, "Twenty-four-Z-four."

"Zebra-four," he answered quickly. He'd been the last to join the four-person SPU, and that had given him the number "four."

"Ten-twenty-one as soon as possible."

"Ten-four."

Ten-twenty-one meant "call base" on a closed line and twenty-four was the number for the main station at San Luis. Del used his cell phone to dial the number. *Who needs to talk with me privately without using the radio?*

"Dispatch," the sheriff's office answered.

"This is Delmar Johnson."

"I'll put you through."

The night sped by outside the Suburban, and Del watched the road. Zebra was the code name for the SPU. *Well, the old adage says "When you hear hoofbeats, think horses, not zebras."* He chuckled to himself. *That works for the usual cases. But we catch the special problems.* He got serious as his superior came back on the line.

"Dex here. Sorry to give you such short notice, but you'll have to handle the Calvin interview on your own."

"Oh?"

"I know, irregular procedure, but we're short-handed

tonight, and I'm still tied up at a situation over on the I-5. No way I can get to Santa Barbara in time."

"Should I cancel? Explain to Mr. Calvin that we could see him tomorrow?"

"No. I don't know what's so urgent, but the word came down from Sandoval that we should speak to Calvin tonight. The man'll probably be impressed by a suit ringing his doorbell so quickly after he volunteered to meet with us."

Del glanced at his sleeve. *Damn. Not wearing a suit.* "Anything in particular I should ask him?"

"No, you know what to do. Standard stuff. You have good instincts. Fill me in first thing tomorrow."

"Will do." Del closed his cell phone and kept his foot steady on the accelerator. Mr. Calvin was in for a little surprise this evening. *One officer, not two—the black one—and in casual clothes, as though I'm dropping by for a chat.*

Del was eager to gauge his response. *You can tell a lot about a guy by his first reaction to the unexpected.*

Delmar Johnson lowered the window of his SUV, inhaling as the aromas of damp eucalyptus and wood-smoke wafted in.

He brushed aside the long tendrils of an enthusiastic ivy plant to find the security button outside the gates of the Calvin estate. *Calma,* a carefully aged metal sign declared. Del had found the place easily, despite the long upward climb along a narrow road etched into the side of the mountain. *Some people call these hills. But just because the Santa Ynez Range starts at sea level doesn't mean these aren't true mountains. And these twisting lanes bordered with lush plantings and high walls must conceal sumptuous estates.* He'd have preferred seeing the scenery in golden afternoon sunlight, but even at night—with uplights illuminating the towering trees—the area was beautiful.

"Yes," squawked the speaker on the ivy-covered wall.

"Deputy Johnson!" announced Del, his voice crashing through the still night air.

A low hum resonated with the smooth motion of a well-oiled gate as it swung slowly inward. The driveway then sloped back down toward the ocean and a Y-intersection came into view with a sign pointing in each direction. A right arrow indicated *Service Entrance;* the left arrow was labeled *Main Entrance & Cottages.* Taking the left, Del stepped on the accelerator to travel the final quarter-mile around and down to the level site of the main house.

This must be it . . . a circular driveway in front of the entrance. Old California they call this. Built in the style of the Santa Barbara Mission.

He noticed that the driveway continued onward, apparently toward the cottages—whoever used them. But he parked at the main house and crunched across gravel, then walked up the three wide steps. By the illumination of wrought-iron wall sconces on either side of the entrance, he took in the details of the heavy carved oak front door and its seasonal décor, an elaborate pine wreath festooned with gilded cones and shiny red berries. *Real, or fake?* Just as Del's hand reached up to touch the wreath, the door opened abruptly, and he yanked his arm back to his side.

Del looked into the cool, gray eyes of a handsome, well-dressed man who stood about his own height of six-foot-two.

Mid-sixties, fit, self-assured. Silver hair neatly trimmed and perfectly groomed; tan sweater, probably cashmere; high polish on expensive loafers. Must be Joseph Calvin.

"Good evening, Detective." The man looked past Del into the dark. "Weren't there supposed to be two of you?"

"I'm afraid Detective Dexter has been detained and won't be able to get here in time. I'm Deputy Johnson."

"I see. Come in. I'm Joseph Calvin, by the way." He paused in the doorway only long enough to let Del enter, then spun on his heel, leaving Del to close the front door. As Calvin led the way into his home, the footsteps of the two men echoed on terra cotta tile, the sounds rising through the high atrium of the central stairway. Del's nostrils flared at the spicy scent of cut lilies that perfumed the chill air from their perch on a foyer table.

As they entered a spacious room lined with bookshelves, Mr. Calvin began, "I appreciate your meeting me this late. I thought we'd talk here in my library. Please have a seat. My butler has the night off, but I'll go get us some mineral water. Please make yourself comfortable. I'll be right back."

Before sitting, Del took the moment to take in the hand-wrought elegance of the home—what he could see of it. *I've only seen a home like this in photographs at the library. It's obvious nothing in here is mass-produced. The exterior is the traditional Spanish style of El Pueblo Viejo, like the County Courthouse and the Lobero Theatre with paseos, courtyards, cornices. And inside, these open spaces, but with alcoves tucked into corners; that arched hallway leading off from the foyer, maybe to the kitchen, but who knows? And I think this fireplace is made from cantera stone.* Though massive, it sent forth a glow that warmed the room and gleamed softly on the oversized mahogany desk.

Del walked toward the desk and, before sitting as Calvin had suggested, he angled one of the carved chairs so his back wouldn't face the door.

Calvin returned, walked to the far side of his desk and placed a tray with two bottles of designer sparkling water. "Hope you don't mind drinking from the bottles."

"No, not at all." *Interesting way to start this . . . with the master of the mansion serving me.* Del twisted the cap off the cold glass container, listening to the hiss of escaping gas. "Appreciate it."

Calvin, now seated in his high-backed leather swivel chair, said, "I . . . I really don't know how much I can tell you, but I want you to know I take this matter very seriously. Chris—Ms. Christian—is a friend of mine. I'm worried about her."

"I see." As Del shifted his weight to reach into the inside breast pocket for his notebook, his leather belt creaked. He adjusted the belt, wincing as his keys and cell phone case scraped against the beautiful chair. Before he could stop himself, Del glanced up at his host, realizing he must look as guilty as he felt. *Last thing I need to do is damage the man's property.* "Sorry if I—"

"Not a problem," Calvin interrupted.

The two men sat in silence for a moment, sipping their drinks. Aware that Calvin was likely taking his measure, Del did the same, using his police training to keep his face neutral. Calvin's expression seemed to him tightly controlled. *A hard man . . . in his own way maybe as hard a man as any I've collared and cuffed. How will he respond if I don't begin the interview?*

Calvin looked at him. "So, shall we get started?"

"If you don't mind." *Doesn't seem uncomfortable even though we're alone . . . or with my being just a deputy . . . or even with my being black.*

Calvin lounged back in his deep library chair, his demeanor suddenly more relaxed, and gave Del an expectant look.

"You last saw Ms. Christian exactly when, Mr. Calvin?" Del held his pen poised over a blank page in his blank notebook, moving it the moment the man spoke.

"It's been a while now . . . seven weeks or so." Calvin shifted position in his chair and crossed his legs.

"Seven weeks? You must've known she was missing. You didn't worry till now?"

"She travels a lot. Overseas, for example. Some of her stories are shot in Asia, some in Europe. She keeps me posted, usually. She was leaving on a trip, going to San Francisco, then to Tokyo. She missed our last appointment, but her plans could sometimes change suddenly. I figured she'd get in touch with me when she wanted to."

"And where did your last encounter take place?" Del looked up from his spiral pad, catching a wistful look on Calvin's face. *The man does seem to have genuine affection for the missing woman.*

"It wasn't an encounter, Deputy. It was a date. She, uh . . . we met at her place in Santa Maria. She'd invited me over—she was working late . . . I didn't get there till about eleven. We'd both been too tired to, uh . . . for any sort of entertainment that night. We simply went to sleep. We both had early appointments the following morning."

"And you left on friendly terms?" Del used the flat tones of a practiced professional, insinuating nothing into his question.

Calvin recrossed his legs and cleared his throat. "Yes, very friendly. We, uh, we were intimate that morning. Although we *were* interrupted."

Del looked up. "By what, sir?"

"A phone call. *Again!*" Calvin looked out the window into the dark, his brows knitting into a deep furrow.

"You find these calls she receives . . . irritating?"

"She doesn't have good boundaries. Be nice if she could turn the damn machine off once in a blue moon."

Now there's heat in the man's voice, color rising up his neck. "Did you have an argument?"

"A disagreement," Calvin admitted, "even though she didn't pick up." He paused. "But she did listen to a voice message. I overheard it. That call altered her mood."

"So . . . Ms. Christian has some kind of voice messaging? There was no answering machine in the preliminary report." Del's mind leaped forward. *Is the message still there? Does anyone else have access? Could they have erased it?*

"Yes, yes, she's a journalist, of course she has an answering machine. She often tucks it out of sight. But she never turns the blasted thing off. Drives me crazy." Calvin's voice dropped, choked off by the anxiety that seemed to rise by the minute.

Del edged forward in his chair. "Mr. Calvin, to your knowledge, did Ms. Christian erase that message?"

"Not while I was there." Calvin composed himself, uncrossed his legs. "We both dressed in a hurry after that," he continued. "She seemed distracted, rushed. I had an early business meeting. We made another date—a make-up date, we called it . . . literally, in this case—for that very evening, before she was due to take her trip. That morning we had a quick bite—toast and coffee, I think—then left immediately. I opened her car door for her in the parking garage—and watched her drive away before doing the same myself." He paused again. "I never saw or heard from her again."

"What was in the message you overheard?"

"It's been a while now. I don't recall the details. But it was a man's voice saying something about a time frame having changed, and that she had to go to some house if she wanted the story."

"Perhaps we should start there, sir."

"I'm sorry, where, Deputy?"

"The last place you were with Ms. Christian. At her residence."

Joseph leaned forward in his high-backed desk chair. "I . . . it'd be terribly odd being there without her—"

"Her permission? I think she'd want your help, don't you?"

Calvin sighed. "I do. Yes."

"In that case, could we make an appointment sometime this week to meet at her apartment? Seeing it again might spark a suppressed memory. You might notice something missing that we wouldn't be aware of. And you could show us where she keeps the answering machine. Could prove helpful to our investigation." *Best to get a commitment from him right now.* "What day would work for you?"

Calvin glanced toward the dark window again and, as though reading his calendar on the pane, he said, "Today's Wednesday. Friday's no good, because we have a big party here that evening and I have to be here all day." Turning to Del, he continued, "I think tomorrow afternoon would work, Deputy. Call my secretary to confirm the time."

"I'll do that. And I'll clear this with Detective Dexter, see if he can come with us, or meet us there."

"Either way, Deputy. It's also fine if it's just you and me at Chris's home."

Del nodded. "All right. In any case, I'll call you to confirm, Mr. Calvin." Del put away his notebook, finished his water, and stood. "The department will appreciate your cooperation."

Calvin saw him to the front door, and as it closed behind him, Del saw the rain had turned to a light drizzle that misted the grounds. He glanced at the circular drive, its exits marked by illuminated end posts. Each lantern seemed to hover, framed by a ghostly rainbow, the particulates of moisture that still hung in the air acting as tiny prisms. *And that's how a case gets solved . . . each clue acting like a lens.*

He inhaled again the pungent aroma from the eucalyptus trees laced with smoke from Calvin's fireplace. *The missing woman probably stood right here, inhaling this same fragrance, enjoying time here with Joseph Calvin.*

Calvin's connection to her . . . the fact that he's now revealed more than we knew. . . . It opens up a whole new avenue of inquiry, gives us something solid. Maybe we can find Christine Christian.

Light shot through the kaleidoscope in her consciousness and made a new geometry of her soul. When had colors been so vivid . . . complexity of design so pure?

Yet even as she yearned to touch it, flow through its matrix, lose herself to the rainbow of light and become its prism, something tugged at the edges of memory.

Christine. *It seemed a nice name—a familiar one.* Pristine Christine … *a childhood song echoed but she regarded the taunt as though from a great distance.*

Now an urgency began to press like a weight against her chest. A few moments ago—or was it a few weeks?—she'd wanted to breathe. Now that seemed irrelevant.

But something else prodded insistently. Yes, there it was— the need to tell.

She remembered now. The story—she had a story to tell, but she didn't have all the details yet. She'd tried to write it. But first there was more research to be done.

The details began to come back into focus, and with them the anxiety increased. What had she done wrong? She'd been smart, diligent, kept her priorities: delayed her dinner date, gone to the house on the bluff to follow the lead, meet her source.

The reporter's instinct that still pulsed within her said danger was still coming closer. That story was the urgency pulling at her, dragging her back to the human circumstances, holding her in the dark. She had to get this story done in time.

Deadline.

The word carried with it the weight of the world.

Chapter 1

The winter storm that lurked just off shore pummeled the Central Coast, punching the already bruised sky and jabbing without mercy at the little town of Milford-Haven.

Miranda Jones shuddered in the chill, startled each time the wind rattled her studio windows. It'd wakened her in the pre-dawn, moaning through the eaves, shaking the trees near her deck and chasing her from her cozy downstairs bedroom. Her new kitten had preferred to stay snuggled in the covers. *Shadow had no interest in coming with me. I knew she was a smart kitty.*

A persistent dripping beat a rhythm from somewhere nearby. *Don't know if this is a new drip or an old one. Depends how well the landlord keeps up with maintenance. I suppose it's no surprise in this storm. I'm still getting used to winter here . . . maybe this is typical.*

The rain that cascaded down the mountains slapped the siding, drenched her tall pines, and tumbled down her small yard, gathering speed as it raced to join the surf pounding at the rocky coastline half a mile away.

Yanking again at the wool socks that'd fallen to pool at her ankles, she zipped up her fleece top, then carefully stepped around the edges of the maps she'd spread out. She sat cross-legged on her studio floor to examine them more closely by the hinged light clamped to the edge of her desk.

The scattered sheets made as colorful a display as if she'd chosen eclectic prints for a possible gallery showing. Were she to arrange them end-to-end, they'd actually look something like her favorite quilt over on the daybed.

Such a special gift. I love it now even more than when Mer gave it to me. The quilt of puffed cotton squares—printed with reproductions of her own landscape paintings—had been a house-warming gift. In good weather, it kept the chill away when she relaxed in the hammock on her deck. Now that winter had truly arrived, it draped cozily at the foot of the daybed occupying the studio's far corner.

Her gaze returned to the maps—more representational than much of her own work, yet in some ways more richly layered, and certainly more embedded with metaphor and meaning.

Representational . . . yes, the art of cartography, where each printed object represents a thing or a thought. Red lines stand for interstate highways, thin orange indicate state roads; pale blue for ocean and lakes contrasts with tan for land that's punctuated with light green areas for state and national parks, dark green for mountain ridges.

What else made them different? She scooted closer to her desk, then reached up to grab the magnifying glass she kept handy. Holding it over the closest map, she bent over to inspect the image.

The lettering! Yes, unlike my work, these art pieces contain words. Moving the lens over different portions of the image, she pondered the significance of the written designations. *Of course, they give the names of the streets, the counties, the highways. But these are not just words, they're graphical elements too.* Fascinated, she focused on one of the tiny words. *They're fonts, carefully chosen so each style of printing represents something specific, just the way colors do.*

Fatigue seeped around the edges of her mind as she bent over the maps, and as her eyelids drifted down, the images blurred for a moment as she pondered the blues of the waters, the greens of the terra forms . . . almost as if they were under water.

Colors swirl in liquid patterns, funnel into rivulets, form into drops. Drip . . . drip . . . Where am I? In a boat. Is water getting in?

The thought jolted her awake—which is when she realized she'd nodded off. *Did I hear more of that dripping?* She stood to walk the perimeter of her studio, touching windowsills to ensure nothing felt wet.

That's good. But my miniatures are leaning against the desk windows. Maybe I'll move them for now. She took the one finished image in its small frame, and the five studies for the new one, and slid them away from the panes. She also moved away the short stack of postcards, picking up the top one to study it for a moment.

It really is a good reproduction of my Milford-Haven

watercolor—the colors vivid, Main Street beckoning, Pacific sparkling blue at the end of the street.

Her manager Zelda had ordered a thousand of them to be printed—and distributed that many in a week. They'd been so well received, sales of Miranda's full-sized paintings had spiked, at least temporarily. Marketing of her work was beyond Miranda's ken, but Zelda seemed to know exactly what she was doing.

Between them they now seemed to have created a monster. "It's time for the next postcard," Zelda had announced recently. *That's Zelda McIntyre—always has an angle.* Furthermore, she wanted it in time for Christmas. Miranda'd resisted at first, not liking the notion that commerce would drive her artistic endeavors.

She thought back to why she'd started creating the small images. Her idea had been not only to celebrate her new home, but to chronicle what was turning out to be a significant internal journey. *Not so much a logical one. More of an intuitive adventure, a heart-journey.*

At first, she'd been inspired to paint something for each season. These were—literally and figuratively—external works, and she'd satisfied that urge by completing four Japanese calligraphy pieces. When it came to the miniature watercolors, her concept had expanded to mark something more internal: the seasons of her life. They were becoming visual metaphors. *First was the season of finding my own home; now it seems to be the season of remapping my life.*

That's why maps had captured her fancy for the second postcard. The more she studied them, the more she understood they stood for both journey and destination, content and context. She wanted an original watercolor by her own hand that'd be not of the town, but of the whole California Central Coast. Somehow it seemed a perfect bridge from past to present, and from her own roots to the branches she was developing. She'd done rough studies of the image. Now she was refining it.

She thought about the inevitable postcard Zelda would print of the new image. *Of course, Zelda took the "seasonal" idea literally. She's probably expecting Christmas trees and a Santa walking down Main Street. She probably won't approve this image at all. But it feels right to me.*

Miranda did a quick mental checklist on her current works, dividing it into what she thought of as "elsewhere" and "local." On the "elsewhere list," the San Diego Zoo commission had been very well received; her painting of Lia the Cheetah was now being reproduced in their marketing material. And, according to Zelda, they would be doing an opening at which Miranda would be honored. *That leaves the Cove commission for Zack . . . and I seem to have painter's block on that one.*

Skipping over the uncomfortable subject, she checked through her "local" list. *The sea otters painting is finished, and already at Finder's.* A whimsical piece, she'd titled it *You Otter Sea Me Play*, which Nicole at the Gallery had liked even better than Zelda. *I got the heart cockle shell done for Shelly for her store.* And she smiled as she thought of the last thing currently on her local list: a mural at Sally's Restaurant. Her friend Sally had asked for a *trompe l'oeil* painting to cover one whole wall. *I've got it sketched out. When I've added the color, I'll take a photo, then develop it as a slide. That way I can project it onto her wall as I paint it.*

Miranda stretched and glanced around her work space. Reassured that her home was tight and secure, she also felt gratified at the increased order she'd managed to establish since autumn. She took a moment to assess this artist-zone. Two walls were taken up with windows, which was why she'd chosen this room as her studio.

One wall she'd left as a hanging area where pieces could dry, be examined or compared, or just be enjoyed until they were shipped out to a gallery, bought by a client, or framed and hung elsewhere in her own home. *The four long, tall sumi-e studies I did last October—one for each season—I sort of miss them on that wall. But they look perfect framed in my bedroom, almost like a Japanese screen.*

Against the upper half of the fourth wall, she'd had her friend Kevin construct a built-in set of shelves. Below it nestled the daybed, which she sometimes used as another surface for spreading prints or paintings, and sometimes used as a reading nook. *And if Mer or anyone else ever comes to visit, this can be a guest room, I suppose.* As her gaze lingered on the daybed, it suddenly seemed so appealing. *Sure would be softer than the floor.*

She bent down to scoop the maps up and onto the more comfortable surface. As she did, the crisp papers rattled, triggering a childhood memory of road trips with her family. Her mother would have a map spread out in her lap, her father would ask, "Here? You're sure you want me to turn here?" "Yes! For heaven's sake, Charles, why else would you entrust the job to me?" Dad would jerk the wheel to the right. Mother would press herself back into her seat. She and her sister would giggle at the whole thing. *Well . . . now I'm my own navigator.*

Settling herself against the cushions, Miranda spread out the improvised atlas she'd assembled. The largest sheet was her road map of California—the very one she'd used on her first drive down the coast from San Francisco sixteen months earlier. Her finger traced the familiar landmarks of the Bay Area: San Rafael and Mill Valley, Berkeley and Richmond. But at this scale, distances were deceptive, with Interstate 5 a cheerful red slash tracing the length of the state. Small cities were nothing more than dots, and smaller communities, like Milford-Haven, didn't even appear. *Better that way . . . a secret haven.*

Switching to a Bay Area map, she smoothed its folds, saw its shapes and colors . . . the narrow waterway leading in from the Pacific . . . the matched set of bays, San Francisco's to the south, and to the north, the San Pablo. Her gaze traced back down past San Rafael to the next peninsula, easily identifying Tiburon, then Belvedere, where she'd grown up in her family's home. The "Jones Joint," her childhood friends had called it, making light of the fact that she and her older sister had lived in a mansion. It also referred to the well-appointed game room she and her friends had turned into a private club of sorts.

But that was twenty years ago. There were plenty of wide-open spaces where we played outside too. Now the area is getting so densely populated. Heard there were public hearings last May . . . a group trying to get permission to build fifty homes on one hundred twenty-five acres. At least the Tiburon Uplands Nature Preserve is still there.

That whole area of Marin County—oceans and bays, foothills and mountains—had been her proverbial "oyster" when she was a kid, a safe place full of natural beauty that taught her to love colors and shapes, birds and animals, hiking and biking.

Yet, somehow that same region—and its sparkling city across the Golden Gate bridge—had taught her sister to value elegance and style, money and power. *Mer used all the irritations of childhood to make herself a pearl. But for me, the place was a shell from which I needed to escape.*

"Home" now meant something different than it had before her move here, more than a year earlier. Her parents' objections at her relocating to an obscure and faraway town had at first been lengthy and loud; now her folks were sullen and passively disapproving. She'd argued the town was closer than it seemed on the map. But secretly she'd celebrated at how much distance she'd been able to attain.

Miranda glanced up at one long row of windows—black rectangles that glistened with rain spots, but offered no exterior view at the moment, not with her interior lights on. *Doesn't sound as noisy out there now. Maybe the storm's passing.*

Turning her attention back to her collection, she reached for the map labeled "Los Angeles." The scope of the urban sprawl set her teeth on edge. *How do people there deal with the freeways, the traffic, the distances?* She glanced over at the 1996 Thomas Guide map book for Los Angeles and Orange Counties. *The book is twelve-by-nine and at least an inch thick! How will I ever find my way? Well, maybe if I just stick close to the coast?*

Thinking about navigating the California terrain reminded her of the new miniature she'd decided to paint, and she zeroed in on a regional map of the Central Coast. *What'll be the borders for my own small piece? Monterey to the north and Santa Barbara to the south? Yes, that seems about right.* To confirm, she looked at the topography just to the south, where Oxnard and Port Hueneme appeared to be the start of the next region, paired with the Channel Islands. Of course, according to her friend Kuyama, a Chumash elder, the whole of this coastal area from Monterey to Malibu had originally been home to her tribal people. *I'd love for my watercolor to include the whole Chumash area down to Malibu. But that would make everything so small.*

She yawned and her eyes began to water. *So tired. Maybe I'll just lean back against the pillows . . . rest my eyes.* She slid the maps carefully to the floor and grasped the edge of her quilt, pulling it up over her shoulders.

I wanted to go for a bike ride this morning. But not in this weather. After this storm, it'll be days before the mud subsides enough for the trail to be passable. It was as she pictured herself clicking on her helmet that Miranda sank into sleep.

As the dream began, Miranda steered her mountain bike to the side of the dirt trail and put one foot on the ground to steady herself in the wind. She wiped sweat from her brow, took a long pull of water from her bike bottle and looked up to see how much farther she'd have to climb.

She stepped back into the pedals and kept her derailer in its lowest gear to negotiate the rest of the hill. About a hundred more strokes'll bring me to the brink. *Standing in the pedals, she pulled at the handlebars and lunged for the top, allowing herself an anticipatory smile. But when she crested the hill and looked down, she was startled to find the town she expected to see nestled below her was, in fact, still only a dot on the horizon.*

How can that be? I know this coastal trail so well.

She paused and faced west, trying to orient herself. To her right, the edge of California snaked its way north against a dull winter ocean. To her left, the southbound trail curved back into coastal pines and darkening woods.

This should be the turn. Why can't I see the homes in Milford-Haven?

Confused, she argued that if she just kept going, she'd recognize her location. Yet, in the back of her mind, a nasty suspicion murmured. You're lost. So lost, you'll be stuck out here on the trail for days. First you'll run out of water. Then you'll run out of steam. You'll never get home. It's much farther than you think.

Ignoring the voice, she rode on and came to a clearing. She could still hear the waves lapping below, but now she also heard a wind sighing high overhead through the hundred-foot pines.

This clearing . . . I'm here again. But how did I actually get here? *She knew why the place looked familiar. She'd first seen it in her mind as a young teen. Mrs. Flood's assignment in seventh grade: design your dream house.* My favorite assignment—ever. *Under her drawing Miranda'd written the words: "where mountains meet ocean, where art meets science, where heart meets heart." Later she'd added sketches to her teen diary: a mountain at the edge of a sea; two overlapping hearts; a constellation reflected in a well.*

One of the drawings appeared in front of her and, as she watched, the original black-and-white began to morph into a colorful image. I recognize this. It's my first miniature, the one of Milford-Haven that became the first postcard.

But here, lost in the woods, she tried to make sense of the three phrases. "Where mountains meet ocean." Okay, I'm riding a mountain trail next to the ocean. *"Where art meets science."* That makes sense. My work is my art. My art is a science. But "where heart meets heart" doesn't track because I'm still alone here. Maybe if I could get a higher perspective.

Suddenly Miranda felt her body lighten and the ground begin to fall away. Higher and higher she rose, watching breathlessly as the coastal region below her resolved itself into . . . my map! My mind couldn't locate it, but my heart knew the spot instinctively, intuitively. This is just what I needed . . . a bird's eye view so I can find my way home. I feel like I'm an eagle, able to see everything in such detail!

She spread her arms, thrilling at the sudden ability to embrace the horizon and hover in the sky. But then, just as suddenly, a horrible realization began to dawn. I may feel like I'm flying . . . but I'm no eagle . . . I can't really fly! *She flapped her arms in a futile gesture, panic beginning to engulf her.* How will I get down safely?

Something tugged at her shoulders and she lifted her hands, touching straps. I'm . . . in a harness. . . . *She looked straight up, where a silken cloud seemed to billow.* I have a parachute!

She watched as, over her head, white fabric filled with air until it formed a perfect dome. Now, she looked down. Sunlight threw a circular shadow on the ground, its darker perimeter outlining Milford-Haven as the circle's center began to glow. Like it's showing my safe landing zone.

She breathed a sigh of relief as the ground drew closer, until she began to drift off course. It's okay . . . I can use my toggles. Use your head! *Reflexively, she pulled on the right toggle, but it took her further off-course.* No . . . I want to use my intuition!

Now she yanked on the left toggle, but it was too late, the ground approaching too fast as she veered helplessly away from the drop zone.

When she landed, she took a moment to breathe. The parachute has disappeared . . . and here's my bike. *She looked down the long slope ahead and blinked in disbelief, for there, stretched out below, she saw the unmistakable angles of her family home: the gabled roofs, the high surrounding walls, the long curving private drive.*

This doesn't make sense. The whole time I was biking, was I pedaling in the wrong direction? *She reached into her rear pocket for her compass, but somewhere along the way, it must've fallen out.*

It's not fair. All that work! And I haven't gotten anywhere! *How could all she desired seem so much farther away than ever before? How could she be so much closer to what she'd already outrun? She nearly succumbed to a sinking feeling of dread as she watched the gates to her parents' home open like the mouth of a dragon.* "No!" *she declared, and the tableau froze to a still photograph.*

I did create a new home for myself, *she insisted.* I found a new sense of self, forged a new sense of faith. All that cannot have disappeared!

Grabbing the handlebars, she mounted her bike, but her legs seemed heavy as lead, her neck welded to her body. Using every molecule of strength she could summon, she forced herself to turn away from the house, but the trail seemed to have disappeared. Where is the path? There must be a greater Spirit. If so, I need your help!

Then, in a dull thicket, a dim vestige of the path appeared. Without hesitation, she plunged into the overgrown trail. Head down, eyes nearly closed against scraping branches, she pedaled, pushing till her thigh muscles burned and tears streamed down her cheeks. It might have been moments or it might have been days, but she pressed on till the trail opened and she made her way back to the high, windswept clearing. Trees towered on nearby mountains and the ocean undulated far below.

Where mountains meet ocean. *She'd seen it before—yes, in another dream. A place to paint, a place to chart with her mind and map with her heart. She had work to do! For this place must never again be lost.*

And then she knew she wouldn't be here alone. She'd met him here before, could remember his touch, as though born recognizing it.

She knew his voice, the scent of his skin, the warmth of his hands where they held and stroked. She remembered the weight of him pressing on and into her, heart beating to heart till the rhythms overlapped. Where heart meets heart.

But where was he now? He didn't come to meet her this time. There was no reunion, only the memory. Or was it a foreshadowing? Am I supposed to wait for him to find me? Or maybe he'll call me to meet him another time.

And how would she find this place again? She could sketch these trees, the lay of the land . . . pencil in boulders, distinctive branches, broken stumps. But she'd have to do more—draw a detailed map to scale, using tools for measurements and a magnifying glass. Where art meets science.

In the distance, a bell began to ring. No, not a bell. A phone? Maybe that's him calling me now.

Miranda reached from under the quilt to grasp the handset. Placing it to her ear, she said nothing, waiting to hear his voice.

"Hello?"

Something's wrong. That's not a man's voice.

"Miranda? Are you there?"

Miranda's eyes flew open. *What? Where . . . in my studio! And I'm holding my phone!* "Uh . . . hello?"

"Well, *there* you are. Good heavens, I thought something was wrong when the machine didn't pick up. But I'm glad you're hard at work already. I just wanted to tell you I have a brilliant idea, and it just couldn't wait."

The voice of Zelda, her artist-rep, had plummeted into the depths of Miranda's dream, yanking her back to the surface. Heart pounding, mouth dry, she blinked and sat up on her daybed. *Nothing like a call from Zelda to bring me back to reality. Sunlight's still pale, so it can't be later than seven.*

"Miranda? Are you still there?"

"Yes." *Wish I had a glass of water.*

"That miniature you told me you're doing—the map—well, at first I thought you'd missed a golden opportunity, given the holidays are almost upon us."

"I figured you'd think—"

"Yes, yes," Zelda pressed on. "Well, I've changed my mind. It came to me, you see, if you really care about this little town of yours as much as you say you do, this could be quite the golden opportunity."

"Sorry, Zelda, I'm not sure what you mean."

"Putting Milford-Haven On the Map!"

Miranda considered for a moment. "You're right. That'd make a nice title for the piece."

"No, no, it could be much more than just the title. This postcard can be their marketing piece for the new year!"

"I'm not sure who you mean. Isn't this postcard going to be sent out like the first one to market my paintings?"

"You're not grasping what I'm saying, Miranda dear."

When she calls me "dear" she's just about out of patience. "No, I'm not."

"So." She spoke more slowly now, as though enunciating would elucidate her meaning to her dim-witted client. "You're going to the trouble of creating a map of Milford-Haven so people can actually *find* the town, am I right?"

"Well, I suppose—"

"That's it, you see. This could be of tremendous benefit to the town itself, the town fathers, or the Chamber of Commerce, or the Town Council, whatever governing body exists in such a small place. It could be their new campaign: 'Putting Milford-Haven On the Map'!"

"Oh."

"Yes! Think of the synergy!"

"Uh-huh."

"In fact, *I* could take this to the Town Council, if you like. I imagine they'll be so impressed they'll swoon."

Miranda couldn't imagine Lorraine, the octogenarian head of the Town Council, swooning over anything—not even a boa constrictor in her bathtub.

"Marketing and PR gurus plot for a year to come up with something this cleverly multipurposed! I just had to let you know. Now get back to work! Ta-ta."

Still speechless, Miranda sat there holding the silenced phone for a moment longer, then replaced it in its cradle. *Is she always that high-energy? Probably. But I'm usually awake for the onslaught.*

Her gaze fell to the maps on the floor. *Did I just dream about them?* She darted a glance out the window, as though that's where she could find a dream-fragment, but it eluded her, as dreams usually did.

Just then the sound of a tiny "Pew" reached her, and she looked toward the studio door in time to see her kitten step around its edge, the black fur giving her the appearance of a small shadow in the lightening room.

Last fall, when Miranda'd nearly finished the fourth of her oversized sumi-e paintings, she added a final flourish near its bottom edge, not quite sure why she had. At the time, she'd thought it resembled a small cat.

Now, she watched the tiny feline staring up at her. *She really does look like that little brush stroke. Talk about foreshadowing.* Laughing at the serendipity of the joke, Miranda stood, then bent over to scoop her pet up to her shoulder, where baby-claws sank into her fleece jacket.

"Hungry?" Miranda asked.

"Pew!"

"Okay, let's go get breakfast."

Moments later, the kitty was contentedly munching kibble, oatmeal was heating, and the kettle was on for tea. Miranda glanced past the kitchen toward the sliding doors that faced the ocean. *The new miniature will have the same tonalities as the first one . . . a theme for the series. Cobalt teal for the water, chromium oxide green for the topographic hills.* She was beginning to paint the new postcard in her head.

Chapter 2

Sally O'Mally pulled shut the door to Burn-It-Off, checking to make sure it locked. The work-out facility she rented—just one mirrored room with step-platforms and floor mats—spent most hours empty. *This mornin' it was jus' the three of us: I, myself, and me.* Sally chuckled. *But bizness is startin' to pick up. If I could jus' get someone else to teach classes again, I bet it'd do jus' fine.*

Between offering step-aerobics two days a week, and running her restaurant six days, she kept a busy schedule. *Busy as a farmer with one hoe an' two rattlesnakes, like Mama'd say.* Sally felt a wistful smile reach her lips. *Actually, she'd prob'ly say I'm about as busy as a farmer's wife . . . jus' like I woulda been if I'da stayed in Arkansas like she did.*

She shook her head and ran fingers through her curly blond hair—still damp from the quick shower she'd taken in the Ladies' Locker Room she shared with other tenants. She'd traded her leotards and the leg-warmers Mama'd knitted for her, and now wore her serving clothes and sensible shoes —ready for another day of standing, taking orders, chatting with customers and sharing some of the gossip and kitchen duties with her staff.

As she stepped into the parking lot, she looked up at the eastern sky, where a faint gleam was just edging over the rim of coastal mountains. *Love this time of day . . . got the world all to myself.* She unlocked her bright yellow Chevette and slid into the driver's seat. *It'll jus' take me five minutes to drive to the rest'r'nt, and then I can put up the first pot of coffee.*

But as she walked in through the back door of her diner, the fragrance of fresh brew already filled the air.

"June?" she called.

"Mornin', Sal!" June called back.

Her faithful friend and waitress June Magliati still sounded like she'd just arrived from Brooklyn, though she'd lived in California for half of her forty-odd years.

What'd I ever do without her? "Mornin'!" Sally answered, checking things over as she slipped past the gleaming stainless steel counters and the rows of shiny pans hanging from their overhead rack.

Since June's got the coffee goin', I have a couple minutes before I have to get the biscuits started. But I feel like there's somethin' else I need to check on. Just can't think what it is. Oh, well, it'll come to me.

Stepping past the counter, she patted the life-size Santa doll that occupied the last stool, fastened there by his belt. *Wonder if Mr. Hargraves will worry 'bout Santa the way he did about "Mr. Hay" who sat there in the fall.* She smiled at the thought of the elderly gentleman who owned the hardware store next door, a regular customer and a colorful local who loved teasing her about the seasonal "characters" who sat next to him at her counter.

She flipped the switch that illuminated the row of blinking holiday lights outlining the front door, then glanced over next to the door, where her always-full bulletin board now held a large, colorful poster. *Doobie Brothers*, it said in bright orange letters across the top. Under that, a photo of the several band members showed hunky guys wearing tight jeans and I-Dare-You expressions. *They'll be playin' at the Central Coast Bowl next week. Betcha they'll get a big crowd!*

Turning her head toward the large wall that currently held her chalkboard—filled with multi-colored letters listing her menu items—she tried to picture what it would look like when Miranda'd painted the mural.

When I asked her to do it, I told her I wanted it like a window. Maybe a view of the ocean. Or maybe a picture of the farm . . . somethin' that'd make it feel more like home. Wistful for a moment, Sally shook her head as if to wake herself from the reverie. *Here I am day dreamin' in the daylight. Time to get to work!*

Samantha Hugo slipped into a steaming tub, letting the hot water sizzle along her skin as she slid down on the Epsom salts that were rapidly melting under her. Submerging herself in the heat had been the only antidote she could think of to the chill of the storm outside—and the turbulence of the one roiling through her mind.

Taking a morning off from her work as head of the Environmental Planning Commission was a rare occurrence—even when she didn't feel well. But, thanks to the Mental Health Parity Act—signed into law only this past September—she wouldn't even have to list this as a "sick" day.

Not sick. Just swamped. Buried. Underwater. Physically. Emotionally. Mentally. This morning had found her clear about only one thing: that she needed some time to herself.

Pressing her eyes shut, she inhaled, then let out a long breath, willing the tension to seep out of her limbs. Though she loved her job, running the EPC single-handedly was, in actuality, impossible. Her budget did allow her to hire an assistant, but dealing with young Susan Winslow was proving to be nearly as difficult as managing the work without her.

As if all that weren't enough, the holidays were almost here, a time Sam always found oppressively stressful. The pageantry and magic of Christmas always spoke to her, yet left her wanting. Though she enjoyed finding special gifts for others, she really had no one with whom to share the holiday, and through the years had developed what could only be described as a love-hate relationship with Christmas. *It's really a time for children. But there are no children in my life, thanks to my own inability to care for the one child I bore.*

Not to mention my nemesis! Jack Sawyer . . . the ex-husband who just won't go away. At this point, they were professional adversaries, which didn't used to bother her particularly. But now, she found herself constantly irritated by his very presence. *Is it because he's an environmental scofflaw, and I can't catch him at his bad behavior? Or is it our personal history that's bugging me more than ever?*

He'd never known about their child. Neither of them had been aware Sam was pregnant at the time of their divorce. And she'd seen no reason to inform him all those years ago—especially since he'd made it abundantly clear he didn't want children.

And then there's that *issue.* Her decision to look for the son she'd given up as a baby weighed heavily on her mind, dredging up old feelings of inadequacy that she had to stifle in order to keep working efficiently.

And while she tried to press on with her life, regardless of her personal issues, she found that at this time of year, others in the business community were busily deserting their posts: taking half-days to shop; closing early for office parties; or actually closing for several days.

I'm about as close to burn-out as I've ever been. This hot water feels divine, but I can hardly stay in the bathtub all day. And helping the body doesn't always help the soul. The emotions had knotted in her gut and the only way she could think of untangling them was to use her two standard techniques: escape her familiar surroundings, and write in her journal.

Had she been able to summon her courage, she'd have followed the advice of her most-admired author. The great nature writer and explorer John Muir had felt the best time to see nature was in a storm. *Couldn't keep up with you today, John. But at least I can follow your example and write.*

Sam pushed herself further down into the water. When she thought of places that offered solace, the one that always came to mind first was the Cove. She could make herself a thermos of coffee and head there to write for a while. *In this weather? Too cold, not to mention wet. I wouldn't last very long. Besides, if any other hardy soul chanced by, I'm in no mood to chat. For that same reason, I don't want to be caught off-duty walking around Milford-Haven.*

Allowing herself to muse for a moment, she tried to imagine what the ideal morning of playing hooky would include. *I'll need some coffee and toast... a place to sit and write for a while. Then it'd be nice to do a little window shopping to distract myself... maybe even get some Christmas gifts. Finish up with a bite of lunch, and a walk on the beach. That sounds like a plan.*

I'll dress in something comfortable, grab my journal, my short Christmas list, and drive down to Morro Bay for the morning. Who knows what I'll discover?

Samantha knocked sand off her tennis shoes and slid into the driver's side of her Jeep Grand Cherokee. *Oh, that beach walk felt good. And I did find some perfect things.*

Six hours ago, she'd driven the twenty miles south, exited off Highway 1, then taken Harbor Boulevard almost as far as the water before parking in Morro Bay.

While fog still swirled along the Embarcadero, she'd toted her purse and journal till she found the Starfish Bakery —treating herself to a steaming-hot latte and a slice of fresh banana bread—she scribbled her private thoughts till her hand ached. By the time she looked up, the fog had burned off, and she headed out to begin her stroll through town.

She spent a good half hour at Coalesce Bookstore—first opened in 1973—a wonderful spot that'd long been a fixture in the community. She saw a display of the wildly-popular

Celestine Prophecy, which her book club had chosen to read last month. *Miranda loved it. I thought it was a rehash of real spiritual works. Personally, if I wanted to take the time for fiction, I'd rather have read Grisham's new* Runaway Jury. *Oh, well. To each her own.*

For December, their group had decided to read *Timepiece,* mostly because of its holiday theme. Picking up a copy of the small volume, she read the flap. *Sounds sentimental, but maybe it'll be a cozy read, given the time of year.*

Sam paused at the Native American section of the store, her attention drawn to a new book: *Tribal Voices* by Elizabeth Cook-Lynn. The author, a scholar and a poet, had written provocative essays that questioned who was actually telling Native stories. *Would Susan read this? She might. The righteous anger of the book might draw her in . . . give her a sense of belonging.*

When Sam stopped at the non-fiction aisle, she sighed. *I could happily spend a year here, reading in the corner.* Tracing her finger across the *M's,* she found the John McPhee books, where *Assembling California* seemed to leap into her hand. *Gotta have this. I've been meaning to read it since it came out three years ago.*

After a pleasant conversation with the booksellers—who wrapped the book for Susan in holiday paper—Sam wandered into a gift store to peruse eclectic items crafted by local artisans. *This store would fit just as well in Milford-Haven. Lovely things.* On a glass shelf she saw a collection of carved boxes that caught her eye. *This one's designed to hold watercolor supplies . . . would Miranda like it? She probably has all she needs. Still . . . something about this is special.* The rosewood box was carved with a mountain scene. *Not exactly her usual subject matter. But somehow it feels right.*

Now with this purchase wrapped, Sam had enough packages that she decided to walk back to her car. She glanced at her watch. *Already eleven. At this point either I need to feed the meter . . . or feed myself. Maybe I'll drive to a restaurant for an early lunch.*

She started the car's engine and thought for a moment about where to go. She'd stopped in once at the Pacific Café, but it struck her as more of a place that Cal Poly students might enjoy. Instead, she chose her longtime favorite.

Dorn's Original Breakers Café had opened its doors in 1942. *Talk about a fixture in the community!* Granted, the place was filled with memories. She'd eaten there years ago with Jack. Still, much more recently, her friend Kuyama had joined her there for lunch. *They have great food and a great view. What's not to like?*

During her lunch—seafood chowder, green salad, and hot bread with both a crunchy crust and a soft interior—she'd felt her shoulders relax and her mind begin to process details in a logical fashion. And now, as she started her engine to head for Milford-Haven, she felt almost human again.

Great lunch. Lovely morning. But the thing that made it all possible was the journal writing. She never knew why it helped, writing down the random thoughts just as they tumbled forth. But she trusted the process. *Miranda's always talking about the head and the heart. When it comes to writing in my journal, no doubt there's a "head" reason why the intellectual process works. But I just accept that my intuition knows what it needs to write down.*

It's not me who likes to dissect things. That's Jack's purview. How he'd belabored every little thing when they'd been married! Of course, it hadn't changed much, now that they'd ended up in the same town, lock-stepped into this "build/no-build" dance. As a contractor, he always wanted to build. It was what *he* did. As an environmentalist, she always wanted to protect the land. It was what *she* did. They both did their jobs well. *But we never danced well together.*

The Jeep's turn signal clicked off as Sam aimed the car north to travel the miles back to Milford-Haven. The town appeared as she rounded a long, graceful bend. Windows of seaside houses flashed gold as the clouds parted to offer a brief moment of noonday sun. *Bathed in radiant light, homes set like jewels along a picture-postcard coastline, tall pines marching up steep hills—this seems a perfect place to live. Almost too perfect. Sometimes I can't believe I actually live here . . . a dream come true.*

Yet, Samantha knew, with the dazzling light came deep shadows. Even her pristine little town had its share of unforeseeable perils.

Samantha pressed down on the brass thumbpush of her front door, then leaned her shoulder against the varnished oak. "Oh, come on," she muttered, aware that in damp weather the door tended to swell and stick.

Give it a minute, she told herself, standing back to adjust the holiday wreath that hung over the oval etched glass window set into the door. She tried leaning against the door again—careful not to press on the glass, but unable to avoid the prickle of pine needles poking into her scalp.

Eyes shut, she shoved off from the front stoop until the heavy door finally gave way, flinging her into her foyer. "Oh, for heaven's sake!" Catching her balance, she looked down at her wet, sandy canvas shoes and the mess they'd left on her floor. Sighing, she untied the shoes, yanked them off and flung them into the umbrella corner, then padded in her stocking-feet to drop her bag and journal on the entry table, and grab paper towels to sop up the mess.

Her phone was ringing, but she made no effort to lift the receiver before the machine picked up. *"Hello, this is Samantha Hugo. I'm sorry I'm not available at the moment."* Her voice sounded unnaturally warm and cordial: her phony-phone-voice. Gazing into her entry hall mirror, she stabbed at spikes of red hair, grown wild with moisture and wind.

"It's Susan, Samantha. I got your message that you're not coming to work this morning." Her assistant's voice, as usual, was full of attitude. "Even though you're not *here* this morning, I thought I should tell you I heard from the Chernaks again. *If* you can be back in your office by two this afternoon, they're supposed to call back—in case you're interested, I mean. Bye!"

The Chernak Agency. . . . Based on a recommendation from Southern California Associated Adoption Agencies, Samantha had left a message. *But that was six weeks ago. Now apparently they're finally getting back to me. Well, I can only assume they're working on a number of other cases. Who knows, maybe it's a good thing.*

Samantha replayed her assistant's message. *Now, there's a girl who can deliver an insult even when she leaves a simple voice mail.* Frustrated that as her unofficial ward and apprentice, Susan was ungrateful and belligerent, Sam had to admit the girl did have potential. *It's not that she isn't smart. She just has such a chip on her shoulder.* Her tone had grated on Sam as it always did, and yet she felt curiously numbed to its minor irritation at this moment. Something else was causing a slow, toxic bile to surge through her system: the prospect of churning up her long-buried past.

Deputy Delmar Johnson opened the window-paned door of Sally's Restaurant, closing it behind him against the chill. *This time of year I kind of miss the screen door's screech-and-bang.* Glancing at the counter, he confirmed his favorite corner stool was free—the one that allowed him to keep an eye on the front door and those who entered and exited. *Probably a holdover from my days in South Central . . . still, not a bad habit to keep.*

He glimpsed a few familiar customers at scattered tables as he settled himself on the tall stool. Hooking the heels of his boots over the foot rail, he cataloged the details of the room: the variety of local business calendars hung on the wall next to the white-board with today's specials; pine sprigs poked into the small table vases; and, of course, the Man-of-the-Hour himself seated at the counter's far end.

"I see Santa stopped by for a cup of coffee," Del remarked as Sally swung out of her kitchen and headed in his direction with a fresh pot of java.

"Oh, ye-yus," she confirmed in her Southern accent, regarding the life-sized doll fondly. "And soon's I turn my head,

I know he'll be helpin' himself to one of my fabulous gooey sticky cinnamon buns, too."

"He *does* have to keep up his strength," Del added, managing to keep his tone serious.

"Well, you're jus' full of the dickens today, Senior Dep'ty."

She's been teasing me ever since my promotion. But she does have an extra twinkle in her eye. "And is this an official complaint from Senior Management?"

"Not a complaint atall, jus' sayin'. Does this good mood of yours come with a good appetite?"

At that very moment, Del felt a rumble in his stomach and couldn't keep his gaze from following the progress of a steaming plate being served by June. "It does indeed."

Sally whipped the notepad from her apron picket and held the stub of a pencil poised over it.

"Eggs over easy," he began. "Bacon, whole-wheat toast and—"

"Grits," she supplied. "Got it! Back in two shakes—"

"—of a reindeer's tail."

That remark got a nice giggle from Sally as she walked away. Smiling himself, Del wasn't sure whether he'd already been in a good mood when he arrived, or whether it was their banter that'd cheered him. *The black city-boy from L.A.-mean-streets and the white country-girl from an Arkansas farm. Even though our ancestors and relations would probably never've been friends in the South, we must have some common roots back there somewhere. Now she's one of the reasons I'm starting to feel at home on the Central Coast.*

He thought again about her uncanny ability to read people—her customers in particular. *Might be a skill she developed as a business woman. But I don't know. Seems like she might've been born with it.*

In October, he'd asked her to work with a Sheriff's department sketch artist to generate an accurate depiction of a man Sally'd seen right here at her restaurant. Apparently, the man had come in asking for the now-missing journalist Chris Christian. Despite the decent sketch they now possessed, there were still no real leads. *Unless I find something when I go through her condo with Joseph Calvin this afternoon.*

Del realized he must've been lost in his thoughts, because he was startled when his steaming plate of breakfast landed on the counter in front of him. He bent to inhale the fragrance rising from the grits, in which a pat of butter was melting to a golden pool.

"Thanks, Sally. Looks great. And thanks again for helping us—you know, with the sketch artist."

"Wish I coulda done more. And awful sorry that gal's gone missin'."

As Sally hurried back into the kitchen, Del took a bite of the grits, unable to resist closing his eyes to savor the homemade flavors. When he looked up he glimpsed Kevin—all six-foot-eight of him—come through the front door, closing it behind him, so as not to let it bang. *A careful fellow, deliberate in the way he does things. What's his last name? Rand? No, Ransom.*

Nodding at Del, Kevin took a stool mid-counter—dwarfing both it and the countertop—yet graceful for all his size. Sally came spinning backwards through the kitchen door, and he watched as she balanced plates on her arms and glanced behind Kevin, as though checking to see if someone had followed him in.

She's looking for his boss, Jack Sawyer. The two men almost always eat breakfast together. He must not be expected today. And Sally almost looks relieved.

While Del enjoyed his own breakfast, he watched as Kevin nodded to Sally. He didn't actually order, but moments later, Kevin began to devour the plate of food that arrived. *That must've been what the nod meant—that he'd have his usual. And that guy eats fast!*

In fact, Kevin caught up to him during the meal. Del glanced at his watch, surprised at how the time had flown. *I gotta get going.* When he noticed Sally busy across the room with other customers, he stood, while Kevin did the same, and both men left their money on the counter at the same time. They reached Sally's door simultaneously, and Del held it open for the taller man.

"Off to Sawyer Construction?" Del asked companionably as they walked toward their vehicles.

"Nope. Gotta get to the job site." Kevin turned to face the Deputy Sheriff.

"So, you must be glad to have a break in the rain, even though it's still foggy. Do you guys work no matter what, just like postal deliverers?"

Kevin raised his eyebrows in question.

"You know, 'Neither snow nor rain nor heat nor gloom of night stays these couriers from the swift completion of their appointed rounds.'"

Laughing, Kevin replied, "Yeah, and that goes for mud too."

Kevin Ransom pulled his truck into the muddy tire tracks, rocking back and forth in the cab as the vehicle heaved over the future driveway of the Clarke mansion.

At this time of year, he felt torn about the weather. On one hand, he relished the chill and welcomed the rain—California always seemed to need the water. But on the other hand, not only were the rains an inconvenience on a job site, but also the moisture proved an unwelcome intrusion into unfinished structures, where it could cause damage.

Damage . . . that's the last thing Jack needs on this job. He's already so angry every time the client calls with another change order. Jack used to be so happy about building this house! Now I worry he'll blow a gasket before it's done.

Leaving his ten-year-old Ford F-150 pickup, Kevin stepped across the slick, oozing mud until he could leap onto the gangplank that bridged the gap between ground level and front entryway. He inhaled the familiar odor of fresh sawdust and, against the din of hammers and saws, nodded or waved the usual greetings to fellow co-workers.

Inside, he trained his gaze across the expanse of the home's great room. *The under-flooring should still be fine if it'll just stay dry till we get the next layer in place. But it's already starting to buckle, so we might have to rip it all out and start over.*

Stifling a groan, he glanced over at the job site phone booth. *There's Mole Guy making another call. Geez, I better not use that name out loud. How many times has he used the phone this week? More than anyone else, that's for sure.*

This was Burt Ostwald's first job with Sawyer Construction —one of several extra guys hired to handle the workload for the enormous house. He wasn't exactly a local, at least not in the usual sense. As far as anyone could tell, he didn't have roots in the community, apparently preferring instead to go as a direct-hire from job to job as needed. *That's what he did with us. And he seems a decent sort—usually willing to sub if some other guy's out sick.*

Kevin turned away, reluctant to make the man uncomfortable if he happened to glance around. *The guy does turn in a good day's work. But lately . . . seems like he's on the phone, or out sick himself. Who knows what all he's dealing with in his personal life? Hope everything's okay.*

For now, Kevin had such a full schedule, he turned his back on Burt and walked toward the kitchen area. *It's gonna be a full morning. Better get started with the first thing on my list.*

Chapter 3

Samantha Hugo sat at her office desk, feeling out of synch as afternoon sun cast a glow over her daily stack of work.

Each morning, she expected to see papers neatly piled and labeled with sticky-notes, gathered the day before by her assistant, Susan, as she'd been trained to do.

Sam looked again at today's work, puzzling over why it didn't appear the way it normally did. *Well, for one thing, it's now afternoon.* Yes, that was it. On sunny days, a lance of morning beams hit her desk, and today she'd missed it. *Like missing a lighting cue in a play. Maybe that's why this pile doesn't seem urgent.*

She stared down at her hands, motionlessly poised on her wrist pad, then lifted her gaze to her blank computer screen. *I may be done with playing hooky, but I guess it's not done with me.* Obviously she hadn't fully reentered her office world.

She still seemed to feel the chilly air, the freedom to browse through shops . . . even a pleasant touch of the holiday spirit. *I do feel better after my "mental health" morning. But now I can't seem to get my head in gear.*

Forcing herself at least to glance through the several inches of paperwork, she saw that a sticky-note identified the upper-most document as "Coastal Erosion Research." *That's an ongoing subject, so it can wait.*

Others were more pressing: permits needing her signature; responses to environmental meeting invitations; a memo from Lorraine Larimer regarding a proposal requiring urgent discussion, even though the Town Council wouldn't meet again until January, taking a break during the busy holiday season.

The next whole layer was composed solely of Sawyer Construction schematics for buildings. *Now that actually sounds like fun.* She relished the thought of poring over Jack's proposed projects, nitpicking the flaws, finding ways to stop his tricks for noncompliance.

But I don't even feel like tackling that at the moment. I only came in because of Susan's message about being here by two o'clock. Too important to ignore, the call from the Chernak Agency felt like a reply to the soul-searching she'd done over the past several weeks.

Good thing Susan called me. But where is that girl? She should be back from lunch by now!

The exterior door slammed, and Samantha pushed back from her desk. *Speak of the devil . . . no, I shouldn't even think that.* Sam walked to the outer office and watched as Susan arrived—sauntering casually as though she had all the time in the world—dressed in her omnipresent leather jacket, her skin-tight top, mini-skirt-over-tights, the latter two items inappropriate for a professional setting.

As Susan looked up, her mouth pulled to one side in a sneer. "Like my outfit, Samantha?"

"If that was your lunch break, don't you think it was rather long? It's not Christmas vacation yet." *Why do I do that . . . always take the bait?*

Susan threw her boss an insolent look as she flung off her jacket. "Happy Holidays to you too, Samantha. I didn't think you'd come into the office at all today. I didn't know you were so desperate to talk to the Chernaks."

"I am not desperate, Susan." Sam sighed, trying not to escalate the frustration. "Thank you for leaving the message so I could be here in time."

"So, when they call, you *do* want to speak to them?"

"Yes!" Sam tried to keep her composure. "I want to speak to them." She paused to take a breath. "But please don't disturb me until their call comes through." Sam spun on her heel, retreated into her private office, and took satisfaction in closing her door firmly.

Susan Winslow was glad to be left alone. She preferred it that way anyway, and could barely tolerate the interruptions and barked orders from Samantha. *Bad enough we're forced to work in the same space for hours at a time. And now, my, my, in a foul temper today, aren't we?*

Susan flung her long, straight hair over one shoulder and pouted for a moment. *If I didn't need this job, I'd be outta here so fast. But I only got the cheap rent and the college tuition because of this stupid mentoring program through the Chumash council.*

She slumped back in her chair and looked down at the

sleeve of her leather jacket. *I couldn't have afforded to buy this. Plus, I've saved a hundred-fifty toward my camera.*

Susan opened the middle drawer of her desk, slipping a dog-eared brochure out from under the pencil tray. "Canon PowerShot 600" read the glossy letters above a picture of the coveted device. Then she glanced through the press release that went with it, dated last May, tracing her finger over the familiar descriptors: "storage of up to 2,000 images . . . flash modes auto On Off . . . max resolution 832 x 608."

The sleek, silver body with its offset lens looked like something from a Sci-Fi movie. She imagined herself backstage at her favorite rock concerts, taking photos and videos of band members, getting them to pose for her while they admired her tight body, skinny legs and shiny black hair. *They'll just think I'm cute, till I show them my fantastic shots. Then they'll start to hire me and I'll have a real career.*

She looked again at the brochure, her gaze trapped by the listed costs. "Original price 128,000 yen, or nine-hundred-forty-nine-dollars." *At this rate, it'll only take me another seven years to have enough to buy it! As if! Obviously, I gotta find a way to get it faster.*

Sobered by the reminder, Susan slid the sales materials back into their hiding place, her renewed desire for the valuable tool igniting a grim determination. She thought back to Samantha's sour mood. *As long as I'm stuck working for her, no reason I can't have a little fun. And I do enjoy getting her going, especially now, just in time for the holidays, too. Hmm, what can I do to annoy her?*

What sprang immediately to mind was Samantha's current

dilemma: the fact that she'd given up a child for adoption and now was trying to find him.

This has to be the juiciest secret in Milford-Haven. And she told me all about it. Thinking back to their surprising conversation last fall, Susan remembered her own jaw dropping when she heard her employer's tale—including the unbelievable fact that none other than Jack Sawyer was the father!

Samantha had requested—no, demanded—confidentiality. And, so far, Susan hadn't betrayed her trust. But sometimes she felt herself practically vibrating with the desire to *tell.*

Nah. That'd screw up my job for sure! So instead, I can just play with her a little. I mean, what could it hurt? After all, she's the one who gave up her own kid. If my mother'd lived, she'd never have given me up. I know that. It was my evil, selfish, brutal, stupid drunk of a father who ruined everything!

Susan felt the heat rising in her cheeks, her breath heaving through her chest. *Anyway, that's beside the point. This is about Samantha getting what she deserves.*

And this morning's phone call from the adoption agency was the perfect place to start. While Samantha'd been out having fun, Susan had faithfully been at her post, and had answered the phone with her professional voice. "Environmental Planning Commission."

A foreign accent had greeted her ears. "Hello, I would like to speak to Samantha Hugo, please," it said.

"Sorry, Ms. Hugo is out now. This is Susan Winslow."

"Ah, Susan Winslow." The woman had pronounced it Vinslow. "How do you do? This is Stacey Chernak. I am calling from the Chernak Agency. I understand . . . that Ms. Hugo wishes . . . that is, she desires help to find a missing child, yes?"

The woman stumbled all over her words while at the same time sounding buttery, like a confused Mrs. Klaus calling from the North Pole. Susan tried to remain polite. "Well, you could put it that way but . . . "

"You see, uh, we can find any long-lost child you are looking for, no matter how difficult to find they may seem to be." Now she sounded like she was reading from a script, except that every *w* was a *v*, and every *d* a *t*. "We will go to any lengths to ensure our customer's satisfaction."

Between the stumbles, the altered consonants and the sing-song voice, it was practically impossible to understand what she was saying, this egg noodle from the land of yodelers.

"Before you go too much further," Susan burst through the woman's prattle, "shouldn't you be talking directly to Ms. Hugo?"

"Ye . . . yes." The stuttered words were interrupted with a burst of nervous laughter. "It is only that you mentioned she is not right now in her office. Is this correct?"

"Yeah. I mean, yes. Correct. So why don't I take down a detailed message and I can have her call you back?" *At last*, thought Susan, *I can get rid of this puff pastry.*

"Ye-yes, it is always best to discuss these matters directly with our client. My husband and I will call back."

"Okay, and before you hang up," Susan prodded, "can I confirm your number so—"

"Thank you so much, Miss Winslow. We will call back at two o'clock. Until then." And the line had clicked dead.

Susan glanced over at her boss's closed door. *We'll see what happens when they call back, won't we, Samantha? And you won't have anyone to trust about this but me.*

Delmar Johnson squinted as he walked toward the Suburban. Low, winter sun struck the Sheriff's gilt emblem painted on its white driver-side door, accentuating the contrast with the vehicle's black body. *No matter where the job takes me in the 3,400 square miles of San Luis Obispo County—and beyond—it's not like folks won't know who I am. Some days, I'd just as soon have an unmarked car. But this one comes with the job—and the territory.*

He'd left Milford-Haven after breakfast to spend most of the day in the SLO Sheriff's office—checking in with Detective Dexter; using the research library to fill in some more background on his several current cases; and reviewing the original search report on the Christian home generated in October.

Now he climbed into the SUV, and enjoyed the deep growl as the powerful engine turned over. Leaving from of the County parking lot, he began his forty-mile drive south to Santa Maria.

Joseph Calvin's secretary said he'd meet me at Ms. Christian's condo at four p.m. We won't have much time before it gets dark, but at least we'll be able to find her unit and check the surroundings. Dex is tied up, so it'll be just me and Calvin again. I'll call to confirm the time, once I'm on the highway.

Del found it interesting that he'd essentially been put in charge of this case of the missing journalist and wasn't sure what to make of it. *Seems like it's a low priority at this point. Yet they've assigned me to deal with this high-profile man.*

It'd been only two months since Del made Senior Deputy— the first African American to make that grade in San Luis Obispo County. He appreciated the vote of confidence from the

Captain—if, in fact, that's what it was. The department had been short-handed, leaving a slot open for someone who happened to be "in the right place at the right time." But it was always hard to tell, when you were the new-kid-on-the-block, if a potentially sensitive assignment meant you were being given a chance—or being thrown to the dogs.

He'd done his one-year probationary period with the Sheriff's department in San Luis Obispo County, and had spent it on patrol in all three sub-stations: Templeton to the north, Los Osos in the middle and Arroyo Grande, which encompassed everything south to the Santa Barbara County line. The year of patrol work meant he'd learned a lot about the area—enough to know he'd fallen in love with the Central Coast.

The SLO County Sheriff's Department had no budget for its own office space north of its hub. But the California Department of Forestry had a new building in Milford-Haven. At first, the CDF had only been willing to allow the Sheriff's department the use of a desk and phone. But when they'd learned of Del's technological expertise, and found out he had his own computer system, they'd become much friendlier. With his recent promotion he'd been given his own office, and it suited him down to the ground—as his mother Ruby used to say.

By any standards, his promotion had come quickly—quickly enough to cause some resentment. But that didn't worry Del. His five years with the L.A.P.D. on the streets of South Central had prepared him as few officers are ever prepared. Now he'd been assigned to the SPU—Special Problems Unit. It had the potential to be the ideal job. He answered only to the Captain and was assigned to work with detectives—or anyone else—when needed. In this unit there was no caseload, as such. The idea was to keep its members free to respond when necessary. *So now I've earned the title Senior Deputy Johnson . . . and have more responsibility and more freedom than I've ever had before in my professional life. That's an enormous vote of confidence. Or not.*

Joseph Calvin resisted, at first, the idea of the late afternoon drive all the way to Santa Maria. But if he were ever going to satisfy his own curiosity about Chris's condo, this would probably be his only opportunity.

On his car phone, Joseph had received a confirmation call from his secretary. And as he pulled through the open gates of Villas in the Oaks, he saw the Sheriff's Department vehicle hulking in the corner of the parking lot.

Exiting his Mercedes, he inhaled the afternoon air, now freshened by today's rains. He watched as Deputy Johnson stepped from the Suburban, waiting while the man approached.

"Afternoon, Mr. Calvin. Thanks again for agreeing to meet me here."

Joseph nodded in reply, ambivalent about the venture.

"Glad the rain's stopped, for now."

"Right."

They approached the entrance to the complex of several two-story buildings, each with four condominiums that were built end-to-end, their front doors staggered for variety. Joseph inspected the stucco arch under which they paused. It showed signs of wear including water stains from previous and recent downpours. An effort had been made to give the place a certain pscale look. *But this is a far cry from the old-world elegance of*

Calma.

Interrupting his musings, the deputy asked, "Shall we? I'll follow you."

Joseph nodded again, taking the lead through the metal gate—a painted-aqua monstrosity matching the railings that paralleled the various exterior staircases.

"Do they call this South-Western?" Johnson asked.

"What? Oh, the salmon-colored stucco and 'faux' turquoise accents?" Joseph pressed his lips together, unwilling to imply any further criticism of his missing friend. "I suppose that's what they were going for." *Always wished Chris's landlord would at least paint the railing black. But it wasn't* my *home.*

As Johnson kept pace with him, it struck Joseph as odd that he knew the location of Chris's unit as well as *he* did. *Of course he does. But not the way I do.*

Arriving at her front door to unit A111, Joseph unsnapped a leather key holder until he held its single key, then handed the open case to the deputy. Wearing gloves, Johnson took them, apparently noticing the smooth leather case was embossed with "J.C."

"A gift from Chris," said Joseph. "Ms. Christian. For my birthday last year. When she gave me her house key."

Delmar Johnson nodded and turned the key. As he stepped through the door, his nostrils flared at the cool, feminine fragrance of the rooms. He turned around in time to see the expression on Mr. Calvin's face and his attempts to swallow. *Is that a lump in his throat? Definitely pain in his eyes.*

"You understand, Mr. Calvin, that I'll have to keep you in sight while we're in the apartment?"

"I see. Yes." The words were clipped.

"I spoke with the property manager. He's due to meet us here."

Calvin nodded.

Del intended to do a slow, thorough walk from room to room. Removing his leather gloves, he exchanged them for the latex pair he took from his pocket. The small foyer gave way to a great room with two areas—living room with two couches; dining area with round table and four chairs. A bar with tall stools created the boundary to a small, open kitchen. *Everything looks normal here. There was certainly nothing in the report about signs of a struggle.* A set of stairs in the corner led upward, and Del climbed to a small loft that served as her office. He looked back down to see Calvin standing by the kitchen, apparently lost in thought.

When Del returned to the main floor he followed Calvin's gaze. *Unwashed dishes on the counter by the sink . . . looks like the remnants of toast. Maybe that's what grabbed his attention.* Turning back toward the foyer, he noted a hallway that led off to the right in a perpendicular direction. "Bedroom this way?"

Calvin nodded, then followed.

Del watched as Calvin entered the bedroom, then stood transfixed by the sight of the unmade bed.

"It's exactly as we left it," he mumbled. "Exactly."

"That seems to confirm she never returned to her condo."

"She couldn't have . . . it's where she threw her . . . the morning she threw her underthings." He pointed to a pile of delicate blue silk on the floor. "That's where they landed."

Del's eyes searched Joseph's for a trace of deception, but found none.

Joseph turned, walked away, headed for the living room.

"Mr. Calvin . . . please." Del admonished.

"Right," said Calvin, swallowing the word and returning.

Del moved around the bed. Noting the bed clothes were in disarray, he pulled them back to reveal the bottom sheet. At a glance, it looked like recreational aftermath. If he played out a worst-case scenario, he might have just enough to suggest a situation. *Coercion? Rape?* He lifted one edge of the sheet. *No blood, but there's residue from other bodily fluids.* He hoisted the bed skirt to peer underneath. *Nothing visible from this vantage.* He crossed to the far side. *Night stand. Phone. But where's the answering machine Calvin talked about?*

Just then, Del heard a tentative knocking on the condo's open door, accompanied by a voice calling, "Hello!" Moving back toward the entrance—but keeping Calvin in view—Del saw a suntanned man, dressed in chinos, with a sweater over a Hawaiian shirt. Taking off a pair of aviator sun glasses, the man walked in, stuck out his hand and introduced himself. "George Silver."

Instead of offering his own—still clad in latex—Del simply nodded in reply.

"I'm the property manager." Puzzlement creased his face as he added, "I see you got in with no trouble. Didn't realize you had your own key."

Del caught sight of Calvin heading toward them.

"Ah. Mr. Calvin, isn't it?" George Silver inquired. At the nodded response, he continued, "Good to see you, sir. Good to see anyone who knows Chris." When neither man spoke, Silver went on. "Of course, she goes off on these long trips, and her monthly fees are paid up through this time next year. So it's not like I've actually been worried." He gave a short bark of laughter that did little to convince Del he wasn't, in fact, concerned about the missing woman.

Del said nothing for a long moment.

"But, since you're here again . . . something I should be worried about?"

Del inhaled. "Ms. Christian's employers have concerns. She still hasn't shown up for her next assignment."

"Oh! Well, prob'ly just means she took a little vacation time. Like I said, she does some serious traveling." Apparently eager to leave, he held up a ring with three keys. "Well, I guess you won't need this extra set for A111?"

Del glanced at the set the property manager dangled in front of them. "Three keys? I suppose one must open the back door. But what does that third key open?"

"Oh," Silver answered, peering at the one in question. "That's to the storage unit."

"Storage unit?" Joseph repeated.

"Yeah, there's a row of units with roll-down doors on the south side of the complex."

"Thanks, Mr. Silver." Del spoke quickly, but kept his tone light. "We might have a look in there too. And the department will need to keep that set of keys for now."

Silver handed them to Del.

"We'll lock up after we leave. Appreciate your help."

"Sure thing!" Relief washing over his face, Silver turned and strode out of the condo.

Del watched him go, then glanced over at Calvin. *He's not saying much, not even making eye contact. He seems pretty unnerved by this whole trip.* "You didn't know about it?"

"The storage unit? No, but no particular reason I should've."

He chewed his lip.

"Let's take a look."

The two men walked in silence around to the south-facing row of storage units. Then moved along its face till they found A111 stenciled in black. Using the key to open its padlock, Del rolled up the wide metal door and peered into an open area bordered by stacks of cardboard containers.

"Boxes," Calvin muttered.

"No surprise there."

"All neat and orderly as you please," Calvin added.

Del stepped inside to touch the top of an uppermost box, then rubbed his finger and thumb together. "Dusty, though. Like they haven't been used in a long time."

"That's no surprise either, is it?"

"Mmph." Del trained his gaze in a slow, careful arc around the room, about ready to leave until one box caught his eye. Partially obscured in its position midway along one wall, the box with its open flaps was barely visible. Walking over, he lifted it down from the stack to rest it on the ground. *The only unclosed box in the whole array . . . and no dust to speak of, so it hasn't been open very long. Notebooks . . . file folders. Might be notes on the stories she was working on. And I wonder if she keeps a list of incoming messages?*

Calvin's shadow fell across the contents. "Find something?"

"Just some papers I should go through. By the way, you'd mentioned an answering machine. But I didn't see it in the condo."

"Oh, I can show you where she keeps it. And there's one other thing I noticed, too."

"Okay, good." After closing and locking the storage door, he hefted the box to carry it inside, where he placed it on the foyer floor. Then he reentered the bedroom, Calvin close on his heels.

Calvin pointed. "There, on her side, see the headboard?"

Del nodded.

"It has a sliding panel. She keeps the answering machine in there."

Del slid back the small door to reveal the device. "It's off."

"Well, there've been some storms. It's not unheard of for the power to go out in this neck of the woods. In fact, Chris used to complain that her machine wouldn't turn itself back on."

Del hit the power button. Its red light began to glow, its message light to blink. The LED readout gave a continuously flashing "12:00" for the time. "Power's been interrupted, so the device reset itself. But that doesn't mean the actual incoming tape was erased." Calvin nodded and Del hit the Play button.

The machine beeped and a mechanical voice said, "October eighteenth, one p.m." Then a real voice followed. "Ms. Christian, we got that water leak repaired. Should be good to go."

"October twenty-first, two p.m.," noted the machine. "Ms. Christian, this is Coastal Cleaners. We did get the stain out of that dress. You can pick it up any time."

These sound routine enough. Calvin seems impassive.

"October twenty-first, nine-twelve p.m." Then, a man saying, "Chris, I got stuck in a late meeting, but I'm on my way now."

Calvin's voice . . . and he looks like an electrical shock just zapped through him. The recorded voice . . . it's intermingled with static, as if he'd called from his car phone.

"Should be at Calma in oh . . . fifteen. See you, doll."

The machine beeped.

"October twenty-second, six-thirty a.m. Ms. Christian, you know who this is."

A strange rasping voice. Not deep, not high, not natural. Calvin's pointing . . . okay, this must be the one he told me about.

The machine continued. "The time frame has changed. If you want to get the story, you now have only twenty-four hours. Meet me at the house—you know the one—but not before ten p.m. Trust me. This is it."

Sounds ominous as hell. No wonder Calvin was upset by it back when the call came in.

The machine beeped again. "October twenty-third, twelve-thirty a.m." And then, "Hey, doll, where the heck are you?"

Calvin's own voice again.

"Our midnight supper's been served, and it's getting cold. I know you said not to wait past twelve, but this was supposed to be our rain check, remember? You can run but you cannot hide."

A prickle of ice trailed down Del's spine. As the tape stopped whirring and clicked off, Del stood still, considering. *Evidently no more messages before the power went out. In this last one, Calvin had ended his call more abruptly . . . an edge to his voice. How obsessed had Calvin been with this woman? Had he followed her? Caught her with another man? Killed her—or them—in a passionate rage?* Nothing in Calvin's demeanor thus far suggested any such behavior. Yet, stranger things had happened. Murderers often started out as stalkers. Stalkers often started out as boyfriends.

Keeping his thoughts to himself, Del hit the Save button and glanced over at Calvin, who was shaking his head as if saying a silent *no.* "Mr. Calvin?"

"That's the end of the tape, right? The machine must not've reset after the outage. No wonder the damn thing wouldn't take my other messages."

"You called Ms. Christian again?"

"Well, when she didn't show up . . . I got worried. Then . . . well, I suppose I got irritated, figured she'd made other plans without telling me."

Sounds plausible, Del thought. "You mentioned there was one other thing?"

"Her suitcases—the ones she would've taken to Tokyo—"

"What about them?"

"Well, that's the thing. See there?" Calvin pointed. "Where the bedskirt is pulled back a little? They're still here."

Del joined Calvin as he knelt, then lifted the bed skirt up out of the way to reveal a matched set of luggage. He pressed his lips together before asking, "She doesn't have other bags?"

"Not that I've ever seen. And I've picked her up at the Santa Maria airport several times."

Del yanked on the handle of the larger bag until it was free of the bed. *Black, soft-sided roller bag. Obviously well-worn. Tag with her business card inserted.* He unzipped it and lifted its lid. *Pair of shoes. Clothes.* He pulled out the second, smaller bag. *This must be her carry-on. Cosmetic kit already packed, and a Tokyo travel book. But the laptop compartment's still empty, so she wasn't quite finished packing. Still, she was ready for her trip.*

The two men stood, and Del studied Calvin's face. *He looks distraught. Finding her luggage . . . well, it's hit him hard.* "I'm going to have to seal the condo," he said quietly. "The Department will need to go through the place again, this time with a fine-tooth comb." He inhaled. "So we can exclude you, we'll need to get your fingerprints, and collect a sample of your DNA."

"Of course."

Del reached into his pocket. "I'm returning your key. But I must ask that you not enter—"

"No, no, I won't be coming back here." Calvin's expression turned stoic as he allowed himself to be ushered out of Christine Christian's apartment, perhaps for the very last time.

Chapter 4

Miranda Jones had spent most of the day painting in her studio. She'd made some good progress with the watercolor map for her postcard, but now set that project aside until her upcoming trip to Los Angeles. *I'll actually be using maps as I drive. That'll give me more ideas.*

For a brief moment she imagined the route, noting that she'd be driving through Santa Barbara, where Zack Calvin lived. They'd shared a remarkable day back in October: a sudden meeting when he'd come to inquire about one of her gallery paintings—*The Cove*; an impromptu hike at her favorite spot, the Enchanted Forest; an almost-romantic evening with dinner at Michael's Restaurant and a cozy cup by her fireplace; and a real kiss goodbye at her front door. *Not to mention, he commissioned me to create a painting for him. But have I ever heard from him again? No! And he never followed up with Zelda to sign the contract either.*

With no contract, of course she'd never started the so-called commission. If he didn't have time for her, neither did she have any time for him. Suppressing the irritation, she stretched her back, rotated her shoulders, then walked toward her easel, where her nearly completed wildlife portrait faced the wall. She turned the piece around, then walked to the far corner of the studio. *Need to see him from a distance, get some perspective.*

When she brought her gaze to the canvas, a spark of recognition seemed to arc across the room, as if the painted image had come to life while her back was turned. The massive head-and-shoulders of a Siberian tiger hunched there, amber eyes staring back at her. *Powerful . . . unconcerned. . . . He might be seated in a docile pose—but he certainly isn't tamed.*

Miranda exhaled, realizing she'd been holding her breath. *Well, he speaks to my heart. Now . . . what does my head say? Got the proportions right. And acrylics were the right choice for him. That thick fur, the vivid contrast of his markings—the bright white between black striations above his browline and on his cheeks; the golden-orange forehead and nose. Yes . . . I'm getting close to completion. I'll miss young Tony when it's time for him to go.*

When this latest piece had been commissioned by the San Francisco Zoo, Miranda'd been ambivalent at first. For one thing, she always struggled with the idea of wild animals being held captive. *But many of them wouldn't be alive at all, had they or their parents not been rescued.* For another, she worried that returning to her own home territory so soon after settling in Milford-Haven would make her feel like a captive herself.

I know my folks mean well. They just have such a huge agenda for my life! She'd managed the problem by not telling them she was in the Bay Area at all, until it was so close to Thanksgiving that they just assumed she'd be headed home for the holiday weekend.

In fact, she'd flown up to San Francisco a week before the holiday and stayed with her sister Meredith. *And that was a mini-drama unto itself. I had to get Mer to promise not to tell Mother and Dad. But she finally agreed, and it was fun to have a little time with her.* By day, Miranda—camera and sketch book in hand—had made visits to her tiger friend.

Three years earlier, the zoo had welcomed a new resident—this huge male Siberian Amur tiger, then just one year old. Born in Tucson's Reid Park Zoo in March 1992, he'd been moved to San Francisco at the end of June 1993. *Who knew there was a real "Tony the Tiger"?*

Since, as an artist, Miranda specialized in landscapes and wildlife, she spent much of her time on outdoor expeditions, to capture on film what she would later interpret on paper or canvas.

But early last September, she'd received her first commission from a zoo. Wild Animal Park, a division of the San Diego Zoo, had hired her to paint Lia, their born-in-captivity cheetah. At this special park, there were no cages. All the animals lived in a huge expanse of protected property where they roamed free—as close to a wild habitat as they could get while cleverly concealed barriers protected species from each other.

The thrill of being so close to the cheetah—separated only by the monorail on which guests rode through the park—had been extraordinary, and Miranda'd snapped several rolls of film. But later, painting Lia had been a challenging assignment: her wildness seemed to defy the static medium. *She was probably almost as hard to capture on canvas as she would've been if I'd actually been chasing her—her quicksilver moods running as fast as those fleet limbs.*

Happily, the Park was tremendously pleased with her work, confident her painting would fetch a handsome price at their annual fund-raiser next spring, where Miranda herself would be honored. *Kinda dread that event. What in the world am I supposed to say? Well, at least I don't have to solve* that *right now!*

Bringing herself back to the present, Miranda sat at her desk and gazed over at the tiger's portrait, the soft eyes a surprise in the powerful face. *Painting Tony has been just as exciting, but in a totally different way. I wonder why, exactly? Of course, he's a heavy male where Lia's a light female. Also he does live in an enclosure, and she doesn't. Maybe that's why it was so much harder to connect with Lia. Meeting Tony was like meeting an old friend.*

Encountering a beast of his size—360 pounds when last weighed—she'd expected to find either the heat of a latent ferocity or the coolness of a cat wound tight and ready to pounce. Instead, when he trained his huge eyes on hers, she'd stared into liquid amber lit from a warmth within. *There's something about him. They tell me everyone who meets him feels it.*

That's not to say Tony wasn't still a wild animal, who presumably had all the instincts any tiger would have—to protect, to hunt, to attack. Yet some animals in captivity seemed to go far beyond the behaviors typical of their species.

Just this past August at Chicago's Brookfield Zoo, the gorilla Binti Jua had made herself famous all over the world by her heroic rescue. A toddler, who'd dashed away from his mother near the gorilla enclosure, had leaned too far over the protective fence, fallen more than twenty feet and been knocked unconscious when he landed. Before workers could reach the little boy, the mother-gorilla—carrying her own baby on her back—had tenderly lifted the human baby to safety, where keepers could easily reach him.

Maybe animals take on some of the qualities of their benevolent human keepers. Or maybe they don't acquire new qualities at all. Maybe their wisdom gets activated because we acknowledge who they truly are. Either way, Tony the Tiger already had a reputation, not as a dangerous predator, but as a giant pussy cat.

As if responding to the sentiment, Shadow popped onto Miranda's desk and padded up onto the art supply bag. *Now she's looking at me with a question in her eyes, like she's confirming I'm about to pack that bag for my trip.*

Unable to resist the tiny companion, Miranda lifted the kitten and held her nose-to-nose. "You're right, Shadow. I'm going away, but not for long. I promise."

When Shadow purred in response, Miranda plunked her onto one shoulder, where the kitten used her tiny claws to secure purchase. Miranda settled in her desk chair to review the information she'd assembled for her upcoming trip.

The brand-new Los Angeles-area non-profit *Palos Verdes on the Net* had chosen her to create its first two art images: one of their historic lighthouse, the other of the gray whales that migrated offshore twice a year.

In their packet of information they'd included maps, hotel options, a contact sheet, the center's hours, and a letter

assuring her the staff would make themselves available to
answer any questions she might have.

But she always widened the circle of her studies beyond the
specifics of the animals or landscapes she was painting, to give
her subject context and background. Over the past few years,
her range of interests in flora and fauna had inspired her to
create her own collection of research folders—locations or
species she might want to paint sometime in the future. *My four
file drawers of research folders are a drop in the ocean compared
with Sam's . . . but they're very focused.*

From her friend Samantha, she'd learned something about
"species suppression": when native plants are displaced by
invasive—sometimes called "exotic"—species. It'd happened
closer to home, on the Piedras Blancas peninsula where their
own local lighthouse stood. In the early 1900s, when California
was busily building railroads, iceplant was introduced to
stabilize soil along the tracks. As the sturdy succulent was also
a fire retardant, it'd seemed a good idea to plant it at Piedras
Blancas, where it eventually took over, becoming a dense
blanket of shiny fingers with intermittent lush blooms of bright
yellow and pink. *The iceplant is beautiful and it has its good
points . . . but when it choked off the native plants, a lot of the
wildlife left too.*

According to Miranda's research, something similar had
happened near LAX, the sprawling Los Angeles airport, where
a combination of urban development and invasive species had
nearly wiped out a tiny blue butterfly known as the El Segundo
Blue, so named for the sand dunes it'd once populated in the
hundreds of thousands. The gorgeous insects had a single
location because their only food source was coastal buck-

wheat—a plant threatened by iceplant and other invaders.

The butterflies—squeezed between urban construction and the airport—had dwindled drastically in the 1970s. But restoration efforts in the 1980s had begun to reverse the trend. The strangest part of the complex environmental equation was that of the three new preserves, one was managed by Chevron. *An oil company . . . protecting a butterfly! I just find that so hard to believe. This is something I need to see for myself.*

She'd never had the time or the budget to explore this species for herself, but now, with the PVNET invitation, it occurred to her she could spend an extra day or two and perhaps come home with some basic photos for a future painting. *Maybe I could get permission to explore and take photographs of the area. The butterflies won't be in season now, they'll be in the sand. Wonder if I could see them in their chrysalis stage?*

The PVNET non-profit organization's letter indicated they'd provide a stipend for her accommodations. In their list of local motels, they'd included a brochure from the Hacienda Hotel because of its proximity to LAX. *They must've thought I'd be flying down. And it's not that far from there to Palos Verdes.* But what caught her eye about the hotel was its El Segundo location. *That'll put me near the Dunes . . . and right where I need to be for all three projects. The little butterfly, if that works out. And a job painting both a lighthouse and the whales . . . all in one trip!*

She marveled at the unlikely convergence—whales, lighthouse, butterflies, and a hotel in El Segundo that would put her adjacent to Palos Verdes. *Some would call it coincidence. But there has to be more to it than that.*

Just then, afternoon sun burst through the clouds and

struck her rain-speckled windows, each water drop becoming a tiny prism that cast rainbows across the room. *And the sun has to be at just the right angle, the droplets in just the right positions . . . another convergence.*

Shadow opened her golden eyes and tilted her head, reaching out to paw at the dancing lights. Delighted at the sudden show, Miranda searched her memory for a specific word. *Synergy? No. Synchronicity! Yes, that's it—the word coined by Carl Jung.* She thought back to what she'd read about his concept while in college—that life wasn't a series of random events, but an expression of a deeper order.

I know that's true. But how to prove it? She let her gaze travel over the multi-colored illuminations playing across her studio walls. *Maybe it's as simple as looking more deeply into the details of life, so the patterns begin to emerge.*

The lighting shifted then, wider beams apparently freed by a further break in the clouds. Wind pushed and gravity pulled at the water droplets coagulating into fist-sized circles on the window panes.

Miranda studied the beams and the shapes they now cast down the walls and across the floor. On the partially painted coastal map she'd left there, a lens seemed to magnify Milford-Haven.

Samantha Hugo's hand hovered mid-air when the EPC phone rang at two p.m. Yet, rather than snatch up the handset, she ground her teeth and waited for Susan to answer first.

Sixty seconds later, her assistant's voice lifted into a shout. "Samantha, it's the Chernak lady."

"Got it!" she yelled back, composing herself before depressing the illuminated button on her phone. "Hello? Is this Ms. Chernak?"

"Stacey Chernak, here."

Susan did tell me the woman has an accent. "Oh, good. This is Samantha Hugo."

"How do you do!" The woman sounded a little breathless, almost as if she'd been running. "And first I should explain, or, apologize, actually, for not returning your call much earlier."

"Yes, I'd begun to wonder—"

"You see," the woman pressed on, "my husband Bill was in Europe on a case, and I was handling previous commitments on other cases that were concluding urgently."

A click indicated another extension had been picked up, and a man's voice interrupted, "Mrs. Hugo?"

"It's Ms., actually."

"Ah, yes, Ms. Hugo. I am on the line now. Bill Chernak, at your service." *His accent sounds the same as hers . . . but with half the charm.*

"I'm speaking with your wife. Thank you for joining us."

"Yes, Bill," the wife added. "We were just beginning, and it is good you are on the line with us."

Something awkward about this call, but now that I finally have both of them. . . . "Uh, why don't you begin by telling me about your agency?"

The husband interjected, "I can tell you that we have a very high success rate of locating children who have been missing for extended periods of time."

"That may be," Sam allowed, "but there's a complication in my case."

"Oh, and what is that, Ms. Hugo?" Mrs. Chernak asked.

"I contacted the original adoption agency," explained Sam. "Apparently, all their records were destroyed in a fire."

"That was only *one* set of records, Ms. Hugo," the woman reassured her.

"Yes, very possibly we can find others for you," added the man.

"I'm relieved to hear you say that. When I began this . . . this project, there was no actual urgency, and now there is."

"I see," continued the husband. "Let me ask you first exactly what kind of documentation do you have about the child?"

"I have a copy of the birth certificate, and of the foot prints as a matter of fact, locked away in my safe deposit box."

"Ah, good, this is excellent. That is a very good place to start. I think it is time we arrange to meet in person. And we can receive these important papers from you."

Sam hesitated. "I do want to see your credentials first, Mr. Chernak."

"Of course. We will bring those."

"Before we agree to meet—"

"We will be in touch soon about the time and place."

Samantha heard a click. "Hello? Mr. Chernak?" *I can't believe he actually hung up on me.* "Mrs. Chernak?" *No reply, but I heard a second click.* Sam had gotten used to that sound. It usually meant her own assistant had been listening in. This time, however, it'd sounded different—which could only mean it was on the caller's end. *Did the wife feel she couldn't continue the conversation without her husband's participation?* Sam replaced the receiver, her brow creasing as she considered the odd way each of them had behaved.

The wife had seemed nervous at first, rushing to pour out some sort of explanation before her husband joined the call. But the open eagerness had disappeared the moment he came on the line . . . *almost as if she was afraid to talk freely in front of him.*

When the husband first spoke, he'd seemed to want to take over the case. And when Mrs. Chernak chimed in, he'd seemed to want to control her comments, seemed even to want her to be silent. Finally, when it came to offering confirmation of his credentials, he'd hung up on her.

She'd encountered this kind of behavior before. But only from companies and individuals who'd been anxious to avoid environmental regulations. With thorough research and dogged determination, she always got the information she needed in the end.

This was different, though. This was personal. She'd wanted to hire the Chernak Agency to investigate the whereabouts of her long-lost son. Why? To gain some peace of mind.

But instead, this has made me feel more unsettled than ever. Maybe it's time I get some help turning some professional investigating skills on the investigators themselves.

Susan Winslow parked her dented VW bug at the edge of the gas station parking lot near her apartment. Grabbing her small leather backpack before locking the car for the night, she watched her step where the pavement's edge broke into shards.

She glanced up the long flight of weathered-wood stairs that clung to the steep adjacent hill leading to the studio apartment pole-house where she lived. *Like, the climb isn't gonna get any easier just because I'm staring at it.* She huffed her way up the fifty steps, then stood shivering in the dark, waiting to catch her breath. *If I hadn't stopped at the deli, it wouldn't be dark yet. Oh, well. At least they'll have those sandwiches ready for me tomorrow.*

Once she managed to get her front door unlocked, she dropped her backpack on the floor, then clomped over to the built-in electric heater. *Doesn't help much, but geez it's freezing in here!* As the heater tinked to life and its ancient coils began to glow, Susan slid out of her black leather jacket and placed it lovingly on the back of one of her two chairs. Sitting, she undid the laces of her Doc Martens and stepped out of her boots, then padded across to her kitchenette to yank open her refrigerator door and review her dinner options.

"Perfect," she said aloud. "Two stalks of celery. And I'll have soup with that."

Laughing at her little joke, she peered into the sink, scrunching her face at the pile of crusted plates and flatware. *Be nice if someone would do the dishes once in a while.* She laughed again. *And who might that be?*

From her cupboard, she took out a small cardboard box containing cubes of bouillon individually wrapped in foil. Dropping one cube in the bottom of the only clean mug she could find, she ran water into a pan, then put it on the stove to boil.

While the water heated, Susan threw off the rest of her clothes, then riffled through her drawer of T-shirts to find one she could wear to bed. She pulled out a dark green shirt with "I Believe in Winter Solstice" faded lettering across its front. *Well, this is the right time of year, at least. I mean, it's not like I actually believe. And I don't believe in Christmas either. But . . . whatever.* The soft cotton felt good falling against her skin, the oversized shirt as large as a nightgown. But, still chilly, she pulled back on her leather jacket and yanked on a pair of tall wool socks.

She could hear the water bubbling on the stove, and went over to turn off the burner and pour the steaming liquid over the condensed knot of soup stock. When the little block had dissolved, she stuck the end of her celery stalk into it. She munched loudly over the sink, nibbling the exposed end till the vegetable was consumed, then carried what was left of her warm broth to her bedside table.

That's another laugh. The bed's just a mattress on the floor, and the table's just a stack of old phone books. She placed the mug on the floor, then settled back against bunched pillows and rumpled covers, pulling the black comforter over her bare legs.

She sighed. *This is the only part of the day I actually like. Well, almost the only part. I kinda liked irritating Samantha today.* Her mouth pulled into a sideways grin at the remembrance of her boss's tension earlier.

Susan reached for the album she kept nearby, enjoying the crackle of the plastic sheets that covered clippings of her favorite rock bands, interspersed with some of her own photographs. *There he is again . . . Ken Casmalia, that guy from the Res. Can't really see his face, though. Wonder if he'll be at the concert? If he is, don't know if I'd recognize him.*

Dismissing the notion for now, she turned the page. "Slash," she intoned reverently. "He is *so*, like, amazing. He's even *more* amazing than he was when he played guitar with Guns N'

Roses." Her hand touched the image of the long-haired, top-hatted, shade-wearing musician whose bare, muscular arms held an electric guitar vertically, an intense expression on his face. *And he's only, like, ten years older than me, or something. If I could only meet him, and take his picture myself!*

But I will *be taking pictures backstage at a big concert . . . next week!* Her heart thumped against her ribs at the thought of the upcoming concert. *Who knew Samantha would actually be right about something, for a change? She told me to ask the Milford-Haven News if I could, like, write about the concert and take photos. And they said yes!*

The Central Coast Bowl hosted concerts on a regular schedule. But with the offerings more likely to be some symphony playing classical stuff, Susan rarely paid attention. But this would be different. The Doobie Brothers were coming to town! *I mean, they're, like, a little older and stuff. But they're incredible!*

Access to the backstage area was already arranged. She'd be picking up her official Press pass at the will-call window, according the newspaper's editor. But how would she know where to go? How would she make herself heard over all the noise? And what if she got lost in the dark and couldn't even find the stage door?

She pushed away at the sudden feeling of vulnerability. *I mean, I could go by myself. But, like, I don't exactly trust those people. I need somebody big to go with me, somebody who can, like, see over the crowd. Somebody who's on my side.*

Earlier today, she'd hatched the idea of getting Kevin to take her to the concert. He could drive her there, wait for her after the show, and drive her home. She wouldn't be alone, like some groupie. She'd have her own person. *That way, they'll know they have to take me seriously, and everything.*

The next thing to figure out was how to get Kevin to agree. *Shouldn't be* that *hard. I mean, he already likes me, and stuff. So, like, what should I wear? I mean, I know what to wear to the show—one of my usual rock-concert outfits. Yeah, but I can't wear that stuff to work. Still, I wanna wear something to get his attention. I mean, not with the nosering—he already doesn't like that. With, like, a really hot skirt, or maybe tight pants.*

Susan looked up at her postered wall. From where she lay across her unmade bed she could admire her rock-star icons in all their leather, dyed, and pierced glory. But Kevin didn't fit the image.

He was taller than most men. She liked that, liked being so much shorter. None of the boys she grew up with on the Chumash Reservation were especially tall, and she sought out guys who were as different as possible from any of them.

Her own mother had been Caucasian, and Susan could sometimes pass for white—when it suited her. On the other hand, it sometimes came in handy to take advantage of her Native heritage.

She didn't think Kevin minded one way or the other, which was cool. *But Kevin is so ... straight! No facial hair. And, like, he has no long ponytail. But he also has no buzz cut, like some of the cute guys he works with. And if he keeps anything else in that pocket protector, he'll fall over on his face! What a strange dude he is.*

She felt in her heart that "strange" wasn't really the right word for Kevin, because she felt too comfortable with him to feel he was strange. Yet there was something she couldn't identify at first. *I know . . . it's because he's always in that terminally nice mood.* It was enough to make a sane girl puke. But that wouldn't get her the favor she needed.

She'd already found out one thing—that she could get him going. She'd seen him get all fidgety that time in Jack Sawyer's office. She'd gotten close to him for a few minutes before Jack had interrupted them. But it had been long enough to *know.*

She sometimes imagined sleeping with him. She knew she'd get bored with him fast after they did it. That's how it always went. First she'd make contact with a guy, usually at Wing Ding's. "Eye waving," she called it. She'd "wave" with her eyelashes and the guy would start staring at her. Next thing she knew, he'd be walking over. They'd talk, if they could hear themselves over the music. He'd ask for her number. She'd never give it. She'd ask for his instead. Most guys liked that, found it different, maybe a little mysterious. She liked it because it put the power on her side right from the beginning.

Then the fun part started. She'd call the guy—if and when she felt like it. It would catch him off guard. He'd accept her invitation to go dance at Wing Ding's. Or sometimes he'd have ideas of his own. Sometimes she'd accept.

Sleeping with someone for the first time was always exciting. Sometimes it would be fast, sometimes slow, but always new. She enjoyed seeing the guy's face as he looked at her tight body for the first time. Some guys were shy and she'd become confrontive, forcing them to look at her. Some guys were hungry and self-confident. She loved challenging them. It made her feel daring and brave, and she blocked the thought that she was using the men she met to fill the hole that gaped where her soul lay dormant.

After sex, she could never sustain her interest. The thrill of discovery was gone. There wasn't much point in continuing. She'd go through the motions maybe once or twice more. But then she'd stop calling. If she ran into him at the bar, she'd be distant. No hurt feelings. No feelings at all.

Kevin doesn't fit into this pattern. He isn't exactly a friend. He isn't exactly a colleague. When she really thought about it, she had to acknowledge that he was, in fact, a member of a rival "gang." She was a Samantha-Home-Girl. He was a Sawyer-Disciple. She laughed at her joke, rolled off her bed, and padded over to her bathroom. She leaned toward the mirror to finger her new nose ring. *Still a little sore. But way cool.*

Tilting her head to one side then the other, she imagined she stood in front of Kevin—in which case she'd be looking up. *Way up.* She knew Kevin had been told by his boss to "keep tabs" on her. She'd gotten him to admit that much. *Mr. Sawyer prob'ly thinks I'll let something slip about Samantha that he can use against her. But he won't get a thing outta me.* Still, the fact that Kevin was actually *supposed* to spend time with her made it all the more likely he'd accept her invitation to the concert.

My plan's gonna work just perfectly. Kevin liked music. In fact, he even liked the Doobie Brothers. *Anyone who's into classic rock can't be all bad.* She couldn't have afforded the extra ticket to the Central Coast Bowl. *That's another cool thing. They gave me a comp for a guest.* For sure, she couldn't count on her decrepit car to get them all the way to Santa Maria. *So we can go in his truck.*

Satisfied with her strategy, Susan danced the few short steps to her closet to review her limited wardrobe options. She pulled her short purple skirt out of the closet, and held it in front of her, checking herself out in the thin mirror on the back of the closet door. *Not bad.*

I'll take a long lunch break tomorrow, and surprise Kevin at Sawyer Construction. Is he gonna agree to take me to the show? She smirked at her reflection. *Oh, yeah. It'll be a piece of cake.*

Chapter 5

J ack Sawyer pushed open the door of Sally's Restaurant and
stepped inside. Despite the annoyance of blinking Christmas
lights, the place seemed a little calmer than usual—no doubt
because he frequented the establishment during peak hours.
No one sat at the counter, and the few customers still seated at
tables were finished with their meals and lingered over cups of
coffee.

*She'll be closing soon. Looks like I was right to come at this
time of day. I can catch her when she's tired and not geared up
for one of her "conversations."*

Closing the door behind him, he took a moment to glance
around the room. *She must be in the kitchen.* He hesitated
before he made his presence known. *I've already put off this
irritating issue for weeks. Now that I'm here, I should just get on
with it.*

In the four years they'd been dating, Sally'd never put him

on the spot until last October. Her behavior'd seemed out of character. *How would I even describe it? Emotional blackmail? Yeah, that's what it was.* She'd marched into his office, claiming she had information about "a child." When he demanded to know what *that* meant, she'd said she wouldn't tell him until he signed a certain piece of paper.

That paper had turned out to be a formalizing of an agreement they'd already made—that he would build an addition onto her restaurant. The tiny existing office being little more than a closet, it'd been clear to him at the outset he'd need to break out her wall, then expand the few feet to the western edge of her property, which bordered the hardware store. *It was a fun challenge to do the design. But now, I've been putting it off for a couple of years. Time I put it on the schedule and got it done.*

He'd ruminated about the letter of agreement for the first three weeks of November, but then it seemed to have slipped Sally's mind as she'd prepared for their early Thanksgiving holiday. In fact, they'd had a great time taking it easy at his place. *Good eating. Good times in the sack. Not a lot of talking. My kind of long weekend.*

Except at the very end. As she'd hefted her overnight bag to head home on Sunday night, she'd tossed off that comment: "I guess you're not interested in hearing about the child, and you obviously have no intention of building my addition!" She'd slammed her car door and ever since then, Sally'd been making excuses about being too busy to spend time with him. Even when they ran into each other at the restaurant, the tension was palpable.

My heart about stopped when she first brought up this

matter of the child. But, obviously, she's not pregnant, just as we always agreed. So if her "big" tidbit of info isn't about any child of ours, it has to be someone else's, and who cares? But . . . if I don't go along with her, we'll never get past this awkwardness, and I'll be sleeping alone every night.

So, against his better judgment, he'd signed Sally's letter of agreement. He was here to hand it over, and he looked forward to resuming the normal pattern of their casual liaison. Now, Jack hitched up his slacks and sauntered over to the counter that Sally was polishing, determined to keep anxiety from his graveled voice. "Hello, Sally."

"Why, Jack! I didn't know if I'd ever talk to you again."

"Aww," he growled. "That's overstating things, isn't it? I mean, we just spent a holiday together—"

"—twenty-two days ago. But who's countin'?" He saw her eyes dart to the paper in his hand. And then she started humming that maddening nondescript tune of hers as she dragged her moistened rag the length of her counter.

So, Sally's gonna play coy. He pasted a smile on his face. "Yes, well, you're the one who delivered the ultimatum."

Her gaze snapped up to meet his.

Good. That got her attention. Waggling the paper, he asked, "Uh, can we talk privately for a few minutes?"

She lifted her chin, then cocked her head to one side trying to suppress a smile. *The gloat doesn't become her.*

Gripping the counter edge to keep from squirming, he glanced around uneasily, feeling as if every customer's eyes were boring holes through his back.

"Why, certainly, Jack. Step into my crowded, cramped, nasty little office, won't you?" Her hips swayed under her apron strings as she led the way. When they entered the office, she closed the door and gestured to him to be seated in the only chair. That would leave her standing over him, but Jack felt he had best comply—for now at least.

"All right, Sally, you've got me where you want me. Here's your damnable piece of paper. It's pure extortion. But I'll build that infernal addition of yours."

"Oh, Jack!" Sally plunked herself onto Jack's lap and fastened her lips on his.

Now she's going sappy and sentimental. And you never know who might walk in here. Time enough for her gratitude, and our private fun, later. He held her away. "Let's don't start that right now, Sally. All right. What's this information you feel is *so* valuable?"

She withdrew her arms from around his neck, but remained sitting sideways across his lap. She twisted a finger in her apron as she settled down. *She's looking at me with those adoring eyes. Best not to think of such things now. She'll have me tied up in those apron strings.*

"What I have to tell you is pretty big news, Jack."

He couldn't keep from laughing out loud. She always found it necessary to heighten every tidbit of gossip with exactly the same sort of fanfare. "Big news." He laughed again. "Well, for the price, it'd better be." Feeling himself relax, he rested a hand on her hip.

"This might prob'ly upset you, Jack."

He sighed. "That's never stopped you before!"

"All right, all right." She cleared her throat. "You have a child."

Jack stood so suddenly that Sally slid off his lap, nearly

hitting the floor. He made no attempt to keep his voice down. "I have a *what*?"

"Now, Jack," she reminded him as she stood. "I told you this would upset you."

"Damn it, Sally! We had an agreement!" He looked for a place to pace but found none in the tiny room. "Didn't we discuss all this before? Didn't we agree this would *not* happen?"

"Oh, no, no, Jack, it's not what you think. *I'm* not pregnant!"

Jack rooted himself to the floor and trained a laser-like stare into her. "Then what the devil did you mean?"

"I meant that, somewhere in the world, you have a child."

For once, Jack was truly mystified. "Somewhere in the world?"

Sally O'Mally stared up into the man's face. *So good lookin' most o' the time. But right now he's got an ugly mad on.* She took in the sight of his solid, muscular six-foot frame. Suddenly his salt-and-pepper hair seemed coarse, his face weathered. His blue eyes began to burn from within as if powered by a terrible current.

A fear ignited in her gut, and she began to talk fast. "It's true, Jack. I overheard Samantha and Miranda talkin'. And Samantha was . . . she was pregnant when you got divorced, and. . . ."

Sally swallowed. *Moon in the mornin', seems like his face might just turn to stone. But if I don't ask him now, I jus' never will!* "Why didn't you ever *tell* me you were married to somebody else right here in town . . . Samantha, of all people?" *She ignored the tremor in her own voice.* "I mean you'd think, with all we mean to each other, that you could at least tell me somethin' so important as that!"

His eyes . . . they look different now . . . like he's seein' right through me to the wall behind my head. Like he's tryin' to see backward through time.

"A *child!*" he muttered. "Samantha. So it happened all those years ago. . . ."

"And you never even trusted me enough to tell me."

"Oh, shut up, Sally. You're not the one dealing with a crisis here." Jack seemed to try once more to pace the tiny area, taking no notice of her own heaving chest. "Why didn't Sam ever tell me?"

"I know you're mad, Jack, but that Samantha doesn't matter any more. You have someone else in your life now. You have me."

Smacking his fist into his other palm, he exploded with "*Blast* that woman!"

Sally placed a hand on Jack's arm, hazarding a smile. "We got so much to look forward to our own selves. And we could start with building something together, like my addition."

Jack brought his glare back to her as if he had no idea what she was talking about.

"You know, now that you've signed our agreement, and all."

Thrusting an arm past her, he flung open the door so violently that it swung wide and banged her desk.

Through the sudden opening, Sally saw glances from her remaining customers fly in their direction. She murmured, "We should keep the door closed till we're—"

He charged from the small room.

"Where're you goin'?" Sally managed.

He strode toward the front door. *It's like his pants are on fire.* "Jack!" Sally called after him. "You promised!"

He banged out of the restaurant.

"You promised," she whispered. Mustering a smile for her customers, Sally quietly closed the door of her private office just as the first tears pooled. Seconds later, hot tears stung as they streamed down her flushed cheeks.

Perhaps her calculations about Jack Sawyer had been quite wrong. *I thought he cared . . . cared about* me.

Jack gripped his steering wheel with fisted hands as if he were bracing himself for a hurricane.

Every thought in his head had been swept away, carried in a flood of emotions rising so fast he could barely keep ahead of them.

All his agonizing over how to solve the situation with Sally . . . signing her agreement . . . anticipating they'd resume their relationship . . . none of it seemed to matter now.

He peeled rubber barreling out of the restaurant parking lot as the big engine labored to get him onto the highway. He drove north hoping to outrun the tide threatening to overtake him. But it caught up, deluging him with the sharp memories of his first meeting with Samantha decades earlier.

Jack Sawyer looked up from the research papers in his carrel at the Doe Library at UC Berkeley.

He tossed down his pencil to run stiff fingers through his thick, black hair, absently noting he was overdue for a haircut . . . a luxury he could seldom afford on his student's stipend.

From where he sat, he couldn't see a clock. Must be getting late. *He stacked his papers and books together and pulled on his leather bomber jacket. It was his father's, technically, but his mom had agreed that Jack should have it, now that Dad was gone.* It's pretty much all I have of the old man's. So much for his returning home from Korea as a war hero.

Jack easily lifted the heavy stack of books and made his way toward the reference desk. That middle-aged librarian would be absorbed in reading something highly intelligent, and he chuckled at the thought of making her jump. She fusses at me, but in the end she always breaks a smile. *Knowing the power of his charm, he moved quietly, staying hidden behind a tall bookshelf till the last minute, then edged around its corner hands first, hiding his head behind a potted plant.*

He let go of the books and they hit the desk with a thwack.

"Oh!" a woman's voice rang out.

He began to laugh softly, catching a glimpse of raised shoulders. She got a pretty good scare ... breathing hard while she presses a hand to her chest. Probably the most excitement the poor thing's had all week.

Yet, from what he could see of the librarian's torso, something seemed different this evening. That blouse . . . thin fabric over the ample chest. Silk. And slightly see-through! Either this gal's had plastic surgery, or. . . .

She cleared her throat, the sound startling Jack, who managed to stop staring at those breasts straining the delicate silk to identify the woman seated behind the tall desk. His eyes were met by the steady gaze of a red-headed goddess. Those eyes . . . amber? Cognac? She's glaring. No . . . she's emanating.

"Shh!" she hissed. "This is a library!"

"That's good technique."

"What?"

"The stage whisper. It actually works much better in a

cavernous space like this." He kept his voice low, his most engaging smile in place. "You must be an actress."

The exasperation that washed over her face delighted him. She flipped her hair over one shoulder and said sternly, "If you're not here to study, please leave!"

He continued to stand at the desk, studying her, *taking in the magnificent architecture of her long bones, the voluptuous sculpture of her flesh. As he watched, hues of peach and orange tinged her golden skin, the color rising until she appeared luminous.*

Got it . . . got those dimensions and gradations memorized. This first time, I just want the visuals.

He stood for a moment longer and she seemed to be waiting for him to say or do something. All he gave her was another smile. Then he turned and, with long easy strides, left the building.

Jack yanked the wheel of his truck to the left and sprayed gravel as he pulled into the Lighthouse Tavern parking lot. *The place looks nearly deserted. Good.*

His boots crunched through the loose gravel and hammered the flagstone entry. He pushed open the heavy door and angled left toward the bar.

"Jack Daniels," he pronounced.

The barkeep gave him a long look. Then in one smooth motion, he took down a bottle, spun a glass, poured the drink, and placed it on the counter.

Ignoring the "Ho ho ho" from a mechanical Santa, Jack slapped a twenty-dollar bill on the bar, making it plain he intended to keep drinking for a while, then moved off to a solitary window table.

As a sluice of alcohol strafed down his throat, he thought back to that first year with Sam, a year in which they'd both been studying like maniacs—and been just as maniacally in love. *We could barely keep our hands off each other, except when we'd get into those marathon talks. Never knew anyone who actually got me. Never before. Never since.*

Now the slide show in his head skipped forward in time. As the orange ball of the sun sizzled down into the sea, fiery streamers lit its surface reaching for him across the water like long tendrils of her mane.

Jack, gripping the convertible's gear shift, glanced over to watch Samantha toss her head and let her thick red hair stream into the wind.

He laughed, feeling the big engine respond. A gift passed along by his mom, the turquoise-and-ivory '55 Bel Air, with its gleaming chrome and hood ornament, was his pride and joy. He'd tinkered with it until Chevrolet itself wouldn't have recognized what was under the hood. And he'd put in the Hurst heavy-duty clutch and shifter. He shifted now, just to see Sam's chest bounce again under that Angora sweater. She caught him looking, but it only made her laugh—a throaty sound he'd come to love.

Only one person knew where they were going: Sam's roommate Ruth, and she was sworn to secrecy. Ruth was a good kid, but full of the devil. As she'd seen them slide into the car that morning, she'd asked him, "Are you sure you didn't get her pregnant?"

"Why?" Jack had taunted. "Should I?"

Sam had been listening to all this, and hit him on the arm. "You know, Ruthie," she chided, "that's not the only reason to get married."

"I know, I know," Ruthie intoned, twirling a finger through her Afro. "It's true love. I 'Second That Emotion.' Well, have a good time 'Going to the Chapel,' children. I won't wait up. And I won't tell the Dean."

Now, as the turquoise car sped north, they were headed not to a chapel, but to a small farm, where a Justice of the Peace had agreed to marry them. "Just ring the dinner bell by the porch," he'd said.

When they did, a man in overalls came around the side of the house, brushing dirt from his hands. "Go on into the house. I'll be right with you," he promised. The Justice disappeared, apparently to clean his hands and don a black robe. When his wife brought in the Bible, the transformation was complete. "You ready?" The Justice seemed eager to get back to his fields.

Jack's stomach felt suddenly queasy. "Ready?"

"Do you have the rings, he means," Mrs. Justice asked.

"Oh! Right here." Jack unbuttoned his breast pocket, and produced two silver bands they'd picked up at Woolworth's. The rings suddenly seemed as cheap as they were.

But then he looked over at his radiant bride, glowing as if lit by a sunset. A calm filled him. He took her hand.

During the brief ceremony, a hush came over the room. As they exchanged their vows, that holy thing that was supposed to happen at weddings . . . what was it . . . the water turning to wine? It happened in that Justice-Farmer's front room.

"You may kiss the bride." Jack did, losing himself for a long moment, sensing a completeness he'd never known before.

While they'd all signed their witness papers, the woman excused herself and Jack paid his fees. Then the bridegroom pumped their host's arm a little too vigorously, and took the hand of his brand new wife.

They stepped out onto the front porch, where they were startled by a shower of birdseed. Mrs. Justice stood there, ready to let go with another handful. "You two have a long and happy life together," she called.

Jack and Sam grinned at each other, then made a dash— through the next sprinkling—to the car. They knew they were heading for the nearest motel and their first legal night of passion. As they drove away, Sam's joyous laugh sounded every bit as celebratory as would be the clanging of cans tied to the back of the Chevrolet.

Jack swept a hand down his face and squinted out the window of the Lighthouse Tavern, noting that the scenery had all but disappeared. The darker it got, the less there was to see, as there were virtually no coastal lights this far north.

Nor was his own interior landscape getting any better. A slight liquor haze had risen up around the edges of his brain like a low lying Tule fog on Highway 1. Though he could no longer think clearly, a perverse codicil of universal law dictated that he could *remember* even more sharply than usual.

As another belt of bourbon lit a fire down his gullet, Jack stewed about how he might rid himself of the memories and knew, with the certainty of his impending heartburn, that he'd do just about anything to be free of Sam.

Before he got too drunk to drive, he marched himself to his

truck, making it crawl at twenty miles an hour up the hill to his house.

Stacey Chernak had stayed late at her job as the secretary at Clarke Shipping in Morro Bay, clearing both her own desk and the conference room before she finally left for the day.

This was a big task ... the printing, collating, stapling, hole-punching, placing into binders. ... but it is all complete.

She'd hurried home and now hefted her purse from the passenger's seat, locked the car door behind her, and took the concrete sidewalk to the apartment she shared with her husband.

She inserted her key and turned it to open the door into a small, nearly dark foyer. She clicked on the cheap wall fixture that only partially illuminated a long hallway leading to the study, where she expected to find Wilhelm. *It used to be lovely to come home to him. Now, I never know what to expect.*

"Wil ... Bill? Are you here?" They spoke English, even when they were alone. It was one of his rules. "It is a *schlechte Gewohnheiten*—bad habit," he'd say, "to speak the mother tongue when we are Americans now." He'd insisted they Americanize their names as well, so she no longer called herself Stasia.

A gruff voice emerged from the study. "What is it, Stacey? I am very busy here." *Oh, dear. A nasty mood ... but not one of his worst.*

She smoothed her short blond hair, calmed her expression, and walked toward the back of the apartment, switching on another light as she did. "I am sorry to bother you. I am just seeing if you need anything. Would you like some tea?"

He didn't look up. *His hair and beard are silvery now . . . like frost fallen onto a dark blanket . . . but he is still so handsome.*

She tried again to start a conversation. "I thought our conversation with Samantha Hugo went well."

He looked up sharply from his work. "Of course it went well. I had that prospect all arranged."

His mood is worse than I thought. "Yes, dear," she offered in a conciliatory tone. "We did perhaps end the call rather suddenly. I could not think of what to say next." *The English still feels awkward. I cannot yet determine the contractions. I think of them after I speak, not before, as I should.*

Wilhelm squinted up at her. "You almost did it again, Stacey."

A trace of fear skipped through her heart as her husband's tone worsened. "I . . . almost did what again?"

His black eyes peered at her over the top of his glasses, and he began speaking in dreaded, instructional tones. "You nearly said too much to Mrs. Hugo."

"But it was you, dear, who did most of the talking to her."

"I am referring to before I joined the call, when you thought you were by yourself on the telephone."

She drew her eyes away, trying to piece together those few moments. "So, you are saying that you—"

"Yes, I listened, Liebchen. I, of course, monitored your words, your tone of voice, your eagerness to make the best impression."

When she brought her gaze back to his, she nearly winced at the grin that failed to reach his eyes.

"I have warned you," he continued, "about your

incompetence at business. But you *will* do better, yes?"

"Yes!" She tried to settle her fluttering stomach. "I am always learning, because you are such a good teacher, Wil . . . Bill."

"And speaking of learning, why is it your English is still not improved? After all the lessons and the coaching you have received, you should now sound like a native speaker."

I do not sound native, but my English is actually better than his. Of course, I will not mention this.

"For me, it is too late, I am older. But you are younger. It should be easy."

"Perhaps with more practice, dear, more chance to talk with other people. . . ."

"I will see that you receive the proper opportunities for contacting *other* people. Meanwhile, you do have very important employment, which you sometimes seem to forget."

Horrified, Stacey interjected, "But I never forget my job!"

"Good! Because I procured this job for you at Clarke Shipping only because Mr. Russell Clarke is a very important colleague. Employing you he did only as a personal favor to me."

She gathered her strength, chafing at the unfairness of her husband's claim. "I did have to pass the hiring criteria of his personnel director. And she and the others in the office always compliment my work. You know I take very seriously this excellent position. That is why I asked you if I could stay later tonight, to prepare the special presentation materials for them."

Now Wilhelm gave her a genuine smile.

Encouraged, she pressed on. "I do wish to mention again,

dear, that I still feel uncomfortable doing our own agency business at their office. This does not feel correct."

His expression tightened. "I have told you, *I* know what is correct. What I have already arranged with Clarke is for you to initiate our conference calls from there, when necessary."

"We should pay them for these calls. Is not that true, Wilhelm?"

He pointed his finger at her. "You know you are to call me 'Bill.' And of course this is not true! I will not explain again, I have this all arranged!"

Stacey shifted her weight from one foot to the other. *He no longer likes for me to appear too sexy.* She kept her hip from arching to one side. "Yes, of course . . . Bill. I understand. You do not need to worry."

"Listen to me, Liebchen, I will give you something to worry about. You say too much to a client again—where you risk contradicting me, where you give people a poor impression of our agency—and you will be sorry." He glared up at her again. "I have very good reasons why you must behave exactly as I say. I have told you before, I am working on a critical project."

Stacey broke away from the piercing stare and moved back from his desk. Gently, she dared to ask, "You know, Bill, you still have not told me what *is* this project of yours."

Now he didn't bother to look up. "That is right, Liebchen, I have not. And that is the beauty of it, you see? I have everything under control, and no one else knows what I am up to, so no one can interfere. Not even you! You see?"

Stacey recoiled and retreated to the kitchen. The meatloaf she'd made yesterday would serve as tonight's dinner as well. She'd make fresh mashed potatoes to go with it, even though the lack of a potato ricer made the task more difficult.

The ricer my aunt gave me when I first moved away from Geneva . . . it is in a box in storage now, along with so many other precious objects. Best not to think of them. But later . . . I will bring out the Christmas box. It will make me feel better . . . and maybe Wilhelm too.

She put five small potatoes on to boil. She preferred cooking with gas, and the electric range was difficult to work with, but it was adequate. *Adequate to boil water. Adequate to burn flesh.*

It had been two weeks since he'd forced her wrist onto the burner. Or had it been three? She fingered the scar gently. *Not so noticeable now. Perhaps it will fade even more with time.* Or perhaps, as she became an old woman, it would disappear into one of the creases. *I will always know it is there.*

A hissing sound startled her. She looked down to see water boiling over onto the hot coils. "*Scheiße*," she said quietly, lifting the pan, and attempting to adjust the burner. As she soaked up hot water with a dish towel, she suddenly realized Wilhelm was standing in the doorway.

"Daydreaming again, are we, Liebchen?" And with that, he began his deep, terrifying laugh.

Jack Sawyer spent worse than a sleepless night.

Twisting himself in sweat-stained sheets, he tried his best to strangle his dreams. Instead, he managed only to wake himself fitfully—torn between downing a sleeping pill or another drink—in the end, choosing neither. Giving up the effort entirely at 3:45 a.m., he struggled into his threadbare robe, then stumbled out to sit on his deck in the chilly dark—the night birds silent, the stars no solace.

Shuffling back inside, he went in search of the cigarettes he'd hidden somewhere. He knew he wouldn't succeed in his effort to quit now, any more than he'd succeeded before. *And this is no time to try.*

Standing on a stepstool, reaching far into the cabinet over top of the refrigerator, he found a stash of mis-matched and long unused paper plates and napkins. *Sally's summer picnics.* Angry at the idea of festive times, he flung the useless things to the floor. Reaching back into the cupboard again, he felt for a familiar shape. *Got it. A half-finished carton of Camels. Five packs left.*

He made a ceremony of the moment, retying his belt, reboiling some old coffee, pouring it into a chipped mug, and heading outside with his fresh old pack of nasties. He sat on the deck now, the wrapper crinkling in one hand, the cancer stick curling plumes in the other. With the deep, addictive sense of satisfaction only a smoker can know, Jack dragged on his cigarette and blew smoke at the trees.

He couldn't tell whether his anger was subsiding, or just getting started. He didn't really know, yet, how he felt about having a son—or a daughter—some grown person he'd never known. With the septic high afforded by the tobacco's nicotine, his focus began to sharpen, however. He knew, now, that he wanted to confront Samantha.

He remembered she was an early riser. He crushed out a second cigarette, then headed back inside where he rehid the box, tossed the open pack into the back of a drawer.

Might as well shower now. Hanging the bathrobe on the

back of the door, he assessed himself briefly in the mirrored bathroom wall above the sinks. His body, even with its extra pounds, was still taut, packed with muscle, sinew, and a toughened layer of fat that gave him extra heft on the job.

His can of shaving cream sputtered its last bit of foam into his hand, and he lathered his face more deliberately than usual. He reached for his razor and dragged its edge carefully down his cheek. *Sam likes to use my razor for her legs.*

Damn! Jack threw the razor into the sink and exhaled, his buttocks tight with tension. *Sam hasn't used my razor in decades, and Sally always used her own. What the hell!*

Jack looked in the mirror and glanced to the empty, unused second sink. *It's like being haunted by a ghost.*

Chapter 6

Susan Winslow had made a particular effort to arrive well before the EPC office opened this morning. For one thing, she had to take off during lunch so she could pick up her deli order and have her special meeting with Kevin. And for another, she was hungry and had no food at home. *The fresh rolls Samantha usually brings in are fattening, but eating for free is better than springing for my own breakfast.*

She knew Samantha would be there *way* early, after taking off a half-day yesterday. To avoid calling attention to her own early arrival, Susan opened the outer door quietly. A glance toward her boss's office confirmed that a crack of light appeared along the bottom of the door. Though it was difficult in her clunky shoes, Susan tried tiptoeing across to the small office kitchen, where she lifted the top on today's fresh bakery box.

Lucked out! Susan exulted, her eyes wide at the assortment of filled rolls. *Hah! Breakfast* and *dinner!* Grabbing a recycled paper bag from the cupboard, she stuffed it with two savory cheese-biscuits for tonight. Next, she chose a jelly donut and opened her mouth for a first bite. Just then, a loud bang startled her so much she dropped the treat back into its box.

Stepping from the kitchen alcove, she was just in time to see Jack Sawyer burst through the outer door. "Uh . . . good morning, Mr. Sawyer." Susan stood transfixed as Jack barreled on across the room. "Oh, Sir—you can't go in there!" He didn't break stride until he'd thrown open Sam's office door.

Jack bellowed, "You should've been a bit more discreet if you didn't want to be overheard."

Oh, boy. I think I know what this could be about! Susan hurried to her boss's open doorway where she saw the two facing off over the desk. "Sorry, Samantha. I tried to stop him."

"I know about it, Sam." Mr. Sawyer stood in front of Sam's desk looking like a volcano about to blow.

Before Susan could stop herself, she asked, "You know about what?"

Without looking at her, he muttered to Sam, "You better close this door unless you want the world at large to know about it too."

Samantha Hugo would've liked to throw them both out of her office. She began with her assistant. "Susan, could you please leave us alone, and close the door behind you?"

Susan pulled a pouty face, then did as she was told. Sam then turned an icy stare on Jack. "Who do you think you are— barging into my office, and what are you huffing and puffing about?"

Jack stood across from her desk, feet apart. "It's no good, Sam. I know about it."

"About *it*?"

"*Him*—or *her*—I should say. The child!"

Oh, my God. How could he already have heard I'm looking for Gregory? Hoping she might be wrong, she asked quietly, "What child?"

"Yours."

She froze.

"Ours," he continued.

"Oh, no."

"Mine."

"I see," she said simply, then collapsed in her desk chair.

Jack put his fists on the desk to lean on his knuckles, bending toward her, his bulk adding menace to his anger. "Well, I don't! I don't see how you could keep this from me for thirty years. How could you think I wouldn't find out?"

As many times as Sam had played out this scene in her head, this was not at all as she had imagined it. "You *didn't* find out, Jack. You never even cared enough to find out if I was breathing after we separated."

"I was angry!" Jack retorted. "You were so damn busy with your thesis tutor, it was clear you had no time for me!"

"I had a doctorate to complete. What was I supposed to do, not speak to Richard?"

"Ah, Richard, is it?" Jack fumed. "I thought he was *Professor* Farnsworth. My point exactly."

"No, Jack, it was *my* point exactly. You never trusted me."

"You did sleep with him, didn't you? How do I know the child isn't his?"

Incredible! He still believes I had an affair with my tutor! "I won't even dignify that with an answer." She paused and squinted at her former husband. "I can't believe we're having this conversation."

Jack snorted, took a step toward the chair opposite Sam's desk, and sat down heavily. He pulled at his mustache and glared at her.

Sam stared back at the familiar face. The lyrics of Jacques Brel's "The Song of Old Lovers" coursed through her head. " . . . *les éclats des vieilles tempêtes* . . . claps of thunder from old storms." *So this is what we've come to . . . all our love for each other burned and shattered like a tree splayed by lightning; all our mutual respect redirected toward constant competition, a lockstep of counter-productive checkmates.*

"Where is it, this child?" he accused. "Where have you been hiding it all these years?"

"*Him!* The child was a boy."

He sucked in his breath.

"I haven't hidden him anywhere. I gave him up at age one."

Color leapt into Jack's face and veins throbbed at his temples. "What?" he yelled. "You gave him up? You gave away my son?"

Sam spun the chair away from her desk, and stood. "Oh, so suddenly he's *your* son! Look, arguing isn't getting us anywhere." She moved toward the window to put space between them. "But as long as you've come blundering into this, I should tell you I've decided I want to find him."

"*Now* you want him back again?" he demanded. "What's this, precautionary measures to protect your political future?"

Sam looked at him. "It's easy for you to blame someone else, isn't it? You, who were never interested in children?" She gripped the windowsill and looked out at the sturdy sycamore standing strong just outside, determined not to allow her emotions to swamp her in front of Jack. "Can't we bury the hatchet long enough to discuss—"

"—Long enough to make sure no one threatens your precious political appointment?"

She felt the anger flushing away the conciliatory thoughts she'd tried to hold. "Everything is political to you, isn't it, Jack? Everything is pride! There's nothing sacred!"

He sprang up from the chair. "You talk about something sacred? When you've been deceiving me all these years?"

He's right. I did deceive him. "Jack, I . . . I was scared. It was overwhelming, and I—" She moved toward him, until his eyes stopped her. The clear blue irises seemed to have frozen to a pale, icy hue. And where she usually glimpsed the heat of friction, now her gaze was met by a hollow, flinty stare.

"I do feel I owe you an explanation. It's taken me a long time to—"

"Your time is up. It was up long ago. And I have to get to my office."

Before she could move toward him again, he bolted for the door, yanking it open and startling Susan so badly he nearly knocked her to the floor. He apparently didn't even see her for, despite her yelp, he marched with a military single-mindedness out of the Environmental Planning Commission.

Sam grabbed a tissue and swiped at a tear. "What were you doing, Susan, listening at the door?"

Susan stared back at her boss. "I . . . I was worried about you. I mean, he seemed mad enough to. . . ." Her face, which *had* betrayed genuine concern for a moment, now tightened into its usual smirk. "Never mind, Samantha. You obviously didn't need my help. I'm getting back to work. I have to do an errand at lunch, by the way."

Sam watched her assistant flounce back to her desk. *Not sure what Susan meant just then, but I think she meant well. For now, I've done all the arguing I can.* Closing her door gently, she moved back to her desk and slumped into the chair. Then, she let the tears come.

Susan Winslow, on her way to the deli at noon, glanced up in time to see Jack Sawyer pull out of his office driveway and gun his truck down Main Street. *Obviously he still hasn't cooled down since this morning. Kinda scary how he gets when he's pissed off. Well, at least he's out of my way for now.*

She walked the short distance to the Whale's Belly Deli to pick up the sandwiches she'd ordered: a meatball hero for Kevin, a ham-and-fried-egg for herself. Carrying the fragrant paper bag, she walked back to Sawyer Construction, where her Doc Martens pounded like hammers on the wooden steps.

When she pushed open the door and strode in, she saw Kevin standing at a big table, poring over huge sheets of paper. He looked up with surprise at seeing her. "Hi, Su . . . Susan."

She strutted over to him, punctuating the beats of her shoes by swaying her hips side to side. "Hey, Kevin." She tried to sound casual. "What's going on?"

"Not too much," he answered.

"So, are you busy?"

"Got lots of paper work."

"You're not busy for lunch, right?" she asked, sliding off the straps of her backpack and thrusting a hand in to retrieve her paper bag. "You gotta eat some time, Kevin. Might as well be now. Might as well be free."

Susan placed the backpack and their food over on Kevin's desk where they could sit together, and sauntered toward the kitchen corner. "Got any sodas in here?" Not waiting for his answer, she opened the office mini-fridge, ignored the muck growing around its edges and rummaged inside. She pulled out two generic sodas, made a face at them, shrugged her shoulders, and headed back to Kevin.

Susan eyed a nearby chair, disregarded it, and settled sideways on Kevin's desk. As she did, she watched him fold his long body into his chair. When she'd opened the cans, she yanked at her tiny skirt and handed Kevin his sandwich, then ripped the paper on her own to take a bite.

Kevin Ransom glanced first toward the excellent view of Susan's bared leg, then toward the long, fat sub in its wrapper. As he tried to decide which seemed more enticing, his stomach rumbled and he unwrapped the waxy paper, inhaling the fantastic aroma of the homemade meatballs with their thick tomato sauce.

"Yum!" he cried, hefting the crusty French bread with its seasoned filling. He closed his eyes and opened his mouth wide for a first bite, then chewed blissfully for a long moment.

"How is it?" she asked.

"Mmph oog," he said, his voice muffled.

Susan smiled, took a bite, then guzzled some of her soda.

When Kevin's mouth was finally empty, he asked, "What's the occasion?"

"Doing you a favor."

Oh, boy. That's what I was afraid of. "Oh, yeah?"

"Yeah. So how about doing me one in return?"

This was the part Kevin dreaded. "Sure," he said after he swallowed some of his drink. "If I can."

"Okay. I need a ride to the Bowl. And a ride home. And I need you to wait, like, after the show." Susan took another bite of her sandwich.

"The Central Coast Bowl?" He tried to calculate whether or not his truck would make it that far. "Uh, when?"

"Saturday night. Big concert." Susan reached into her back pack.

"Wait, that's when . . . "

"Got free passes." She waved them in front of his face.

Kevin opened his eyes wide. "No way," he said. "It's the Doobies!"

"Like 'em, huh?" Susan's mouth pulled to one side in a crooked grin.

"They're terrific! Wow. How did you . . . "

"I'm doing a story for the *Milford-Haven News*. Gotta see the concert. Gotta go backstage and interview them too. Thought you might like to go with me." Susan slid off the desk, wrapped the second half of her sandwich, and began picking up the lunch debris.

As he chomped his last bite, he stared at the colorful concert passes, then said again, "Wow."

"That's the second time you've said that, Kevin. Guess that means yes." She went to the garbage container and dropped in the trash.

"Yeah, sure," he said, wiping his mouth and standing. "I have to check the truck, make sure it'll get us there."

"It better," she said, returning to the desk. Now that he was standing, she had to look up at him, and she did so through long black lashes.

Kevin towered over her, his hands thrust as deep into his jeans pockets as they'd go. *She's so pretty. Wish I could hold her. Don't know if she'd let me.* He couldn't help but stare at the side of her nose. "Does that hurt?"

Susan touched the edge of her nostril. "The nose ring? Not much. Like it?"

"I'm not sure."

Susan laughed, and took a step closer to him. A spicy cologne lifted off her skin and tickled his sinuses. "You should bring a blanket," he said.

"Really?" Her eyes flashed. "Why would I do that?"

"Don't have any heat in the truck."

"Oh. Then you can keep me warm. And besides, Kevin, we can have a nice, long talk while we drive over to the Central Coast Bowl." She turned and slid into the shoulder straps of her pack. "Gotta get back to work."

Susan beat a percussive path to the door of Sawyer Construction. She turned to look at him once more. "Later!"

Kevin watched the door slam shut after her. "Wow," he said softly to the empty room.

Chapter 7

Zackery Calvin parked his gunmetal-gray Mercedes 500 SL in the shade of a spreading sycamore in the Santa Barbara Library parking lot. He wished he could've spent the afternoon at home. Instead, after his workout he'd showered at his cottage, zipped into his casual-wear Puma Indie Blue track suit, and chosen the library as a likely spot to find some badly-needed peace and quiet.

This morning he'd asked the Calvin Oil secretary to forward any urgent faxes directly to his cottage, and he'd caught up on his business reading. Then he'd spent ninety minutes in the estate's gym to use the treadmill and weights. From Calma, he'd driven to Starbucks for a bottle of their new Frappuccino beverage, and concealed the unopened drink in his briefcase before making his way inside the library to stop at the reference desk.

The librarian had been very helpful when he asked for environmental references ... perhaps *too* helpful, given the heft of the stack of books he now carried. Finding a remote carrel, he plunked the books on the desk and settled himself.

It'd seemed like such a good idea to read up on environmental matters in preparation for Calvin Oil's upcoming meeting with the Coastal Commission representative. Now he just felt overwhelmed.

He reviewed the selections recommended by the librarian: Rachel Carson's *Silent Spring*; Alston Chase's *Playing God In Yellowstone*; Aldo Leopold's *Sand County Almanac*. According to the dust jackets, each offered horrendous stories of sullying the planet and decimating now-endangered species. *Wonder if any of them offer some hope of redemption.* He looked at the computer print-out he'd requested. "Oil Spills: California." The list went on and on. *No redemption for an oil man like me . . . unless I start a company campaign to contribute to some local ecological charity . . . that's a thought.*

He pulled out his Frappuccino for a sip. *Not only do I feel like a reprobate. I feel like a refugee, hiding out from the onslaught at home.* The whole estate had been taken over by a crew of strangers. At eight a.m., they'd started hammering at tent stakes; at ten, they'd banged open hundreds of folding tables and chairs. *It's anything but "Calma" today! By now, the place will be unrecognizable . . . all for the sake of my so-called birthday party.*

Actually, he'd celebrated his birthday last evening—on the actual day. James, the family butler, prepared a delicious meal; Dad gave him the garage-hoist for his car's hard top— something he'd been wanting. And Cynthia presented him with nice Cartier cufflinks, then later . . . well, she offered her considerable charms in his bed late last night.

She'd left for the main house early this morning to supervise preparations—whatever that might entail. Tonight's party was actually a holiday fund-raiser. *For some reason, Dad's agreed to have the event at Calma. Must've been Cynthia's idea, even though she's not in charge of the charity. I remember that she started out working with the Fine Arts Museum, but then there was some snafu with two charities having their big events on the same night. When the committee realized 1996 was named International Year for the Eradication of Poverty, they switched to Unify, a local charity for low-income residents, which is all to the good. She does seem very excited about it—except for being spooked about the date.*

Friday the thirteenth. She mentioned it over and over again. *Dad thinks the superstition is the silliest thing he's ever heard. But I'm not so sure. I do have an odd feeling about the whole event. Why? Guilt.*

There it was, rearing its head again . . . a lingering discomfort about Cynthia. Mostly, he enjoyed their time together and had been seeing her on and off for two years. They did well at parties and on the few trips they'd taken. *And why shouldn't I date her? Flashy. Beautiful. Fun. Sexy.* Even now, he could feel the heat that radiated from this connection of theirs. *Do we ever really talk? Or is it mostly about the sex?* He never seemed to be able to answer that question.

Maybe that was why he continued to flirt with the idea of contacting Miranda Jones again. He'd *meant* to call her right after they met last October. *Finding that painting of hers when I drove up the coast . . . then meeting her in person . . . hiking across that cove. Heady stuff. I even told her I wanted her to do a special painting for me. Then I never got back to her . . . didn't follow up with her rep, as she requested. Jesus, she must think I'm an asshole. I've gotta make it up to her. How?*

Then it came to him. *Why not invite her to the Doobies concert?* He considered the notion. *No idea if she likes their music . . . but I could arrange something special, like a backstage pass. . . .*

For the last six months, Zack had been helping out with a different fund raiser: a Doobie Brothers reunion concert that would benefit Vietnam veterans. Calvin Oil always contributed to a certain number of charities each year, something he and his dad usually discussed. But he'd never told his father about this one. *Guess I wanted to see how the project developed—not to mention how I felt about working with Rune Sierra. Then, as the date got closer, I felt odd I hadn't mentioned it to Dad. Anyway, not his kinda thing.*

Last year, on a flight to New York, Zack had found himself sitting next to a musician in the First Class cabin. Keith Knudsen, one of the Doobies' percussionists, mentioned his favorite charity, the National Veterans Foundation, and his goal to put together a benefit concert for them. Next thing Zack knew, he'd agreed to help out, though he could hardly imagine what that would involve.

Mostly he'd made phone calls over the past few months, using his contacts to sell blocks of tickets to other corporate sponsors. *It's been fun . . . gave me a different perspective. And going forward, I should generate my own list for Calvin Oil's contributions to worthy causes.*

He'd considered inviting Cynthia to the concert, but she'd made it clear any number of times that she couldn't stand rock-and-roll music. Had he been working with James Taylor or

Stephen Stills, she'd have accepted in a heartbeat. But raucous guitars and men with long hair didn't seem to ring Cynthia's bell. *On the other hand, Miranda might really enjoy them. And it'd be a helluva way to get back in her good graces.*

He peered around the edge of his carrel. *I'm as far away as I could get from the librarian . . . and no one else seems to be here at the moment. Guess I can use my cellular.* He pulled his Motorola Star-TAC clamshell phone from his pocket then fished in his briefcase pocket for the slip of paper with Miranda's phone number. *If I don't call her now I never will.*

He pressed Send and listened to the first ring, startled when she picked up before the second.

"Hello?"

"Miranda? You answered!"

"Sorry, who is this?"

"Zack Calvin." Silence filled the airwaves for a long moment.

"Oh, hi, Zack," she finally said.

"I owe you an apology."

"You don't owe me a thing, Zack. How have you been?"

She sounds distracted . . . or disinterested. Serves me right. "Fine. Busy. But I'm not offering that as an excuse. I just hope you can forgive my not calling sooner."

"Nothing to forgive," she asserted. "What can I do for you?"

"You're painting, aren't you? I've probably interrupted you."

"Uh, I am sort of in the middle of something."

"Okay, I have a question. I'll be up in your neck of the woods next week, and wondered if you might have some time?"

"Depends what day. I'll be out of town till next weekend."

Out of town . . . hadn't counted on that. "Well, if you're back home next weekend, how'd you like to go to a concert?"

"Oh, gosh, that's very nice of you. I thought you wanted to discuss your commission. But I don't think I can spare the time for a concert."

Shoot! I still haven't mentioned her painting! Should have said something about that first. "I apologize again, Miranda. I meant to follow up and contact your rep. It's just been . . . well, I've been working on this concert, among other things."

"Working on . . . you mean, you're performing?"

"No! No, not me. But some guys I know, or have come to know, because of this project. They'll be at the Central Coast Bowl."

"You don't mean. . . ."

Zack heard suppressed excitement in her tone.

"The Bowl? Well, of course, there's the Doobies reunion concert, but I heard the tickets are sold out, so it can't be them."

"Maybe it can."

"Now you're teasing."

"Nope."

"So that's what you do! You were so mysterious when we had dinner. At last, the man of mystery begins to reveal something of himself."

Zack felt a nervous laugh bubble up. "I don't know about that. What do you say? Do you want to go?"

"Yes!" Miranda seemed to collect herself before adding, "I love their music. Just hope I'm back from L.A. in time."

"L.A.? That's where you'll be next week?"

"Right. Actually, I leave tomorrow morning."

"The Doobies are doing a show at the Hollywood Bowl, if you'd rather see that one."

"Which night?" she asked.

"Friday."

"No . . . that's the day I'm driving back to Milford-Haven."

"Okay, so here's another idea. Would you like to come to a rehearsal in L.A.?"

"Really?"

Zack grinned at the almost childlike delight in her voice.

"They have one scheduled at the Bowl—the Hollywood—Wednesday afternoon."

"Okay, let me just check my schedule." He heard the phone hit something—probably the countertop in her kitchen. A moment later, her slightly breathless voice said, "Perfect. That's the one day I didn't have another field trip."

Field trip? Wonder what that means, exactly. Maybe she'll explain when I see her. "Okay, so here's the plan. Come to the Hollywood Bowl at about two p.m. this coming Wednesday the seventeenth. Tell the guards at the gate that you're with me and they'll let you through to the parking lot. Once you park, walk up the concrete ramp toward the auditorium. If I don't come get you right away, ask for Jeff and he'll find me."

Zack heard scribbling. "Just making some notes," Miranda explained. "Okay, got it."

"Sorry I won't be able to pick you up on Wednesday. Know your way around Los Angeles?"

"No. But I have my trusty Thomas Guide."

Zack chuckled. "Yeah, that's the bible for that city. And then on Saturday, I *will* give you a ride from your place. I'll have to pick you up early like, say, at three p.m., and you'll have to wait backstage, if you don't mind."

"Mind? Being backstage with the Doobies? I think I can handle that."

He laughed. "Okay, I'll see you next Wednesday in L.A. Bring your earplugs. It can get really loud near those speakers."

"I'll be ready."

Wonder if she's staying with somebody? "Do you have a number where you'll be staying in L.A., in case I need to leave you a message, or something?"

"I don't have the number right here, but I'll be at a hotel called the Hacienda. It's near LAX in an area called El Segundo."

El Segundo . . . AKA Chevron-town. Why in the world would an environmentalist like her being staying there? Wonder if she knows who runs things there. "Uh . . . okay. And by the way, I'll be at the Hollywood Roosevelt, near the Bowl, if you need to leave a message for me."

"Okay."

"Well, glad I reached you, and sorry again it took me so long."

"That's . . . yeah, it's okay. Thanks so much for the invites. Sounds very special."

"See you soon, Miranda."

"Bye," she said quietly before hanging up.

That soft voice . . . brings it all back. That evening with her at the Lighthouse Tavern . . . how lovely she is, and how shy. Later, that kiss by her front door . . . rather chaste . . . but with a lot of potential.

Joseph Calvin paced the carpeted floor of his office, ignoring the panorama of the Pacific. He'd hoped his fact-finding trip to Chris Christian's condo with Deputy Johnson would reassure him. Instead, he found it had left him even more agitated.

To make matters worse, Zack had failed to send him the promised agenda for their meeting with the Coastal Commission. *Normally, he gives our secretary his dictation and Mary has it typed up a few days ahead of time. But the meeting is set for Monday, and apparently he hasn't yet sent her anything.*

Stopping at his desk, Joseph scanned his agenda book one more time. "I swear if I don't hear from Zack soon, I'll—" His muttering was interrupted by the ringing of his private line, and he grabbed it before Mary could.

"Hello?"

"Hi, Dad."

"Zack, where in blazes are you? I can't believe you haven't done your agenda for the Coastal Commission meeting. Why the procrastination?"

"Whoa, whoa, Dad, you know me better than that. I'm working on it. And since the meeting isn't till late Monday afternoon, right? I figured we'd have the morning—and then some—to review our topics for discussion."

"Aren't you cutting this pretty close to the wire?"

Joseph listened as his son inhaled a breath, then said, "Look, Dad, I'm researching some environmental issues."

"Researching? All the issues relating to the Commission are ones you already know backwards and forwards."

Zack sighed. "There are all kinds of ways to look at the data we've collected, and I'm afraid we've only looked at it one way. How do we know what the index species is for our area?"

"Index species? What the heck is an index species?"

"You see, that's what I mean. We need to demonstrate our awareness of *their* way of looking at things, and they tend to examine the long-term ecological effects."

Joseph's patience felt thin as rice paper. "I have no desire to damage the environment or injure any creatures. But the fact is, we never have hurt them, and never will!"

"I'm not sure that's true."

"What is this, Zack, a new movement called 'Save the Snails'?"

"Look, Dad, I wouldn't be doing this if I didn't feel it was necessary. If we really have our homework done, we're going to look very good in that meeting."

Joseph held his tongue for a moment as he allowed his frustration to dissipate. *Why this sudden interest in ecology? It's never seemed to matter much to him before. And I'm not sure we're really on the same page about it. But he's right about one thing. We will look better in the meeting if we're prepared to discuss matters using their own language.*

Joseph punched the speaker button on his desk phone and raised his voice slightly. "Okay, Zack. You said you were doing research, but . . . are you at home?"

"No, I'm at the library. Who could work at Calma with all the chaos?"

"You're right. A lot more chaos than we bargained for."

"My sentiments exactly. If you hate the upheaval, why did you agree to it?"

"Why did *I* agree to it? Don't give me that, Zack. Cynthia's your woman, not mine."

"My what? Look, Dad, I didn't ask your opinion."

"No, you didn't, not about your woman, nor about taking over the estate for a blockbuster party."

"She's not 'my woman,' and she told me *you* had okayed this, Dad, that's why I went along with it."

"Well, she certainly thinks she's 'your woman,' and she told me *you* had approved this, and that 'we mustn't disappoint Zackery on his birthday.' "

Zack paused. "You know I hate my birthday. She played us both. Typical."

"Yes, it is typical, Zack, typical of the women you get yourself involved with. You know, I was settled down by the time I was your age."

"Thanks so much for the lecture, Father. You were lucky enough to find someone like Mom."

Joseph gritted his teeth and stood to pace the floor of his office, glaring intermittently at the speaker on his phone. *Sometimes I can't figure him out. One minute he's dallying with this superficial girlfriend of his; the next, he's making extra efforts to prepare for a meeting.* After a long moment he said, "I'm . . . I'm sorry, Zack."

"Dad, I don't want to argue."

"Neither do I. It's just . . . I'm—"

"You're wound up tight as a cable. Got the Holiday Humbug?"

"It's Chris Christian."

"Ah. Woman trouble." Zack chuckled.

"Don't laugh, Zack. She's missing."

"You mean she's on assignment or something?"

"I mean I haven't heard from her in weeks and I don't know *where* the hell she is."

"I'm sorry, Dad. Maybe she's got some things to work out."

"Yes. Maybe." Joseph paused again. "So. You'll bring me an agenda Monday morning, right?"

"Right."

"Meanwhile, how are you dressing for this shindig tonight? Is it black tie?"

Zack snorted. "It is. But I'd rather show up in shorts and a Santa hat."

Joseph laughed. "In fairness, your friend Cynthia did choose a worthwhile charity. Unify has been around for decades and their organization does a tremendous amount of good in town."

"They do. I just wish there was a way to help our favorite charities without having to stand around for hours schmoozing society matrons and staring down their leather cleavages."

Joseph guffawed. "I'm with you there, son. But it comes with the territory. And if staring at cleavage is the worst we have to endure, life isn't too bad."

James Hughes called on every bit of his formal training as a butler to keep himself from acting on his fantasy to take Miss Cynthia across his knee the next time she called his name. *Certainly she's earned a good spanking!* In a single morning she'd managed to exacerbate the already disrupted harmony and order of the Calvin estate.

"James!"

He heard his name shouted through the corridors for the fortieth time in as many minutes. Hiding in the second kitchen, he kept his hands in the sink's running water a while longer and prayed for a reprieve.

The tent installation had begun at eight a.m., despite the wet ground. Mercifully the rains had stopped in time for the event. There'd barely been time to clear Mr. Calvin's breakfast dishes before the caterers had begun taking over the kitchen.

He'd watched their parade of deliveries: pounds of iced shrimp; mounds of glistening beluga caviar; rounds of Brie to be left out to soften.

Getting out of the way, James had busied himself with straightening Mr. Zackery's cottage. *That took more time than usual this morning, but at least by that time Miss Cynthia was already having coffee in the main house.* Then he returned to the mansion to tidy the rooms and adjust the furniture for this evening's soirée. *These affairs are always disruptive, but happily are concluded in a day. With good crews, it all goes smoothly enough—unless a random element like Miss Cynthia is introduced.*

As if the thought had conjured her, James heard footsteps that came to rest outside the second kitchen, then he heard a hand on the doorknob. *If only I'd locked it.* He sighed. *No rest for the wicked.*

"Oh, James, there you are." Her voice was sounding more shrill by the hour. "You know those arrangements with the red flowers?"

"The poinsettias?" James enunciated.

"Those're *gor*geous. But the other ones with them, that have a name something like—coyote's stocking?"

James sighed again and turned off the water. "The foxglove perhaps?"

Annoyance flickered across Cynthia's face—beautiful despite her current lack of makeup and the dishevelment of her blond hair. *It's no wonder Master Zackery finds her so bewitching.* "Yes, that was it. Those, and the huge tall feather duster things."

"I think you mean the mondo grass."

"Whatever," she retorted. "They're much too tall. Too long, I mean. You'll have to cut them."

"That will require removing the arrangements from each and every table, and I suspect we no longer have time for that."

She glanced at her watch. "Oh! You're right! I only have a few hours to get ready! Must run. You can do it after I go, okay? See you later!"

"But, Miss Cynthia!" he tried to call after her. "I won't be able to adjust the flowers!"

There was no reply as Cynthia's mules clacked loudly away on the tile. James couldn't help but sigh with relief.

She said she'd need a few hours to get ready. I imagine she'll be quite transformed by the time I next see her.

Cynthia Radcliffe sat at her dressing table rehearsing her pout. *Good. But not quite as fetching as the smile.* Her newly whitened teeth contrasted sharply with the "No-No Red" lipstick she'd finally chosen.

She stood to admire herself in the adjacent full length mirror. *What a shame I have to cover up all the lingerie.* The strap of the backless brassière cut slightly into her flesh just above the panty line. Instead of actual panties, she'd chosen a thong—another bite into flesh at just the right spot—then finished the ensemble with old-fashioned garters that made slight indentations mid-thigh. *Zackery's going to be a very happy man.*

They'd sit together at the banquet. He'd put his hand on her thigh, feel the garter through her satin dress, look at her, roll his eyes, and get all hot and bothered. *I'm getting hot and bothered myself, just thinking of it.*

With a final twirl for the mirror, Cynthia doused herself with her favorite gardenia-scented Fracas, headed for the closet, and lifted her gown from its hanger. She stepped into it, wriggling it into position. By the merest spaghetti straps, it hung from her shoulders and clung to every curve all the way down, making of Cynthia a red satin sculpture. At the back, the dress began at her waist; at the front it began at her cleavage; and from every angle, it dared the viewer to peer over its edges.

She slid a comb decorated with a silk poinsettia to hold the shiny gold hair she'd swept to one side. Then she put on her ruby earrings and ring and slipped into her backless black satin pumps. She paused for a final look. *Last night's private birthday celebration was delicious . . . but only hors d'oeuvres compared with the feast I have planned for this evening.*

Zack Calvin had climbed into his monkey suit and was still yanking at his tie as he arrived at the main house. He entered through the kitchen, hoping to catch James and ask him for help with the stupid thing. He nodded at the caterers, but they seemed too busy to notice him.

The butler spun backwards through a service door, a tray full of champagne glasses balanced perfectly in one hand. "Ah, Mr. Zackery. Trouble with the tie is it, Sir?"

"You know me, James. Never could do these."

"Never mind, sir. With you in two shakes."

James glided off with the glasses, leaving Zack marooned in

the kitchen, like some uninvited guest in his own home. He considered retreating unseen to his own cottage, until he overheard Cynthia's voice berating James . . . something to do with flowers.

God, he thought, *the woman has no boundaries. James has been our trusted family butler for two generations . . . Cynthia, by comparison, is new . . . "new money," Dad would say. I better go put out that fire.*

Just then, she strode in, flashed him a smile and rotated on one spiked heel to be admired.

"Wow! You might get arrested in that dress."

She grinned, posing for him, an Aphrodite in Technicolor. *She really is a vision.*

"Darling, your tie!" she shrieked. Before he could stop her, she began yanking at it in full view of the kitchen staff.

"Cynthia, you don't have to undo the whole thing, I just need help with the knot!"

Cynthia slapped his hand away. "Now, now," she said, giving him her best pout. "Cynthia fix."

She often says that in bed . . . and we both know what usually happens next. In spite of himself, he felt the sudden coil of lust. *Good Lord, not here . . . not now!* He hoped his clothing wouldn't betray him until she could finish knotting his tie.

Chapter 8

Zelda McIntyre drove her black X-type into the *porte cochère* of the Calvin Estate, turned off the motor and slid out. She pressed her Jaguar key fob—along with a folded five-dollar bill—into the eager hand of the valet and waited for his gaze to come up to hers. "You'll park it carefully, won't you?"

"Yes, Ma'am!"

With a nod, she walked carefully to avoid damaging her Bruno Magli pumps on the gravel, then took the stairs up to the open front door. A well-appointed servant stood just inside the spacious foyer. *What a nice touch—a liveried butler. How civilized. He's rather distinguished looking.*

She heard a lovely Scottish brogue as he stood greeting other guests and offering to take wraps. "I'll keep mine, thank you." *Too chilly to give him my stole.*

She stood for a moment taking in the old-world elegance, which bore the imprints of wealth married to taste. *Fascinating that Joseph's home is so different from his office . . . Art Deco at work; El Pueblo Viejo here.*

At the butler's gesture, Zelda joined the growing crowd and began to make her way down a long arched corridor toward the brassy sounds of a Big Band playing holiday carols. When she emerged at the rear of the home, she passed through open patio doors into a holiday circus: a tent large enough for elephants filled the entire back lawn, its center apparently supported by an gargantuan Christmas tree. *Certainly not in keeping with the understated elegance of the home . . . but festive.*

The multi-colored lights of the tree threw a collage of color across the tent fabric. *Like an abstract painting on an oversized canvas . . . I must admit, the effect is rather charming.* The perimeter was set with tall heaters chasing away the chill, and lighted evergreen swags decorated the tent's upper seam. Candles flickered through ruby-glass stars on each table and tiny white lights hemmed the red damask tablecloths. *I can see the decoration committee has made a big effort. And this lighting is certainly flattering, which reminds me . . . it's time to find my host.*

She glanced around, watching as a group of begowned women kissed the air next to each other's hairdos, then caught sight of Joseph shaking the hand of another man.

Without hurrying, she made her way through the crowd till she stood at his elbow. "Good evening, Joseph."

He turned in her direction, a pleasant expression plastered on his face. "Good evening. Nice to see you. And you are . . . ?"

"I suppose I should take that as a compliment, since you've only seen me in business attire."

He seemed confounded. "I apologize. I'm afraid you have me at a disadvantage."

"Oh, but that's just where I want you."

Joseph Calvin watched as the glamorous woman in front of him gave a delighted laugh. *Shiny black hair . . . exotic eyes . . . somehow familiar. And what she lacks in height is more than compensated for in shape.* His gaze fell to the voluptuous breasts that undulated with her laughter, captured like two tidal waves in a shimmering blue decolletage. *Where have I seen that view before?* "Ms. McIntyre!" He felt the blood surging up his neck. "I apologize again! I . . . well, I didn't recognize you until . . . at first, that is."

"It's Zelda," she purred. As she extended a hand, her shawl slipped off her shoulder, revealing, if possible, still more of her spectacular scenery. "As I said, I take that as a compliment. What a lovely party."

"Oh, I can't take any of the credit."

"Still, it's very generous of you to offer your beautiful home. Do you host events often?"

Before he could answer, Zack approached them. "Hi, Dad. Everything looks terrific. Nice party." Joseph would've loved to laugh out loud at Zack's simplistic attempt at party banter, but they were not alone.

Zelda's hand was outstretched before Joseph could utter a sound. "Zelda McIntyre. And you must be Zackery. I've heard so much about you."

"Oh, really? You're uh . . . a friend of my dad's, are you?"

Joseph inhaled as if to explain, but again Zelda beat him to it.

"Well, no. Actually I heard about you first from Miranda."

Joseph saw Zack's expression go blank.

"Miranda Jones, the artist. I'm her representative, you see." Zelda's upturned gaze held steady on Zack.

"Oh, yeah, Miranda Jones—she does interesting work," Zack muttered.

Zelda's making my son uncomfortable . . . and she's enjoying it. What is all this about? And here comes Cynthia in that incredible red dress. Oh, boy. This should be interesting.

"Zackery, darling, here you are. You haven't told me how much you like the décor!"

"It's uh . . . it's very nice, Cynthia."

"Very nice? Darling, didn't you mean to say 'spectacular,' or something like that?" Cynthia hooked an arm through his, and leaned in as if to bite his ear.

Joseph, who'd been mesmerized by the drama unfolding before him, now intervened. "Cynthia, have you met Zelda McIntyre?"

"Zelda! I should have guessed you'd be wearing the most gorgeous gown at the party!"

"How very charming you are, Cynthia. You look stunning yourself."

Joseph couldn't think of what to say next. Time seemed to slow as the awkward absence of commentary isolated the small group in the midst of a sea of conversations. *Like we're caught in the eye of a storm.*

Zelda brought him back into synch. "So lovely to have met you, Cynthia dear. I hope it's a wonderful birthday for you, Zackery. And Joseph, we'll talk soon."

"Yes, Zelda," was all Joseph managed to say. Zelda tugged

the edge of her shawl demurely, gave Joseph a coquettish grin, and disappeared into the crowd, lifting a champagne glass from a passing tray as she went.

Zack, feeling blind-sided, glared at his father. "Enjoy the party. See you later," he managed. Grasping Cynthia's elbow, he began moving across the tented room as if in search of air.

"There's no need to be rude to dear old dad," she protested.

He didn't notice her comment. *That woman . . . Zelda . . . talking about Miranda! Can't believe* her *name was mentioned here, of all places, and tonight, of all times. Two seconds later, and Cynthia would've overheard. I've gotta find out how dad knows Zelda and why he invited her.*

He could feel Cynthia trying to keep up. "I know you're dying to get me alone, but could we slow down a little? I don't think you want me to lose my dress just yet."

Zack stopped propelling her toward the far end of the tent.

"Thank you, darling. My, my, such ardor." Cynthia gave him a smile.

I'm pretty sure Cyn doesn't have a clue what's going on. "How well do you know this Zelda McIntyre?"

"Not very well, but she seemed to be one of the more important people in town to invite to your party, so I . . . ."

He snorted. "*My* party? Hardly. That's something else I want to discuss with you."

"Well, the fact that your birthday party is also a Christmas charity event just shows what generosity you have."

"Yeah, right. So *you're* the one who put McIntyre on the guest list? Without checking into who she is?"

"You're acting terribly suspicious of her. Did she do something wrong?"

"Not that I know of. Not yet. When did you introduce her to my dad?"

"Oh, I didn't. They obviously know each other. He had a little twitch for her, did you see?"

"I don't think so, Cynthia."

"Oh, darling, I know a twitch when I see one." She leaned in just enough for the red satin to hide her hand from view, then reached between his thighs.

A noise escaped from his throat. He turned the sound into a cough, and grabbed Cynthia's arm again, spinning and almost dragging her toward the main house.

Cynthia threw back her head and laughed.

James Hughes patted his damp brow with a pristine white handkerchief, as the party tent had grown quite warm.

He stood at the sidelines observing the ladies jiggling in their finery to the beat of "Jingle Bell Rock," wondering how they kept their dresses from falling to the dance floor.

Earlier, during dinner, he'd pressed himself into a corner of the kitchen and sampled the offerings. *The caterers did a decent job. Beef tournedos not as mouth-watering nor the sea scallops as succulent as my own, but quite acceptable, given the number of mouths successfully fed. Of course the Chardonnay and Syrah donated by Cambria Estate Winery were superb as always.*

Yes, despite his misgivings, the service had been well-executed, right down to the removal of the dessert plates—

which hadn't been easy, given the slippery raspberry sauce over the flourless chocolate cake.

Now, still watching the dancers, he grew misty-eyed when husbands drew their wives close to the strains of muted trumpet, as the sentimental melody of "Silent Night" soared through the evening.

He felt grateful this calmer melody meant the party was now at least half over. To the front of the stage where the band now played, a lectern would soon be added. *The charity speeches will be next—no doubt everyone hoping they'll be brief, though they seldom are. Then Miss Cynthia will give me my cue to bring Mr. Zackery's gift forward.*

And she would *insist on making it a surprise, no matter how many times I warned her that he does not enjoy them. Perhaps tonight will be an exception to the rule. Then again, this is Friday the thirteenth.*

James, having helped the catering staff sort through glasses for several minutes, hurried back to his post where the gift, awkward and heavy as a folded table, leaned against the side of the stage.

" . . . Couldn't have done it without her," a matronly female voice rang over the sound system. "Please join me in thanking Mrs. Gertrude Chance."

A thunderous applause broke out with the mention of this person's name. *Must've given generously.* He glanced to the head table, checking on Mr. Joseph and Mr. Zackery who politely applauded with the rest. Miss Cynthia wiggled as she clapped, squirming in her chair. *She's certainly exuberant.* He sighed as he considered the plight of the two overly eligible Calvin bachelors. *All the wealth they might wish for. Yet it cannot buy them the female companions they deserve.*

" . . . Our co-chairwoman of the planning committee, Miss Cynthia Radcliffe."

His attention came back to Cynthia, whose name evoked a somewhat less enthusiastic response from the crowd. But she soldiered on, negotiating the steps up to the stage, careful not to tread on the satin hem, but unable to avoid pulling up the dress strap that slipped off her shoulder just as she reached the microphone. *I do hope the photographers didn't catch her awkward gesture.*

She stepped too close to the mic and feedback rang throughout the tent. "Well, I believe Mrs. McNally has really said it all. Mrs. Marge, I call her. . . ." With that, Cynthia giggled girlishly. "Mrs. Marge has thanked all of you who worked so hard to make this a special evening. But one person hasn't been recognized." The speakers throughout the tent echoed for just a moment after Cynthia's pause. "I think you'll all agree when I tell you that he has been extremely generous in allowing us to share in his home, and his birthday."

James glanced over at Zackery in time to see him mouth an obscenity, then remembered the word "birthday" had been the cue. Hoisting the heavy frame, he climbed the stairs and carried it, still draped, toward the microphone.

Cynthia beamed, then continued. "I won't embarrass him by asking him to make a speech. I'll just say, Zackery darling, come up here and get your birthday present!"

The poor young man appears as the proverbial deer-in-the-

headlights. When his father nudged him, he managed to stand and take a step toward the stage. *Now I'm to pull away the covering.* When James did, the audience "Ah-h-ed", renewing their applause with still more vigor, apparently impressed with the painting before them. Mr. Zackery, however, froze.

"Zack, they're waiting," James heard Mr. Joseph admonish. Still, the younger man appeared unable to move.

James glanced over at Cynthia, still center-stage under the bright lights, jiggling in her red satin, beaming her white teeth for the cameras. He saw her begin to falter, though, as the applause died down and Zackery remained rooted to his spot. Now James could see reporters, scattered through the crowd, begin to take notice, perhaps sensing the sudden tension near the stage.

To check for instructions, James caught Mr. Joseph's eye. *He's nodding. Good. I'll stay here in case I can help.*

Mr. Joseph stood, threw an arm around his son's shoulder, and walked him up the three short steps. Still holding on, he turned to face the audience and smile for the cameras as he leaned into the mic. "Thank you all so very much for coming. My son, as you can see, is stunned by his surprise." A ripple of laughter broke through the crowd. "And now we'll ask our marvelous orchestra to resume the music. Enjoy the rest of the evening."

The alert band leader signaled the musicians to pick up their instruments and start playing "Joy to the World." Meanwhile, the guests pushed back their chairs, resuming conversations or heading to the dance floor. *The party has been saved. I'm not entirely sure about Mr. Zackery.*

He followed the progress of the two Calvin men. *His father's shielding Zackery from that reporter. Mr. Joseph's savoir faire always comes through.* He glanced again at Miss Cynthia. *Still smiling for the other reporters. She's obviously fine.*

James lifted the heavy painting off the stage and carried it inside to find a safe place for it, deciding on Mr. Joseph's library. Just as he'd placed it, the two men unexpectedly arrived, Mr. Zackery's gaze again riveted by the image.

James himself regarded the splendid coastal depiction, a location he'd guess to be somewhere north of Santa Barbara. "What's the provenance of the piece, sir?" he asked.

"Apparently it's called *The Cove* and the artist is Miranda Jones."

Joseph Calvin, having said goodnight to most of his guests, had returned to the library to try to make peace between Zack and Cynthia.

Through the open doorway, he watched his son pace—tie hanging, jacket flung over one shoulder. "God dammit!" Zack shouted again at poor Cynthia, "I hate that! Don't *ever* do that to me again. I *hate* surprises."

Joseph stepped inside to close the door behind him. The young woman shuddered in the corner, tears streaming down her face, the ravishing party girl now ravished.

"I think she's gotten the message, son," Joseph said calmly. "But it seems that something else is bothering you, right? I mean, can't you tell us what has you *so* upset?"

A quiet knock sounded.

"Probably James with a couple of stiff drinks," he commented, moving to open the library door.

"Anything wrong, Joseph?" Zelda's large violet eyes looked up at him over the blue iridescent shawl, pulled now around her shoulders.

"Zelda!" He looked down at her. "I . . . I didn't realize any of our guests were still here." Joseph stepped out of the library, closing the door again.

Zelda spoke softly. "I stayed because . . . well, there seems to have been quite a strange reaction to the painting, for some reason, and I must say I feel responsible. I'm terribly sorry if I've caused any trouble." She blinked several times, as if batting away tears with her eyelashes.

"Let's sit down over here." He guided her toward a window seat in the spacious foyer. "What do you mean, responsible?"

She smoothed her shimmering blue gown and settled on the cushion. "Surely you realize, Joseph, that Cynthia purchased this piece of art from me. She requested a painting, to be sure, so that wasn't *my* idea, but of course, she wouldn't have had the slightest notion where to get such a magnificent work without my help."

Zelda McIntyre paused to gauge Joseph's reaction. *Better he should learn directly from me that I was the source. Finding out from someone else could ruin our business relationship, at the very least. He's never gotten back to me about my proposal, but I'd rather have the social connection anyway.* "In any case, I just wanted to be sure that everything is all right. I am really quite concerned."

Joseph regarded her coolly. "Let me understand exactly what you're saying. Cynthia Radcliffe contacted you?"

"Yes, she got my name out of the society pages, apparently. I had never heard of her but, of course, she'd heard of me."

"She called you about a painting?" Joseph asked.

"No, no, she invited me to your party. Later, she called me back, and asked for professional advice in choosing a birthday gift for your son."

"So she asked a professional to help her select a birthday present."

"Exactly. You know about my career as an artists' representative. She wanted to make a good impression on Zackery. Or on you. Or on me, for that matter. She wanted to make a splash at the party."

"Well, she did that. Almost swamped the boat."

"It's not as bad as all that." She uncrossed her legs and leaned in, allowing her shawl to slip slightly off her shoulders. "Why don't you let me do a little damage control? Since I represent the artist, I could swap this piece for another, if this one bothers Zackery so much."

Joseph glanced down at her chest, then looked away. "To tell you the truth, I don't know *what's* bothering Zack. It might not be the painting at all. I'll tell you one thing: he doesn't like to be surprised."

"Yes, I got that." Zelda leaned back again, then placed one manicured hand on his thigh. "I don't want to intrude any further. Why don't you send Cynthia out here to me, and I'll calm her down. Then I'll be on my way."

He seemed to consider her proposition. "Yes, I could use a moment alone with Zack. Thanks, Zelda. I appreciate your concern."

He's dropped his guard. One star for me. "I'll wait here for Cynthia." She gave his thigh a pat, then withdrew her hand quickly at the sound of approaching footsteps. James crossed the foyer, balancing a tray with a decanter and clinking glasses.

Joseph stood. "Ah, James, good, we need those."

"Yes, sir," James said, throwing a curious glance at Zelda. "I'll take them right in."

Cynthia slipped into Zack's cottage and closed the door behind her. He'd left it unlocked, as usual. Slacks and a sweater were thrown over his valet stand. James had obviously been too busy to straighten things twice today.

She left the lights on this time. *No more surprises! Not tonight, anyway. Zackery's still in the library with his father.* She'd wait for him—but not in ambush.

Over the last half hour, her new mentor had given her words of advice. "Just apologize to him, dear, and keep apologizing," Zelda had cooed. "There's nothing like a reconiliation to rekindle the flame."

Panic rising at the thought of losing Zackery's affections, Cynthia'd hungrily listened to the encouragement.

"This is nothing," Zelda had reassured her. "We can always exchange the painting. Just explain to him how hard you worked, how you thought only of him. That's what a man wants to hear. Don't undress," she'd counseled, "and don't remove your makeup."

Now Cynthia peered into Zackery's mirror, confirming that she looked a wreck ... her red satin creased with wrinkles, hair flattened and bedraggled, face tear-streaked. *I'm dying to clean up, but Zelda says my looking this way will make him feel sorry for me.*

Resisting the temptation to wash her face, she glanced

around the room for a place she could sit and be *seen* as soon as Zackery returned. Choosing the high-backed regency chair situated near the door, she settled herself and waited for the doorknob to turn.

Zack Calvin entered his quarters, too exhausted to protest Cynthia's presence. Flinging his tuxedo jacket on the burdened wooden valet, he yanked off the bow tie hanging from one side of his neck.

Cynthia stood, kicked off her high heels and moved toward him. But he moved away. She paused, then sat on the edge of the bed. She began to talk quietly. "I just wanted to do something nice for you, Zackery. I worked so hard for weeks and weeks on this party."

Her tears are starting up again. He entered his closet, removed his shoes, and stood in its doorway, facing her.

"Everyone said they were having a lovely time." She sobbed now, her words becoming less intelligible. "And I looked beautiful, and you thought I looked sexy, and we were having fun. And I spent all this money to buy you something really special. And when you just stared and stared, everyone looked at us like we were *crazy!*" She dissolved again into a nasty, guttural gasping and another torrent of tears.

As if I didn't feel miserable enough. I don't like surprises. I don't know why. Why can't people just accept it? Why does someone always feel their surprise will be the exception? Yet, Dad was right . . . something else did set me off, and I'm not sure what. I felt . . . completely engulfed. . . .

It was as if something had tripped a live wire, triggering an explosion deep in his psyche. He couldn't stand to think about it. It was behind him now, over with. He'd gotten past messy situations before. He'd outlive this one too.

I never intended to make Cynthia suffer, even if I didn't appreciate her gift. She doesn't know anything about Miranda, apparently. No malice. Just evil, capricious Fate that would put something of Miranda's into my hands as a gift from Cynthia. I'll repay her for the painting. It's the only thing to do.

He went over to the bed and touched Cynthia's shoulder.

"Oh, Zackery!" she wailed, looking up at him with a ruined face. She clung to his waist, and cried against him, her make-up soiling his white tuxedo shirt.

After a moment, he moved to sit against the pillows, taking her along to nestle. Her red satin was tearstained and crumpled. A wave of regret washed over him, and he held her closer. Her sobbing subsided, reduced to gentle hiccups. He stroked her hair.

"I'm ... I'm sorry, Cynthia. I didn't mean to hurt you."

She looked up at him, her amber eyes puffy and streaked with running make-up. "Really?" she asked plaintively.

"Of course not." He kissed her forehead and touched a sculpted cheek.

"I'm sorry too, Zackery," she whispered. "I thought ... I thought you'd like the painting." A sob started in her throat, and her shoulders began to shake.

"Sh-h-h," he said, stroking her hair again to calm her. "I've gotta get out of this monkey suit and grab a shower." Zack eased out from under her and went to the closet to remove his clothes.

"I'm ruining my dress. I should take it off too." She moved

after him, letting the dress slide off to pool at her feet. A black half-bra cupped her breasts and a matching lace thong bit into her hips. *Never seen those before . . . they're probably new . . . part of her master plan for the evening. But I can't be that easy.* As he left for the bathroom, he heard the rattle of her long plastic bag being slid over her dress.

Inside the stall, he turned on the faucet, allowing the water to heat and fill the space with steam. *She followed me into the closet . . . wonder if she'll join me in here.*

She opened the glass door and stepped under the hot water. He watched as the spray of needles gently cleansed her face of its black streaks. A purer, simpler Cynthia stood in place of the carefully artificed woman he'd seen earlier.

For once, she's not making the first move. She's waiting for me. His eyes traveled down the long, blond hair where it clung to her breasts and separated around the nipples. She trembled now, as he looked at her, despite the steaming water.

He went for her, his mouth colliding hard with hers, his hands cupping her buttocks. She placed one long leg around his waist, and the other leg followed easily as he lifted her. He pushed open the glass door, slammed the spigot off and carried her into his room, tumbling toward the bed, soaking the linens as they landed. He took her hard, pumping into the silken sheath that opened for him so readily, then clamped tight, guiding him home to searing satisfaction.

Minutes later, they lay panting, side by side. As his sexual haze blended into exhausted sleep, he had time for a fleeting thought. *Even if the evening didn't go exactly the way she planned, she still ended up in my bed. And I let her.*

Chapter 9

Sally O'Mally woke up tired. She opened her eyes in the dark and peered at the green iridescent numbers on her old alarm clock: 4:40. *Well, moon in the mornin', I woke up before my alarm.* Too alert to close her eyes again, she stared at the ceiling, barely visible by the eerie green light.

Jack'll be wakin' up at his house by now, either broodin' over the news of his child, or mad enough to punch somebody. Prob'ly both. He'll calm down. Bound to. Can't stay mad as a wet bull more'an a day or two. She took a deep breath. *Makes no nevermind, 'cause I gotta get a move on.*

She swung her legs out from under the warm covers and stood, until a dizziness swept through her, causing her to plunk back down on the bed. *Well, I never. Don't tell me I'm gonna be like my Aunt Ida Sue with her vapors.* Steadying herself, she pushed up carefully, and found she could stand just fine, all trace of the vertigo gone. Yet what remained was a slight feeling of nausea. *Maybe I caught me somethin'. Better have a nice tall glass of orange juice when I get to the rest'r'nt.*

Her soft cotton nightshirt clung to her slight body as she headed for the bathroom. Shivering in the pre-dawn chill, she closed her eyes, flicked on the light switch and squinted against its bright intrusion. When she opened her eyes, she saw the dark circles under them, deciding she'd better add some concealer to her make-up today.

After pulling the pink quilted robe from its hook on the back of her bathroom door and slipping it on, she headed to the kitchen to make herself a cup of tea. As tap water filled her kettle, she glanced out her window to see a silver crescent hanging in the dark sky. "Well, it really is moon in the mornin'!" she said aloud.

Sally closed the back door of her restaurant, flipped on the kitchen lights, and continued through to her office, where she put down her bag. The desk calendar caught her eye and she sat down for a moment, suddenly aware of what had been poking at the edges of her mind.

She turned the page back to November, where, across the second weekend, she'd written *Getaway with Jack*. She'd known that during the real Thanksgiving week, she'd be busy cooking up special holiday orders-to-go, and then would be too exhausted to be good company. So they'd decided to have their own holiday a week earlier. June had covered for her at the restaurant, and with Sally back on duty for the holiday, June had been able to visit her relations for Turkey Day in New York.

Sally and Jack had kept their private holiday simple, but it'd been romantic none-the-less. The one night she didn't cook, he'd treated her to a delicious dinner at Dorn's Restaurant in Morro Bay, which he knew was one of her favorites. During the course of the weekend, he'd rubbed her tired feet, told her funny stories, and even rented a video for them. They'd snuggled in the flickering light of his bedroom television to watch *Tin Cup*, a romantic comedy with Kevin Costner, another of her favorites.

And Jack surely was feelin' his oats the whole time. I'm usually real careful, but he didn't always give me a chance that weekend. Focusing again on the calendar, she placed her finger on the tenth, and began counting down the weeks. *One, two, three, four ... I'm a little over a week late. Well, that could mean somethin'. But then again, it might not. I've been this late before, and it's been nothin' but stress and nerves. Still, I better get me a pregnancy test at the pharmacy. Not gonna let myself worry about it right now, not till I know somethin'. I gotta get my day started!*

Now that Christmas was almost here, she knew to expect more tourists and more locals too, who looked forward to her Christmas eggs or holiday chili. Stepping out into the serving area, she turned on the colored lights and glanced again at the Doobie Brothers poster. *Sure would be fun to see 'em, but who has time? And Jack sure wouldn't wanna go.*

Heading for the kitchen, she scrubbed her hands and began rolling out the biscuit mixture she'd refrigerated overnight. Working with the dough made her feel better, and she began to hum the nondescript song that was never far from her mind.

The phone rang, startling her. *Must be Mama*, she figured. *She knows I'm alone this time of day.* "Sally's," she answered on the second ring.

"Uh, yes, I wonder if I could speak with Sally O'Mally?" The man's voice sounded long distance, just a bit tentative, and a little familiar, too.

"You are."

"I . . . I am Tony Fiorentino."

"No, I mean, you *are* speaking to Sally O. . . ." She paused, her heart beating faster. "Wait a minute—did you say—Tony?"

The voice on the other end of the phone began to chuckle.

"Tony Fee . . . Fiorentino?"

He drew in a breath. "Yeah. Yeah, it's me, Sally. How're you doin'?"

"How . . . how am I doin'?"

"Is there an echo on the line?"

"An echo on the . . . no! I mean . . . well, I'm fine. Absolutely punkin pie perfect. Fine. Ye-yus. Well I haven't seen nor heard from you in that month-a-Sundays, I reckon."

"Yeah . . . yeah, it has been a long time."

Silence fell on the conversation, the white noise of the phone line arcing up to fill the gap.

Tony Fiorentino stared out his apartment window at the adjacent building's brick wall, trying to picture Sally's face. "Hope you don't mind." His voice broke into the stillness. "I just called your mama and got your number."

"Oh, that's nice. Are you still in the big city? I mean, I heard that's where you moved back to."

"Yeah, I moved back to New York after . . . well, later. Got a decent job up here. Working with a . . . a charity."

"That's good. Sounds real nice. I'm keepin' busy too."

"Yeah, I heard that! Heard you started your own restaurant! Wow, Sal, that's really big. Huge."

"Well, it ain't *that* huge, you know."

"No, I mean, it's an accomplishment to—"

"I knowed what you meant."

He chuckled. *Gotta ask her ... before I get lost in small talk.* "Uh, listen, I heard you were out there in Milford-Haven, and uh, I'm actually heading in your direction, and I thought, well, as long as I'm in the neighborhood anyway, maybe you could ... maybe we could ... would you like to get together?"

Geez, I made a mess of that. The woman's gonna think I've gone mental. And after all this time, why would she even give me the time of day? While he'd been busy berating himself, she'd said something. "What? What did you say?" He pressed the phone hard against his ear.

"Sure, I guess so, I said. But I run a bizness now and I don't have much time for socializin'."

"Great! I mean, no, not great that you don't have much time. Listen, I'm not doing this very well. Not used to calling people up for—"

"Me neither."

"Yeah." He took a breath. "So actually I'm calling for something specific. There's a special reunion concert being given by the Doobie Brothers. I remembered that you used to love their music."

"Still do! Like 'em bunches!"

"Yeah. So ... well, they, uh ... they're playing near you—"

"At the Central Coast Bowl."

"Yeah, that's right. Guess you know about it. And, uh ... I've been given two tickets and I thought you might like to go."

"You have? You did?"

"My plane gets into the Santa Maria airport next Saturday

afternoon. I could drive to Milford-Haven and pick you up at, say, four? I'm supposed to be there a little early." He waited through a long moment of silence, sitting unnerved on the other end of the line. "Sally?"

She suddenly broke into a nervous laugh. "Well, you may not like how I look any more—it's been a long time!"

"You might not like how I look either, Sally. I'm in a chair now." *Finally! I managed to blurt it out. She probably knew, and was just being polite. Now she'll beg off. But what the hell, at least I tried.*

"A chair? Well, what a silly thing to say. What's wrong with sittin' in a chair?"

Damn. She didn't get it. Maybe she hasn't heard. "No, no, I mean . . . a wheelchair."

White noise.

After interminable seconds she replied. "Oh." She paused again. "Oh."

What do I do? Let her off the hook? Or plunge ahead. "Okay. So, I'll pick you up?"

"You mean you can drive?"

"Oh, yeah, Sally. I get around just fine."

The white noise arced up to fill Tony's ear, but in it he sensed Sally gathering herself.

"Yes. I'd love to go to the concert with you, Tony."

"Good," he responded. "I'll . . . call you when I land."

"Ye-yus."

He gently replaced the receiver, savoring the remembrance of her lilting accent as he looked out the window again. On this side of the apartment, his only view was into rising floors of closed blinds belonging to unknown neighbors, the windowsills etched now with thinning lines of gray snow, some of them highlighted with colored lights.

On his own windowsill sat a solitary plant. Last August, he'd allowed an avocado seed to sprout in a glass of water. Later he'd planted it, and now a thick, lone stem grew bravely upward, teetering in a small pot of dirt. It was his sole holiday décor this year, wound with a single strand of tiny white lights. Its only leaves poked out from its upper end, angling hungrily toward the seven minutes of direct sun that penetrated to this floor. *The leaves look greener . . . and it's not just the lights.*

He wheeled himself in the opposite direction, out to his narrow, frigid balcony. In fact, the whole city looked clearer, brighter. Through a neighbor's window, an inflated Santa took on the cheering aspect of a benevolent spirit. The decorated spire of a distant office building no longer seemed a blasphemous commercialization. And the fake tree on an adjacent balcony seemed as stately as an evergreen in an alpine forest.

He began to chuckle, a sound of delight that took him by surprise. Then it deepened to a belly laugh, and his deep voice ricocheted off adjacent concrete walls and resonated down the fire escape.

Sally's hand still touched the phone and her heart thudded as heavily against her ribs as a new-born calf's.

I knew it, knew about his wheelchair, and couldn't bear to think of that tall, handsome athlete . . . and those beautiful, strong legs. . . . I just stuffed it far enough down in my memory that I could pretend it wasn't real. Just held onto how things were way back when we were highschool sweethearts. She pressed a hand to her heart. *Think I'll say a little prayer for him tonight.*

Yet much as her soul ached for the man she'd loved so long ago, she'd also heard something strong and healthy in his voice just now. Kindness ... humor ... maturity. Yes, a manliness that shook her down to her sensible shoes.

In her mind, she replayed their conversation, and when she came near the end, she blanched. *The man calls me after all these years . . . and I ask him if he can drive! I'd give away ten batches of my biscuits if I could take that back . . . a slap right in his face! I surely didn't mean it!*

She pressed a hand to her chest again to steady her nerves. *But then—that didn't stop him. He took away my awkward feelin'. So he can still do that, like he always could. Well, I'm gonna show him some good old-fashioned Southern hospitality. After all he's been through, he deserves it. It's the very least I can do.*

Quietly, she began to cry.

Miranda Jones, still wearing her long flannel nightgown, counted the odd assortment of bags lined up by her front door like a group of obedient pets waiting to be taken out for a walk. Shadow seemed confused by the impostors and, from her vantage point on the kitchen counter, peered down at them quizzically.

Miranda focused on each bag in turn, going through her mental checklist again. *Jeans, T-shirts, underwear, socks, toiletries case in the green duffle; camera, lenses, film in their black bag; folding art table in its case with brush carrier, watercolors and small water bottles; cassette carrier is already in the car. HandBook journals, pens and colored pencils in my green backpack. I still need a hat. I probably don't need anything fancy . . . got the hanging bag with the green sweater dress and flats, just in case, though I still can't find the matching purse.*

Despite all these preparations, she still hadn't figured out what to wear to the Doobie Brothers rehearsal. The moment she thought of the band, the song "Black Water" began to play in her head. *When I first planned this trip I never imagined . . . and I still can't!*

Dashing back downstairs to her bedroom, she again stood in front of her closet regarding the modest array of clothing that comprised her wardrobe. Nothing seemed to be right, and she was running out of time.

What do you wear to an afternoon rehearsal? Is it the same as an evening concert? No. But then again . . . it's them! *I suppose I could wear jeans . . . but not stretched out and paint-stained. And what about the concert when I get home? Wear the same thing? Or something different? Well, something warm, since it'll be outside in winter, even though they'll have those outdoor heaters. So I'll need a sweater up here, but probably not a couple hundred miles farther south, especially since the rehearsal's not at night.*

Evenings in the Central Coast tended to be raw and chilly at this time of year. You could always spot the tourists with their goose bumps under thin cotton T-shirts and shorts. They'd come looking for "California sun" and be surprised to find the Golden State actually had weather. *I'll add a fleece for another layer of warmth against the damp fog that usually rolls in at night.*

"Maybe I'll take out my trusty old blue jeans again and look them over," she said aloud. A tiny "pew" from Shadow seemed to confirm this as a good idea. The jeans were fine for a walk at the Cove. They were fine for errands. They were fine for almost anything. They just didn't seem to be fine for a date with Zack to a Doobies concert he'd apparently helped to organize.

What a great job to have. Why was he mysterious about it last fall? She'd find out more in L.A. Even if he didn't tell her, she'd be able to observe for herself. *Maybe he's too modest to brag about his career. And maybe I'm fooling myself and making excuses for him.*

These musings weren't getting her any closer to finishing her packing. Still in a quandary, she stood for another moment in front of the hangers cramming her closet, suddenly remembering she might need a pair of stockings in case she happened to wear the dress. She reached into her socks-and-hose drawer, rummaging in the half-dark of the deep space, startled when tiny claws traced across the back of her hand.

"Kitty! Are you helping me find them?"

Shadow looked up, mischief lighting her amber eyes.

"Oh, you wanna play?"

The kitten seemed to acknowledge this idea by leaping straight up in the air, turning one hundred eighty degrees, and landing again on her human's hand.

"You little dickens!" Miranda cried, continuing the game by pulling a sock over her hand, making it a prey-puppet that lumbered through the ever-tumbling socks. Shadow—a miniature panther in a woolen jungle—crouched, murmured a high-pitched growl, then pounced again.

After another few minutes of play, Miranda said, "Okay,

kitty. Thank you very much for helping with my socks. Maybe you know what I should wear to the rehearsal?"

Shadow popped out of the drawer to sit on Miranda's knee, apparently having nothing more to offer on the subject.

"Well then, who *would* know? Oh! Meredith! She'll know!"

Grabbing the cordless phone by her bed, Miranda pressed the pre-programmed number and the call was answered in one ring. "Meredith Jones."

"Hi, Mer, it's me."

"No!" her sister shouted to someone in her office. "I want to sell short on those!" Then back into the handset she said, "Meredith Jones."

"Yeah, hi, Meredith, it's Miranda."

Meredith shouted, "Take the order for me, will you? I've got someone else on the line." In a normal voice, she said, "Meredith Jones."

Miranda began laughing. "Not busy, are you?"

"I'm sorry, this is our busy time of day. Who's calling, please?"

"Your sister. Remember me?"

"Mandy? Oh! Sorry, it's just crazy here today. What's up? Anything wrong?"

"No, I'm fine, but I do want your advice about something."

"Shoot."

"Gotta figure out what to wear."

"Ah, a wardrobe consultation. My personal favorite." To someone else, she yelled, "Hold my calls, okay?" Then back to her sister, she asked, "What's the occasion?"

"Rock concert."

"Oh! Jeans."

"Even if my date is the organizer?"

"Oh, *no*, you're not dating some slimy rock star manager or something, are you?"

Miranda laughed again. "No. Well, maybe. I don't know."

Her sister paused. "If *you* don't know who you're dating, Mandy, who does?"

Watching Shadow tiptoe across the phone cord, Miranda sidestepped the question by asking, "What kind of jeans?"

"Um, if you have any with rhinestones down the sides. . . ."

"No, fresh out."

"Didn't think so." Meredith seemed to consider for another moment. "What about *black* jeans, instead of blue ones? Looks a little fancier."

"Oh! That's a great idea! Thanks, Mer!"

"What's the concert? Is this part of your trip to L.A.?"

"Yes. And no."

"Not sure you're making a lot of sense today, Mandy."

"Sorry. The concert is actually up here, after the trip. But while I'm in L.A. I'm seeing a rehearsal. And it's the Doobies."

"Fantastic! You love them!"

"Oh, yeah. I've had their songs in my head ever since the invite came."

"So, where will you be staying in L.A.? Since you love the ocean so much, you should really stay at Shutters. Know about it? Like its own little city of cottages, each one decorated with white shutters and wicker, little fireplaces, right on the Santa Monica beach. They just built it in the early nineties."

"Before or after the earthquake?"

"Oh . . . before, it must've been. It *is* a little pricey."

"Lord, if *you* think it's pricey. . . ."

"Well, you're a successful painter now, Mandy. And you deserve to stay someplace special, not at some hostel."

Miranda chuckled. "I *am* staying someplace special. Historic too. The Hacienda, near LAX."

"Why in the world would you stay near the airport?" her sister demanded.

"Because it's also near the only habitats for—"

"—some rare species, right?"

"Right. Tiny creatures."

"Smaller than hummers?"

"Smaller."

"Ugh, not some kind of bug?"

"Yes, but the bugs become the most gorgeous endangered blue butterflies."

"Ah," she sighed. "The world's a better place for my sister being in it. Hey, Kiddo, I gotta get back to work. They're looking daggers at me."

"Yeah, me too. Gotta go, that is. Ever coming to visit me? I really want to show you my place, my new town."

"I'll get there soon—promise. Love you!"

"Love you!" Miranda hung up smiling, and ran back to her closet. Pushing the double sliding doors all the way to the left, she rummaged in the semi-dark of the lower rack. She yanked a hanger out. *Yes, here they are.* Pulling up her flannel night-shirt, she slipped on the black jeans with silver rivets. *They still fit and, as far as I can tell, no spots. Okay, so much for the bottom. And on top, I could wear that red sweater. Yeah, it's warm, looks great with black, and besides . . . 'tis the season.*

Wearing the nightdress over the jeans, she ran up the

stairs—the kitten racing her to the top—to the hall closet next to her front door. The tightly packed space held a motley array of outerwear. "Don't you get lost in there, Shadow," she admonished. "Somewhere in here, there's got to be ... yes, here it is." She held up her black acid-washed denim jacket with silver buttons. *Tucked in at the waist, and flared over the hips. Okay, this'll be perfect for the actual concert up here at the Central Coast Bowl. But for a daytime rehearsal in L.A. I do have a relatively new pair of blue jeans.*

Now she thought of something else. Still holding the jacket, she ran back down the stairs and opened the upper right-hand drawer in her bathroom. A wooden felt-lined jewelry box served as a holder for her pins. Just as she began to use her index finger to push pieces out of the way, a small black velvet paw joined the effort. "What do you think ... a pewter pin for a pooder?" Miranda laughed at her pun, which, however, was lost on the kitten, who continued to explore the shiny collection of silver pins.

"Japanese paintbrush, hummingbird, pinecone, Golden Gate bridge, kitty cat." *None of these seem to fit the occasion. Oh well, maybe I'll find a new pin while I'm on my trip.*

Cornelius Smith, eager to begin his trip north to Mendocino, steered his Dodge Durango down the hill toward Highway 1.

Mom and Pop seem to be doing just fine ... as if time doesn't really touch them. Well, they do need help with their seasonal decorations. But that gives me a good excuse to visit four times a year. And this year, it'll be five times, because I'll be back in just a couple of weeks for Christmas.

He had to chuckle at his mother's tradition of switching things around at the start of each new season. For the past couple of days, he'd been helping her put away the front door autumn wreath, the rust-colored throws on the sofas, and the various silk florals that'd brightened the rooms. Then, he and Pop had hefted boxes down from the attic, standing patiently while Mom remembered where each holiday item belonged, then carrying the decorations wherever she pointed.

Now, the Smith home emanated a jolly Christmas spirit, perhaps more Celtic than Christian: fairies and elves dangled from a convincing fake fir tree in the corner; cushions Mom herself had needlepointed years earlier dotted the sofas and chairs; fresh poinsettias bloomed on the front porch. *I can't even remember all the rest of the stuff she had us put around the house. But it made her happy. And when she's happy, Pop's happy too.*

As his SUV reached the corner where Village Lane connected Main Street to Highway 1, he pulled into the right lane, ready to turn north. While he waited, motor rumbling, for the light to change, he noticed a dark green Mustang pull into the left-turning lane. He noticed something in his peripheral vision and glanced down through the passenger-side window to see a woman's graceful hand flip a swatch of long silky hair over her shoulder. *A beauty . . . wonder if she was just visiting . . . or whether she lives here?*

Miranda Jones heard the purr of a big motor idling to her right as she pulled up to the traffic light at Highway 1. The moment the signal turned green, she made the left turn to head south.

Ten minutes later, she glanced to the right as Highway 1 carved a wide arc to parallel the terrain at Morro Bay.

Thinking back to her departure a short time earlier, she mentally reviewed that things at home had been left, more or less, in order. *So great that I can call Kevin if I need to, not just to check on Shadow, but to close a window or take care of anything I forgot about.*

Her tall friend from Sawyer Construction loved animals as much as she did, and was delighted to cat-sit for her—though he'd decided to take the kitten to his own house.

Shadow had seemed concerned when her carrier appeared, and quite upset to be placed inside. From her vantage point behind the mesh, she'd meowed in a surprisingly loud voice, until Kevin had plucked her out to place her on his shoulder. "It's okay, girl," he'd cooed. And the kitten had immediately agreed, obviously intrigued to be on such a high perch. The large-and-small friends had trotted off happily, leaving Miranda utterly reassured, and curious as to what kind of adventures they'd have together.

Speaking of adventures . . . I'm about to have a few of my own! To help put herself in the mood, she reached over to the cassette carrier resting on the passenger seat, feeling across the hard-plastic case edges until she could pull out the one she'd loaded in the first position: Pat Metheny's "Letter From Home."

From the moment she popped the cassette into her player, his haunting, dreamy guitar filled the car, the underlying rhythm synchronizing itself to the cadence of tires-and-asphalt, the soaring electrified solos underscoring the golden clouds highlighting the sky over the bay.

The songs kept her company through the familiar coastal towns. *What's that tune? "Are We There Yet"?* She laughed, the child in her remembering the eager phrase.

Even with the music flowing around her, gently pushing her forward the way a following sea carries a boat, she had to admit the prospect of driving in and around Los Angeles tended to give her a case of nerves. Yet the good news was that every time she thought about her new commission, concerns about driving in the huge city eased in the wake of her excitement.

She recalled PVNET had sent that thick manila envelope containing, among other things, their own brochure. Unfolded, it revealed a detailed depiction of the coast just south of LAX. The wide Palos Verdes peninsula protruded from the diagonal coastline with two important landmarks highlighted: the Point Vicente Lighthouse and the American Cetacean Society Observation Post Number Six.

This time of year, the gray whales will be on their southbound journey to bear their young. Then in April, they'll start heading north again to feed in the Alaskan waters. It'll be so interesting to compare the experience with my time last month at Observation Post Eight at Piedras Blancas . . . just twenty minutes from home.

A month earlier, she'd been thrilled to be invited to the eighth in the long string of observation posts that stretched from Point One at Magdalena Bay in Mexico, to Point Twenty in the Chukchi Sea, just south of the Bering Sea in Alaska. Something most unusual had also happened, though, involving not the grays, but sperm whales. *Knew them from the Planet Peace voyage but never thought I'd see that species so close to shore! I'd read about that behavior, but never imagined I'd see it.*

That's something I'll never forget . . . the male rescuing the female. That'll be a painting one day.

She mentally reviewed the Center where she'd be working. It'd opened in 1984 with a mission to present and interpret the unique features and history of the Palos Verdes Peninsula. She knew it offered a premier whale-watch site for amateurs, but also greatly admired the volunteers who'd be sitting for long hours each day, peering through their binoculars, tracking the number of adults heading south.

She knew there'd still be plenty of the graceful behemoths to be seen off the California coast. Their annual migration from frigid Arctic feeding grounds to Mexico's balmy birthing lagoons generally began each October or November, the forty-ton giants plowing south by the hundreds completing a five- to six-thousand-mile trek in an average of fifty-five days by swimming nonstop.

Imagine their strength, their endurance. We could learn so much from them.

Miranda's Mustang sped down Highway 101 as it hugged the coast between Santa Barbara and Ventura, then angled inland through Thousand Oaks at the outskirts of Los Angeles. Even this far away from the center of the city—if this city could be said to *have* a center—traffic steadily increased. *I had the road to myself when I started out this morning. Now I've got a lot of company. No matter how many more lanes they add, they're always full.*

She could feel the tension increasing in her muscles, see her grip tightening on the steering wheel. *Just keep calm. According to the California map, it's about two hundred fifty miles from Milford-Haven to the Palos Verdes Peninsula . . . so I must have about another fifty miles to go.*

She always found it interesting that—although everyone imagined the California coastline as, more or less, a straight north-south line—in fact the coastline meandered, with many segments actually traversing east-west.

Have to pay attention now . . . make the interchange from the 101 to the 405. Later today, she'd find her hotel and get settled. But first, she wanted to head directly for the Point Vicente Interpretive Center, where she'd be working tomorrow. *Is it the lighthouse . . . or the whales that're pulling at me so much? Both, I guess.*

An hour later, never having taken her focus away from freeway signs and braiding traffic, she'd negotiated the exit onto California 107—which actually turned out to be Hawthorne Boulevard. She traversed a segment of densely populated city-grid, and felt the straight lines give way to the gentle curves of Rolling Hills Estates, a serene assembly of amoeba-shaped cul-de-sacs dotted with orange-tiled roofs. *Income level must've jumped about five-hundred-thousand in the last half hour . . . manicured and sculpted . . . golf courses and private pools . . . neighbors living too close for comfort . . . but, no doubt, great views.*

Arcing through another turn, she took a moment to gaze upward where the land was carved away to reveal a profile of multi-layered sediments. *Like a wedding cake where each sheet is made of different ingredients.*

The compressed layers had then also been up-thrust through the eons, until they now rose from the sea, angled wedges tilting toward higher altitudes, defining the coastline. Yet it wasn't that the land actually ended. "Land's end" was, indeed, just a linguistic euphemism. *The land doesn't terminate; it plunges downward into the ocean . . . and what the whales are seeing on their journey is just like what I'm seeing on mine!*

She mentally reviewed the underwater terrain she'd seen sketched on maps . . . shelves and benches . . . canyons and valleys . . . some as famous as their land-side counterparts. At the far edges of the Pacific, she'd heard of the Mariana Trench; and here, just offshore, stretched the Southern California Bight. Point Conception in Santa Barbara marked the boundary between Central and Southern Cal, and that's where the Bight began, extending all the way to a point just south of the U.S.-Mexico border. The long topographic bench served as a catch-point for many creatures including the miniature shrimp called krill, making the area a favorite feeding ground for the blue and the fin whales, the largest of the species. *I bet Sam has all kinds of data on this . . . I'll talk with her when I get home, maybe even take her some new info. And to make my postcard map image complete, I'll have to add the underwater topography. Yes! The mapping of the terrain will be in greens-and-browns above water, shades-of-blues offshore.*

As the Mustang swept around the next corner, Miranda gasped. The Pacific spread itself as a panorama before her, diamond white caps sparkling across a sea of sapphires. *Like a dreamscape . . . almost too beautiful to be real.*

Making her final turn left onto Palos Verdes Drive, she slowed to pull into the parking lot, then turned off the motor. *What do I want to take in with me? Fleece jacket . . . backpack.* As she exited the car, a gust of wind nearly snatched the jacket from her hand. Long hair suddenly trailing across her face, she managed to wrestle her arms into the sleeves and close the door before it crashed against its hinges.

Wow! I had no idea it'd be this windy out here ... wonder if it's always like this? Backpack in hand, she headed toward the angled building nestled on the point until she stood cliffside on the patio of the Point Vicente Interpretive Center. A small group of observers—bundled in hooded parkas and severely buffeted by the strong gusts—sat faithfully at their post, tracking gray whale migration data for the American Cetacean Society's Los Angeles census.

Miranda didn't disturb them—not today. There'd be time enough for that tomorrow. For now, she clung to the railing 125 feet above the kelp beds and imagined the whales swimming just off the rocky shoreline, navigating the multi-leveled seafloor.

Of course, they communicate as they swim. But what do they think about on that long journey of theirs?

Chapter 10

Zack Calvin had left a softly snoring Cynthia nestled in a canyon of pillows, then quietly slipped out to head for the Calma gym.

The separate athletic building held an indoor pool, weight room, pair of squash courts, open workout space and two locker areas, one for each gender. This morning, while the party's rental tables, chairs, flooring and tent were packed up and carted away, he'd done a half-hour run on the treadmill and a solid hour doing the weight-machine circuit.

It wasn't until he'd stood in the steam-shower that he allowed himself to think about the previous evening. *Didn't want the party to be here in the first place; sure as hell didn't want some surprise thrust upon me in front of a crowd . . . especially the particular painting I'd tried to buy from Miranda. That was my own private business . . . nothing to do with Cynthia. Rotten luck that those two wires had to cross. I'll make sure they never cross again. And I don't know what the hell to do about the painting . . . but I don't have to decide that now.*

After donning a gray running suit he walked the pathway toward the main house, hoping to find the rental people gone and James ready with a strong cup of coffee. When he slipped through the kitchen door, he inhaled the rejuvenating scent of java and poured some into one of the waiting mugs.

He took a sip and brought his gaze to the little holiday touches around the many kitchen surfaces. On the center island, a brightly trimmed miniature Christmas tree stood where a bowl of fruit usually rested. His mom had always loved the season. Ever since she'd died, James had always made sure to bring out her favorite decorations. *Kind of reassuring to see them. Means the elves are still at work and Santa still flies.* He listened for a moment to the soft whirring of the two refrigerators. *The house does seem quiet . . . guess the trucks have left.* When he glanced through the windows, he caught sight of his father sitting on the deck reading the Sunday *New York Times.*

Carrying his mug, Zack headed out to the terrace. "Morning, Dad."

Joseph looked up from his paper to peer at his son with a trace of apparent concern. "Sleep okay?"

"Yeah. Cynthia's still in bed. But I've been up for a while. Went to the gym for a workout."

"Good. Good. James'll be out in a few minutes with breakfast. Hope scrambled eggs are okay."

"Yeah, sounds great."

The two men sat in companionable silence, enjoying the cool

morning mist that clung to the trees and lightly coated the flagstones of the terrace. Zack finished his coffee, choosing not to pour himself a glass of orange juice from the half-empty carafe already on the table.

His dad stood to retrieve the thermos-pitcher left on the sideboard, then refreshed both his own cup and his son's. When he was seated again, he remarked, "Well, it's nice to have a day off to recover from the party and get ourselves ready for a busy week."

"Right. Think I'll actually go into the office for a while, get the rest of my memo ready for the Coastal Commission meeting."

"You and Cynthia don't have plans?"

"Not really." Zack thought back to the exotic woman who seemed to have made such an impression on his father last evening, and couldn't help poking at his dad. "What about you and Zelda?"

Joseph Calvin pressed his lips together while he tried to think of how to respond. "Not that I know of."

Zack snorted. "Some women . . . have a way of making plans first and letting us know about them later."

Joseph grinned. "Knowing that is the beginning of true wisdom, my son . . . though I suspect women will always remain something of a mystery."

"I don't know. They're a weird combination . . . subtle one minute, obvious the next." Zack took another sip of coffee. "As promised, we did get plenty of cleavage last night."

Joseph felt heat rise up his neck as he thought of Zelda's plunging neckline, those full, round breasts undulating in her blue silk.

"Dad, if you feel that way about her, you should ask her out."

Joseph cleared his throat. "What? Oh. Yes. The thought had occurred." *Didn't know I was the one being obvious.* He brought his gaze up to Zack's, where he saw a glint of humor.

Suddenly the two men began to laugh, the release of tension as palpable as steam escaping from a high-pressure valve. James opened the door from the kitchen and Joseph saw him smile, apparently enjoying his employers' merriment as he wheeled out a serving cart.

"Are you all right, Mr. Zackery?"

"Yes, great," Zack confirmed, his voice weakened by laughter.

"You'll find bacon, eggs, halved beefsteak tomatoes grilled with breadcrumbs, and whole wheat toast on the warming platters. More orange juice?"

"No, we still have plenty," Joseph answered. "Thanks."

As James returned to the kitchen, the Calvins stood, served themselves, then returned to their table and placed fresh linen napkins on their laps.

Zack Calvin took a first bite. *Now's as good a time as any to tell Dad I'll be away.* After another slug of coffee, he said, "Glad you're in a good mood, because I wanted to mention I've got to take off next Wednesday through the end of the week."

Joseph looked up. "Half the . . . during such a busy week?"

"Actually, I'm all caught up, for once. I'll be back the following Monday morning. I'll leave all the numbers with Mary."

Before they could continue, James opened the kitchen door. "Mr. Zackery? You have a phone call, sir."

"Who is it, James?"

James paused for a moment. "It's Mr. Rune Sierra."

Zack paused, looked at Joseph. *Bad timing. Damn, another ten minutes and I'd have had this covered.* "Uh, tell him I'm in a meeting and I'll call him back shortly."

Their butler returned inside and Zack felt the shift of energy in his father.

"What the hell," Joseph muttered under his breath.

"It's not what you think."

"I don't really care what it is, Zack, it doesn't look good. You don't *know* who he really is. He's the son of Domingo Sierra, who's done everything in his power to ruin Calvin Oil. There's no enemy like a former friend. Domingo taught me that. If you insist on speaking to the son, you better at least record the conversation."

Zack ran his fingers through thick, blond hair. "I'm afraid I'm going to be doing more than just talking with Rune, Dad."

"Oh, for heaven's sake, we've been all through this. Williams has advised against any further contact pending litigation."

"He advised against any further *professional* contact."

"Well, what the hell other kind of contact do you propose to have with the boy? You two get alone in a room and I'll give you ten minutes before one of you throws a punch."

"Under normal circumstances, that would be true."

"Normal circumstances. Hah." Joseph chomped through a piece of bacon in three bites, then swallowed. "Normal circumstances always means some woman is involved. You're going to tell me this *isn't* about a woman?"

"No, this has to do with a concert."

"That was always one of the problems, that Rune spends too much time with these extracurricular activities. Believe me, I can understand his father's frustration."

"The man started his own company. It's the American Way, isn't it? Besides, this 'extracurricular' activity's for charity."

Joseph stopped eating and turned to face Zack. "I can't believe I'm sitting here listening to you defend Rune Sierra. You two have been sworn rivals for years."

James reappeared on the patio. "Mr. Zackery, sir, Mr. Sierra said to tell you thanks, and that he'll see you Wednesday afternoon."

Zack felt himself flush, shifted his weight in the chair, and thanked James. Now he waited for his father's voice to raise the hairs on the back of his neck.

Sure enough, his dad shouted. "What the hell, Zack, what have you gotten yourself into?"

Zack glanced around to check that James had closed the patio door behind him, then he waited as his father's tirade continued.

"You mean to say you've gotten yourself involved with one of Rune's goddamn rock concerts? And you've taken *company* time to do it?" Joseph pushed back from the table, the wrought iron chair legs screeching against the flagstone.

"Look, Dad, I can't really explain. But this concert is something I had to do."

His father glared into his face as though looking at a stranger. "Your logic is beyond me, Zack. I just don't know where your priorities are anymore."

Zack stared back at him without anger. "I don't want to fight, Dad."

"This is the second time you've said that in the last few days. But it's as if you *are* fighting. In fact, you've got some . . . I don't know . . . internal war going on."

Zack considered the irony of what his father had just said. "Well, speaking of battles . . . that's what happened to a lot of guys. That's what this concert is about. It's for veterans." Zack pushed himself up from the chair, then stood.

"Like I said, Dad, this is just something I had to do." *I'd hoped he'd understand . . . I can't fight his battle with the Sierras. I've just gotta fight my own.* Turning, he left the patio and walked inside.

Joseph Calvin sat where Zack had left him and stared out at the stunning vista of mountains trailing down to the sea. While his anger continued to subside, he had to admit he'd heard a sense of purpose in what his son had said—a quality he hadn't heard from him in a long time.

Where does a young man find his core mission? Is it something he learns about from his parents? It'd been no easy task, raising a son alone, Joseph reflected. Joan's death had been a devastating loss for all of them.

The loss had hardened the boy prematurely, but all in all, Joseph felt it had served Zack as well, given him his mental toughness, prepared him for the cutthroat world of business. *A man needs an edge to survive in this arena.*

Zack had always played as hard as he worked and, although he attracted the wrong women, Joseph believed this was temporary. It was Zack's method of keeping himself out of any serious relationship until he was good and ready. *Someday he'll find a good woman—an equal, a supporter.*

Work. Women. Relaxation. They were all part of the plan, part of Zack's grooming as Joseph readied him for taking the helm at Calvin Oil. Though by oil company standards she was a small firm, still she was a big ship. Zack would be ready to steer her course when the time was right. But only if he stayed focused.

Rock concerts should be the least of his concerns. Zack could afford the occasional dalliance. But actual involvement with the Sierra family was another matter. Rune Sierra was not part of Joseph's plan, nor would he ever be.

Cynthia Radcliffe fumbled her key ring with her one free hand while pressing—between her other hand and her chin—an enormous stack of boxed purchases.

But, with apparent energy of their own, the boxes bulleted away from her chest to sail across the hallway outside her condo. "Shit!" she cried. *I really don't want to use that word any more. Doesn't suit my self-image.* "Damn, I mean."

It also didn't suit her self-image to have strewn packages all over the corridor, so she hurried to collect them. Through the front door at last, she made multiple trips to the hall, flinging them into her tiny foyer until all its floor space was taken up with the multi-colored paper bags and boxes of the stores she'd visited.

She closed her front door, picked her way through the disarray, then kicked off her shoes. The closest piece of furniture was the fake-leopard-skin-covered love seat. She sank into it and began massaging her toes, which were now happily free from the torment of the high-heeled pumps she'd worn on her shopping spree.

It'd been a long day, driving the round trip to Beverly Hills to find decent fashion items, and she felt entitled to a glass of chilled wine. Standing, she padded to the tiny bar over which a few stemmed glasses hung upside down, and plucked one free. Carrying it, she stepped into her compact kitchen and opened her refrigerator door, where a half-bottle of corked Riesling rested on its side. She grabbed its neck, pulled out the cork, and watched the golden liquid swirl into the glass.

Unable to decide where to sit, she stood for the first sip, allowing the cool burn to drift down her dry throat. *I suppose I spent a little too much. But I want my next outfit for Zackery to really pop, especially since we'll be at some big rock concert.*

As she sipped at her wine again, she remembered their evening together and a thrill ran down her spine. Something about last night had been different. The drama . . . the fear . . . they hinted at a new vulnerability between them—both her own, and his. Just when their relationship had seemed ready to stall, it'd turned volcanic. It could've been her greatest defeat, those dreadful hours after the party she'd worked so hard to create. Instead he'd seen her naked—body and soul—and had taken her voraciously.

My big mistake . . . surprising him with the painting . . . turned into my big victory. Zelda was sooo right about how things would turn around. There's just nothing like make-up sex. No matter what problems arose these days in her relationship with Zackery, they always seemed to get solved in bed. *What could be better?*

And with the upcoming concert, she'd had a perfect excuse to go shopping. Feeling rejuvenated, Cynthia put down her wine, hobbled on sore feet toward the unruly pile of goodies, and yanked open two of the bags from Neiman Marcus. *Needless Markup the skeptics call it . . . but for me it's the ideal store.*

It'd been brutally crowded this time of year and, of course, gorgeously decorated. From the signature mobile that hung down through four levels, oversized golden balls had been carefully draped; every floor had its own Christmas tree; lighted swags dripped across every banister; and every employee was dressed like a decoration.

She'd tried to appear nonchalant as the escalator pushed her through the crowd—all the while scrutinizing the wealthy young matrons and starlets of 90210, taking mental notes. She'd seen plenty of Jimmy Choo shoes—and that was one thing on her "must" list for the day. She'd been aware of the young Chinese designer since his first 1988 splash in *Vogue.* But this year, she'd read all about how he'd gone big-time when he partnered with British *Vogue* fashion editor, Tamara Yeardly Mellon, so Cynthia knew this was the time to add a pair of his sleek footwear to her collection.

Skirts, she'd confirmed, were incredibly short and sleek, often worn over opaque tights—a look that perfectly suited her own long legs. *Love that all-black look . . . easy to duplicate with less expensive pieces, and oh-so classy.* What bothered her, though, was the growing trend toward "grunge"—jeans and T-shirts, torn-this-and-ripped-that, mis-matched colors. . . .

I suppose it's mostly college kids being rebellious, or something. But really . . . how can they make a fashion statement with no real sense of design?

Dismissing "grunge" as irrelevant, she'd focused on the featured designers in the store. Having just worn her primary holiday formal, she'd skipped the top floor where the gowns were exhibited. She'd spent some time—just for fun—on the third floor where the suits hung in their respective designers' areas. The Ungaros, the Karans, the Versaces, all beckoned, and she'd found two that fit her divinely. But she wouldn't really need a power-suit until some future occasion demanded it. So she'd spent most of her time today on the second floor where the trendy, fun outfits hung like funky fabric-art collages. Here she'd found herself grabbing hangers off racks like a child snatching tasty morsels from a Christmas dinner table, then wriggling in and out of them in the mirrored dressing room.

Now that she was finally home with her treats, she opened her first bag anxiously and, with a crinkling of tissue paper, lifted out the first outfit. "Delicious . . . like pistachio ice cream." Skin-tight stove-pipe jeans, with two matching tops: the deep-V'd shirt, and the cropped denim jacket, all in that distinctive green. *They'll certainly see me coming in this . . . and it* is *this year's rage as a Christmas color.*

Grabbing for another bag, she yanked out the next outfit: holiday-red vinyl skirt with its fake-leather jacket. *Maybe this is better. In a skirt this short, I'll probably freeze. That could have its advantages too. Zackery would have to keep me warm. Very distracting, though. He might not want everyone gawking. I want him focused on me . . . but not everyone else.*

Something stirred at the back of her mind. Focus . . . yes, that was it. Until last night, he'd been losing focus lately. With no warning, he'd suddenly go off to Mill Pond, or whatever it was called. And now he was suddenly tackling research in the library. *He never used to do that sort of work himself. He's got a whole staff to do it all for him.*

She opened the last of the Neiman bags, and pushed paper away from a midriff-baring silver lurex number. Tap pants and a loosely fitting tank top. *This isn't for the concert. This is just for us on Christmas morning when he wants to unwrap me. . . .*

Feeling heat rise through her, she thought again of last night. *One of our steamiest . . . more intense than I've ever seen him . . . like he had something to prove. The more I think I know him, the more of an enigma he seems to be. I mean . . . what did happen when he saw the painting I gave him? He went cold. Then later, he was so hot. . . .*

She supposed he might be having some sort of "male crisis." She'd read about these in her women's magazines. Yet this could be a very good sign—a signal that he was preparing to leave behind his bachelor days and embark on a committed relationship. Yes . . . that made sense. And all the truly *important* things about him were perfect. *Plenty of money to support me; ambitious and successful, which makes him feel good as a man; his handsome and my stunning looks are complementary; and we have a great time in bed.*

Yes . . . I can always get a rise out of Zackery. She laughed at the thought of it, humor blunting the edge of worry. *He must be finding me more and more irresistible.*

Having reassured herself, she returned to the task of choosing concert clothes. Hoisting a Fred Hayman, she whipped its contents from tissue paper and excitedly flung brown satin hip-huggers with their matching cropped top across the sofa. *That's it. These and the platform shoes. The only question now is . . . what do I wear on top to keep warm?*

Rummaging for the next bag, she suddenly remembered she hadn't checked her machine for messages since returning home. She grabbed the satin pants and held them to her body, looking into her full length mirror as the messages began to play.

At the sound of Zack's voice her heart thumped.

"Hi, Cynthia, it's Zack. That was, uh, fun last night. Listen, I just wanted to let you know I won't be around this week or next weekend. I've still got a lot to do on the rehearsals and concerts, so I'll be very busy. Besides I know you hate that kind of music. So, stay out of trouble, have one of your spa visits, and I'll see you next week."

Cynthia froze, one hand still holding the phone. The other hand let go of the brown satin pants, which slid to the floor and remained in a heap at her feet. "Shit," she said. "Damn!" she yelled. "Fun?! Damn! Damn!!" Her voice rising with each word, she grabbed the first thing in front of her—a delicate glass vase. She hurled it across the room, where it hit the living room wall and broke into smithereens.

Breathing hard, tears of rage seeping from the corners of her eyes, she yelled some more. "I have just spent the entire day shopping for something to wear to your stupid concert, Zackery Calvin, and you have the nerve not to invite me!!"

She glanced at the shelf unit that held figurines and framed photos, scanning for something else to throw. Her hand reached for a paper weight but as she lifted it to throw, something about it caught her attention.

The glass ball was etched with words, which she squinted to see through hot tears. "Third Annual Dirt Bike Rally for Starving Children." She smirked at the notion. *Perfect thing to throw!* But then, images of the event flashed through her mind.

Me in tight stretch pants and a visor . . . Zackery in shorts . . . and that guy Rune in a helmet. She remembered then, the way the stranger'd looked at her. Even through his goggles, he'd made it clear he appreciated her every angle. And she remembered something else too. His attentions had bothered Zackery. *Yes, that bothered Zackery a lot.*

She hadn't thought anything about it at the time, eager only to attend these charity events with Zackery because it meant they were establishing themselves as a couple. But now she considered the possibilities. She'd overheard enough talk between Zackery and Joseph to know there was some sort of problem with this man. And in Zackery's face she'd seen the unmistakable look of jealousy.

Cynthia glanced down and kicked away the satin pants still near her foot. The plan formulating in her troubled brain brought a new focus, and a false peace began to descend on her raging spirit. She knew how to make phone calls too. And she knew just where to begin. She looked again at the words on the paperweight. Etched in glass was the name Rune Sierra.

Zelda McIntyre's stomach began to rumble indelicately. Tempting though it was to reach for one of the synthetic—but deliciously smooth and sweet—non-fat puddings she kept refrigerated, she pondered instead a delicious notion, rolling it around her tongue like a piece of butterscotch candy.

I never thought I'd have the slightest interest in attending a rock-and-roll performance, but now it's become such a focal point for the Calvin men . . . even though Joseph doesn't realize it yet. I simply must attend the Doobie Brothers concert at the Central Coast Bowl; and I have to be there with Joseph.

Zelda had heard about the event first from Miranda, who'd told her breathlessly not only that she'd been invited to the concert by Zack, but that she'd be attending a big rehearsal while in Los Angeles. Zelda had simply filed away this inforation as an unimportant detail ... that is, until Cynthia had *also* mentioned the Central Coast event during her tearful tantrum last night. *Surely Zackery wouldn't invite* both *his women . . . which means Cynthia still apparently has no idea she will* not *be invited. My word! I need to see this chapter of the Miranda-Zackery-Cynthia drama played out first-hand.*

In addition, there was the matter of Joseph. Since she'd heard nothing at all about the event from him, she wondered whether he'd been told little-to-nothing about this venture on the part of his son. Yet she already knew Calvin Senior felt himself to be close enough to Calvin Junior that the omitted invitation would be hurtful, or even damaging.

Joseph needs to know. And he needs to see it with his own eyes, not be told about it. So if I suggest that I need to attend—but can't possibly go alone and need his help—he can find out everything he needs to know while saving face ... and without my being the one to tell him. Can't have him blaming the messenger.

Granted, it'll be quite forward of me to invite him ... still, he should really know what his son is up to. Besides, I saw him making eyes at me last night. Best to strike while the iron is hot, before some other likely female grabs his attention.

If she could pull it off, she'd have less than a week to prepare herself. Fortunately, she'd colored her hair just yester-ay; but she'd have to schedule another manicure and have the girl take the length down on her nails again, they grew so fast. One thing she couldn't abide were the long, polished claws women in California favored.

And if Joseph and I do begin seeing each other . . . eventually he'll come here to my town home. She glanced down at her waxed parquet floor, suddenly noticing a spot. Wetting her index finger with her tongue, she bent down and rubbed the spot away as carefully as if she were cleaning a pair of glasses.

He's a fine man with a good life. But I can make it ever so much more exciting.

Joseph Calvin had left Calma to spend some time at his office, relishing the prospect of being there alone on a Sunday afternoon.

He crossed the foyer from the bank of elevators toward his private suite, appreciating the well-appointed entry. Though normally too preoccupied to pay it any attention, today he glanced down and noticed the geometric design of the floor, executed in alternating marble and carpet, hearing the uneven sounds of his own footsteps—a sound he found oddly comforting.

On his way through the foyer, he glanced at his secretary's unattended desk—completely cleared, as it always was before she left each day. Mary Meeks was in every way the perfect secretary, past retirement age now, but stalwart and trustworthy. He found it impossible to imagine Calvin Oil without her, and was grateful he didn't yet have to consider that eventuality.

The phone ringing behind his locked office door startled

him out of his reverie. *Why would anyone be calling on a Sunday?* The line continued to ring. "Oh, hell," he muttered, turning the key in the lock. He flung open his office door and grabbed the receiver on the eleventh ring. "Hello, Calvin Oil."

"Joseph? Marvelous, I've caught you. It's me, Zelda."

"Oh . . . Zelda, I'm trying to . . . could we talk on Monday?"

"Monday? Oh, I wouldn't want to keep you guessing for the rest of the weekend."

In spite of himself, he laughed. "Okay, Zelda, you've piqued my interest. Guessing about what?"

"What I was going to invite you to," came the reply.

"Oh, it's very nice of you to think of me, but really I've had a bellyful of events for the time being."

"This one won't have nearly so dramatic an ending, I'm sure," she countered.

Joseph snorted. "That wouldn't be difficult."

"No."

"By the way, thank you again for last night. You seem to have calmed Cynthia down in very short order."

"It was my pleasure to be able to help, truly."

Admiring her apparently modest reply, Joseph continued, "Well, I suppose you have me curious enough to at least ask what this shindig is you're calling about."

"A rock concert."

Joseph burst into laughter. Noticing she did not join in the merriment, he reined himself in. "Sorry, Zelda. I can't picture you at a rock concert any more than I can picture myself there. Your business has more angles than I was aware of."

"Oh, I mean business, but not in any financial sense."

"Oh? Now you *do* have my interest."

She pressed on. "I need to be there, you see, and I did buy two tickets, hoping to convince someone to go with me. To be brutally honest, I'm slightly terrified to go alone."

Joseph guffawed. "That'll be the day . . . when you're terrified of anything."

"I'm tremendously flattered you think of me as a brave woman. But I assure you, being at this event worries me. I keep imagining parking miles from the door, attempting to navigate my way through presumably rabid fans, and getting crushed in a thundering crowd."

He tried to picture her in that setting, and began to see her point. *She's not very tall . . . and in that crowd, wouldn't know her way around.*

"And believe it or not," she continued, "this concert is in a worthy cause. It's a fund-raiser for veterans, you see."

That detail pricked his ears. *This has to be the same fund-raiser Zack told me about this morning. What are the chances?* "It so happens," he said, "I do know about the concert. Tell you what. I'll go to this shindig with you, but for reasons of my own."

"How mysterious of you."

"Not really. Let's just say I can help you and help myself as well."

"Sounds ideal. So, you must already know the concert is up north in Santa Maria."

"Yes, at the Central Coast Bowl, so we'll need to allow a couple of hours' travel time."

"Exactly. So what time should I be ready Saturday night?"

"I'll pick you up at five p.m. What's your address?" As she told him, he grabbed the notepad on his desk and jotted it down. "You're close to downtown . . . let's have a quick bite at Café Français first."

"I look forward to it. Ta-ta." Zelda's end of the phone line clicked off.

No lingering on the phone. I like that. Good Lord, what am I getting myself into with this woman? Well . . . it's just a date. And to have this fall into my lap . . . a chance I couldn't refuse.

His gaze came up to the bookshelves' leaded glass doors that now reflected the ocean view with a bright band of orange at the horizon. He surveyed the gleaming Art Deco furnishings, remembering how Zelda had looked here in this room at this same time of day—when they'd first met last autumn— fetchingly aglow in the warm afternoon light.

Only this morning, Zack was teasing me about her . . . he picked up on our attraction so fast. And now I'll be at this concert of Zack's, have a chance to see firsthand the extent of his involvement with Rune Sierra. Wouldn't have gone on my own. That'd smack of spying on Zack, something we agreed years ago neither of us would do.

And now I have an excuse—a date with Zelda the live-wire. Still feel disloyal to Chris, even though she's now officially "missing." He imagined she might suddenly reappear and show up at the concert to interview the band for some television piece. *Is that what I'm hoping? That she'll see me with another woman and get jealous?* He pursed his lips. *That'd be awkward.*

One thing was certain. Spending next Saturday night with Zelda would be a helluva lot more interesting than facing yet another evening of carefully prepared meals awaiting him in the estate kitchen's well-stocked refrigerator.

Chapter 11

C ornelius Smith rounded the last bend before Highway 1 took the local name of Shoreline Drive. *Good timing. Sunset's at 4:45 today . . . I'm just in time to see the red ball plunge down into the Pacific. In this clear, clean air, I might even catch the green flash.*

On final approach to Mendocino, he'd stopped a few yards short of his turn-off to take in the picture-postcard view of the lovely town atop its peninsula. Pulling off the road onto a wide shoulder, he'd stepped out of the Durango. Across a slice of a small bay, lights began winking on in the Victorian buildings, bright spots between dark trees, the peaked roofs matching the steep angles of the cypress stands.

He brought his gaze to the horizon. *Yes! There it is . . . the flash of emerald.* He took a deep breath, rotated his neck, then moved back into the car. *Time to check in. I should be just in time for dinner.*

He edged the SUV back onto the highway until he made a

right turn onto Comptche Ukiah Road, soon thereafter entering the grounds of the Stanford Inn.

Since first receiving the invitation last fall to create two lectures and a star-gazing experience for guests at the Inn, he'd done his homework—not only on his own program, but on the history of the hotel itself.

Founders Jeff and Joan Stanford had bought the original Big River Lodge in 1980, grasping with both hands the unexpected opportunity to live in their dream location. With help from the original owners—who still lived in the 1850s farmhouse at the front of the property—they began the wildly ambitious project of expanding the inn, and designing and constructing organic gardens, as well as having two children.

Their premise had been to build a place in harmony with the land, sensing the indigenous energies of their unique location, and working as much intuitively as logically to create a home for themselves and for guests they would treat as family members. Now their eco-resort was truly on the map, with their vegan restaurant supplied by their own organic gardens, and with canoeing up the Big River Estuary and biking the nearby lanes all included.

The Durango climbed the steep hill to a lot behind the wide two-story main lodge, where dark wood framed squares of lighted windows and doors. When Cornelius had pulled his olive drab backpack from the passenger seat, he headed inside to check in. When the paperwork was completed, the clerk gave him an envelope containing a hand-written note, which he opened. "Dear Cornelius, Welcome to our Inn! We look forward to meeting with you tomorrow. We hope you enjoy a restful night. Joan and Jeff Stanford." *Well, that's a charming touch.*

After thanking the clerk, he headed back out the front door, and a few minutes later he went to move his car closer to his quarters. He climbed the stairs to the second floor and opened the door of number 110 to a cozy, welcoming room: parchment-shaded lamps showed off knotty-pine paneling; a fireplace stood ready with stacked wood; and at the far end, a balcony overlooked a V-shaped valley that framed the ocean beyond, now barely aglow in the last light of day.

Tired from his seven hours of driving, he dropped his backpack on a low dresser and opened wide the French doors to his balcony. The evening chill bit through his corduroy jacket even as it pierced the fatigue. Below him stretched the raised beds of the garden, and from somewhere in the lodge inviting cooking aromas reached his nostrils, mixing pleasantly with the tang of ocean and kelp.

Don't know whether it's the smell ... or the visuals ... but I'm suddenly reminded of the Miramar. When he was a young teen, Santa Barbara's resort had been a favorite family vacation spot for his parents and their only child.

In a bygone era, it'd been a posh destination with its own railroad stop. In his youth, it'd slipped quietly into disrepair, the stucco of its individual bungalows cracked and water-stained, a faint odor of mildew clinging to the closets. Yet it'd retained something of its charm—the orange blossoms and salt spray becoming a pungent mix that overwhelmed the musty molds—and the entire surrounding infused with nostalgia. *Amazing that would all come back to me so vividly. Last time we were there must've been . . . at least twenty years ago. But its name—"behold the sea"—makes sense why I'd think of it.*

Now Cornelius thought about the nearby estuary and

wondered if he'd have time for a short canoe trip in the morning—depending on the tide schedule. It'd be a busy week. He'd be giving two short lectures here at the Inn, and with the several articles he had to write, he planned on some quiet time in his room. Plus, he'd visit the site of that historic observatory he'd read about.

Tomorrow I'll meet with the Stanfords to discuss this week's lectures and figure out where to set up for the Star Party next Friday. He inhaled the enticing food odors again and his stomach rumbled. *Think I'll go to the dining room and grab some dinner, then make an early night of it.*

Miranda Jones blinked her eyes open, uncertain for a moment where she was. *Hacienda Hotel . . . and it must be the jet that woke me up.* She'd forgotten about the proximity to L.A.'s huge airport. But at least the planes didn't roar directly overhead, instead taking off toward the ocean. *Hope that doesn't disturb the coastal critters too much . . . but, of course, they'd all be used to it.*

She glanced around her room. *It's been so long since I stayed at a hotel . . . almost forgotten what it's like.* She drew her hand across the high-thread-count sheet, then glanced around her nicely appointed room: hot-pot with its tray of individually wrapped coffees and teas, sugar and powdered cream; a compact desk for writing notes or letters; a chair and footstool for reading; and, of course, the requisite television, which she so rarely watched. *But since I'm here in "Hollywood," maybe I should watch something when I get back to my room tonight.*

Closing her eyes again, she let her thoughts drift back to

family vacations. Throughout her childhood, her parents had chosen one grand hotel each year—sometimes in the States, sometimes overseas: the Broadmoor in Colorado Springs; the Biltmore in Ashland, North Carolina; the Greenbrier in White Sulfur Springs, West Virginia; the Fujiya Hotel in Hakone, Japan; the Château D'Artigny in Montbazon, France.

Each had been a place offering a complete vacation, with built-in daytime activities like swimming and croquet, horse-back riding or tennis lessons. In the evenings, they'd all dressed for dinner, then taken turns at ballroom dancing with Daddy.

She had to acknowledge those were wonderful times. For herself and Meredith, the vacations had been full of the excitement of meeting boys from other wealthy families, impressing various grown-ups with their manners and well-spoken conversation. *And the dreaming . . . that was the most fun of all . . . dreaming about who we'd be when we grew up, where we'd go, what we'd create. Mer always wanted to be the first woman president of a big bank; I always wanted to be the artist famous for being the first to visit the North, then the South Pole.*

Lingering for one more moment in the comfortable bed, she wondered about those dreams now. *Meredith is still on track with her financial work. And I am too . . . I'm still on track with my painting, though for me it's not about being famous any more, and my goal-destinations might be a little more modest . . . but just as intriguing. Like today's visit to the lighthouse!*

Throwing back the covers, she stood and moved to the window, where she opened the black-out curtains. By the pale light of near-dawn, she peered into a lovely central courtyard dotted with blue umbrellas over wrought-iron tables and chairs. At the center of the open space a round fountain splashed water over colorful Mexican tiles.

She smiled at the charm of the setting, remembering how bright and inviting it'd looked in yesterday's afternoon sunshine. *It might not be as swanky as my parents' vacation spots, but this is special . . . and it's mine.*

Miranda parked her rental car in the lot of the Point Vicente Interpretive Center. With no morning rush-hour traffic, the trip from El Segundo had taken only thirty minutes on this blustery Sunday morning. For the final few hundred feet of her drive it'd been difficult to keep her gaze from fastening to the tall, white structure punctuating land's end.

Despite the wind, she'd decided to begin her day outside, then gradually work her way in. *My meeting with the Center's Director is set for nine-thirty . . . that gives me a solid two hours to walk and draw first. Now I've gotta get ready for those not-so-gentle breezes.*

To hold her painting journal pages in place, she secured them with rubber bands; and to keep her hair from streaming across her face again, she gathered it into a French braid from the crown of her head to the nape of her neck. Now—fleece jacket zipped, hood drawn snugly and backpack over her shoulders—she stepped out of the car to hike the short distance to Bluff Cove Overlook at the north end of the peninsula.

The tumbling air . . . the brisk walk . . . the incredible scenery . . . it all feels like a movie . . . or a novel. Well, I am in the City of Stories. When she grinned, a gust of wind snatched at her breath and tugged at her backpack as if it were a sail.

After a few minutes she arrived at the Overlook and stood facing north to admire the trailing coastline. *Spectacular . . . the whole of Santa Monica Bay is laid out in front of me, arcing northwest.* Finding a perch on a flat rock, she slipped out of her backpack and from it grabbed her journal and colored pencils. *Never be able to manage my paints in this wind . . . that's okay, the pencils with their high pigmentation will work fine, and I'll also snap photos from this vantage.*

When she'd settled her journal on her lap, she opened the case of Blick pencils, choosing the Brown and Burnt Ochre, and with quick strokes sketched in the coastal rocks and jagged cliffs. Next she used the Azure and Cobalt—plus the colorless for blending—to capture the white-capped chop of the ocean and the froth at the shoreline. *And for the pale morning sky, I can use the Sky Blue . . . nice synchronicity.*

Now she took a deep breath to settle her spirit. It was then she began to *see* the creatures around her stirring in their subtle movements. *There's a plover . . . and another.* She used the Slate Gray and Black to capture the sweet black-and-white snowy plovers that hopped and swooped along the shore. *If I remember right, they were put on the endangered list three years ago. I wonder if they're in this cove for the winter, or all year round.*

A willet, marching along the wet sand at water's edge, grabbed her attention—its large body and long bill showing the resemblance to its sandpiper cousin. As another of these bigger shore birds lifted off the beach, she admired its beautiful black-and-white wing pattern, sketching quickly to capture the decorative design before the bird soared out of sight behind the next bluff.

When she'd filled two facing pages with a wide depiction of the panorama before her, Miranda stood, stretched, and found another perch—this time facing south. *Yes . . . I want to capture the lighthouse from this distance first . . . in its context.*

The coastal escarpment seemed even more rugged from this perspective, the rocks just offshore merely surface expressions of underwater ridges that would be so treacherous to ships venturing too close to land.

Atop the jagged 130-foot cliff, the lighthouse stood tall and straight, but not alone. Next to it stood a palm tree almost exactly matching its 67-foot height—the closest of a grove of palms that filled the lovely twelve-acre grounds.

Like all lighthouses, this one stood sentinel: with the brightest light along the southern California coast, it warned of danger to those who approached by sea; and with sheltering trees and buildings, it reassured with its offer of safe haven to those who arrived by land.

When her second panorama was completed on the following two pages, Miranda packed up her materials and hiked south until she passed through the open gates to the lighthouse property, eager to accept the hospitality of the Light Keeper.

USCG Auxiliarist Stephen Cantwell had occupied the post since 1992. But the accomplished Coast Guard officer also frequently traveled the West Coast with the Aids to Navigation Team, to help repair and maintain California's lighthouses.

Miranda stepped into the cozy outbuilding that housed the office he shared with his fellow officers and was greeted with a firm handshake and a steady gaze.

"How may I help you today?" The voice was surprisingly

soft-spoken, laced with an accent she'd read was Argentine.

"Thanks so much for meeting with me. As I wrote in my letter, the Interpretive Center has commissioned me to do two paintings for them—one of this lighthouse. Before I do, I wanted to learn more of the Point Vicente particulars."

Already, he was standing and walking toward his tall set of file cabinets, searching through them to withdraw printed sheets, which he handed to her. "'History of the light' . . . 'California Lighthouses' . . . 'Aids to Navigation Bill'. . . . Thank you so much! All this will be helpful."

"There are twenty-nine lighthouses in California," he said, "each with its own history."

"Yes. From what I've read, many of them were built in response to a shipwreck."

"You could say that," he gently corrected, "but it might be more accurate to say each came into existence in response to the particular terrain. Some were designed and built in place; some were built elsewhere and moved. But each has its particular mission. And each has its own requirements as well, particularly with regard to restoration."

He speaks not just technically but elegantly . . . this is more than his job, this is a passion.

"I happen to live near the Piedras Blancas Lighthouse," Miranda shared.

"That light has quite an interesting history." A fondness crept into his voice. "You know, it was first damaged in 1948 by earthquakes—three in a row, actually."

"Oh! I didn't realize that."

"Yes. The top three stories of the structure, as well as the lens, had to be removed. That was a First Order Fresnel lens—extremely heavy. By comparison, our light here at Point Vicente is a Third Order."

"I see, and so the tower here is shorter?"

"Yes, here we have a 67-foot structure. But at Piedras, the tower was originally 104 feet. When it was capped, the height was reduced to 74."

"It's always looked strange—the Piedras light, I mean—like a rook in a chess game."

A wistful expression came over his face, but then he added with conviction, "We're committed to restoration, as are most people who serve at lighthouses."

Miranda smiled.

"There was quite an interesting problem when Piedras was capped. Here was this magnificent Fresnel—and no place for it. It was abandoned and was to be destroyed. But in 1951 the Lions Club took it to Cambria on loan from the Coast Guard."

"Right, I've seen it there, outside the Veterans Building."

"Ah, outside—this became another problem. The exposure was damaging the lens. So six years ago, it was refurbished in Monterey. And in 1992 the Friends of the Lighthouse built a housing. So, it is once again in Cambria."

"On Main Street. At least people get to see it."

"Now here at Point Vicente, this lighthouse has found an expanded purpose."

"Oh, really?"

"Of course, we are primarily an aid to navigation. But now we are training Coast Guard cadets; we have special events throughout the year; we are becoming a landmark for the city of Los Angeles."

After thanking the officer profusely and shaking his hand,

Miranda slid the papers and pamphlets into her backpack. Outside again, she stopped at another small building to buy postcards and a Point Vicente pin. *Guess this means I'm starting a lighthouse pin collection. What'll I put them on? Maybe a hat?*

She gazed up at the light tower, remembering an eerie piece of history she'd read. Shortly after World War II, Southern California experienced a huge building boom, mostly created by servicemen returning home from the Pacific theatre. The homeowners near the lighthouse were then disturbed by the powerfully bright beam that strafed through the windows, so the lighthouse keepers coated the land-facing windows of the light tower with white paint.

No sooner had the paint dried, than locals began to observe the silhouette of a woman who appeared to be pacing the tower's walkway. There were several theories as to who she might be—the first lighthouse keeper's wife, who'd lost her footing one foggy night; or a heartbroken woman who threw herself over the cliffs when abandoned. In any case, she came to be known as "Lady of the Light". *Maybe I'll meet her up there,* Miranda joked to herself as a shiver ran up her spine.

Now she walked the short distance to the tower. She climbed the spiral staircase, pausing at each landing to glance at the rising view and orient herself. When she reached the top, she found herself face-to-face with the five-foot-diameter lens itself, rotating immediately in front of her as if she'd stepped into a house of mirrors. In fact, she *had*—each carefully ground piece of glass perfectly angled to magnify and reflect the central bulb. *It's like a complex sculpture . . . no, more like a mobile, only instead of the parts hanging free, they're framed to move synchronously, like the internal workings of a clock. And with the light magnified by this complex lens, it shines twenty-four miles out to sea.*

Standing inside the tower—feeling almost as if she were inside the light itself—she paused for a moment, groping to identify the odd sensation moving through her. *I've only ever experienced a lighthouse from the outside . . . never really imagined being inside one before . . . let alone being here, in the tower.*

She let the revolving lens wash its prismed light over her, while through the clear windows she absorbed the expanding view of etched coastline and varnished sea.

So this is what it feels like to be at the core . . . the center . . . where everything synchronizes . . . where the smallest movement amplifies to a 360-degree rotation. And where a single bulb magnifies to a two-million candlepower light.

Awed by the new awareness as much as by the staggering view, she wound her way back down the tower, then hiked in the wind back to the Learning Center.

Miranda walked through the double glass doors of the Interpretive Center and stood transfixed by what hung from the lobby's ceiling: a gray whale's skeleton.

All art students through the ages had studied interior structures of whatever creature they intended to draw or paint. "Ze inside determines ze outside." She could hear Monsieur Gilroy's French-accented voice even now, repeating this as a mantra to his students at Bennington College. *Perfect to have the chance to see this close-up and to scale, right before I start my whale painting . . . another synchronicity.*

Just by walking quickly through the exhibits, Miranda could see this center was as much a small, focused natural history museum as it was a working center for wildlife study. It'd opened in 1984—twelve years earlier—and she imagined had more than proven its worth, with its programs for children, guided tours, and support rooms for the American Cetacean Society.

After her brief self-guided tour, she spent the afternoon with the Director—learning more about the center's mission and its local history—in particular, listening carefully to exactly what the Director expected of the new painting Miranda would create for them.

"Accurate, but evocative," he'd explained. "We don't want a photograph. We really want people coming in here to imagine the whales swimming less than a mile from where they're standing."

They went on to discuss the high drama sometimes observed from the point: orcas harassing the grays on their migratory journey; grays occasionally entangled in fishing nets.

In both scenarios, the whales were at risk. In orca attacks, at least the grays were in a position to defend themselves from these naturally occurring predators. But when entrapped in manmade devices like nets, the whales became powerless, frustrated, imperiled, and—without human intervention—left with no solution and in danger of drowning.

Yet these events would not be the subject of Miranda's painting, which would instead depict the ocean floor, a migratory group of males, females and calves, and an accurate positioning of the cetaceans with regard to the coastline and to one another.

After her meeting, Miranda stopped at the intriguing little gift shop, eager to see if they might have a pin she could add to her collection. Indeed, they did have pins and she chose a pewter double-stick model depicting a migrating gray whale. *It'll go right onto my heavy denim jacket, next to the sperm whale pin I bought after the voyage.*

Next she went out and approached the group of volunteers, asking them questions and snapping photos of the setting. Then, to complete her day of research, she found a seat, dug out her own binoculars, and waited through an hour's vigil—nose red and hands stiff with cold—but thrilled each time she saw a tail fluke or a shooting spray rising above the waves.

An hour later, Miranda's Mustang threaded its way through Palos Verdes until she reached Highway 1—almost a country road, compared with L.A.'s network of freeways. She noted scrubby vegetation clinging to the rising hills to her right, a dirt trail paralleling the road to her left, dotted with intermittent scrub oaks and short, squat palms. But beyond, stretched the wind-whipped ocean, its dark surface flecked with the vermilion reflections of a rapidly sinking sun.

She pushed another Pat Metheny cassette into the player, and he resumed his concert with "Offramp"—a piece as turbulent as today's ruffled sea. His electric guitar now seemed uncannily to mimic the wails and moans of whalesong. Wildly varying melody arced and plunged against clusters of percussive drumbeats and rhythmic clankings that suggested an underwater chaos of wave-churned rocks and shells. *Perhaps the grays don't like the turbulence any more than we do.*

The Mustang hummed along the road past houses and lawns, but Miranda kept the gleam of the ocean in view as another piece began to play . . . she couldn't recall its name . . . peaceful, evocative paintings of sound . . . high-pitched humming that plummeted to low tones as if the notes were echoing off the uneven seabed.

"We're here for a reason," the whales seemed to intone in the deep resonances humans couldn't hear above water. *"Watch us . . . heed our journey. We have much to share."*

Be patient with us, she wanted to say. *We're slow . . . but we're learning. We may be more alike than we are different . . . we may be on parallel roads . . . like two species who are the very best of friends.* The song ended on two gentle notes that sounded like "Amen."

Sally O'Mally opened her oven door, pulled the rack half-way out, and inhaled the fragrance of the sizzling beef roast while she basted the meat again.

Pushing the rack back inside, she surveyed the kitchen. She'd always known the quickest way to a man's heart was through his stomach. *Not for nothin' did Mama teach me the cookin' secrets every good farm woman should know. I'm nowhere near the farm now, but that ain't gonna stop me.*

Sally needed to cook. It was the thing that brought her back to center, and she was very much in need of finding that part of herself that seemed to have wandered off and shut itself in the pouting house.

"If you're gonna be stickin' that lip out that way, you best go do it in the poutin' house," Mama would say. By turns, family members would spend the needed time to sit alone and think things through. When they were ready, they'd return to the main house, usually drawn by the unmistakable smell of supper. Perhaps the aromas of her own kitchen could call back her pouting soul now.

Sitting at the center island, she began snapping green beans, enjoying the ring of the stainless steel pot as the first one hit bottom. *Why do I need to cook green beans today?* Miranda would say beans meant strength, or purpose. Sally chuckled at her friend's sense of things, where everything in life had a double meaning. *She ain't far off this time.*

Below the surface, the language of the soul simmered like a fine soup. Aspirations had been added like cut vegetables, and now her own need was heating the whole cauldron to a boiling point.

Got about an hour before Jack gets here. I got the house and food ready to go. But how in tarnation am I gonna get myself ready for what I have to say?

Sally'd decided early this morning that she'd had quite enough of the hollow, rattling silence between herself and Jack. So she'd picked up the phone to declare that dinner would be served at five p.m.

I knew it wouldn't do no good if I asked him, so I just had to tell him. Without argument, he'd mumbled gruffly in the affirmative.

Next, while some of the locals were at church and others enjoyed brunch in one of the restaurants, Sally'd scooted off to the market to do her shopping. She'd bought the roast, russet potatoes, fresh green beans with some bacon fat to season them. Next, she'd driven down to Cambria to stop by Linn's

Fruit Farm for a fresh olallieberry pie. *Jack prefers theirs to my own. But it don't make no never mind, long as I can scooch that man back into a good mood.*

While at the supermarket, she'd pushed her cart down the women's products aisle to pick up a pregnancy test. Once home, she set out the groceries she'd need, inhaled a deep breath and marched herself to the bathroom.

Five minutes later she stared at the test result. *Positive. Well, I'll be a mashed potato pie!*

When she quit staring at the stick, she stared instead at her own face in the mirror, watching the slow smile work its way up from the corners of her mouth until it reached her blue eyes.

I'm gonna have me a baby! She whispered it to her reflection like she'd share a precious secret with a very best friend.

Then, in a daze, she walked out to the living room to plunk herself on the sofa. *Diapers . . . lullabies . . . pinafore dresses or maybe soccer shorts . . . prom dress or a long-legged tuxedo . . . and pretty soon it's graduation.*

She reeled from the projected passage of time, growing dizzy from the exercise. Then she brought herself firmly back to the present. *First things first, Sally-girl.* That's what Mama would say. *And she's right. Well . . . I'm healthy. I got me a good income and a decent place to raise up a little one. Never quite pictured it coming on me so quick. But then again, I ain't gettin' no younger. This baby's gonna have a devoted mama, just like I did. But . . . what about its daddy?*

Her thoughts shifted to Jack, so lately infuriated by the news of the child he'd known nothing about. *I'm sure enough not gonna make* that *mistake! In fact I'll do just the opposite of what Samantha did. I'll tell him the very same day I found out myself. I know it'll make him happy. This is his big chance to have what he lost out on. I think we're gonna have us one special celebration this very night.*

Sally heard the loud knock at her front door. Rather than rushing to open it, she stood still for a moment, collecting herself. *Table's all set . . . salad's gettin' crisp in the fridge . . . I've got on my good dress . . . and the whole house is filled with nice cookin' smells.*

The cry of a linnet pierced the evening. When the knocking came again, the bird seemed to complain about having his song interrupted.

Now she remembered she had to light the candles, and reached into her apron pocket for the matches. She dropped the first one on the table. "Oh, fiddle," she mumbled. As she finally got the candles lit, the knocking started again.

"Well, I'm comin'! Just hold your horses for one more little minute!" Sally dimmed the lights, smoothed her skirt, then sauntered to the door. When she opened it, she put on her most welcoming expression. "Well, good evening, Jack."

"For heaven's sake, Sally, I just about gave up, you took so long. What in the world is going on—did you forget I was coming over?"

"Does it look like I forgot?"

Jack looked her over from top to bottom. A smile played across his face. "Well, are you going to invite me in, or do we conduct this little meeting of yours out here on the landing?"

"Please come in." *I do feel a might silly, acting sorta like a*

Southern belle whose servants just happen to be busy. But I'm tryin' to set the tone for our evening.

He stepped into the room. "Sally, what's happened to your lights? You didn't forget to pay the light bill, did you?"

"Why, Jack, don't you recognize a candle-lit supper when you see one?"

He paused a moment, his expression softening when he saw the table gleaming in candlelight. "It's . . . it's been quite a while. Is, uh . . . all this for me?"

"Um hmm," she said as she walked toward the kitchen counter. *Now it's time to put my cut gladiolas in water. I knew Jack wouldn't think to bring me any flowers, so I bought 'em my own self.* She made sure he noticed the crackle and squeak of the paper around the flowers as she unwrapped the red blooms.

"It seems Christmas came a little early this year."

When she glanced back to see him standing in the center of the room, he looked a little sheepish.

Good.

"I thought you were mad at me."

Typical! He's turned it all around. "Well, land sakes, and here I thought it was *you* who was mad at *me!* Anyway, you know if I was, I can't really stay that way. I just . . . well, I get a little emotional, you know?"

"Emotional" was one of their words. It'd taken the abuse of his complaints and her tears, and—like a favorite child's blanket that had been through too many spin cycles—it was now a soft and pliable rag. But it was theirs, and it was a signal. *If I'm playin' my cards right, that'll kick-start things.*

He moved in on her. "As a matter of fact, I rather like it

when you get a little emotional." He stood over her, his barrel chest inches from her chin.

She threaded her arms around his waist and looked up into his now receptive face. "First off, I wanna say I'm sorry."

"No need. It's forgotten."

"No, I mean . . . sorry she . . . you know, the one you used to be married to . . . sorry she kept it from you, such an important thing."

She felt the muscles of his back tense.

"I don't want any secrets between us. 'Kay? I promise right here and now, I'll always tell you right off whatever's important." Before he could pull away, she slipped out from under him, beginning their dance. "Sooo, I'm just going to check the roast again."

Everything's ready . . . everything 'cept me! I gotta find my moment. But I will. And he's real smart. He'll prob'ly get the picture without me even havin' to spell it out. He followed her now, obviously delighted by the prospect of their nice dinner . . . and by more than that, she hoped.

Jack Sawyer inhaled and felt his mouth begin to water. "I thought I smelled roast beef." He stood close to her. "I suppose I better be getting suspicious now. You've cooked my favorite meal."

"Suspicious? Of little old me? Oh, fiddle."

He admired her shapely backside as she bent to open the oven. When she'd lifted out the heavy roast and placed it on the counter, she sang, "You know one thing I can do is cook, and if I feel like cooking, I can just cook, can't I?"

Jack smiled at her impudent tone, then leaned toward the pan to inhale the heavenly aroma again, watching the meat and roasted onions sizzle in their juices. "Oh, you can cook all right." Again he moved closer to her. "Want any help with that?"

She smiled. "Since you mentioned helping, why don't you take that roast over to the table? Everything is ready now."

What is she up to? That was a pretty little speech but I have no intention of discussing Sam with her. Is that what this dinner is all about? Making me feel better?

He delivered the roast as requested, then observed as she efficiently carried serving pots of steaming vegetables and side dishes to the table. When he noticed her removing her apron, he held out her chair. *That's something I haven't done in a while. The occasion seems to call for a little gallantry ... though I'm not sure why.* She smiled appreciatively and took her seat. When e'd seated himself, she handed him the bottle of wine that'd been left open to breathe. "Well, now I'd like to propose a toast," she said, lifting her glass.

"I can't wait to hear this."

"Well, I know you're going to like this just as much as I do."

Regarding the feast spread before them, Jack said, "Yes, I'm sure of it."

Sally's eyes glistened as she continued. "I wanted to have a special celebration just for the two of us tonight ... on the very day I found out my own self."

"Found out?"

"This is somethin' I've wanted for a long time."

Either she's talking about my building the addition again, or she's finally agreed to my proposition ... I just can't tell which. Or maybe she's planning that trip to Monterey we'd once talked about for Christmas. Whatever it is, she thinks I know. I'll just play along till I can figure it out.

He looked at her closely, trying to conceal his speculations. What he caught in her expression were the soft, seductive qualities that first drew him to this woman. *It's been how long since we started up? Four years now . . . and at least two since I delivered my proposition.*

Over another candle-lit dinner he'd asked if she'd be his mistress—though he'd used the word girlfriend. He'd never marry again, he knew, but a regular and convenient exchange of favors would suit him perfectly. He was sure she'd understand. She was an independent business owner herself, past the usual marrying age, but still much younger than he.

She'd turned him down that night. But he continued his attentions—not too blatantly, but persistently, sure she'd relent eventually. The first time they slept together, she'd cried. That'd been flattering in a way . . . and disturbing. That's when they began using "emotional." Eventually, they admitted they had something that worked. She kept a low profile and brought unpretentious, feminine nurturing into his life. He promised to build an addition onto her restaurant.

It'd worked well for a long while. But lately she'd seemed restless. *Now, at long last, she must be about to accept our convenient relationship whole-heartedly.* All privileges, no strings—as close to commitment as he could get. With relief and anticipation, he felt his excitement growing. "Not nearly as long as I have," he said, his gruff voice a deep whisper.

She touched his glass with hers. "Well, here's to a new life!"

Their glasses clinked, and he took a long sip of the excellent Burgundy. A slight confusion at her choice of words was washed down by the pleasant prospect of the meal—and the sex—just ahead of him.

"A new life! Well, you could knock me over with a feather. I'd almost given up hope. I've wanted this little arrangement between us for years."

Now tears brimmed in her big blue eyes and spilled over their edges. "You have?" she sang. "Oh, Jack! Why didn't you ever tell me you wanted a child?"

A thrill of fear raced down Jack's spine, as though someone had thrown ice water at his back. "A child! I'm talking about— you know, what we've been talking about, about you and me having an arrangement."

A trace of confusion painted itself across her features. "But, Jack, this is the arrangement—where you're the daddy and I'm he mommy and we take care of this new life we have going between us."

"So *that's* what this was all about!"

Sally seemed baffled. "Yes!" she exclaimed.

Jack pushed his chair back from the table, the scrape of wood-on-wood jarring. He continued to sit heavily, his breath coming hard, catching in his chest. "I thought we'd settled this."

Sally O'Mally squared her shoulders. *If ever there was a time for truth-tellin', it's right now.* "Jack, you're upset about a kid who's all grown up and doesn't even know you. I know it upset you. I know it hurt, her keepin' that secret from you and you never havin' the chance to know your own offspring." She reached out, took his hand, and placed it on her belly. "Here you've got a kid on the way that you *can* know, right from the start. No secrets. No keepin' you away from what's yours. I know that's what you really want."

The only sound in the room was Jack's breathing. She

watched as his chest expanded like it hurt, and a raggedy red color climbed up past his collar, blotched his ears, and overtook his face, which was now an alarming red. Horrified and helpless, Sally watched as he began to hyper-ventilate.

He jerked his hand away from her body. When he spoke, it was at first in a hoarse whisper. "What I really want is none of your concern. Nor is it anything you understand." Jack's voice grew in volume. "What happened between me and my ex-wife is none of your business, and how you imagine that I would consider involving myself with some brat of yours. . . ."

Anger flooded through Sally. "It's yours too, Jack, not just mine!"

He stood from the table, knocking his chair over backwards as he did. "Don't bother me again. Don't trouble yourself with imagining I take an interest in you or your little problem."

Sally's mouth fell open as she listened to him rant. He threw his napkin on the floor, and marched toward the front door. "And don't imagine I'll build your damned addition on that restaurant of yours, either, even if I am one of your best customers!"

With that, he slammed open her front door and marched off into the dark of the Milford-Haven night.

Sally ran after him and, pausing in the open doorway, called out, "Jack! Jack, you're making a terrible mistake!"

She waited, still not believing he would end things this way. *He's always come around before.* Awash in her own mix of denial, anger, and concern, Sally continued to stand in her doorway. *But I ain't never seen him so upset.*

"Jack!" she called out one more time, but by then, he was long gone.

Chapter 12

Stacey Chernak glanced at her watch and her heart began to thud. She'd arrived at her job at eight a.m. and in just over an hour had completed most of her filing. But nerves began to pinch at the edges of her mouth because she knew that, in a few minutes, she'd be deserting her post to place a conference call upstairs.

She took a deep breath and glanced over at her colleagues. *No one is paying attention. But I must not lose this job!* Working at Clarke Shipping company might be much the same as working at any of the other of the companies where she'd typed and filed. *And yet here there is excitement in the air. Ships are leaving, and on them, people are getting away.*

Quietly, she opened the drawer where she kept her own Samantha Hugo case file. Slipping it in her oversized handbag, she stood as if to make a brief trip to the Ladies Room. *Again, no one is watching me.*

The first floor where she worked lacked any real view,

except of shrubs planted close to the windows. But the second floor offered a 180-degree vista of the famous Morro Bay itself. Four minutes later, she pushed open the second-story conference room door and walked toward the wide array of windows. *Such a großartige Aussicht . . . spectacular view!*

Suddenly a toxic blend of feelings swamped her, part guilt at taking a moment to enjoy the beauty, part nerves at the prospect of being found in this important room normally reserved for the company officers—despite Wilhelm's reassurances that they had permission to use it for their own calls.

Es fühlt sich an, als würde ich mich in den Konferenzraum schmuggeln. Warum sollte ich mich deswegen schlecht fühlen? I must think in English! I feel like a sneak creeping around the conference room this way, but why should I feel guilty?

The office phone began to ring, with one of several lights suddenly blinking on the instrument at the oversized table's far end. Hurrying to catch the call, she depressed the button for line one and answered, "Clarke Shipping. May I help you?"

"Yes, Liebchen, you may."

"Oh! Wilhelm . . . Bill . . . it is you." She brought her hand up to her heart as if to make it slow down.

"You were expecting someone else?" His voice rasped.

"No! No, it is just . . . it is still a bit early for our call, and I thought *I* needed to initiate the conference from—"

"That is correct, you do. I am just calling with small reminders. You will make plans to meet Mrs. Hugo—but not at Clarke Shipping, and not in Morro Bay."

"I understand."

"And, of course, if she has any serious questions, you will allow *me* to answer."

"Yes, of course."

"I will hang up now, and you will call me back at 9:29, one minute before the conference is to begin."

He terminated the call before she could reply.

Samantha Hugo looked up from the report on her desk and glanced again at her watch. *It's after nine . . . where's Susan?* She peered down at the report, but her gaze skipped to the window where she glimpsed the trunk of her sycamore.

She'd found it difficult to concentrate ever since her unpleasant visit from Jack last Friday. She'd had a rough weekend: hikes, yoga, baths, reading—nothing had made any difference. It seemed all she could do was suffer through one Jack Sawyer flashback after another: that insolent first meeting at the library when they were students at Berkeley; endless talks with her roommate Ruth, one day about getting *with* him, the next about getting *rid* of him; and then . . . getting married to him; *I may as well call them "Jack-backs."*

She knew she shouldn't have been surprised at his outburst. In a way it was a relief. Inevitably, he'd have find out one day. But when it hadn't happened in the first year . . . then the first five years . . . then decades . . . she'd convinced herself it never would.

Did I bring this on myself? Of course I did. I can even name the steps. I called Miranda, asked to meet at Sally's Restaurant. My own big mouth met up with Sally's big ears, and now . . . the proverbial cat is out of the bag.

Perhaps this was cosmic justice. She'd stirred the elemental pot by asking the Universe to grant her request. It was answering—but, of course, in its own way, and with a price. *"Sure,"* it seemed to be saying. *"You'll find your son. But you won't believe what else you'll find along the way."*

Pushing back from her desk, Sam wandered to the window for the tenth time this morning. *This does change things, at least somewhat . . . makes them more urgent. What if Jack starts to look for him? I mean, he doesn't even know exactly where and when the baby was born, but still . . . what if he finds him first?*

Of course she had no knowledge that Jack might actually look for their lost son. But that was the problem. *There's no way to predict his behavior. There's probably no way for him to predict his* own *behavior.* He'd been turned into an active volcano by her own carelessness, and now she'd just have to get ready for a series of eruptions.

This Chernak Agency seemed promising. They'd gotten off to a slow start, but now at least they seemed to be following through. It might not do any good, but she'd have to try.

She glanced at her watch again. *They're due to call at ten a.m.—just half an hour from now. What's happened to Susan?*

Susan Winslow made every effort to slink into the EPC office unnoticed, now that she was a good half-hour late. But the paper cup of hot coffee she was carrying nearly slipped out of her hand and, to save it, she let the door slam. By then it was too late to be quiet, so she swore while she put down the coffee, dropped her backpack on the floor with a thud, removed her leather jacket, and sank into her chair.

As usual, she saw light under Samantha's door, and felt glad her boss was too busy, or too disinterested, to open it. The phone rang, and Susan stared at it. She never liked to answer too promptly. It could set a bad precedent.

"Hello, Environmental Planning Commission."

"Yes, Ms. Samantha Hugo, if you please."

It's that woman with the accent again, from the Chernak Agency. I'm not in the mood to play Christmas Elf to Mrs. Klaus. "I'll see if she's in." Susan put the phone on hold, and pounded across the floor to Samantha's door. Before she could knock, the door opened.

"Glad you got here, Susan."

Whatever that means. "That Mrs. Chernak is on the phone again."

"Right. Got it."

Susan returned to her desk, sat back in her chair, and stared at a stack of paperwork she was expected to do. Her gaze moved over to the phone, and to the lighted button. She'd gotten good at lifting the receiver undetected.

" . . . if this would be convenient."

Susan could now overhear perfectly.

"But have you actually found out anything?" Samantha asked, sounding impatient.

Mrs. Chernak paused. "I can tell you it is very unlikely your son was adopted outside the United States."

"Well, that narrows it down," Samantha said.

Susan smiled to herself. *Now, now, Samantha—don't be sarcastic.*

"Yes, it is true."

Geez, Mrs. Chernak thinks Samantha meant it! She's even

stupider than I thought.

"I was being facetious, Mrs. Chernak." Samantha corrected.

"I am sorry. I do not understand."

"Never mind. Where is your office? I'll meet you."

"Oh, we do not spend money on the big office, Mrs. Hugo. We put our resources to work for our clients. Also it is better we should meet where you are comfortable."

Samantha seemed to consider this remark. Susan wondered, *Comfortable? What was that supposed to mean?*

"Also we are in Morro Bay," Mrs. Chernak continued. "No need that you should come this far. I will be happy to meet you in Milford-Haven."

"I see. Well, this time I agree. I suggest we meet at Pelican's Landing, the little park overlooking Touchstone Beach. Do you know where that is?"

"I will find it, Mrs. Hugo. I will see you at the time we agreed, yes?"

"That's fine. Goodbye."

The Chernak woman hung up. Susan waited, holding her breath, until Samantha put down the phone. *Rats! I didn't pick up the extension in time to hear when they're meeting. I don't even know what day!* She did, however, have access to Samantha's business appointments. One way or another, she'd be able to figure out when her boss and the strudel-woman were going to have their not-so-secret meeting.

Samantha Hugo hung up the phone and stared out her office window at her favorite sycamore, its branches bare of leaves but dangling with some remaining brown seedpods. Something about the Chernaks struck her as odd, and she couldn't put her finger on what it was.

She'd play along for now—take the meeting with Stacey Chernak and see where it led.

But it also occurred to her she should go to the meeting armed with a clearer sense of where the law stood on matters of information about adoptions. On such an emotional issue, even small events could be flashpoints, and each state would have legislation in place to protect all parties. But what those laws were, she didn't really know.

She could make phone calls to various state agencies, read texts in the library, or try to find something on the Internet. *No . . . that would take me weeks.*

There was, however, a lawman in town who might be able to help her. She could call him and test the waters. Deputy Delmar Johnson struck her as a man of discretion. She'd have to test her theory.

Rune Sierra's right hand arced upward and jabbed vigorously at thin air as he spoke toward his office phone.

"We did, Paul. We *did* have this discussion with the Bowl." Traces of a Mexican accent punctuated his speech more than usual as he managed his frustration. He ran his fingers through shoulder-length black hair and leaned toward the mic built into his speaker phone. "We had it last month. They promised the rewiring of the board would be completed by last week."

A strained voice issued from the tiny speaker. While Paul spoke, Rune's assistant Sojourner set a steaming mug of *café con leche* on his desk and he mouthed a "Thanks."

The offices of Sierra Promotions were quite informal: one large room shared by all the firm's members. Of the several desks, only two were in full-time use: Rune's and, at the far side of the office, that of his trusted confidante and secretary, who bore the title Executive Assistant.

From the tinny speaker, Paul spoke again. "This is a pain in the ass, Rune."

"I know it, man—but, bottom line, they didn't solve it, so . . . we have to."

"Again."

"Again. But you know what this means."

"Means I gotta pull people off other installations to get this board operational."

"Yeah. And it also means we're buying into the action. That was the deal. We fix it again, we own twenty percent."

"Sure you still want the piece of junk?"

Rune laughed. "That's not what we're buying, Paul. We're buying into the rental company. That's a nice piece."

"True."

"So you got it handled, right?"

"Yeah, I got it," Paul said with resignation.

"Hey, not only are you a good man. You're making *me* look good."

"Well, it's a dirty job, but—" he said.

"Thanks, Paul."

"You got it."

Rune hit the speaker button to terminate the call, took a loud sip from the hot liquid and flipped through his day-planner. A carefully printed grid was overwritten with scribbled reminders as well as being pasted with sticky-notes.

Sojourner Carr, sitting within earshot, smiled at her boss's charm. *The faint accent doesn't hurt . . . and I do admire how he nurtures his staff. But about one minute from now, he'll lose something on his desk and yell for me.*

"Soj?" he called out. "Where's my list of incomings?"

Make that one second. She stood from her desk and ambled to his, feeling sleek in black leggings, an oversized persimmon-colored silk blouse, and large, stainless steel earrings. "They're all right here," she said, lifting the edge of his oversized day-planner and showing him a neat array of orange message slips, "in the order in which they were received."

Rune began rummaging, destroying the neat chronological display. "Gotta see which fires to put out first," he mumbled.

"Personal, or professional?"

Rune darted a glance at her, but she kept her face blank. "Come on, come on, what d'you know?" he asked, returning to his rummaging.

Her mouth pulled into the merest smirk. "I'm not saying a word," she told him, retreating to her desk, "but you might want to look at message number six."

"Message number . . . but these aren't in order now. . . ."

She made her getaway.

Rune Sierra continued skimming through the messages. *Two calls from Zack. Those can wait. Let him sweat a little. One from Paul. Already handled.* He balled up the orange slip, aimed for the wastebasket and missed. Several from friends, all of them wanting last minute tickets, of course. He'd deal with those later. One from Sarkisian at the Bowl. *Gotta return that one fast.* Just as he began to dial, his eye fell on a message from Cynthia Radcliffe. He noticed it because his assistant had a habit of drawing innovative cartoons on some of his messages. This one looked like Veronica Lake.

"Let me guess," Rune called out.

"You always said you wanted blond Mexican kids," Sojourner intoned from her desk, without looking at him.

"Nice one, Soj." He grimaced, but she didn't notice. She had put her headphones back on, and was busily typing. Her drawing —if not her comment—served to bring the memory of Cynthia sharply to mind.

It'd been quite a while since that obvious flirtation at the bike rally. *It was fun to see how irritated Zack was that day, when his date made eyes at me. Whoa, the legs on that babe. But the last thing I want is to tangle with him again over a woman. Of course she'll be at the concert with Zack—unless he's bringing someone else. On the other hand, maybe Zack put her up to calling, trying to get something out of me . . . in which case, she can wait too.*

Miranda Jones finished her breakfast of fresh-squeezed orange juice and an omelette of tomatoes, feta cheese and dill. She'd been charmed by another instance of synchronicity: the Hacienda Hotel's restaurant had been named by the employees "Mariposas"—the Spanish word for "butterflies."

After signing her bill, she carried her backpack out to the parking lot and climbed into the Mustang. Her painting supplies were still in the car, and a couple of bottles of water. *I should have everything I need.*

She flipped to page 702 of her Thomas Guide and consulted

the map, a little startled to realize she was only a mile and a half away from Southern California's largest oil refinery. She headed south on Sepulveda, then turned right on East Grand and took it to Vista Del Mar, which bordered the local beach, amazed to be in a neighborhood of cozy houses one moment, and driving past huge industrial storage tanks the next. She'd read that the refinery covered one and a half square miles, and that "El Segundo"—meaning "the second"— referred to this being the second local oil refinery, built in 1911.

I've always been so ambivalent about the oil business. . . . On one hand, they're the source of pollution, oil spills, greed . . . on the other hand, they provide so much of what we need and want. Who am I to talk? I'm driving a combustion engine car and I'm carrying water in plastic bottles. Sure never thought of a big conglomerate like Chevron as a "neighborhood" presence. Yet here, they've apparently done something truly good by saving these coastal butterflies.

According to the research she'd done, the fragile species depended for its existence upon a single food source: coastal buckwheat, a plant that grew in the high-sand-content soil of the 3,000-acre El Segundo Dunes stretching from Santa Monica down to Palos Verdes. Historically, 750,000 butterflies had roamed this habitat each year. But gradually, development and environmental degradation destroyed so many acres that the "blues" numbers plummeted in the late 1970s. In the '80s, restoration began and scientists now estimated the terrain capable of supporting 100,000 annually.

Three preserves were making this possible: Magala Cove at Palos Verdes; Airport Dunes by LAX; and the refinery, where the endangered El Segundo Blue Butterfly now had a permanent home on the two-acre Chevron Butterfly preserve. To support the beautiful creatures, the company planted new buckwheat seedlings each year.

She pulled the Mustang into the refinery parking area, finding a slot for visitors. *Time to see for myself if this place is as remarkable as they claim.*

Miranda put down her paintbrush and journal to flex her hands. After adjusting her wide-brimmed hat, she rotated her shoulders and stood for a couple of Tai Chi moves.

All morning she'd been training first her camera, then her mental lens on close-up details, glancing from flower to leaf to page. The buckwheat plants had the look of blooming wild grasses—flowering off-white or pink other times of the year, but maturing to a chocolate color by autumn and lasting even till now, in December. *When the bright blue wings flutter over the pink flowers it must be quite a sight. I'd love to come back in March or April when the tiny blue wings start to emerge. But these more subtle colorations are beautiful too. And they match the pupae, hidden in the sand.*

As far as she knew, at the end of their larval stage all butterfly species burrowed in somewhere for protection: some rolled up in a leaf; some lined a small hollow with silk; in the case of these local insects, they dug into the sand.

She felt around in the soft granules for the smooth pupae, her eyes widening when she found one and lifted it for closer inspection. Brown enough to blend with its surroundings, the tiny inch-long spindle lay in her palm, a tightly wrapped package that—despite its inert appearance—seemed to hum with life. *So many lessons from one little creature . . . protect an idea while it's still developing . . . it's why I never show a painting until it's nearly complete; transformation requires quiet and solitude . . . every artist knows that. And then . . . there will come a time to spread your wings. Is that what I did when I left San Francisco? Slipped out of the safe little cocoon of my parents' environment? Was San Francisco my chrysalis? Yes! That's where I lived with my sister long enough to get a foothold in the gallery world. And now that I've found Milford-Haven is where my heart lives . . . I'm spreading my wings.*

She placed the pupa carefully back in its tiny sand cave and dusted her hands, then sat for a moment reviewing her artist journal. The scale of the creatures she'd been painting and studying these last two days struck her—the behemoth and minikin, the huge and miniature, the "grays" and "blues."

Location would be another contrast between the whales and the butterflies. The cetaceans migrated nearly the full length of the northern hemisphere, identifying both their northern and their southern zones as "home." Yet these tiny Lepidoptera lived their entire life-cycle in one place.

Is that what I'm looking for in Milford-Haven? I grew up traveling . . . and still love to go to new places. So I'm more of a migratory species. But I'm intrigued by some of the native-born folks in my little town whose whole universe is right there.

Though the sun was now high overhead, she still felt the coastal chill that'd penetrated to the bone while she'd been working outside all morning. As usual when at work, she'd been so focused on the close-up details she wanted to paint that she'd lost track of time. *But it must be about noon. Time to find a spot for lunch.*

She'd already packed her camera back in its bag, ever so careful to keep sand away from it. Now, after packing up her journals and paint supplies, she hefted her bags and slogged out of the dunes till she arrived at the car. *I promised to send photos and at least one sketch to the PR contact at Chevron. No need to speak to him again today. But when I do, I'll have to acknowledge they're obviously doing a good job protecting an endangered species.*

Miranda edged the Mustang past the refinery's borders and navigated to Main Street. *Wonder if there's some cute local place where I can get a bite?* When she saw the sign for the Blue Butterfly Coffee Shop, she had her answer.

Cynthia Radcliffe hadn't heard back from Rune, and time was running out. Deciding the only solution was to show up in person, she'd poured herself into a tight skirt, then slid behind the wheel of her snappy lipstick-red Miata convertible.

Streaking up highway 101 from Santa Barbara to Goleta—blond hair flying, sunglasses gleaming—Cynthia grinned, enjoying how the coupe handled. *Pure sex. The car, not the man.* She felt herself squirm, realizing she was thinking about Rune.

In the parking lot of his modest office building, she pulled into the one available slot labeled *Visitors*. After checking her make-up in the rear view mirror, she shut off the car engine, took a deep breath and stepped out.

She smoothed her butterscotch leather mini-skirt, tossed her hair to one side, grabbed her purse and strode through the glass door stenciled with the name *Sierra Promotions*.

An exotic-looking woman with caramel-colored skin, a bright orange silk shirt and huge earrings sat at a desk wearing headphones. *She must be the receptionist, but how do I get her attention?*

Just then, the woman glanced up from her work, widening her eyes as she apparently cataloged the details of the visitor. She took off her headphones, stood and walked toward Cynthia, yet kept some distance between them. *Is she afraid I'll scratch her with my claws?*

"May I help you?" The assistant was polite, even a bit formal, yet Cynthia felt somehow this was an act.

"Thank you. I need to see Mr. Sierra. Right away. I'm Cynthia Radcliffe. I called earlier." She could see Rune sitting across the room at his desk. But his back was toward them, and one hand gestured in the air while he had some animated conversation on the phone.

"I'll let him know," said the assistant. "Would you like something to drink?"

"Oh, I'd adore an espresso."

"We have bottled water. It's right over there." She pointed, turned and moved toward Rune's desk.

Bitch, Cynthia thought. *No,* she stopped herself. *Stay focused. This is about connecting. Don't alienate the secretary.* She took another deep breath and opened a mini-fridge in the corner. One shelf was well-stocked with small bottles of an inferior domestic water. She took one, snapped the twist cap, and took a dainty pull, being careful not to disturb her lipstick.

She glanced around at the décor. An attempt at holiday cheer was manifested by elegant vanilla poinsettias. But the chrome-framed chairs seemed garish. *At least the flowers don't clash with the orange fabric seats and the beige shag carpet. Not a single antique. To think this man tries to give Zackery a run for his money.*

"But that's the whole point, man."

Cynthia couldn't help but overhear as Rune's conversation grew in volume.

"Both the bands are playing for free; all the crew is kicking back ten percent to the vets. What makes you feel you're the only guys who should be paid full price?"

Rune sounded vehement. Cynthia worried her timing was off.

"Yeah. Well, go back to them and work this out!" He was almost shouting. "Call me back." Rune slammed down his phone, squeezed at his temples and turned to look at his assistant. While he did, Cynthia saw him steal a glance at her. *He must wonder what in the world I'm doing here. Now I feel nervous, dammit, and exposed in this short skirt.*

He nodded at his faithful assistant, who turned toward her and said, "Come this way."

Cynthia walked to the front of Rune's desk, offering her best smile. *He's even more handsome than I remembered . . . but he's not even standing to greet me!*

"Long time no see," he said jovially. "It's a *real* busy day. What can I do for you?" His posture said he wasn't surprised to see her, but his dark eyes said something else.

"Do you think I could sit down?" Cynthia asked.

"No problem. Soj! Bring a chair for our guest, when you have a chance."

Rude to me, polite to his secretary. Thanks so much.

When the assistant returned with the chair, Rune said, "This is Sojourner Carr, by the way. Soj, Cynthia Radcliffe."

Sojourner nodded, then left them to converse on their own. Cynthia peered down at the steel edge of the seat, afraid it might mar her leather, but then decided sitting was more important than standing in front of Rune's desk. She eased down, then crossed her legs, offering an expanse of sleek thigh. She settled back as Rune took in the view.

"Well, here you are," he said, a smile playing across his mouth.

"Here I am," said Cynthia, uncertain what he meant. She took a sip of water. An awkward pause hung over them.

"Yeah, here we both are." Rune spent another long minute observing her, while she did her best not to fidget. *He's practically licking his chops, like I'm his next four-course meal.*

"So," he continued. "Are we here for a date, or are we here on business?"

"A date?!" Heat rose up her neck and for a long moment she was too offended to think of how to answer. But his dark eyes and unflinching gaze met hers without anger . . . and apparently without judgment. In fact, his startling perception and brutal honesty had cut through her pretense. She knew, now, none of her carefully rehearsed lines would work. Suddenly deflated, she said simply, "I have a favor to ask."

Rune Sierra continued to stare into Cynthia's amber eyes. *The eyes of a cat . . . unafraid . . . yet suddenly uncomfortable at being found out.* "This favor . . . it's for you, or for Zack Calvin?"

She sat up in her chair. "This has *nothing* to do with Zackery. In fact he has no idea I'm here."

"Uh-huh. So what's the favor?"

"I . . . I find I've taken an interest in some different kinds of music lately. Surprises even me." She threw out a nervous laugh.

I don't have time for games . . . not today. "If you want tickets, just ask me. I still have a few set aside for friends, but only for the Central Coast Bowl."

"Oh, that's so nice, Rune," she oozed. "I accept! And I do appreciate it. Actually, though—there's something more."

He couldn't help but laugh. "It's only five days before that show, and you want a ticket, but something else too? What the hell. Fire away."

"I'm a singer, you see. I was wondering if you'd care to listen to a tape I happened to bring along."

"You just *happened* to bring along?" He ran both hands through his hair and blew air through inflated cheeks. "I'm going to run something by you, Cynthia. All I ask is that you be honest with me. Fair?"

She nodded.

"This is how I see it. Zack is probably being an asshole, as usual. This is his first big outing in the land of charity events and rock bands. Not his usual thing. You've been left out of his big night. Not only do you want to be at the concert, you want to be my date. Nothing else would spell revenge so clearly. How am I doing so far?"

Her jaw went slack, her eyes widened. She flung her hair to the opposite side and looked away.

"Come clean. That's it, isn't it?"

She dropped her head, then brought her gaze back up to his—barely. "That's it." She stood to leave. "I'm sorry, Rune, I—"

"You'll have to drive yourself. I'll have to be at the Bowl all day."

She paused a moment. "All right," she said.

"Get there an hour before the show, go to the Will Call window to get your ticket, and also a backstage pass."

"A backstage pass? Oh, that's perfect!"

"And as long as we're play-acting, wear something . . . interesting."

A smile began to light her face. "Not a problem."

The office phone rang and Sojourner answered quietly from her vantage point across the room. "For you, Rune," she called out to him. "Tony F."

"Great," he answered. "Tell him I'll be right there." He looked at Cynthia. "There's just one condition," he said.

"Which is?"

"That you don't ever try to con me again. ¿Comprende?"

She bit her lip. "I'll do my best."

"Okay, then. See you Saturday."

"Yes, you will," said Cynthia. Still holding the water bottle, she slung her small purse over one shoulder, and turned to go.

"Oh, and Cynthia," Rune said. "I'll listen to your tape after the concert is over. If there really *is* a tape."

Cynthia cast a sidelong glance at him, then walked back to his desk where she set down the water bottle. Sliding a hand into her purse, she brought out a cassette tape and slapped it down beside the water. "Yes, there really *is* a tape." She smiled as she made her way out the front door.

Rune sat still, aware that now his own face must show surprise. *Feel like I just had a close call with a feral cat. No, with a lynx. Those eyes . . . and I bet she knows how to purr. Got away with it this time, but. . . . ¡Por Dios! . . . beware the claws. Oh, who am I kidding? Beware the whole animal!*

Chapter 13

Zelda McIntyre, opening her office curtains to bright morning sun, looked down below her office window. She studied the *trompe l'oeil* murals she'd commissioned Miranda to create for her exterior courtyard. The painted vines blended so perfectly with the live jasmine, she couldn't tell where one began and the other ended. The real plants climbed upward from large pots and wound through trellises. Winter rains had kept the leaves green, but there were no blossoms in December and she missed their scent. *But their fragrance would be too delicate for this time of year, and the Waterford bowl of Sweet Bergamot potpourri matches my perfume so well. Must remember to order more from Marks & Spencer.*

Though the morning was chill, she rotated the handle on her office window. As it opened, from the corner bakery the aroma of the fresh brioches prepared each Tuesday morning wafted in, and she couldn't help but inhale. *Merde. Now I'll have to ignore my rumbling stomach.*

She pictured the bakery where it sat immediately adjacent
to her own center-block Spanish Colonial Revival building. She
rented out her first floor to two businesses that fit nicely as
part of an appealing parade of shops. Her tenants—one a
gallery and the other an antiques emporium, were also
businesses synergistic with her own and nicely covered her
mortgage.

She'd divided her second floor into two segments. The
offices of Art Placements & Artists Representations overlooked Victoria Street. Her private apartment faced the alley,
which bisected the block between Anacapa and Santa Barbara
streets, offering private access to parking and an inner
courtyard not visible to passing traffic.

Ascending either by elevator or staircase, she, her clients or
her guests arrived at a marble-floored foyer where an antique
table held an azalea that in spring would burst with white
blossoms. From there, one chose either the door into APAR, or
the one into Zelda's private residence—though once inside
either, another interior flow-through door could be used
between the two spaces.

She'd furnished the suite with French antiques. To both the
full kitchen in her private apartment, and to the small, efficient
kitchenette next to her office, she'd added hand-painted tiles.
She'd bought an ornate table-top lamp and sideboard fashioned
from a small, early-eighteenth-century desk of carved oak with
legs terminating in *pied de sabots*. Since she loved those clever
scrolled animal-footed legs, she'd found similar ones on a Louis
XV desk. Though large and substantial, it was distinctly
feminine with veneered and inlaid flowers that relieved the
dark wood with lighter tones. Both pieces were edged in gold

that glinted in the morning sun streaming past floral drapes gathered between the windows.

When she heard the morning mail drop through the slot in the foyer, she went to retrieve it, came back into her office, then crossed to her desk. Sorting through, she slit open three pieces that pertained to wildlife art. The first was confirmation that Miranda's work had been accepted for display at the eighteenth annual San Dimas Festival of Arts National Western Art Exhibition. The second was a notice Miranda had been accepted in the "Wilderness Realized" art exhibit next June at the Wilbur D. May Museum near Reno.

Good. Miranda needs to spend more time with her public, not sequestered away in her studio in that little town. If only she had one tenth the marketing sense of Sue Grafton with her "Alphabet" series. Brilliant. Zelda glanced over at her copy of *M is for Malice,* published last April, and ignored the fact that the examples springing to mind were writers, not painters. *And think of what that author James Redfield has accomplished!* The man had self-published *The Celestine Prophecy* in 1993, and in the last three years he'd sold 100,000 copies. Now he'd been picked up by Warner Books. *If he can do it out of the back of his Honda, surely Miranda can make a success from the back of her Mustang.*

Zelda walked over to the kitchenette where she put water on to boil, then poured a small amount of whole milk into a pan. While the water and milk heated, she ground some French roast beans. Tapping the ground coffee into her Melior, she poured in first the warmed milk, then the boiling water, topping the glass canister with its filter press. When the mixture had steeped, she depressed the plunger, then poured out the fragrant café au lait into a white and gold Limoges cup, swirled the contents and took a sip.

As she walked back to her desk she thought some more about Miranda, whose career continued to show signs of acceleration. Attending art shows versus working in her studio—this was a chronic argument with her client. Miranda had significant talent as a painter. Of that there was no doubt. Zelda wouldn't represent her otherwise. But what Miranda failed to understand was that the painting itself was at best only half what it took to have a career. The rest was the marketing. And unless Miranda could learn to be more personable and show her face at important art events, she would never enjoy the success Zelda expected of her.

She opened the third piece of mail. It began with "Dear Miranda Jones, Congratulations! It is our distinct pleasure to inform you that you are a Finalist for the Nevada Wildlife Art Award." Zelda paused for a moment. *Excellent! I knew I was right to submit Miranda for that show!*

The fact that she hadn't told the girl yet was a minor detail she could now gloss over with the good news, while deducting the entrance fees from the sale of the next piece.

Zelda glanced at her calendar. *Miranda's in the wilds of Los Angeles now, off on a painting adventures. No point in trying to track her down.* Instead, Zelda reached for her phone book. *Now I have one more "kudo" to use as leverage when I pitch my idea.*

Ever since Miranda'd mentioned her next postcard—the miniature map of the Central Coast—Zelda had known this should be built into a campaign, one that would bring attention not only to her client, but to a larger entity, one that would benefit Zelda and her own company.

Though not a fan of little beach towns like Milford-Haven, Zelda'd had to accept that her client had now chosen it as her home. *Might as well make something of it.*

Research had revealed that a Lorraine Larimer served as head of the Town Council, and had for at least a decade, after retiring from a career working for the State and then the County. Zelda saw no point in starting anywhere but at the top, so she placed the call.

"Milford-Haven Town Council," announced a salty, mature female voice.

Unless everyone on this Council is as old as the hills, I bet this is she answering her own phone. "Do I have the pleasure of speaking with Lorraine Larimer?"

"That remains to be seen, I'd say," the woman replied.

Zelda offered a small chuckle, then continued. "My name is Zelda McIntyre. I'm the CEO of Art Placements & Artists Representations in Santa Barbara and—"

"That's one fancy name." The brusque voice cut her off. "What can I do for you?"

"I'm coming to that." Zelda took a breath. "I happen to represent one of your local artists, Miranda Jones."

"A fine young woman and a fine talent."

"I agree! How very nice of you to say so."

"Not really. Just true."

"You may have heard," Zelda went on, "that Miranda painted a miniature portrait of your lovely town last autumn. I then created a postcard campaign on her behalf, which was quite successful."

"For whom?"

"Successful for Miranda, in that it sparked a boost in sales.

But also successful for your town in terms of tourism."

"Pretty hard to document that," the laconic woman countered.

"To your point, I propose to do a campaign that is both more focused and more synergistic for her next miniature. She has painted a delightful watercolor of a map, you see, with your town at its center, circled by the image of a magnifying lens. I thought we'd call it the 'Putting Milford-Haven On the Map' campaign."

White noise shot through the phone line for a moment. Then Lorraine said, "This has potential. We'd need to see it. And we'd need to know the specifics."

"I'd be happy to present the idea at your next meeting. When would that be?"

"No meeting this month, what with the holidays looming. Next meeting is mid-January."

"I'll be there. With your permission, of course."

"That'll be fine, Ms. McIntyre. Send a fax with your contact information, and a brief outline of what you want to present. We'll see how it goes."

When the woman hung up, Zelda gently replaced her own hand set. *Well. A bit unceremonious. But it's a foot in the door.*

Miranda Jones began her third full day in Los Angeles with slight trepidation at the prospect of traversing the entire city, then venturing way beyond it into the notorious Mojave Desert.

While enjoying breakfast in the Hacienda's coffee shop, she opened the thick Thomas Guide and began placing sticky-notes starting with page 702, her current location, and following the numeric edge-markers that led through the grid.

When her waitress stopped by the table to offer a hot tea refill, she asked, "Need some help with directions?"

Looking up, Miranda answered, "Oh, no, thanks. Just checking my route."

"Off to do some more painting today?"

Miranda smiled. "Thanks for asking. Yes, I'll be visiting the Exotic Feline Preserve today in Rosamond."

"Oh, way out in the desert. Pretty country. You know, you'll be passing the Vasquez rocks. They might look familiar from so many movies and TV shows." The waitress leaned in slightly, as if she might be sharing a secret. "Named for a famous outlaw who'd make his way into those rocks to hide."

"Really? Thanks! I'll see if I can spot them." *Seems like everyone who works at the Hacienda has a sense of L.A. history. And they take a real interest in their guests.*

Sipping the last of her tea, Miranda went back to her map book. From her present location near LAX, it seemed to make the most sense to travel east for a short distance on the 105, then transfer to the 405. *I'm sure local people do this all the time, but yikes! I'll have to use two freeways just to get started!*

She'd be driving for about thirty miles before the 405 seemed to blend into the 5, which she'd only use for three miles before she exited onto California highway 14 North. By then, she'd have crossed the entire San Fernando Valley and traversed a mountain range, and would be heading out toward the desert. *Well, sitting here staring at the map won't take me there. Better get rolling.*

Miranda had unwittingly joined the weekday rush hour at seven-thirty this morning, making her drive both worse and better than she'd anticipated. True, she hadn't had to deal with switching freeways while traveling over sixty miles an hour. But she'd been shocked at the overwhelming volume of cars traveling in every direction. *Is this worse than San Francisco? Probably not. But how do people deal with this every day? I think I'd lose my mind.*

The urban distance she covered was about thirty miles before she veered right on the 14 and began climbing northeast through the San Gabriels, the road opening up into a beautiful valley of folded mountains as she climbed two thousand feet past evocative monikers. *River Valley . . . Agua Dulce . . . Sand Canyon . . . Soledad Canyon . . . Shadow Pines . . . love the names! They all sound like they come from cowboy movies or Louis L'Amour books. And those rocks over there . . . they do look familiar. These foothills . . . sometimes the road cuts through as if someone has taken slices of bread from the center of a loaf.*

She'd been noticing snow on distant ridges but now, as she passed through Palmdale, she saw these larger mountains were completely white-capped. As the highway made a wide turn north, the mountains slipped behind her and a desert vista opened ahead. A sense of vastness struck her. *This could be Utah, or New Mexico . . . but it's still California. This is what the L.A. people brag about—being at the beach, the mountains, and the desert all in one day. It's true!*

She noticed signs for Lancaster, and for Edwards Air Force Base, where the Shuttle landed. *So this is where Uncle Arthur brought us for the very first landing. When was that? Oh yeah, 1981 . . . when I was eleven. We heard the first double sonic boom.*

Absorbed in the memory, she nearly missed the sign for the *Cat House*, but saw it in time to turn right onto Rosamond

Boulevard. Commercial buildings and then residences thinned until she arrived at the isolated location and pulled into the dirt parking lot. She walked into the adjacent building where the gift shop—filled with adorable stuffed cats of all descriptions— also served as the entrance. After buying a ticket she introduced herself, and a friendly employee explained they'd been expecting her and that her guide would join her shortly. Meanwhile, she was invited to begin her self-tour.

Miranda stepped outside again and walked a shaded pathway. In the first cage, a serval paced; in the second, an ocelot napped. As she rounded a corner, a glimpse of a sleek black leopard took her breath. *He'd be a fearsome creature in the wild, fully capable of taking down a water buffalo four times his size.* Here in his generous enclosure, he paced his territory just as he would in the wild, pounding down the loose dirt with his massive paws. As his haunches rippled through shafts of sunlight, she saw the distinctive but nearly-invisible spots on his coat—the same shape and size as the large rosettes more visible on his tan cousins.

A man with an embroidered emblem on his shirt appeared, talking to his feline charges as he walked the path. After he introduced himself as Phillip, he addressed the jaguar. "Hey, Doc. Ready for your snack?"

The cat opened his mouth as if to answer, a gentle growl indicating his eager anticipation. And even while Miranda noted his power, she couldn't help but respond to a quality she hesitated to name as "cute." *But he is adorable—talking to his keeper, asking for his treat, delicately licking the fingers that fed him through the bars.*

She suddenly flashed on an image of her tiny black kitten

prowling through the drawer in pursuit of Miranda's sock-clad hand. *The behavior is so much the same . . . I suppose in a way I have my own tiny jaguar at home.*

"The jaguar is the third largest of the feline species," Phillip explained, "and the largest in the Americas. He makes a roar that sounds like a cough deep in his chest. We might hear him later. The jaguar won't cohabit with any other creature. Were he to take a mate, she'd occupy a contiguous piece of property, and the two cats would designate overlapping ground as their mutual space."

Wonder how the invitation is given? "Hey, gorgeous, I'll meet you at our rancho tonight"? Miranda grinned at the thought. *Just so long as you make some beautiful cubs just like yourself.*

Phillip added, "This spectacular animal himself has siblings right here at the center—but unlike his black coat, theirs are the more traditional ivory or tan with brown markings."

"Oh, I didn't realize brothers and sisters could have the different coloring."

Phillip led her to the next enclosure, where a splendid Amur leopard began parading. "While the jaguar is built for power," he pointed out, "the leopard is built for speed." The moment he said it, she could see the difference in their structure and proportions. "The leopard has a variety of sounds—spits and hisses, snarls and rasps. But, unlike the so-called big cats, it doesn't actually growl."

She noted the leopard's glossy coat—its spots slightly different from the jaguar's, which were larger "ringed" rosettes. Though many people probably didn't notice the difference, both of these feline hides had become universally beloved designs throughout the fashion world. Indeed, some species of the leopard—the Amur in particular—had become endangered largely for the profit in selling their pelts. *Thank God, no one in America uses the real pelts anymore. And the synthetic versions could be seen as a tribute. I'll never see a purse or a blouse again without imagining these majestic creatures displaying the genuine article.*

Miranda followed Phillip to the larger snow leopard enclosure, where her heart beat faster at the sight of a regal male sitting—paws crossed in front—staring silently from his high mountain perch. Granted, the "mountain" was artificial, but it allowed him to live in surroundings resembling his native Himalayan habitat. While the male remained stately and aloof, his female partner was obviously a natural performer.

To the delighted grins of her audience, she first revealed her shiny claws, then flopped on her back to show off her tummy, then finally flashed her teeth with a smile. *All I want to do is take her home! But that would never work.* She knew this snow leopard—unable to live in the wild for whatever reason —already had the best home she could have.

Miranda spent the next three hours at work: first photographing and sketching, then interviewing and discussing the status of these endangered cats and the mission of this Exotic Feline Breeding Compound, while getting a sense of the overall Zoological Association of America's purpose and goals.

Before gathering her belongings, she walked once more through the compound, saying farewell to the cats she'd met, overhearing the conversations with their keepers. She watched as one of the employees calmly entered a cage to clean it, talking to the leopard who leapt politely out of her way. *These are amazing relationships . . . and I wonder who's teaching whom? These cats can't help but express their grace and power. If they were ever threatened, of course they'd respond. But there's no malice in them.*

On her way back through the gift shop, she stopped to buy three pins, justifying her purchase with the knowledge that proceeds would help the center. *Pewter pins for the three cats I befriended today: the jaguar, the Amur leopard, and the snow leopard. They're charming . . . and I'll think of them when I wear these.*

Miranda sat in her car and studied the map book one more time before starting her trip back to West L.A., tracing her finger from page to page and adjusting her sticky-notes. *If I take this cut-off, I can see a little of the National Forest and maybe get a glimpse of Mount Wilson. It's been an adventure so far . . . might as well try something else I've never done.*

"Bye, kitties!" she said, glancing around to make sure no one had actually heard her. She aimed the Mustang south to retrace her route on the 14, also called the Antelope Valley Freeway. But this time, at the twenty-five mile marker, she exited onto the Angeles Forest Highway, which soon began to climb steeply up into the Angeles Crest. Gentle curves gave way to hairpin turns and the relative warmth of the desert chilled as she continued through the frosted ravines.

Hope a big fire never burns through here . . . but I suppose it'll happen some day. The chaparral, yuccas and mesquite are all designed for it.

When the Angeles Forest Highway met the T-intersection of the Angeles Crest Highway, she crossed to take advantage of the rest stop, then reviewed the map again. *If I wanted to climb higher into the Forest, say to see Mt. Baden-Powell—or even go to Wrightwood, which looks like a small mountain town—I'd go left here. But I wanted a glimpse of Mt. Wilson, which would lead me down toward the city.*

Several miles later, she smiled as a gleaming white bubble appeared on the next ridge—the historic Mount Wilson where she knew Albert Einstein had visited. Nearby the ridge bristled with tall transmitter towers. *Hope I can visit sometime. Hope I can get to the Griffith Observatory sometime too.*

As she continued to wind down through the mountains, she began to notice how hungry she'd gotten. *People at my hotel mentioned the Farmer's Market as a local landmark with every kind of food imaginable. Think I'll go there for an early dinner.*

Ahead of her, she caught sight of downtown Los Angeles's skyline, a grayed-out silhouette veiled by a pale purple haze appearing as mythical as a movie set backdrop.

Miranda spent Wednesday morning at the Hacienda, first enjoying another good breakfast, then back in her room, adding comments and sketches to her painter's journal while recent events were still fresh in her mind.

When she'd finished catching up with her chronicle, she went for a walk, heading west on Mariposa, then north on Washington, where she passed two small urban parks and scores of one-story single-family houses. Though she had to admit the eclectic variety and high energy of L.A. had some appeal, by now she longed for the bright, clean air and the rugged simplicity of the Central Coast. *Still . . . this is an amazing trip. And it's not over yet.*

While returning to the hotel, she reflected on how much

she'd enjoyed establishing her own travel rhythm this week: driving to new locations, reviewing research notes, preparing questions, taking photographs, making sketches. Now she felt a strafe of nerves at the thought of seeing Zack Calvin again, mixed with a jitter of excitement at the prospect of meeting the Doobie Brothers.

At least I know what to wear. Figured that out before I left home. Back in her room, she took from the closet the heavier of her two denim jackets, the new-ish blue jeans and the dark green sweater she'd chosen, laying them all out on the bed. She fastened her new whale pin to the jacket. Then she showered and washed her hair, letting it dry while she reviewed the map book.

East on the 105 again . . . skip the 405 . . . head north on the 110 . . . pass over the 10 . . . then take the 101 North to the 5. Brother . . . six freeways and I won't even be there yet! I'll have to keep my eyes glued to the road and watch for the signs or who knows where I'll end up? Before I go, I better have a quick lunch here at the hotel.

Miranda knew she'd driven through downtown Los Angeles because the signs had told her so. But, terrified she'd miss one turn-off or another, she'd barely spared a glance for the tall skyscrapers and historic buildings as they'd whizzed by.

She'd allowed herself one distraction: switching to the Doobies cassette and listening to it all the way to Hollywood, the band's rocking rhythms enveloping her in their infectious joy.

She knew when she got near the Bowl, she'd recognize the

concrete and granite, multi-tiered, multi-figured statue-fountain that landmarked its entrance. She'd read about this elaborate art piece that'd virtually replaced the original hill-side, built between 1938 and 1940—the largest of hundreds of WPA projects in Southern California—by George Stanley, depicting the Muses of music, dance, and drama. The upper-most figure, the Music Muse herself, knelt, playing a harp; standing elsewhere on the structure stood the other Muses.

Sure enough, when Miranda exited at Highland Avenue, she followed the well-marked designators that had her looping over the freeway, and she spotted the entrance immediately. *The Muse looks serene . . . as if she knows the musicians will be listening, following her guidance.*

Following Zack's earlier instructions, Miranda pulled into the nearly empty parking lot, then on foot began to climb the hill leading to the amphitheatre. As she topped the rise that allowed side access just past the first ring—where VIPs and season-ticket holders probably sat in box seats—she walked to the center of the semicircle.

Bathed in bright California sunshine, the bare bones of the theatre stood revealed: the rainbow-shaped white band shell the focal point; quarter-circles of seats fanning outward and up the hill; the entire seating area framed by a living wall of trees. She looked behind her up the hill at row upon row of seats, believing this venue would indeed hold more than seventeen thousand, the largest natural amphitheatre.

She stood still for a moment longer, sensing vibrations of concerts past . . . as if they'd been absorbed by the stage and seats, hills and trees—and, long held, were on the verge of releasing. *This is sacred space . . . artist space . . . I can feel it. The hopes and dreams of careers . . . the magical moments of connection between performers and audiences.*

Miranda's eye was drawn to a man who wandered alone onto the deserted stage. *Tall and lanky . . . a shock of dark hair with a trimmed beard to match. He must be a sound tech because rehearsal doesn't start for a little while.*

She watched with interest as he scrutinized the four platforms that each held a full drum set. *Four drummers? That'll sure rock the house.* Now the man paid particular attention to one of the drum sets, shifting the racks and bouncing on the stool before adjusting its height. *Didn't realize anyone but the drummer himself would adjust the instruments . . . but what do I know?*

He began to play. *Curious to be hearing an acoustic instrument when it's surrounded by speakers the size of library bookshelves.* Drawn by the sound, Miranda walked down a few rows closer to hear him better. Rat-tat-tat-tat ta-tat-ta-tat-tat. Then he repeated the pattern. *I know that figure . . . it's the opening of "I'm Here to Love You." Oh! That's not a techie, that's one of the Doobies!*

She took another few steps closer. He changed songs. *What's this one? So fun to identify a song just by the percussion—no melody, no lyrics.* She almost recognized it. She noticed his lips were moving. *He must be singing . . . he's still too far away for me to hear.* Now she saw he was staring at her as he sang. She'd been seen, and felt she should leave immediately, and yet he was holding her there with his gaze and with his music. She knew the song now. "One step closer," he sang, while he hit his drums in magical cadence. She laughed out loud at the joke, and stood beaming at him while he played.

When the song finished, the musician continued to look at her for a moment, then stood from his stool to place his drumsticks carefully in preparation for the rehearsal. When he looked in her direction again she gave him a nod and turned to go in search of Zack, but he called, "Don't run away."

Miranda waited as he came toward her with an easy gait. "Hi," he said, extending his hand. "I'm Keith."

"Hi . . . hi," stammered Miranda. "I'm . . . I'm Miranda. I'm . . . I'm here with Zack."

"Cool," said Keith. His eyes shone. "Here for rehearsal?"

"Yes . . . I'm sorry. I didn't mean to disturb your practicing. I mean your preparation."

Keith laughed. "It's cool. Zack told us you'd be here. Glad I had someone to play for."

She chuckled. "Oh, I don't think you're going to lack for people to play for."

"Been to one of our shows before?"

"No, this'll be the first. But I've loved your music for a long time."

"You're not coming to the show Friday night here in L.A. You're coming to the Central Coast Bowl, right? Live up there?"

"Yes, in a little town called Milford-Haven."

"Beautiful area. What do you do there?"

"I'm a painter."

He nodded as if he understood. "That's great. My wife is an artist too. So, hey, enjoy. And we'll see you after the Saturday show."

"Great." Miranda smiled up at him. "Thank you."

"For what?"

"For the concert. The one you played for me, and the one

you're about to play."

He smiled, then left the amphitheatre, she imagined to go backstage.

"Miranda!"

She turned to see Zack waving from mid-auditorium. "Come on up . . . want to show you something!"

Zack Calvin watched her climb toward him. *She looks great . . . that long glossy hair, the tight jeans.* He kissed her on the cheek when she arrived, inhaling her fresh, spicy scent. "I see you found it okay."

"Yes! I wouldn't say I've mastered the L.A. freeways, but I'm managing to get around."

"So you met Keith Knudsen."

"Had my own private concert." She giggled. "Very nice of him."

"Nothing like an appreciative audience. So this is what I wanted to show you." He pointed to the middle row of seats where lighting technicians had established a temporary control center, electrical conduit and a maze of wires draping across seats, lighted panels glowing across a complexity of dimmers and sliders. "Thought we'd show you some of the lighting effects we're going to be using." Zack nodded to a lighting tech. "Of course, you can't see it clearly until it's dark, but this will give you some idea."

She looked toward the darker inner portion of the band shell. "Oooh!"

"Bring it up a little brighter on the Cyc, Brian," Zack asked.

"What's a Cyc?" Miranda asked.

"It's short for psychodrama," replied Brian, "which is what I'm about to be starring in, if I don't get this thing working."

Miranda stared at him, confused.

"No, actually it sounds like 'psych' but it's short for 'cyclorama,'" the technician corrected. "It's the wall all the way upstage—at the back of the stage, that is."

"It's a canvas," Miranda said, "and you paint with light."

"I like that. Hey, man, where'd you find her? This one's a keeper."

Zack chuckled and saw Miranda blush. Remembering her strong aversion to attention, he quickly made their excuses. "Look, Bri, are you okay for a few? Rune should be here any minute, but call me if there's a disaster. I'm on the two-way."

"Rune's around here somewhere, and I'll do what I can, but don't wander off too far, even if you do have a beautiful date."

Zack looked at Miranda. "Shall we?"

He led her on a short walking tour of the Bowl's vast backstage area. *Hope she's not bored. Hard to tell, she's so quiet.* "So that's about it as far as the sight-seeing goes. Rehearsal should start in a couple of minutes. Want to stay?"

With a huge smile, she answered, "I wouldn't miss it!"

Miranda Jones followed Zack, resuming her original spot mid-audience. *He seems kind of formal today, like he hardly knows me. Well, that's true, he doesn't. And I imagine he's got a lot on his mind with the rehearsals, the shows, moving from one venue to the next.*

"I apologize," he said, "for being, well, distracted. Enjoy the rehearsal, and I'll find you afterward to say goodbye before you take off."

She looked up at him as he paused for a moment, noticing a shift in his expression. *Wistful? Worried?* "It's okay, Zack. Don't be concerned about me." She thought for a moment he might lean down to kiss her, but instead he turned to go.

A moment later, her attention was grabbed by watching the band members arrive on stage and begin to pick up their instruments. She tried to identify each of them from photos she'd seen on their album covers.

She reached into her backpack to grab her artist journal and a pencil, then began sketching the stage and musicians, her hand moving fast to capture what she could of the quicksilver flow of energy.

"One . . . two . . ." she heard, and then the familiar strains of "Long Train Runnin' " began to play, Tommy Johnston taking center stage to sing his strong lead. Then the focus shifted to Michael McDonald as he sang "Minute by Minute," the syncopation and minor chords a contrast to the straight-ahead rock. Yet the focus was never really on one musician. They shared the spotlight, traded phrases. Michael's piano riffs . . . John McFee's haunting guitar solo . . . Pat Simmons's clear tenor. . . . *Love the variety. These guys really do rock.*

Just when the song was reaching a crescendo, it fizzled out —a stray note here, an isolated drum strike there. And Michael, who'd been anchoring the tune with his signature chords, began instead to play the theme song from *Leave It to Beaver.* She couldn't help but laugh out loud. After a brief exchange of words, they started the song again. This time Miranda couldn't sit still, so she stood and began to dance in her aisle, carried away by the vibrant energy of the music.

Chapter 14

Deputy Delmar Johnson rolled his shoulders, cracked his knuckles, and wondered whether he should take his dinner break now, or later.

It'd been a busy day, keeping up with several cases. For that matter, it'd been a hectic several days. He'd closed a boat theft case in Morro Bay and he had good leads on a white-collar crime ring that was using private mail boxes in SLO.

Following his visit to the Christine Christian home with Joseph Calvin last Thursday, he'd reported the matter of finding her luggage still there—the luggage she presumably would have taken with her, had she actually embarked on her planned trip overseas. That'd been enough to get the necessary search warrant for her premises, and the team had now gone over her place meticulously. *Haven't seen their report yet. I'll give it a week, then check back with them.*

Meanwhile, he'd been keeping track of two upcoming local events: the Chumash Winter Solstice gathering and the Doobies concert at the Central Coast Bowl.

Learned a lot, meeting with Kuyama Freeland, the Chumash Elder. What a remarkable woman. I won't mind talking with her again any time.

As far as the Doobies were concerned, he enjoyed their music just fine, and looked forward to catching at least a glimpse of their performance. But he was well aware that, when it came to rock concerts, you never really knew what might happen. *We don't expect any problems. The Cap doesn't want any extra personnel assigned. So it'll just be a matter of keeping an eye open in and around the Bowl. Maybe I'll actually get to see most of the show.*

Hunger suddenly gnawed at him and his stomach rumbled. *Guess that answers my question.*

Del ate dinner at the Bird's Nest. When he'd first tried the establishment some months earlier, he'd felt foolish eating in a place with powder blue walls and little wicker baskets full of antique silver-plated flatware. But he was getting used to it. They served a greaseless chili and a down home cornbread, and they kept the coffee coming.

While he ate, he thought about paper work. *It never ends. Never has, for as long as I've been on the job.* Report after report after report had to be filed. *If the public knew how many hours police officers spent consumed with paper work, they'd probably be outraged.*

Although he'd never made Detective back at the LAPD, he'd memorized the sequence of reports that had to be filed on every homicide: Robbery-Homicide Division report, major incident report, evidence report, press release and autopsy report. And for solved cases, a close-out report; for unsolved cases, a follow-up report. *Wonder how many reports I'll be filing on Chris Christian.*

At least he wouldn't be writing them longhand. Those days were long gone for him, though not for his buddies back in L.A. The LAPD had eighteen divisions, and had never had the budget to provide a computer network linking them together. Separate, incompatible, and outdated computers sat on random desks. So Del had done what several other officers had: bought his own system.

Del had liked computers from the first time he saw one. A friend at the precinct in L.A. had gotten an early PC, and Del asked to borrow it. They'd watch a game after work, and Del would stay on, typing letters and reports, saving them on huge disks. *That was when floppy disks really did flop.* He'd carried them carefully in his worn canvas bag, adding to them whenever his friend asked him over.

The technology changed so fast that by the time Del had saved enough money for his own system, it was outdated in six months. Then he'd started the upgrade game. He knew that would never end either. *I'm state-of-the-art now. That'll last three months. But my timing's good.* He figured part of the reason for his promotion might be that he'd brought a new system along with him, and he knew what to do with it.

Del, dinner still settling in his belly, let himself back into the office. He looked forward to these quiet hours when he could prowl the timeless cyber-realm of the Internet while Milford-Haven slept.

He sat for a moment in the ghostly light of his computer screen waiting for the current page to load. The modem labored as if groggy, issuing forth brief but unreassuring messages that promised graphics would soon appear. While he waited, he brewed a fresh pot of dark roast.

Since the case of the missing journalist didn't seem to leave him alone, he figured he'd see if the computer could get him better results than the telephone had.

He'd called the FBI and, at first, been reassured when a real person answered the switchboard. He'd been dismayed, though, when she almost immediately transferred him to a pre-recorded series of messages.

"Welcome to the FBI voice information system. Please listen carefully and choose from the following options."

He pressed Three.

"As a part of its public affairs programming, the FBI radio show focuses on a variety of topics including counter-terrorism, gangs. . . . "

Wrong choice. He pressed Seven instead. But the seven no longer applied to the current menu, and now he found himself deeper into the broadcast information.

The more numbers he pushed, the farther into the maze he wandered. *"If you would like information about the FBI Laboratory, press Four."*

He did.

"Laboratory examiners and technicians conducted 543,556 evidentiary examinations of 149,556 specimens, not including latent print examinations. Fingerprint specialists performed 1,760,779 latent print examinations."

The voice was all business, but had no drama. *Where's Joe*

Friday when you need him?

"Polygraphers conducted 9,671 polygraph examinations. Photography technicians processed 1,492,906 photographs."

Didn't the FBI know the difference between statistics and information? He hung up in disgust. He knew how to do homework a better way.

He rubbed his eyes and stared at the screen. The graphics had finally finished loading now, and the publicly accessible portions of the FBI were laid out before him in detail, as a series of choices and sub-choices.

"Infrastructure Protection Task Force."

That looks interesting.

"Created in 1996 by Executive Order . . . a government and private sector collaboration to protect the likes of water supply systems and gas and oil production."

Brand new . . . and a little high up the food chain for me. But where there's big game, there are likely to be big predators lurking. He made a mental note of the IPTF. *Might come in handy some day.*

He continued to browse the site. *"State Your Opinion"* appeared as he scrolled through one page. *"This space is provided for authorized criminal justice agencies and prac-titioners to provide commentary. . . ."*

He cracked his knuckles. *Now we're talkin'.*

The NCIC was planning a major upgrade, and this was his chance to put in his two cents. In his opinion, the National Crime Information Center was one of the most important government services offered. As with every good service, there was also plenty of room for improvement.

He began his comments by admiring the Illinois VITAL

program. The state's new image-based Violent Crime Tracking and Linking system would eventually provide officers in their vehicles with images of identified gang members. He described how helpful such technology would've been during his tenure in South Central. He went on in some detail about the importance of federal standards, and the necessity of increasing officer safety. When he finished his epistle, he hit "save," and then "send." *That's a satisfying sensation.*

It had been only hours since he himself had used the NCIC's national computer database to enter all the information he had about Chris Christian. Two months earlier, he'd gone through all the routine procedures for missing persons, checking hospital admissions, jail bookings and accident reports. He stared again at the computer screen. The NCIC accepted reports from any originating agency. *If I get lucky, I'll get some sort of response.*

What frustrated him about the case was that so little was known. There was no body, no evidence of homicide. But even more basically, there was no evidence of forced entry, no damaged property, no blood, apparently no altercation, not even a nosy neighbor who'd seen anything amiss. There was no ransom note. There was simply a missing person. *And now, there are the suitcases which should be missing, but aren't.*

He reflected on what he'd found at her condo. *Wish I could send her answering machine tape to the FBI laboratory for analysis.*

Unfortunately, it wasn't that simple. For one thing, voice-print technology didn't work the same way as fingerprints, contrary to popular opinion. *You can't send in a voice, the way you send in a print, and run it through the system to see if there's a match nationwide.*

Voice printing was more like a bad photocopy of an original painting—it was hard to tell, under the best of conditions, whether or not it matched the original. And if there was no original to compare it to, you had nothing at all.

Despite what we've found so far, I'm treading on shaky ground. The woman was missing, but with nothing to indicate foul play, that could simply mean she was on a long-overdue vacation, and had been so burned out she told no one she was leaving town.

And yet his gut told him that Chris Christian was on no vacation. *I always listen to my gut. It's saved my life more than once. Maybe it can still save hers.*

He'd thought of one concrete avenue he could pursue: the stories Christian had been working on at the time of her disappearance. *I'll need to talk to her editor, for one thing. For another, go through her notes. And maybe she has tapes I can review too.*

Del dragged his mouse to the sign-off button on his computer screen, and glanced at the clock. Small red digits read "2:41," and a tiny light was illuminated next to the letters "a.m." As he headed toward the parking lot, he looked up to see a sprinkling of stars over the sleepy coastal town.

Cornelius Smith had spent his Tuesday using the bike provided by the Inn for a ride.

He'd ridden north to Point Cabrillo, first hugging the shoulder of Highway 1 until he crossed the Big River bridge, then veering left onto the old highway for five miles until he took a sharp left on Lighthouse Road. He followed the dirt trail through open meadows until a blue horizon popped breathtakingly into view, punctuated by a Victorian house whose peaked roof was topped by a light tower. *Must be the shortest lighthouse I've ever seen . . . and maybe one of the most charming.*

During a visit inside the gift shop, he learned the Friends of the Lighthouse had recently received a grant with which they planned a complete restoration of the historic building. *Love to come back when they've made some headway. This is a piece of history that really should be preserved.*

A couple of hours later, his bike ride took him through the carefully tended streets of Mendocino, the Victorian buildings decorated now in an "Old-Time Christmas" theme. *My folks would love this. Maybe I should bring them up next time.* He locked his bike outside Mendo Burgers, where he enjoyed a fish sandwich on their outside deck.

After lunch, he rode the perimeter of the Mendocino Headlands State Park, glancing from the peninsula out to sea in three directions and grinning at glimpses of gray whales on their migration south for the winter.

On Wednesday, he'd embarked on a day-long canoeing excursion up the Big River Estuary, returning to the Stanford Inn tired but exhilarated.

Today he'd planned to work in his room for the morning, then—in the afternoon—go looking for that historic observation site he'd read about.

In concert with his future plans to someday build an observatory in Milford-Haven, he was always on the lookout for coastal locations that had served well in the past. So, during the course of his usual spare-time research, he'd come across a place called Observatory Hill.

The map he'd found indicated the site was only ten miles from here—in suburban locations a very short drive, but here he'd be using a country road that would give way to what might be an even *smaller* country road, heading up into the trees. *Need to drive there in daylight so I can be sure to find it . . . but then I'd like to stay well past dark to check the night sky from there.*

Already packed in his Durango was everything he'd need, including a tent, if he decided to actually stay through the night. He'd filled his thermos with hot coffee ordered from the kitchen, where he'd also bought a roasted-pepper sandwich, now carefully wrapped and placed in a paper bag. *In case I decide to stay up there and get hungry later.* He had his battery-powered Coleman camping light, writing materials, maps and, of course, his portable telescope.

Now he walked to his truck, climbed in and started the motor. As he trundled down the hill toward Highway 1, he mentally reviewed his route. *Cross the bridge, third right onto Little Lake Road, stay on it four miles, then left on Thompson Gulch Trail. After that I'll either find something . . . or I won't.*

He loved these excursions, which seemed to happen far too infrequently, given his work load at NASA Ames. Whenever he managed to find possible observation spots that had potential, he had a pet name for locations like this: sight-sites. *It's weird most of my pet words are hyphenated . . . maybe because I'm originally from a hyphenated town.*

The Durango made its way along Little Lake, which paralleled Big River just to the north. He found a scattering of buildings, but once he passed the big bend at the start of

Thompson Gulch, he found none.

A few minutes later, he reached the designated coordinates and, sure enough, found only the remnants of a small clearing in the trees where the historic observatory had once stood.

He parked the truck facing east, then opened the rear hatch, giving him a west-facing place to sit. *It'll be twilight soon . . . good time to look at that photo again before I lose the light.*

From his backpack he pulled out the thin file—thin because he'd found such scant data. The most interesting thing among the papers was a sepia-toned photo labeled *Observatory Hill.*

The photo showed two wooden buildings: one, some sort of house; the other, the observatory building itself. With horizontal wood slats below the roofline, above them rose a white dome—almost invisible against a pale sky—with a tall, narrow window open to allow a telescope lens access to the heavens.

When this photo was taken, it must've been during the time the local redwoods had been logged off these hills. The trees I'm seeing here now have to be second growth.

In the old photo, in a courtyard between the buildings, nine men busied themselves: two sat on folding chairs scribbling notes; another knelt on the ground adjusting a case of some kind; one read a book; the rest stood looking down at the sextants they held. *Wish I could talk with them . . . share some data, let them look through my own telescope.*

Cornelius shivered. *Evening chill? Or a visit from a departed colleague?* Which it might've been, he'd never know. But he put away the file and poured himself a cup of coffee.

"You were onto something," he said aloud. "This *is* a good sight-site." Laymen, when they imagined suitable locations for observatories, sometimes focused on altitude or ambient light. While these were appropriate considerations, Cornelius always came to his observing mantra: *the seeing is a measure of the air.* To be more precise, it was a measure of the air's lack of turbulence.

And this is where the Pacific could be one of the astronomer's best allies. The ocean would "uniform" the air temperature, calming it. So at a site like this, his bygone colleagues would've had a west-facing view of the sky in which the stars, rather than sparkling, would appear steady—perfect for good observing.

As the sun sank, he looked again for the green flash. *Yes! Just caught it.* Zipping his jacket, he watched the evening star show begin. *Might as well give myself a rehearsal for tomorrow's star party.*

Reaching behind him, he pulled out the telescope, unfastening its case and beginning to set it up. A hush came over the trees as birds began to settle for the night. At the horizon, he could just see a distant glimmer of the ocean. *Such a gorgeous spot. It'd be great to share this with someone.* But, content with the moment, he tuned in to the joy of his solitary pursuit.

Chapter 15

Stacey Chernak glanced at the office clock. *It is almost time to leave for the day.*

"Good night, Stacey. Take care of that wrist." Gladys stood over her desk, staring meaningfully at the injury. Then, more quietly, she added, "You don't have to take that, you know."

Flustered, Stacey asked, "Take...the medicine, you mean?"

"You know what I mean, Stacey. Like I said before, you need anything, you call me." Gladys placed a business card on Stacey's desk, her sleek black fingers accented by elaborately painted nails.

Stacey looked up at her colleague one more time, smiled weakly, and nodded. Gladys left, her skirt swinging as she waved to another employee.

Stacey dropped the card into her handbag, then stacked papers neatly and filed the report she'd just finished typing. Her desk in order, she stood, pulled on her coat, and began the dreaded journey home.

Stacey opened the door to a quiet, dark apartment. Even the string of Christmas lights she'd hung were unplugged. Not calling out his name this time, Stacey tiptoed carefully to the back room—where Wilhelm usually secreted himself—relieved to discover he wasn't there. Quickly, she checked the rest of the rooms. *Oh, I had forgotten! He did say he would be home late this evening, and wanted to have dinner about an hour later than usual.* She heaved a sigh of relief, hung her coat on the rack next to the front door and plugged in the tiny lights to brighten the evening.

Next she went into the small kitchen to make preliminary preparations for dinner. She opened the refrigerator, lifted the lid on the stuffed cabbage she'd made that morning, checking its color and fragrance, then leaving the crockery container on the counter so that it would come to room temperature. *This will be a lovely meal.*

Briefly and efficiently, she set the small kitchen table for two, making certain the napkins were still unstained. Her chores completed, she went into the living room, sat at her small pull-down desk, and stared at her stack of bills. She removed the rubber band from around them, and examined each invoice again. She'd already carefully slit open each envelope and circled the amounts due. *I will check the balance in my checkbook. Now that I have received another paycheck, perhaps I can pay another few bills.*

Her handbag hung over the back of her chair, and she reached into it for her wallet. As she opened it, a card fell out onto the floor. "Safe Haven," it said. *What extraordinary words.*

Gladys had meant well, giving it to her. She stared at the words some more. *What would happen if I called their number?*

But I cannot. Such a number, and such a place, was for other women, women who were in serious trouble, women who had children, women who had no choices left. She was in control. She earned her own money. She had her own acquaintances.

And yet, it was tempting. Perhaps just a simple inquiry, calling as if on behalf of a friend. She could find out what they offered, be prepared in case someone she knew needed such a place. What did they do there? Did one receive lectures? Was one told what to do, blamed for not having done it sooner?

Stacey looked down at the card and saw her hand tremble. *Perhaps just the briefest call. Yes, purely for information.* She stared at her hand as it dialed the number on the card. After one ring, the phone was answered. "Safe Haven," said a woman's voice. "Is this an emergency?"

"Oh, no," said Stacey to the stranger. "I was simply calling for information."

"I'll connect you," said the voice.

"This is Gladys Wilson. How may I help you?"

Stacey sat in stunned silence.

"Hello? May I help you? Are you in difficulty?" The warm and compassionate voice made it impossible to hang up.

"Uh . . . no, Gladys, I am fine."

"Stacey? You called! I'm so glad. Are you all right?"

"Me? Oh, yes, of course—I am just fine, Gladys. I . . . well, I was thinking perhaps it would be good to know . . . to know what you do at this place, in case I ever know someone who needs . . . who needs to know."

"Oh, yes, of course. I can tell you all about it. I can describe our services over the phone. But it might be more interesting if I could just show you in person. It would only take a few minutes. Then we could have a cup of Christmas tea."

The warmth in her friend's tone was inviting, reassuring. It seemed a small thing, a normal thing, to meet a friend for holiday tea. She would be able to explain that to Wilhelm. Surely one cup of tea with a friend wouldn't be punished. "Uh . . . that would be very nice, Gladys."

"Good! I'm here till nine this evening."

"Oh, no, I could not be late. I would have to come. . . ."

"Come right away! Now would be a perfect time. You have the address on the card."

"Yes, I know that street. I believe I could be there in ten minutes."

"I'll be waiting for you."

Stacey hung up the phone and sat at her desk for another moment, looking at the card. *How strange. I really made the call . . . and discovered that my own colleague works at the place.* That made things so much easier. She could go there, see what it was, and yet really just be meeting a friend for tea. *Sometimes things work out very well.*

Dropping the card back in her handbag, she saw the small pieces of scratch paper stacked neatly on the desk. She lifted one, and wrote a note to Wilhelm. *"Must meet a friend from work,"* she wrote. *"Dinner will be ready at 7:30." No . . . even though it is close, that will not be enough time.* She slid the piece of paper off the desk into the wastebasket. Using a fresh sheet, she re-wrote the note to say *"Dinner will be ready at 8:00."*

She stood, lifted her handbag from the chair, and glanced at her watch. It was now five-thirty. Her meeting would still have to be brief. She headed to the front door and placed the note and her handbag on the tiny hall table. As she lifted her coat from its rack, her arm caught in the sleeve. Unable to free it, she looked over her shoulder to see what was wrong.

Stacey froze where she stood. Wilhelm was holding the sleeve of her coat, a bitter smile locked onto his face.

"Going out, Liebchen?" He lifted her captured arm suddenly, pressing it so far out of position she was sure it would break. With his free hand he snatched her note from the table. "Must meet a friend. Dinner will be ready at 8:00," he read. "Oh, how thoughtful. We will give dinner to the husband, but we will make him wait an extra half hour for it."

Stacey's heart pounded. Though her mind raced, she tried to slow it down by thinking in English. *How did he know my first note had said an earlier time? He had been in the apartment all this time! Where had he hidden? What did he hear?* Her mouth was almost too dry to speak. "No, Wilhelm . . . Bill . . . it is not to make you wait . . . it is . . . my friend . . . she asked me. . . ."

"You do not have friends, Liebchen. Remember? That is something you are not able to do. No one would want to be the friend of someone so incapable. Do you agree?" He twisted upward on the arm.

Stacey cried out. "Yes," she said in a trembling voice.

"What else does the little note say? 'Must meet a friend.' Aha. 'Must meet.' But *I* did not tell you to do this, so how could it be that you 'must'?" Wilhelm yanked down on the sleeve, ripping it from the coat and releasing her arm. She cried out again as her arm dropped.

"I am sorry, Wil . . . Bill. If this is not a convenient time for me to meet my friend, I do not have to go. I will prepare your dinner." She took one step away. He grabbed a handful of her hair and yanked her back. She stood patiently, her neck arched backward, her throat exposed.

"Convenient?" He stood breathing on her. "No!" he bellowed. "It is not convenient!" Chernak released her hair, and her neck collapsed forward. Holding it, Stacey dared another step away from her husband. He seemed to be letting her go. She entered the kitchen.

Her glance fell on the knives stuck into the side of the cutting block. She could reach one. She could pull it out. But then what would she do? Would he knock it from her hand? Use it on her? He seemed pacified for the moment. *Best to light the oven, heat up the dinner.* Her hands shaking, she lit a match and pulled down the squeaky oven door. Her hand still trembling, she held the match over the pilot. With a hollow inhalation, the old oven lit. As she began standing, he came at her from behind.

He rushed her, trying to ram her head into the edge of the stove. She fell, clawed away, and managed to stand. She glanced back just in time to see the fist coming at her face and turned to deflect the blow. It caught her on the upper left cheek, nearly knocking her down again. She scrambled to get behind a kitchen chair.

Chernak flung the chair out of her reach, grabbed the fabric of her blouse, and reached his fingers around the front of her two bra straps. Hoisting her upwards, he propelled her against the kitchen wall. "Safe Haven, is it?" he bellowed. "What a nice little card I found in your handbag! You are not feeling that you are safe, Liebchen?" He released his right hand, then slapped her bruised cheek, so hard her ear began ringing.

"N . . . n . . . no . . . Wilhelm!" she tried to speak through swollen lips. "It was my friend. . . ."

"You do not have friends!" he yelled. He encircled her throat in one strong hand. He spoke quietly, his mouth inches from her face. "You have only me, Liebchen." He spoke as softly as a caress. "Am I not right?"

Her head made a small motion up and down.

"That is right. That is so much better, Liebchen. I like to see you this way—so quiet, so obedient."

Stacey stood pinned to the wall, her eyes downcast. *This could all be over in an instant,* she thought. *Slight pressure on the trachea and I would stop breathing. Perhaps it would be better that way. Certainly, it would be easier.* And yet she remained in the submissive posture, her instinct to survive still winning.

Suddenly he released her and backed away. He rubbed his hands together and regarded her with contempt. "Now, fix this dinner," he said and strode from the room.

Stacey raised a shaking hand to her face. Already she could feel the flesh swelling. *It will be bad this time. I will have a difficult time disguising it for work.* Unsteady on her feet, she stumbled to the refrigerator and reached into the freezer for a small piece of ice to hold to her battered face. She had to make sure the swelling wasn't too bad to keep her away from her job. *I can stand almost anything but that . . . anything but being unable to leave this apartment.*

Stacey retired as soon as she finished washing the dishes. Wilhelm voiced no objection. He'd said nothing during dinner and she'd avoided eye contact, glancing only furtively in his direction to make sure he was no longer angry.

Now she lay in their bed, water leaking from the ice she'd wrapped in a washcloth. She held the cloth against her left cheek and practiced the deep-breathing exercises she'd once known.

The door to the adjacent room was open and she did not dare close it. A shaft of light from Wilhelm's office fell across their bed. She would have preferred perfect, healing darkness, but it was not an option. She placed the cold cloth across her eyes and winced as it touched her bruised flesh.

Hearing Wilhelm open a file drawer, she wondered again what he could be so consumed with day and night. His "project," as he called it—the project he would never discuss with her.

She heard him muttering. *Perhaps he is talking on the phone? But ... this does not sound the way a phone conversation sounds, with pauses while he is listening. So he must be talking to himself.* She felt too tired to care what he might be saying, and yet in spite of her fatigue, her curiosity was still awake. She tuned in as best she could.

"Oh hear, oh hear," she thought she heard. He repeated the phrase again and again, but that wasn't quite it. He was saying "So near, so near." Again and again, he was saying it. He was ranting, she realized.

"So close, so close!" Wilhelm said this phrase louder, and she heard his fist pound his desk.

As Stacey lay alone in the dark, she admitted that the man in the next room was quite mad. He had, in fact, become a raving lunatic. Not only was she was married to him; he had taken control of her very life.

She hadn't gotten to Safe Haven tonight.

She did not know when. She did not know how. But somehow, someday, she was going to get there. In her exhaustion, she drifted at last into an uneasy sleep.

Chapter 16

Miranda Jones awoke in her darkened room at the Hacienda Hotel. She turned her head to see the luminous green digits of the clock read 5:12 a.m.

Perfect. Now I can get an early start on my drive home. In the few days she'd spent in the L.A. basin she'd learned that traffic was always a factor. If she were on the road by six a.m., she'd sail beyond the city limits; if she waited till an hour later, she'd sit bumper-to-bumper on the freeways for a good two hours before she could actually spring the traffic trap.

Having mostly packed the night before, she took a quick shower, placed the last of her toiletries in her bag and zipped it shut. With bags on both shoulders and in both hands, she made her way down to the parking lot where she settled everything in the Mustang.

Now she walked back inside to the coffee shop, where she inhaled the enticing aromas of fresh pastries. She ordered a bran muffin and a cup of hot tea to-go. Walking one final time through the colonnaded lobby, her gaze was drawn to the wide, blank wall panels. *I still think this is a perfect place for murals. Hope they hire an artist to create some one day.*

Miranda clicked on her headlights and pulled out onto the now familiar Sepulveda Boulevard to find an onramp for L.A.'s major north-south artery, the 405. *Sunrise has been happening at about 6:45, so . . . another half hour of dark. Even this early, there's plenty of traffic . . . at least it's flowing.*

Her car joined the thousands of others streaming in orderly lines up the four-lane, a darkened box linked to the others by eerie streaks of headlights. They all seemed connected to the electrical-emotional energy that pulsed through this huge city. *Funny, I've been feeling like a total stranger all week, but now that I'm leaving I almost feel like an Angelina.* She laughed at the term she'd overheard for the first time at the Blue Butterfly Café. *Kinda like it, though it'd be more accurate now to call myself a Milford-Haven-ite.*

In an hour and a half, she left L.A. County and crossed into the beach town of Ventura, passing under a Lego-like railroad bridge and getting a glimpse of a tall hotel that seemed to rest right on the wide sandy beach, its highest windows catching early rays of light.

A patch of vivid green revealed a grove of perfectly tended agricultural plantings, these most likely orange trees. She'd skipped Oxnard, so had missed the vast fields of strawberries and other fruit. There, the terrain was flat enough for a profitable agri-business that fed much of Los Angeles.

Overhead, the first shiny green sign mentioning San Francisco appeared, reflectors highlighting the words like white marbles stuck to a piece of construction paper. And to her left, she caught glimpses of the Channel Islands looming like a mirage at the horizon.

Just past the town, the 101 blended with Highway 1 for a stretch. The two roads squeezed together where the mountains and the sea approached each other again, with escarpments and bluffs, rolling hills and canyons—lit now by a brightening sun piercing the clouds.

Her painter's eye continued cataloging visual details whenever she could dart glances away from the road. *Those moisture clouds hanging heavily in the sky—two tones of gray, charcoal on the bottom, pearl on top.* Ragged, scrubby mountains tumbled to the sea, interrupted by the swath the highway cut across their descent to the water. When she could catch a closer glimpse, she noticed the hillsides were fuzzy with new growth, the winter browns being overtaken by rich greens.

No irrigation on these wild mountains, so they're a true measure of rainfall . . . now, in December, it jumps from one inch a month to about four.

To her left, a row of two-story wood-frame dwellings paralleled the coastline, and a line of bearded palms standing like *Bürgermeister* assessing the passing cars and reporting on the tides. At the Seacliff Exit, an artificial island stood offshore, connected to the mainland by a series of submerged pillars. To her right were storage tanks and oil pumps, a small but obviously industrious oil operation. *A lot smaller than the Chevron installment in El Segundo, but all part of the larger California oil production picture.*

As she approached Santa Barbara, a bank of clouds nestled against the coastline and hovered over the ocean like a puffy quilt floating on a waterbed. *Wonder what kind of bed Zack sleeps on? He's not home now anyway . . . still busy with the band in L.A. I suppose I could stop to have a cup of coffee with Zelda . . . but I'm eager to get home. Lots to do before the Doobies concert tomorrow night.*

She pressed on, winding up the San Marcos Pass, memorizing the colors: celadon grasses in the foreground; malachite broccoli-shaped oaks dotting the meadows; slate-blue hills arcing away; and in the far distance, granite-gray mountains pushing up into drifting clouds.

It was mid-morning when the Mustang drew near the Milford-Haven turn off Highway 1. Before she headed up the hill toward home, she paused at the Village Lane stop light. *Right back where I started from . . . as that old song says . . . but with a whole new perspective.*

She glanced overhead at a jet contrail streaking through a clearing sky. Then she noticed a second line of powdery white, crossing the first. She grinned. *Like a giant map showing me where home is . . . "X" marks the spot.*

Cornelius Smith had discussed various locations for tonight's Star Party with Joan and Jeff Stanford, and together they'd chosen the front lawn for the gathering, as it offered a view cut through the widest gap between the stands of coastal trees. As the event began, guests would be gazing low in the sky, so ideally a bit more altitude would've been desirable. But he was confident he'd be able to show a splendid variety of celestial treats to the hardy souls who'd venture into the evening chill.

For use during the event, he'd brought along his portable twenty-inch telescope and now had it set up and trained on the first of several heavenly bodies. Guests would line up by turns as he described each object on tonight's program.

As he'd outlined the event, he'd thought carefully about what would be above the horizon, when it would appear, and how clear the available magnification would make it. He'd decided the ideal time to begin would be just at twilight.

Thing was, most people didn't realize that, from an astronomer's perspective, there were actually three kinds of twilight. The first was known as "civil," the time of day he'd witnessed himself when he'd arrived in time to see the green flash. This period—which today would begin at 4:47— extended from when the sun ducked down, until stars just became visible.

About an hour later, "nautical" twilight began, so named because both the horizon *and* the stars would then be visible— vital for the use of navigational tools aboard ships.

Another half an hour past that, "astronomical" twilight began, by which time no horizon would be visible, yet the barest glow would still hang in the sky. This was when he'd begin tonight's party, because the final glow of day would provide a theatrical backdrop, and the darkening sky would allow a kind of visual crescendo as stars began to pop more clearly into view.

We'll be about half-way along in the party by eight p.m., at which point the moon will still be 62 degrees above the horizon. But it'll be 169 degrees azimuth—or almost straight south, as I'll describe it—so from here, not sure how late we'll actually be able to see it. Today's the twentieth . . . tomorrow's winter solstice . . . then it'll be Christmas!

Cornelius glanced at his watch and zipped up his jacket

against the chill. *Four-thirty. I'm all set, and folks will be arriving soon. Before they do, think I'll test the magnification of my lens from this location. What'd be a good challenge to pick out of the twilight sky? How about Uranus? Well, better still, how about Miranda?*

He adjusted the angle of his telescope, training it on one of the moons of Uranus and doing mental calculations as he did. *My limit with this instrument is 14.8 magnitude . . . Miranda's magnitude is at 15.8. At 17 degrees above the horizon, she'll be tough to spot. I'll have to use averted vision.*

Practicing astronomers knew looking directly at an object often wasn't the best way to perceive it, particularly when the celestial body in question was obscured. So they cultivated their peripheral sight, and learned to trust it.

There she is! Gotcha, even if I did have to use averted vision to see you. Pleased with himself, he straightened just in time to greet the first of his guests. They arrived bundled in warm clothes and carrying various blankets and extra sweaters, then began to sit in the plastic folding chairs the staff had placed on the lawn. The group was larger than he'd imagined it would be: four couples; a family of five with kids ranging from about ten to seventeen—each of them wearing a Christmas sweater; and two middle-aged sisters. He was pleased to see the Stanfords sit in the last row, flattered they'd take the time to attend.

After he welcomed them all, he said, "I'd like to get started right away since it's the sky, not me, setting our agenda. Can everyone see the moon?"

They all nodded except the teenager, who rolled his eyes as if the lecturer had lost his marbles.

"At this point the moon is about four days from being full.

Or to put it in scientific terms, a waxing gibbous moon 150 degrees away from the sun."

The teen blinked while everyone else's eyes widened.

"Observing a crescent moon is great for two reasons. One is that along the terminator—which is the line between light and dark—you can see the shadows of the mountains; the other is you can see bright spots within the dark area. These are mountain peaks where the rising sun is beginning to illuminate them. Okay, who wants to look through the telescope first?"

He couldn't help but be delighted when the slouching teen stood, shrugged his shoulders and stepped up.

"Great. Just lean over and look through, without touching the instrument. Those bright spots you see are the peaks of the mountains where the sun is hitting them."

"Cool," the young man murmured.

"I wanna see!" yelped his younger brother.

"Everyone will get a turn," his mother reassured quietly.

Several minutes passed as the attendees took turns at the telescope, most of them coming away with pleased expressions barely visible in the day's final glow.

Now Cornelius aimed the lens at 36 degrees above the horizon, shooting over the trees to find Albireo, a double star in the constellation of Cygnus the swan. "Next we'll take a look at our first star of the evening—a particularly beautiful one. The light reaching us from stars isn't actually white. But our eyes correct for the color usually, which makes all stars *appear* white. However, this one is what's called a visual binary, a blue and gold double star, which your eye can't correct."

"I bet mine can!" the younger brother piped up.

"Jeesh!" the teen muttered.

"Well," Cornelius continued, "it's kinda cool if it can't, because it lets you see the gorgeous colors. The tail of the constellation is Deneb, by the way, the brightest star in Cygnus."

"How far away is it?" one of the men asked.

"About three hundred eighty light-years away. So to calculate … we'd subtract three hundred eighty years from this year, 1996. So what we're seeing is how this star looked in 1616."

"Incredible," one of the women commented.

While the group again took turns looking through the telescope, a rhythmic clanking drifted across the grass and he saw several of the group members turn their heads. The new guest arrived aglow from the flashlight she carried—which did nothing to improve everyone else's night vision, but quite a lot to show her own features.

He estimated her to be somewhere in her twenties, attractive enough in a bohemian way—wild blond hair spiraling off like a nebula; long, colorful skirt; bright green sweater and too many bracelets to count. *Those are what must've been clanking.*

She walked right up, nearly overwhelming him with some sort of incense-perfume, and stuck out her hand, which he shook reflexively.

"Hi," she said in a breathy voice. "Sorry I'm late." She sat in the chair closest to him, not moving when its original inhabitant returned from the telescope.

"Think you could turn off your flashlight?" Cornelius asked.

"Oh! Anything for you!"

He winced at her suggestive tone, then pressed on with the program. "Saturn will be our next object, and—"

"Oooh, I *love* Saturn!" the bracelet woman cried.

"Yes. Good, I mean. It is a great thing to see. It's 49 degrees above the horizon now. When you take your turn, look at the rings." *Saturn's rings are almost always the star of the show. Who knows, seeing them tonight might turn another kid or two into a future astronomer.* "Then also see if you can spot Titan and the other moons."

Bracelet-woman bounded out of her chair to stand in line first, brushing his hand when she passed. Happily, one of the couples came to chat with him, which restored his equilibrium. When they returned to their seats, he glanced over at the family and noticed the kids were beginning to sag in their chairs, the youngest already cradled in her mother's lap.

"Anyone up for a snack?"

The ten-year-old piped up with a "Yeah!"

"Good, because you see those lights heading our way?"

"The bouncy lights?" the little girl asked.

"Yup. Those are nice people from the Inn bringing us goodies. I'd like to invite the Stanfords to introduce themselves, in case you haven't met them yet."

Joan came forward, welcomed the guests to the Inn's inaugural Star Party, and described the culinary offerings. "We serve a vegan menu, so tonight we're offering star anise cookies—they're star-shaped and flavored with star anise. And we're serving them with hot coconut cocoa."

As Joan resumed her seat, a waiter and waitress brought trays of the hot drinks and confections through the aisles, everyone apparently glad for the pick-me-up, since by now the time was well past nine p.m.

"Look!" cried the little girl. "The star cookies are so cute!"

After finishing their treats, the family made their excuses and gathered their blankets to head for their rooms. But before leaving, the teen slunk over to Cornelius. "That was way cool, man."

"You're welcome. Glad you could join us." To the group he said, "Still with me?"

"Oh, absolutely!" bracelet-woman exclaimed.

I suppose I shouldn't be surprised she was the one who answered loudest. Everyone else does still seem to be game. "Okay. So up next is Andromeda, a nice spiral galaxy at 78 degrees above the horizon, and about two million light years away. This is the closest spiral galaxy to the Milky Way, which, incidentally, is also a spiral galaxy and is about the same size."

"So, since the universe is expanding," Jeff Stanford began, "Andromeda is moving away from us, right?"

"Actually, unlike the rest of the expanding universe, it's heading *our* way. So in about three billion years, these two galaxies will collide. I'll be selling tickets after the Star Party."

Laughter rippled through the group.

"What about comets?" another man inquired.

"Well, comets don't enter our atmosphere. Some meteors do come from comets but they're evidence of the Earth passing through material from a former comet tail. Comets weigh billions of tons but meteors, or shooting stars, are actually only about the size of grains of sand.

"Seeing a comet, though, can be quite spectacular. Earlier this year, we had the Comet Hyakutake. You might remember, it was discovered just last January 31 and it did pass very close to Earth in March. In fact, it was dubbed The Great Comet of 1996—one of the closest cometary approaches of the previous two hundred years. It's more or less being upstaged, though, by the anticipation of Hale–Bopp next year."

He glanced around, put down his now empty cocoa mug, and rubbed his hands. "Okay, we have three heavenly bodies to go. The first is Pleiades—"

"But I have a question." He could hear the bracelets and knew exactly who was speaking, despite the lack of light.

"Go ahead."

"I wanna know what sign you are."

Snickers filled the lawn.

"Well, the brochure *did* say you'd answer our questions."

"Lady," one of the men chimed in, "there's a difference between *astro-no-my* and *astro-lo-gy*, in case you didn't know."

"Of course I know, but they're both sciences based on the stars, so they have more in common than most people think."

"Hmm," Cornelius offered. "Let me ask—what sign are you?"

He could almost hear her smile. "I'm a Sagittarius. And my birthday was the twelfth!"

"Congratulations," he said. "Well, since your birthday is December twelfth, you're an Ophiuchus."

"A what?"

"Ophiuchus, meaning serpent holder in Greek."

"Huh? No no no. I've known *my* sign for a long time."

"What I mean is, astrology doesn't take into account the degree to which the earth has precessed."

"You mean, processed? I get that. Life is a process."

"No, *precession* is a change in the orientation of our

rotational axis. So the North Star didn't used to be the North Star; it used to be in the constellation Draco. The pyramids, for example, line up with Thuban, not with Polaris, our current North Star. The sun presently scoots across an additional constellation in the first couple of weeks of December."

"Are you sure you know what you're talking about? I mean, I've never heard anything about the sun 'scooting.' For *sure*, I've never heard these names, and I've been studying for years. I don't know what sign you are, Mister, but I'm a Sagittarius."

With that, she gathered her long skirt and began clanking her way back across the dewy grass.

Another satisfied customer. Yeah, I really handled that one well. He sighed.

"They say there's one in every crowd," one of the sisters remarked quietly.

He smiled in the dark. "So, I was just starting to tell you about Pleiades, the tail of Taurus the bull."

"And that's no bullshit," one of the men muttered under his breath.

This time everyone burst out laughing, including Cornelius. When he could manage, he began again. "Pleiades is an open star cluster, only one hundred million years old, which means it's very young. Here we can study stars as adolescents."

"Too bad the teenager had to leave," one of the sisters commented.

"Well, I think we already *know* his behavior," her sibling added. "By the way, isn't the Pleiades also called the Seven Sisters?"

"Yes, that's right. Good point, from one group of siblings to another."

The few remaining guests chuckled some more, and Cornelius pressed on, again adjusting his telescope. "Orion is up next, the Great Hunter. The central star on Orion's Belt isn't really a star at all." He glanced at the luminous face of his watch. "It's nearly one a.m., so we'll end our party tonight with the Orion nebula—a stellar nursery where we actually study how stars are born. And this is the closest stellar nursery to the Earth."

Most of the guests now seemed a bit subdued and might even be bleary-eyed, with the notable exception of the two sisters, who seemed ready to stay up the rest of the night.

But Cornelius—though usually a true night owl—now felt tired himself, and eager for a good nap on the comfortable bed in his hotel room.

He shook hands with each of the guests, accepting their thanks and enjoying connecting with them. But as he packed up his telescope, he thought back to the woman with the bracelets. *I'm pretty clueless when it comes to figuring out human behavior, particularly where strange women are involved.*

He rubbed his hands together, then hefted his telescope bag and headed up the hill to the lodge. *At least there's one thing I know I'm good at, and that's star-mapping.*

Chapter 17

Zelda McIntyre stood inside her walk-in closet, contemplating tonight's unusual date with Joseph Calvin. *First, it was I who called him. I don't believe that'll be the case next time. Second, we're attending a rock concert and the trick will be not to look like the proverbial fish out of water, mouths gaping. Just how wild will these Doobie Brothers be? I have no idea. But I do know they're very successful, so they're doing something right.*

Arm outstretched, she began to move methodically through her garments hanger by hanger. Yet nothing spoke to her. *I could go by fabric . . . or by color. Wonder if there's a slightly showy necklace that might suit?* In see-through gauze drawstring bags she kept her sets of costume jewelry, mostly necklaces with dangling earrings to match. She skipped over a large gold coin that might work for a costume party, say with a pirate theme; the abalone shell seemed too delicate; then she came across the gold-flecked ammolite pendant. Though it'd never been a favorite, she'd liked it as a little piece of art and thought she might wear it at some gallery opening for a client.

She recalled the vendor in Durango, Colorado who'd sold it to her several years ago, along with the earrings to match. He'd explained that ammolite was extremely rare, going on to say something about how it could be found only in a particular sediment layer in the Rocky Mountains. She didn't recall much about its geological history, but what did intrigue her was that the particular color pattern in this type made it resemble an aerial map, giving it the name "Terrain ammolite."

Now suddenly the pendant brought to mind Miranda's hand-painted map. *That would give me the perfect excuse to tell Joseph about my new "Putting Milford-Haven On the Map" campaign.*

She held the colorful piece in her palm. *Like her map painting, the pendant is mostly blues and greens. Tight blue jeans? Why not? The navy sweater with the plunging neckline? He'll enjoy that. And the pendant will tuck perfectly into the cleavage.*

Cynthia Radcliffe struggled with the red vinyl skirt. Rune had requested she wear something "interesting" and the brown satin pants now seemed too tame.

The skirt had fit perfectly in the store, but this was short, even for her. She tugged at it again, straining at the waist band, doing her best to stretch the shiny, synthetic fabric. *Oh, well, I suppose black tights could cover up the dangerous parts.*

At first, she'd imagined wearing her red stilettos. *But with the opaque tights, why not wear the "naughty boots"? Zackery's too busy for me? Fine. I can be busy too. Very busy.*

She reached up toward the stack of shoe boxes balanced precariously on her top closet shelf, lifting down one after another. *I should label these boxes. I say that every time I go hunting for shoes to wear.*

Finding the pair at last, she snatched one from its tissue paper and slipped it on: smooth black leather, laced up to the ankle. *Very nice. Very naughty.* She paraded unevenly in front of the mirror, one foot lifted on the boot's high heel, one foot flat. *Yes, this will work. Regard and weep, Zackery Calvin.*

Now she'd need a top—something with long sleeves. *Maybe the cropped black sweater.* With the flash of bare midriff, she'd be chilly. She'd see to it that Rune kept her warm, at least when they were in front of Zackery.

How dare you uninvite me to your big concert. How dare you give me only two days' notice! How dare you risk embarrassing me!

She felt again the nasty pinch around her heart that'd been happening ever since that call from him. *Good thing this concert's way up north in some middle class town. More likely no one from our social circle in Santa Barbara will be there. At least I hope not!*

Sally O'Mally couldn't stop pacing and her shoes hammered a steady drumbeat across the wooden floor of her living room.

Nerves hardly described the tangle of emotions braiding their way through her as she waited for her old friend Tony. *Of course I wanna see him . . . I just had to accept his invitation after all he's been through. But here I am steppin' out on Jack. Not that he doesn't deserve it! Still, the whole thing's givin' me the wiggle worries.*

Suddenly the steady rhythm was interrupted by a knock at the door. *I'm not ready! Yes, I am! No, I'm not!*

Ignoring her conflicted inner dialogue, she called out, "I'm comin'!" Stopping for one more glance in the hallway mirror, she saw a thin woman in blue jeans yanking at a blue Christmas sweater with white snowflakes. She put on her most cheerful face, then forced herself not to run to her front door. As she opened it, she cleared her throat and began her rehearsed line. "Well, Tony, it's so nice to see...."

There's no one here. No one atall! Mystified, she continued standing in the open doorway. Then she heard the knock again, coming from the back.

Closing up in front, she ran toward the knocking. When she pulled open the back door, all rehearsed lines vanished. "Tony! What are you doin' back here?"

"Hey, Sally, I'm sorry I couldn't get to the front door. Hope you don't mind."

Awash in embarrassment and guilt, Sally gushed, "Oh, I am so sorry, of course, of course, because of the steps, I'm sorry, I didn't even think of it, what a silly thing for me to...."

"Sally. You look beautiful."

His remark cut through the nervous chatter and the two old friends stared at each other. *Tony in a wheel chair... Lord have mercy. But look how tall he is, even sittin' down. I remember those eyes... dark brown and intense. They look the same, but the fire burns deeper than before.* His hair was still dark, and he'd grown a beard, which suited him. His upper body was not as massive as in his high school football years, but it was sculpted now, and powerful. His hands looked like the Italian marble statues Sally had seen in school books.

Tony Fiorentino relished her scrutiny while he drank in the sight of her. A few delicate lines had appeared around her blue eyes, and her hair had lost some of its fullness. But her waist was still tiny and he could sense the undiminished strength of her spirit. He inhaled deeply of her fresh scent.

"Well, isn't it nice we have good weather!" she prattled. "Not that we didn't need the rain, but don't they have the concerts outside at the Bowl? Yes, I b'lieve they do." Her eyes darted right, then left. "Land sakes!" she exclaimed. "Think I better get us an umbrella? Oh, and I nearly forgot my little cooler in case we want a snack later." She reached to pick it up from the adjacent kitchen counter. "I'll just—"

"Give me the cooler, Sally." He took it from her easily, placing it on his lap. "Ready to go?"

Sally nodded mutely, grabbed her jacket and purse from the counter, then walked behind him as he rolled himself to his van.

Tony opened the passenger door for her. *Lord, the woman's as beautiful as ever. I can hardly dare hope that. . . . Well, either it'll work or it won't. We might be able to start up our friendship again. Or maybe in the hour-plus drive to the concert we'll run out of things to say.*

Miranda Jones had dressed in her red sweater, black jeans, and acid-washed denim jacket, now adorned with her snow-leopard pin in honor of the Doobies' new double album, titled "Rockin' Down the Highway: The Wildlife Concert." Instead of bringing her backpack, she'd chosen a small zippered bag she could sling across her body. *Too small to hold my camera, but the little disposable one fit just fine, next to the small sketch pad.*

She rode with Zack in his Mercedes and now his car turned into the parking lot, reserved for those working with the band, and pulled up to the loading docks at the rear of the Central Coast Bowl.

After turning off the engine, he opened a manila envelope.

"Here, Miranda, you'll need to wear this on your sweater so it's still visible if you take off your jacket." He handed her a two-inch square sticker.

She inspected the sticky-backed fabric, silk-screened with the Doobies logo and the words *Backstage Pass*. She began peeling off the paper backing.

"This won't be like the rehearsal in L.A. You won't be able to get beyond that door without it. Those guards are friendly, but they mean business."

She nodded, placed the badge, then grinned as her excitement began to spark.

He got out of the car and came around to open the passenger side for her. They walked in silence toward the stage door, and a roadie greeted Zack.

As promised, a guard inspected her sticker when she opened her jacket. Then he glanced at Zack's badge. *His reads "All Access" and mine doesn't . . . so I'll be alone at some point this evening.*

As they entered the backstage area, Zack took a moment to survey the progress. She felt out of place in this bustling world of wires, lights, platforms, and equipment. Scores of young men scurried from place to place with perfect focus, each apparently certain of his task, fitting into a huge, complex puzzle. The band members were nowhere to be seen.

"I'm going to check to see if Rune needs me for anything. You all right on your own for a few minutes?" Zack seemed distracted.

"Of course." Miranda smiled at him. "Take your time."

Not sure where to go to be out of the way, she waited several minutes, then wandered a long, curved corridor until she came to a door marked *To Green-room*.

I don't think that's where they keep greens . . . I think that's a special room for the performers. Better not enter. She started back the way she'd come.

"There you are!"

She heard Zack's voice.

"Perfect. Let's go on in."

"But—I wouldn't want to disturb their quiet time."

"Miranda, it's not exactly quiet before, during, or after a rock concert."

She laughed. "I suppose not."

"The green-room's the place where everyone relaxes, meets friends. Some of the guys like to visit before the show, some don't. And there's always wonderful food."

He ushered her down another short corridor until they reached the double doors of a private room—guarded by yet another uniformed Bowl employee—who scrutinized her sticker.

Miranda stopped, turned to Zack, and looked up at him. "I'm not hungry, Zack. But the green-room sounds like a good place for me to be out of the way while you finish working."

He sighed. "I appreciate your forbearance. I shouldn't be

long. But in case I am, here's your ticket." He reached into his breast pocket. "Take your seat, I'd say about twenty minutes before show time." He paused a minute longer. "Are you sure you're all right?"

"Zack, this is fun. I'll be fine."

"Okay, then. See you as soon as I can." He leaned down and kissed her softly on the mouth. She slipped her fingers through his as they kissed, then pulled quickly away and moved through the door.

The green-room was deserted for the moment. *Just as well.* Tiny colorful Christmas lights draped across window frames and wound through potted Ficus trees, giving the space a pleasant glow. Sofas and chairs were grouped into seating arrangements. Across the room, a wide table held a buffet. She migrated toward the food, taking in the sumptuous display: chilled shrimp, hot *shumai*, crisp baby carrots, cubed cheese, stone-ground wheat thins, and sushi.

She glanced around the room. *Still no one.* Despite what she'd said to Zack, her mouth began watering. Impulsively, she grabbed a small plate and began choosing bite-sized delicacies till the plate was filled. Glancing around the room one more time, she chose the unlit corner of a sofa and popped a California roll soaked in *ponzu* sauce into her mouth. Its pungent flavor assaulted her senses and she closed her eyes in a reverie of taste.

"Pretty good, huh?"

Startled, her eyes flew open at the unexpected question. A man regarded her expectantly, but, her mouth completely full, she couldn't answer a word.

He began to laugh. She began to gag.

"Oh," he said. "Sorry. I'm really sorry. I didn't mean to make you choke." He began laughing again, though, unable to stop himself.

Her choking continued.

"I'm . . . uh . . . here. . . ." He began patting her on the back, gently. "Want something to drink?"

Miranda nodded.

He dashed to the side table and popped open a soda, offering the can to her.

She sipped from the chilled drink and at last swallowed. "Thank you," she said in a weakened voice.

"No. No! It was my fault." He looked at her carefully as if reassuring himself she was all right. "Pretty funny, though."

She grinned. "I guess so."

The man, she now recognized, was another of the Doobie Brothers. *I'm pretty sure he's John McFee.* He had wide, hazel eyes, brown hair well past his shoulders, and a huge smile. Her artist's eye took in the details of his outfit: sleek leather pants, ostrich cowboy boots, a cloth jacket with a beautifully painted Native American motif.

"I'm John."

"Miranda."

"You're here with Zack, right?"

"Yes. Seems like word gets around."

"Backstage is like a small town," John said.

"Sounds familiar," she answered.

"Aha." John stared at her, but appeared to be thinking distant thoughts. *Can't tell if he's shy or preoccupied with the upcoming show. Maybe both.*

"I want you to meet my wife later."

"Great!"

"Okay, well, I have to get going. Hope you like the show."

"Oh, I will," Miranda said, still balancing her plate of food on her lap. "I *love* your music."

"Thanks." A shy smile lit his face, and then he was gone.

She became aware now that several other people had entered the room, and a short line had formed in front of the food table. Another musician she recognized as one of the band members sat on the arm of a sofa, laughing with invited friends, and still another shared some mutual backslapping with a leather-clad pal. It was a jovial occasion, full of good will. She could feel the energy rising palpably as the room filled and the concert time drew closer.

This would be an impossible way for me to work. To paint, I need solitude. But maybe, to play music, you need company. Lots of company. Still, she wondered about these talented men, some of them away from home . . . and for long stretches of time. She wondered about the fundamental loneliness of the road, and what a high price they paid for the glamor of being rock musicians.

Rune Sierra practically shuddered with relief. The argument between two of his key stagehands had mounted all day, but now he'd helped them reach detente, if not actual agreement. *A year of work's about to come to fruition. Can't let it derail at the last minute. One more fire's out. Hope I don't have to douse any more tonight.*

Just this afternoon he'd had to argue again with the venue management, who'd wanted to allow their employees and families to attend the show for free. *Hated to sound stingy, but I had to explain—again—that not even the band members' families could come for free this time. Our goal was to raise money for the vets. No freebies.*

He'd received word that a friend named Cynthia had arrived and was asking for him. He caught up with her just outside the green-room. *She looks like she's dressed to be on stage, not in the audience . . . a black-and-red rock-and-roll version of a Christmas tree topper—though no angel—who'll light up if I plug her in. No . . . don't go there.*

As he approached, she beamed. "Rune! There you are!"

"Hi." He plunged his hands into his pockets to avoid the embrace she seemed to be expecting. "You got here just in time for a quick look backstage before we have to send all the guests to their seats."

"Fabulous!"

She followed where he led—though he couldn't imagine how she could walk in those sexy little high-heeled boots. *If we're gonna run into Zack, it'll probably happen now. Don't know whether to hope we do or hope we don't.* The question was settled when he heard a familiar voice. *Think I'll step back and watch the fireworks.*

"Cynthia? What the . . . what are you doing here? You hate this kind of music!" Zack stood staring at Cynthia, an appalled expression on his face.

She turned toward him. "Do I?" Her voice sounded syrupy. "What I really *hate* is being left *out.*"

"But how . . . how did you get backstage?"

"I was invited, Zackery. In fact, when Rune invited me tonight I just couldn't resist."

"Rune invited you to this? You mean. . . ."

"Yes. I'm his date."

Even from this distance, Rune could see Zack seething as he scrutinized her, his gaze stopping at the bottom of the skirt. Rune couldn't hear what he muttered under his breath.

"You seem just the tiniest bit upset." She flashed a smile. "Are you? I thought red was just perfect for a Christmas rock concert."

Zack stood smoldering. "I am *not* upset. Where is Rune?"

Rune stepped toward the dueling duo. "Somebody ask for me?"

"I thought you were taking care of that problem with the stagehands. You left me high and dry!"

Rune tried not to sneer. *You don't know a stagehand from a roadie.* That's what he wanted to say. Instead he managed, "Zack, you have no idea what you're talking about. Right now Cynthia and I have some business to take care of."

"Business to take care of?" Zack fumed.

"See you later, Zackery." Cynthia tugged at her skirt, but as she spun on the heel of one boot, she seemed to wobble.

As Rune grabbed an arm to steady her, he caught the satisfied expression on her face. *She looks like a cat who just lapped up a delicious bowl of revenge.*

Chapter 18

Miranda Jones sat in the dark of the amphitheatre and looked up to see a waxing nearly-full moon hovering in the sky. She snugged the collar of her thin denim jacket, glad she'd at least had the sense to wear a sweater. But now the chill seemed to fade away as she felt the Central Coast Bowl begin to vibrate with the anticipation pulsing through the audience.

This was not the polite murmur of a pre-symphony crowd. This was the purr and growl of the Doobies Fan-Beast, hungry for its next meal.

Tony Fiorentino waited in the wings, sweat pouring down his back.

The sky had grown dark, plunging the Bowl into a state of readiness. A sudden blaze of light illuminated the stage, and the audience began cheering. It wasn't a band member who stepped up to the mic, however. It was Rune.

"Good evening!" The tinge of his accent resonated through the speakers and his own amplified voice seemed to surprise him. He stood back from the mic for a moment before resuming. "Tonight . . . is a very special night. We're going to hear some great music."

Cheering rose from the audience in a crescendo, then subsided as Rune continued.

"And we are here to honor men and women for whom honor is long overdue. I'd like to introduce to you tonight's special honoree, a decorated veteran, Tony Fiorentino."

Tony began to wheel himself toward the center of the stage, becoming breathless from what should be a normal exertion.

The crowd started to applaud. It sounded like thunder. He wanted to run for cover. His usually strong arms seemed weak as he pushed forward again on the two large wheels and he seemed to be making such slow progress, he felt he wasn't moving at all. Rune appeared as a tiny figure in black, backlit by a thousand blinding lights.

And then Tony heard another sound. A cadence had begun in the clapping. His colleagues in the first three rows were giving him encouragement. His nervousness ebbed and strength returned to his arms. He reached center stage, and saw the man who had become his friend ready to hand over the microphone. While the steady beat of applause spread throughout the audience, Rune struggled to lower the mic stand. And suddenly it struck Tony as wrong to be sitting. He edged himself forward in the wheelchair and looked up. "Rune," he said over the noise. "Help me up?"

Rune Sierra stood stunned for a moment. *He can't mean . . . but he does.* His eyes darted over to the darkened wings, where the only person he could see clearly was Zack Calvin. Zack seemed to take in the situation, because he responded by walking on stage. Rune looked at his rival, and set differences aside. "One on each arm, okay, Tony?"

Tony nodded. Rune locked eyes with Zack, and each placed a hand under one of Tony's elbows. In one smooth motion, all three men stood tall.

The crowd's roar rose as a wave of energy and good will. Rune glanced down and in the fifth row saw tears cascaded down the face of Tony's friend in the snowflake sweater. She wasn't the only one crying.

Miranda Jones swept a tear from her cheek and joined the crowd in finally sitting down after giving this man Tony and his fellow veterans a long standing ovation. His heartfelt acceptance speech segued smoothly into the start of the concert, musicians appearing and the music cascading off the stage and through the audience like a tidal wave.

With so much happening in front of her, it was hard to know where to look. Visually, this was a live painting. Banks of lights poured washes of color over the instruments and musicians in perfect synch with the music, making this both a visual and an aural experience.

The light bounced off guitars, drums, boots, buckles, and keyboards. Somehow the guitarists and bassists all managed to cross back and forth, up and down the stage while still playing in perfect time, taking their music to each other, playing face to face, their heads bobbing to the rhythm. The imagery overloaded her senses, and she closed her eyes for a moment.

Then her eyes flew open again when the guys rocked into

"Jesus Is Just Alright." Standing up at their mics, right legs beating time, Pat, Tommy and John strummed out the chords and sang the melody and harmonies. Then her attention went to the men behind them. Two bassists played this special concert—Skylark thrummed the deep tones that traveled down his body and into the planks of the stage, while Tiran Porter anchored the tune with a bass-line that shot into the audience and loosened her hip sockets.

Then, with a rhythm shift from the irresistibly powerful drums of Keith Knudsen and Mike Hossack, the song took a right turn into blues. Cornelius Bumpus stepped up to the mic to sing this slow section like a spiritual, trading solos with Pat Simmons on wailing guitar and Guy Allison on organ keyboards that made her feel like she was in a rock-and-roll church.

The next tune began gently, familiar guitar chords and the sudden melodic lines of a fiddle as John McFee took the lead, playing a lyrically romantic solo spiced with just enough country-twang to make listeners feel a little homesick for a simpler life.

"Black Water," another of their signature pieces, enveloped the audience in a musical embrace, and they loved it when Pat Simmons substituted "Central Coast moon" for the Mississippi moon of the original lyric. Miranda could feel a dreamy sense of hope rising. Mid-song, the band turned the vocals over to the crowd, and she found her own voice joining thousands of others singing. No one resisted any longer, dancing and singing in the aisles, letting the music seep into them and take away the cares of the world. Then, with no warning, the next tune started. *Seems to me they hardly had time to take a breath between songs.*

Michael McDonald—no longer full-time with the Doobies since he'd rocketed to the top of the charts with his own solo career—*was* here tonight for this special occasion. The smokey sound of his voice swirled into the mix of emotions flowing through her—longing and anticipation, a thrum of desire, a spark of mad ambition. *It's like touching a live wire . . . thrilling and dangerous.*

The danger she felt was the raw energy released by the music, freeing everyone in the audience from their usual constraints. *This band and their music . . . they make you lose yourself . . . and find yourself.*

Strong, rich rhythm coursed through her and filled her with the unfamiliar sensation of collective joy. It overflowed and spilled out of her as a laugh quickly swallowed up in the exuberant sounds lifting from the amphitheatre.

Zack Calvin peered out from backstage until he located Miranda, standing with the strangers in her aisle, clapping and swaying to the music.

Talk about contagious joy . . . she's caught the fever.

His own moment on stage with Rune and Tony had done a lot to get him past Cynthia's saccharine-coated tantrum. And Miranda's presence was curiously calming. He watched her for a moment longer. It touched him to see how completely she was transported.

The band sang about "depending on you," and as Zack looked at this woman he barely knew, he wondered if someday he'd do just that.

Zelda McIntyre looked up at Joseph again, trying to gauge his reaction to what he was seeing. *Before the concert started, he seemed quite touched by Zack and his friend Rune's gesture to help the poor veteran stand. I saw that. But he was agitated about something too.*

Their seats were well up the hillside. The performers on stage would have been miniature figures in the distance, were it not for the huge video screens that captured their every move and magnified them beyond their natural importance: a guitar seemed as large as a jet; a fling of the arm across the strings became a plane lifting off a runway. And when one of the young men leapt in the air, guitar and all, he seemed to be flying. The musicians looked like demi-gods of mythological proportion. *Indeed, perhaps in this culture . . . they are.*

Joseph Calvin shook his head, grateful, now, that Zelda had given him a set of disposable ear plugs—not because the music wasn't good, but because it was shockingly loud. The people in the row ahead of them were standing. He glanced around the auditorium and saw that most people were. He stood as well, and Zelda followed suit.

He caught sight of Deputy Johnson and gave him a nod. *Wonder if he's here for any particular reason, other than general security?* The deputy nodded back, then moved off.

Joseph gazed down at Zelda. *She looks good in the fitted jeans and sweater . . . not to mention that colorful pendant plunging into her cleavage . . . and enough make-up to go to work on a soap opera. But she's chic . . . and sexy as hell.*

She had her arm looped through his and had kept it there most of the evening so far. The gesture seemed both formal and intimate. There was even something plaintive about it, as if she ran the risk of getting trampled unless she held on to him. Despite the high-heeled wedge shoes, she didn't have much stature. He found himself responding to her vulnerability . . . a pleasant sensation. Her large violet eyes looked up at him. He enjoyed returning her inviting gaze.

Cynthia Radcliffe felt more comfortable now that the entire audience was standing, because she could keep an eye open for Zackery without being noticed. She hadn't caught sight of him since their fracas backstage, but she knew he must be here somewhere. She caught sight of Rune standing in the wings, watching the audience more than he was watching the band. *Gauging their reaction, I imagine.*

Shifting her eyes back to the show, she had to admit the Doobies offered quite a spectacle. *There are ten musicians on stage, and every one of them's a real man. I could tell that in a heartbeat.* The unbridled male energy pouring off the stage was enough to make her weak in the knees. She yanked down on her skirt again.

She'd seen bands before with *one* drummer. This band had *two.* As she watched, the percussionists sat on high risers, two men with arms of steel hammering huge arrays of drums in perfect unison. The drums sounded like accelerating heart-beats and Cynthia wanted to dance. She started moving slightly from side to side, and checked around her to see what other people in the audience were doing.

Three rows ahead of her, a woman tossed her hair from

side to side, clapping with her hands overhead. *But no one's taking any notice. It's because this is a place to come and be free. Well, for some people it is.*

Someone touched her hand, and she snapped her head to the left, surprised to see Rune standing there watching her, a knowing expression on his face.

What is he up to?

She smiled, then noticed his lips were moving, though she couldn't hear him. "What?" she yelled.

She watched his lips, beginning to notice they moved in synch with the music. She tuned in to the song until she could make out the word "dangerous."

He's smiling at me while he mouths the words. This guy knows me too well.

Miranda Jones stood with the rest of the audience, clapping and whooping. Technically, the concert was now over, but the Doobies were coming back on stage for their third encore. She glanced around to confirm not a single person was left sitting in the entire amphitheatre.

A movement from the side caught her attention and she saw Zack beckoning from the end of her aisle. She hesitated, but when he continued to wave her on, she made her way past her screaming aisle-mates as the band began to sing one of her favorites, "Taking It to the Streets."

The soulful strains of Michael McDonald's voice arced over the sound system and penetrated Miranda like a heart ache. Tonight, with the vets in the front rows being honored, the lyrics were an embrace of these men and women who'd given so much. *Singing like that, Michael makes all of us feel like brothers and sisters.*

Zack took her hand when she reached the last seat. She hated to leave while they still played, but she figured Zack had a plan. They power-walked past the concession stands redolent of hot dogs and relish. The sounds from the stage receded slightly as the music ended. "Thank you very much!" she heard Tommy Johnston say, and with that another roar erupted from the crowd. The corridors leading from the seats began to fill rapidly, pouring forth a charged and exuberant stream of humanity.

Zack clutched Miranda's hand tighter. They could no longer walk side-by-side, so she stayed behind him, careful not to step on his heels. She tried to orient herself. They seemed to be approaching the quiet room where she'd eaten before the show. It was no longer quiet. Already hundreds of people stood in a line that snaked away from the door and blocked people trying to leave the Bowl. These were the fans.

Zack pressed through to the front of the line and flashed his all-access badge. That wasn't enough to get Miranda through, however. The guard stopped her until she managed to turn her body far enough for him to see her backstage pass sticker. The tall guard glanced at the pass, then lifted his head imperiously, pushing her through the door.

She'd expected relief once they were in the room, but that was a laugh. Friends stood shoulder to shoulder and wall to wall. Some had landed near the food table and were eating; some were drinking; all were being jostled by the new arrivals, which sent small side-stepping movements through the crowd like ripples.

She recognized some of the people in the room—a City

Council member from San Luis Obispo, a well-known author who now lived in Cambria. *Stars attract stars, I imagine. I know artists attract artists.*

"Enjoy the show?" she turned toward the familiar voice, and realized Keith had asked the question.

"It was fantastic!" beamed Miranda. "Never seen anything like it!"

"Cool," he said, giving her a big grin. "Really glad you enjoyed it. We sure have fun doing it."

"Are you exhausted?"

"Nope! Well, I'm not saying I'd like to do another show tonight. You know we spend a lot of energy, but we get a lot back from the audience too."

"They really love you."

He chuckled. "They love the experience, which is cool. If they really knew *us*, they'd realize what a bunch of insane guys we really are."

Miranda laughed. "*Good* kind of insanity."

"Hey, man, excellent show." Zack had been talking with someone else, and now turned to Keith. "You played your heart out. The vets will never stop thanking you for doing this."

"It's something we really wanted to do. Wouldn't trade tonight for anything. Thanks for working on this, Zack. Good job."

The two men embraced and slapped each other's backs. In this packed, overheating room, the heartfelt moment sent out its own ripples. *That's Love . . . pure Love.* Miranda snapped a mental picture, knowing she'd keep it as a cherished memory.

Photos! She'd nearly forgotten the disposable camera. As the two men released their embrace, Miranda said, "Smile!"

When she'd snapped that first photo, others followed as she and Zack made their way through the crowd, shaking hands, embracing, and snapping shots with the other musicians. She loved thanking them in person, thrilled to meet each member of the band. She got to tell John how much she enjoyed both his guitar and his violin, impressed he could play both with such expertise.

At one point, she caught sight of the man who'd helped Zack with Tony the vet. *His name's Rune . . . he's standing with a beautiful blonde.* But they were far across the room, a hundred people between, and she dismissed the idea of trying to meet them. *No agenda . . . just go with the flow and let the joy sweep me along.*

Rune Sierra stood with Cynthia by the stage door an hour later, keeping her out of the way of busy stagehands. He turned to look at her again. *For all her strength, she looks so alone, so sad to be left out.* Resisting the urge to hug her, he plunged his hands into his pants pockets.

"Fernando will see you to your car."

"What? But can't you even. . . ."

"I have a lot of things to take care of here before I leave. That's why I told you you'd have to drive yourself. Besides, mission accomplished, right? Zack saw you with me and got ticked off?" *Whoa, struck a nerve. She looks like she wants to slap me.*

"Absolutely," she said with frigid politeness. "Thank you, Rune."

Again, she nearly turned an ankle as she tried to make a hasty departure. When her hands shot out to steady herself, he grabbed them. They stood that way for a moment—held and holding. He dropped one hand to reach up and cup her cheek. "Drive carefully." He turned and strode back inside.

Cynthia Radcliffe twisted her mouth in confusion. *I was sure he was going to kiss me. Then he kicks me out the back door of the theatre!*

A Hispanic man—Fernando, according to the name embroidered on his breast pocket—came up the concrete steps and offered his hand.

She ignored it.

"Be careful of the stones, Miss."

Cynthia looked with contempt at the man's little red coat with the Central Coast Bowl logo. "Where the hell is my car?"

"This way, Miss."

As Fernando led the way into the darkened parking lot, Cynthia picked her way carefully over broken asphalt and loose stones, furious her naughty boots were getting scraped.

Note to Self: no more hare-brained schemes involving dates with Rune Sierra. And if I'm ever really tempted again . . . I think I should just go shopping instead.

Chapter 19

Susan Winslow threaded her way through the maze of backstage corridors at the Central Coast Bowl.

The shouts among crew, roadies and lingering fans made it almost impossible for her to hear. She shifted her backpack to the opposite side and continued to the end of a long hall. As she turned a corner, she nearly had a head-on collision with a huge equipment box being rolled to the loading dock. "Watch it!" she yelled.

"Better clear this area, miss. This ain't a good place to be," said a man in a sweaty T-shirt.

"Better yank up on your jeans before your crack shows," Susan muttered as she passed him. She then thought he might know where the Doobies were hanging out. She called after him. "Excuse me, could you tell me. . . ." The man never even glanced back over his shoulder.

I could go back to the stupid guard. But he already gave me directions once, for all the good it did.

Another box came rolling down the hall, and she pressed herself to one side. "Do you know where the Doobies are?" she asked as the man wielded his heavy load.

"Backstage!" He was moving away fast.

"Yeah, but where?!" Susan shouted after him.

"Next corridor!" he managed to say before disappearing.

Great. Everyone here knows which corridor it is, except me! She'd been assigned to interview the Doobies, and now she couldn't even find them.

Kevin had no press pass, so he was out there somewhere waiting for her and couldn't come inside to help her look. *I should've said I had an assistant, or something.* The thought annoyed her, the self-blame a familiar toxicity that shortly began to morph into blaming someone else. *So what if Kevin has to wait a little longer? He got a free Doobies ticket out of it.*

She recognized the symptoms of her mounting frustration: sweaty palms, shallow breathing, the first edges of a headache. *Unless I find these guys, I can't do my job. I'll wind up back in Milford-Haven with no notes, no article—and never get to write for the stupid newspaper again, even if it is just an insignificant local rag. I asked for the assignment, and if I don't make good, I'll look like a fool. Worse. I'll be called a liar.*

She could feel heat crawling up her neck and into her armpits. She breathed, considering her options. *Start over. Make my way back to the stage door, assuming I could ever find it again, and get the guard to tell me the way again. No, that'll take too much time.*

She began again at square one of the maze. Now the forbidding concrete hallways were mostly empty, the staccato beat of her shoes pounding a hollow rhythm.

She walked the line of closed doors, knocking on one after another. But her knocks went unheeded. Either that, or every single room in this place was already empty.

What if I've missed the band altogether? What if they've already gone to their cars or whatever, and they're gone? No! she ranted. *No, no, no!*

She was shouting now. "Isn't there anyone here who can help me?"

Yet another rolling box trundled down the hallway in her direction, and again she backed up to avoid it. She pressed herself against a door and when it suddenly opened behind her, she nearly fell backwards.

"Geez, next time you open a door, you ought to see who's there!" she complained, turning around quickly to see who she might be talking to. Five men were in the room, all of them staring.

"I recognize you guys! I mean, you're not the Doobies, but you were, like, the opening act, the band who'd played first, right? You guys are called Landbridge. This must be your dressing room." She smiled.

They exchanged looks, then continued to stare, none of them speaking.

"That was nice, to open the door for me."

Four of the five musicians threw jackets over their shoulders, lifted musical instrument cases, and headed out the door, nodding to her and the one remaining musician as they went. Susan was left standing alone with him.

"I liked your music!" she called after the departing foursome, but they seemed not to hear, and disappeared into the backstage maze.

She turned to look at the musician who'd stayed. *It's kinda hard to look at him, he's so, like, intense.* His eyes were dark, his hair long and black. It streamed down over both shoulders. He wore black drawstring pants and soft shoes. The T-shirt said something, but it was obscured by a jacket with multi-colored ribbons fastened on by round, silver medallions.

A strange silence engulfed them. Now that the noise of the hallways had evaporated, Susan had the odd sensation they were standing outside in a forest. She half expected a bird to fly by over their heads. *He's not really saying anything, but it's like I can sort of hear him talking.* She shook her head, as if trying to dismiss the notion.

"Thanks for rescuing me from that crazy hallway. It was … I was lost, kinda," she babbled. "So, you play guitar, right?"

The man said nothing, but a faint smile seemed to play across his mouth. He touched his guitar case, as if answering her.

"Yeah! Right! That *was* you. So is this the dressing room for both bands?" *That was a stupid question. The room's too small.* The man didn't answer. "Cuz I'm supposed to interview the Doobie Brothers for the *Milford-Haven News*. I guess they'll be here in a moment and I can just talk to them here. Do you mind if I wait?"

He shook his head. His guitar case rested on a long bench. He opened it, revealing a beautiful instrument with a feather stuck under its strings. He lifted out the guitar, then removed the feather to place it carefully back in the case.

Putting one foot on the bench and resting the guitar on his knee, he danced his fingers over the strings, creating a single, melodic line.

Enchanted by the sound, she exclaimed, "That was great!" *Geez, I sound like a teenybopper.* She laughed nervously. "So, what's your name?"

He plucked a chord on his guitar.

Maybe he's really shy. She rummaged in her backpack to find her notebook. "You can tell me in, like, confidence if you want. I won't print it if you don't want me to."

Again, the man plucked some notes.

I think those might've been the same notes he just played. But is was getting old. "Look, I can take a hint."

The man looked at her intently.

She thrust one hip to the side and looked up at him defiantly. "If you don't want to talk, you can just, like, say so, you know." *No one's ever flirted with me like* this *before.* When a shiver ran down her back, she couldn't tell if it was fear or excitement. Either way, the element of control was quickly slipping away.

She slammed her notebook shut and stuffed it into her backpack. "Hey, I don't mind getting out of your way here. I'm supposed to be doing a job anyway. Obviously this isn't the Doobies' dressing room." She zipped her bag shut and flung it over one shoulder. "I'd say nice talking to you, but. . . ."

He strummed his guitar strings suddenly, making a sound that was both insistent . . . and plaintive.

"Look, I don't even know why I'm telling you this, but my name's Susan. So now you can tell me yours. That's fair, right?"

Again he strummed a chord—she could have sworn the *same* chord he played last time she asked his name.

"Okay, that's it, I'm outie." Susan opened the door and turned back to face him. "It's not that I don't like your music, because I do. It's just that I'm not comfortable with a man who won't tell me his name. Okay?"

He looked at her almost imploringly, but said nothing.

"I've got interviews to do. With the Doobies. Remember? I have to catch them before they go. Okay? It's my job. Well, I mean it's my job for tonight. Whatever. Where *is* their dressing room, anyway?"

He raised one arm, bending his wrist to gesture a left turn, followed by another left.

"Thanks . . . I guess."

As Susan moved down the hall her Doc Martens rang out on the concrete, and she left the stranger in his island of silence.

Ken Casmalia waited in the backwash of the young woman's departure, his emotions buffeted like a small craft caught in a larger ship's wake. He couldn't bring himself to break his vow of silence. Solstice came but twice a year and he needed its purifying renewal.

But he'd sensed her pain and tried to reach her with his music. *Susan.* There was melody in the way she spoke, a tribal lilt woven through the strident demands. There was sinuous beauty, too, and a defiance that gave him an ache.

How or where he didn't know, but he knew their paths would cross again.

Rune Sierra stood at the first circle of vacated chairs in the outdoor theatre. The stage was dark now, the Bowl quickly transforming. The last of the fans were exiting the only door left unlocked, and by now the band members would be heading for the custom buses that would drive them all night to their next city.

Rune walked onto the darkened stage and looked out at the empty seats. He surveyed the debris strewn across the aisles as a host might calculate the ruins of a wedding feast. It all seemed to have been over in a heartbeat.

The months of phone calls, the weeks of negotiating, the hours of frustration—all were behind him now. He thought about Keith Knudsen, the Doobie who'd first approached him— he'd seen this through all the way, and they'd become friends and colleagues; the band's families, their generosity and enthusiasm; Tony Fiorentino and all he'd done to help the National Veterans Foundation, and how it could change lives. He recalled Tony's speech, what it had taken for him to get here, his determination to stand for his big moment, and his gracious way of asking for help.

He'd learned a lot from Tony over the past year, not least about diseases and disorders he'd never heard of or even imagined until he'd read some of Tony's reports and letters: recurrent and intrusive recollection, amnesia, psychic numbing, insomnia, hypervigilance, exaggerated startle response, survival guilt, psychogenic fugue dissociative disorder, post-traumatic stress syndrome—the list seemed endless.

I knew meeting the guy changed me. Maybe that's why something's shifting in my old relationship with Zack too.

Calvin had been Rune's rival since boyhood. He shook his head, wondering how much of the competition that still existed between them was theirs, and how much was inherited from their fathers. *The two old stallions and their colts.*

The boys had fallen in step behind their old men. They'd gone to the right schools, gotten the right degrees, worn the right shoes. They'd been groomed, these two young men, for the oil fortunes awaiting them. Then Max Petro and Calvin Oil got embroiled in a corporate raid, and the once-friendly bidding wars turned to genuine battle. The fathers no longer spoke.

Then the sons had encountered Heather. They'd met her the same night—that heady, romantic evening during the families' joint vacation in La Paz. She'd lied to both of them about her feelings, playing them both, wrapping one of them around each little finger. Somehow, they'd both escaped from her, but their friendship was never the same. *Zack lied about his relationship with Heather. I never trusted him again.*

Meanwhile, the corporate noose tightened around each of them, disguised as a designer silk tie. In Zack's case, he took his Vice Presidency and ran it up the flag. Written up in *Business Week* as the brightest young exec on the rise, he appeared with his father in a *Wall Street Journal* front page column. Augmenting the professional articles were society mentions in Santa Barbara and L.A.

The scenario Rune's father Domingo had laid out for his own son ran parallel: a high life in Mexico City—"the center of the known universe," as Domingo described it—with multinational travel, high-level business, and every eligible society *señorita* bidding for his attentions. That would mean staying South. Rune had moved North instead.

He'd managed to anger both the Sierra and the Calvin families by opening Sierra Promotions for business in the Calvin family's own back yard. Just by being there, in defiance of his father, Rune was stepping on a sleeping snake that could strike at any time. His father could cut off his inheritance; the Calvins could undermine his reputation through the social grapevine. But the more the noose tightened, the more determined Rune was to find his own persona.

Papá is still angry, Rune considered. *If Papá could see me now, he'd tell me to get a haircut. But . . . if he'd been here tonight— it's just possible he'd also say I did a good job with the concert.*

No one had been more amazed than Rune when Zack called about the benefit. With misgivings, Rune agreed to let Zack become involved, and he'd done some good work. Then, suddenly, something happened to Zack. He was different somehow, and Rune couldn't decide whether the change was good or bad. The old mistrust resurfaced, and once again a woman was involved.

Rune shrugged and looked around the stage one more time. This was a far cry from what his father had planned for the career of his only son. But it was something he had done on his own. He stood there, remembering the cheers and the applause. Somehow, this evening had been both poetically— and politically—correct.

A song echoed in his mind. "Whoa, whoa, listen to the music," the Doobies had sung. He smiled to himself, glanced down, and headed for the stage door.

Susan Winslow sashayed down the corridor, thrilled at how successful her Doobies interview had been a few minutes earlier.

When she'd *finally* found their dressing room, she'd met all the band members briefly. They kept saying she oughtta talk to Keith—that the whole benefit concert was his idea—so she'd taken their advice and focused on him. He'd treated her like a real reporter, taking her questions seriously and giving honest answers. Besides that, he'd been downright friendly. "Contact our office next time we're in the Central Coast," he'd said. "I'll make sure you get a ticket."

With a good set of notes and quotes in her reporter's notebook, and some awesome snapshots on the new roll of film in her camera, she'd floated out of the Doobie dressing room, surprised that in this higher state of consciousness she'd had no trouble at all with the backstage "maze." In fact, on her way to the back door, she'd recognized that her path would take her right past the silent musician's room again. *I could stop and say hello. I'll probably just get the silent treatment again, but at least I can tell him how perfect my interview was. Can't blame a girl for gloating. After all, the guy could've helped me find the Doobies sooner.*

She turned down the right hallway and, when she found the door slightly ajar, pushed it open. "Hey, Mr. Notes?" She laughed at her joke. *Not a bad name for a guy who'd give me nothing but notes on his guitar.*

The room was empty. Yet something she couldn't identify hung in the air. She lifted her chin and fought back the sense of disappointment. *Why should I care about not seeing this weirdo guy? I don't care. After all, he couldn't care less about me.* She turned to leave and nearly trampled something resting on the floor. *That's his feather.* Bending to pick it up, she held it between two fingers. *Where can I put this to keep it safe?*

She thought about how dumb that sounded. *Keeping it safe? It's only a dumb feather. He won't miss it. He probably has lots of them.*

Maybe she should take it with her. Maybe she could get a poster of this guy's band and pin the feather to it on her wall. *A real live souvenir. Yeah, that'd be totally authentic.*

She could even return it to him when she saw him again. *Oh, yeah, fat chance.* Anyway, she wasn't sure she ever wanted to see him again. The more she thought of him, the more flustered she became. Annoyed, she stuck the feather in the pouch of her backpack and made her way to the exit.

Kevin would now have been waiting for at least an hour ... maybe longer. *Hope he's not mad. But it's not like we were on a date, or anything. I've been working!*

Kevin Ransom glanced up at his rearview mirror just in time to see Susan bang through the stage door and start walking ... no, skipping toward his truck. *Interviews must've been great. Means she'll be hungry.*

He jumped out of the truck and rushed to the passenger side to open her door. "Sorry," she said, as he helped her into the high seat.

When he got the truck started, he backed out of the now-empty parking lot and headed for the exit. Susan kept peering at his face, like she was trying to figure something out. "Aren't you going to say something?" she asked.

"Say something? Oh, sure. How did it go?" Kevin had learned to let Susan have her own moods, good or bad, neither judging nor anticipating which it might be, ready to respond to either. He pulled the truck to a stop, checked both ways, and pulled onto the highway.

"It was great!" Susan replied.

"That's good," said Kevin. He glanced over, surprised that, despite her report, something pinched in her face. "Are you okay?"

"Of course." She turned toward him. "Mad, huh?"

Puzzled, he asked, "Mad? About what?"

"Kept you waiting for nearly two hours."

"Yeah, well, I figured it would probably take you some time." Kevin kept his eyes on the road and they drove in silence for several minutes. Then he glanced at her. "I got us some food. Thought you might be hungry."

"Outstanding!" Susan replied.

"Found a good spot to eat too. It's just up here on the right." Kevin pulled to the side of the road and turned off the motor. They had wound up a hill and could see the lights of San Luis Obispo in the distance illuminating a lowering cloud cover. Reaching under his seat, he lifted a paper bag and produced two medium-sized hero sandwiches. He and Susan munched in silence for a few minutes.

"Got something to drink?" she asked between bites.

Kevin reached under his seat again and handed her a soda. "Thanks."

She's being polite. That means she's here, but not here. Her head's still back there with the Doobies. Actually, mine sort of is too. "Those guys are really fantastic. Always loved their tunes, but to see them live. Wow. Really glad you asked me to come."

"Yeah . . . me too."

"Really? That's good." *Excellent. Didn't think she really cared whether I was here or not . . . but I was hoping.*

When they'd eaten, he collected their debris into one of the paper bags and placed it behind his seat. They sat quietly looking at the view and listening to the night sounds.

She's starting to shiver. I can feel it. Slowly, carefully, he reached over to place his long arm around her small shoulders.

Susan Winslow sat stock still not knowing what to do. *Dang*, she thought, *he does think he's on a date! Well, he's right, in a way. But I didn't mean it that way. Guess he is kinda cute, in a hulking sort of way.* She looked up at his face, noticing the square cut of his jaw.

"Special night," he said.

Oh, shit. Now I'm supposed to say something nice.

She liked Kevin. He somehow understood her moods lots of times when no one else did. Besides, having Kevin around was useful. For one thing, with all the stuff going on between Jack and Samantha, Susan needed to be able to pump Kevin for gossip. She had to be a *little* nice to him. On the other hand, if she was *too* nice to him, she could wind up with a real mess on her hands. *Gotta make this clear, somehow.*

She looked up at him, gave him a slight smile, and took a breath. Kevin leaned down and kissed her full on the mouth. Shocked, she reacted without hesitation. She punched him.

Kevin's eyes got very big. For several seconds, his arm still didn't move. She stared at him in silence, her heart pounding, wondering what would happen next. Then, slowly, he removed his right arm from around her shoulders. He used that same hand to gingerly feel his cheek and jaw—where her punch had evidently landed—while he opened and closed his mouth, like he was checking to see his jaw still worked okay. Then he started the truck and backed into the road.

As they began a long, sullen drive back to Milford-Haven, rain began to dot Kevin's windshield.

Tony Fiorentino used his left arm to steer his van while he and Sally cruised up Highway 1. Sally had partially reclined the passenger seat, taken off her shoes, and put both feet up on his dash.

"Tony, you didn't tell me you were gettin' an award tonight. No wonder you got front row tickets." She gave him a you-can't-fool-me smile, and he tossed one back to her. "What a special night for you."

The lights of opposing traffic flashed by their windows, and Tony was enjoying the sound of her accent. "Yeah. It sure was special," he said, "in a lot of ways. I'm glad you were there to share it with me, Sally."

"Still am," she said, but then looked away as if suddenly shy. "Say, would you like something? I've got some sodas right here . . ."

"No, no, that's okay."

". . . in this cooler."

"No, really."

"It's no trouble gettin' 'em out." She reached down between the seats where the cooler now sat on the floor between them.

"Well, if they're right there. . . ."

"Is root beer still your favorite? Or I've got—"

"Yeah, that's great."

She popped the top on a root beer and handed him the chilled can. "Got other things too."

"Oh, no, really, this is fine."

"Got celery and carrots, turkey-and-Swiss sandwiches...."

"You got sandwiches in there?"

"Rye or whole wheat?"

"I'd drive an extra fifty miles for some Jewish rye."

"You're already doin' the fifty, and I got your Jewish rye."

Tony glanced over at her, grinned, and took the sandwich she unwrapped. He sank his teeth into the delicious, soft bread, and pungent mustard tickled his tongue. "Mmm," he moaned, then chewed contentedly for a long minute. "What about you?" he said between bites.

"Oh, no, not—"

"Not hungry?"

"Not really."

"Let's see ... seven hours since you last ate, give or take a couple. Unless you count an apple as a meal."

She glanced at him.

"Come on, girl. Eat up, or I'm stopping the van."

"Tony—"

"No excuses. There's an exit just a mile up the road."

"But I—"

"Let's see, what's that big pink hotel all lit up with Christmas lights there?"

"Tony, no!"

He put on his turning signal. "Yeah, that looks perfect. What are those, palm trees?" He squinted his eyes. "Hey, those are turrets! It's a pink castle! Even better."

"Oh, Tony, that's ... you don't want to go *there!*"

"Well, open your mouth, and put a sandwich in it, or we're going to the Pink Palace Motel."

"Oh, land sakes. . . . "

"Here comes the exit now."

"Mmph . . . ting!"

"You're eating?" Tony glanced her way. "Okay, good. Now keep it up. Don't let me catch you slipping that thing half-eaten back into the plastic wrap."

She chewed obediently for a few minutes, then carefully folded her empty plastic wrap and placed it in the bag she'd brought for trash. Reaching for an orange soda, she complained, "You sound like Mama."

"Your mama! She sounded good."

Sally smiled. "She's the same. She's just . . . you know, she's Mama."

"Oh, Sal, that's great. Glad to hear she's well. Still cooking pies?"

"Never misses a delivery."

"Mrs. O'Mally's pie. Now *that* would taste excellent about now."

Sally reached down into the cooler again.

"You're kidding," he said. "You've got some of your mama's pie in there?"

She laughed. "Now, before you start drooling, you need to know I am not tellin' whether this is Mama's pie, or mine."

"Aha."

"What does that mean, 'Aha'?"

Tony pulled his beard. "Well . . . I'm in trouble either way."

"In trouble? Tony Fiorentino, you're doin' that riddle-speak thing you used to do."

"No, no, I mean if I say *your* pie is better, I insult your mama, and if I say *hers* is better I insult you."

"Oh, moon in the mornin'!"

"So let's just say any O'Mally pie is a pie I'd be proud to eat."

She made a face at him and unwrapped a piece of chilled pumpkin pie. "Can you manage that?"

"Uh . . . wouldn't want to . . ."

". . . drop it. Okay. Now you just keep those eyes straight ahead, I'll get the pie to you." Balancing herself between her seat and his, she stretched a hand toward his mouth.

Leaving his own hands on the wheel, he took a bite, chewed it, then muttered, "Have mercy!"

"What?"

"That's outrageous. Who made this? No! No, don't tell me, I don't want to know."

Chuckling, she offered him another bite.

Tony polished off a second piece, unsure whether it was the taste of the pie or being hand-fed by Sally that delighted him more.

She twirled the empty plastic wrap, dropped it in the bag, and replaced the cooler lid. Then she settled back into the comfortable seat.

They watched the road for a while, the coastal towns zipping by them. A gentle, syncopated rain began to hit the windshield and Tony turned on the wipers, the sound hypnotic and comforting.

Sally O'Mally felt more relaxed than she had in a month of Sundays. Maybe it was the familiarity of being with an old friend. *He knows my background. I don't have to explain myself.* Maybe it was sharing the references to home . . . and Mama.

Maybe it's cuz the man likes my food. Maybe it's a whole lot more than that.

Belatedly, she felt a pang of guilt about Jack. It seemed like forever since she'd been out with anyone else. *It's not like he'd even notice.* Suddenly breaking the silence, she commented, "Heard you got married after you got back."

Tony darted a look in her direction. "Yeah, yeah, I did, but it didn't work out."

"I'm sorry. What happened?"

"For one thing, our politics were different. She'd never approved of the war in the first place, even though it'd all been over before we met. She didn't really approve of me, I found out eventually. I think she also was looking for someone to depend on her, and that's not what I needed." He paused for a moment, staring at the road. "We couldn't find a way to talk to each other anymore."

Sally swiped at a tear.

He glanced over again. "Hey, hey, what's this? I mean, it's a sad story, but it's not *that* sad." He smiled.

"It's . . . it's. . . ." She reached into her pocket for a tissue. "I'm so sorry for all you've gone through—the war, and ending up in the wheelchair." She blotted at her face. "Then you had to go through a divorce on top of all that."

"Hey, Sally, we all make choices. My life may be tougher than the next guy's; it may not. But it's okay. I'm here. I'm learning."

He slowed the van and turned off Highway 1 at the Milford-Haven sign. They rode in silence until he parked in the driveway next to her small, cozy house. He turned off the motor and they sat listening while the metal cooled.

Tony glanced right until he stared at her bare feet. *He used to tell me how pretty they were.* Now his gaze traveled up her legs, her arms, her body, until it came to rest on her eyes.

She felt her heart beating all the way from her chest down into her stomach. She took her feet off the dash, and slid them into her loafers.

"I don't suppose you'd consider . . ." he began.

"What?"

He took a breath. "Going out with me again sometime."

"No."

"Right."

"No, I mean . . ." She pulled her hair back from her face. "I can't."

Tony drew a hand over his beard. "Just . . . just tell me one thing. It'll be easier for me if I know. Is it the chair?"

"What? No, no. No, it's not that, Tony. It's . . . I'm . . . I'm seeing someone."

They spoke quickly, overlapping each other.

"Oh."

"Yes."

"Didn't think to ask."

"I should have mentioned it."

"No, of course not. Why would you?"

"Yes, I really should have."

After the rapid exchange they fell into an awkward silence. Tony filled it by releasing the lock on his seat, moving into his wheelchair, and lowering himself to the driveway. She wanted to kick herself. Instead she lifted the cooler out of the van.

"I'll get that," Tony said, and before she could object he'd taken the cooler from her and balanced it on his lap. She stepped out into the light drizzle, making her way around the side of the house to her back door. He followed, wheeling himself along a narrow strip of concrete. She unlocked her door and Tony placed the cooler just inside.

Looking at his saddened face, she blurted out, "Oh, Tony, it's been so good to see an old friend . . . to see *you*, I mean."

He looked up at her. *Even in this back porch light, he looks handsome.* They paused as rain hit the overhanging roof.

"How about a hug? Think you could hug a guy in a wheel-chair?"

She nodded.

"You want a polite one, or a real one?"

She looked at him, and bit her lip. "A real one."

"Okay, here's how we do this. Stand sideways, and sit on my lap."

"Oh, but . . . you don't want. . . ."

"Sit on my lap, Sal. You can't hurt me."

She sat, and Tony's strong arms came up to encircle her. *Even sitting, he's tall.* Her small frame nestled against him. *It feels so good, so familiar, to be held.*

Release shuddered through her body. He shifted his arms to hold her tighter. Then, slowly, they disengaged and he helped her to stand.

"It's b . . . been a wonderful visit," she stammered.

He rubbed his hand over his face. "Yeah. It has. So, listen. Let me write down all my information for you." Reaching into his jacket pocket, he retrieved a small wallet with business cards. Scribbling fast, he asked, "You don't have e-mail, do you?"

Sally raised her eyebrows. "Me? But, whatever in the world

would I do with somethin' like that?"

He laughed. "Well, it's on here, just in case. You know, for future reference."

"Okay," she said softly. "Happy Holidays."

"Take care of yourself, Sally O."

"You have a real good Christmas and take care, Tony." His name caught in her throat.

He turned his chair, and in three long strokes reached his van. She listened to the mechanical whir as the platform lifted him. With a final wave, Tony backed out of her driveway and drove off into the rainy night.

She stood a moment longer, hearing the hiss of his tires fade into the distance. She looked down at the card he'd given her. At the top of the card he'd written his home number. In the middle, his name, address, phone number, and e-mail were printed. At the bottom of the card there was a logo that read: "Paraplegic Veterans of the U.S.A."

Chapter 20

*S*usan Winslow quivered alone in a dense fog. The mist cold and wet against her face, she could just make out waves crashing far below. Hearing guitar music in the distance, she tried to move toward it, but it seemed to be coming from every direction. Fear seeped into her, as though the fog itself were penetrating her skin, and her heart began to thump.

The music continued, but seemed to be moving away. "Wait!" she tried to say, but could only whisper it.

"Talk to me!" the guitar answered, and she tried to follow its sound. She moved her foot forward, but then heard the music behind her. She turned.

There in the mist hovered a face, towering over her, looking down insistently, judgmentally.

"What?" she whispered. "What do you want?"

The figure pointed a finger at her and she wanted to flee, run from the apparition. But what if she tripped in the fog? What if she failed to see the cliff? What if she plunged to her death?

Susan's eyes flew open in the dark of her room. Still gripped in the terror of the dream, she turned over and flopped onto her back, breathing hard, eyes open. Her at-first-unseeing gaze rested on her black wall and she struggled to dismiss the apparition. But as she stared, she saw with increasing horror that the image was becoming clearer, not fainter. *A man with black hair . . . fierce eyes . . . staring at me, pointing a finger.*

Fumbling in the dark, she reached over to snap on the lamp resting on the floor beside her mattress. When she looked back up at her wall, she recognized the lead singer of Doom Salvation pointing at her with a scowl.

Stupid poster! Stupid dream! She snapped off the light and tumbled again into an uneasy sleep.

Susan—reawakened by the first beams of sunlight hitting her wall—tried to roll off her mattress. The covers had wound themselves around her body, tangling with her solstice T-shirt, and she struggled impatiently, finally freeing herself with an angry thrust.

She hated it when morning light hit this room, and hated the fact that she had no choice about its rude intrusions at this ungodly hour. She'd been hoping for more rain, but even the dark clouds had left her to the merciless solar blasts.

She yanked the frayed black comforter off the mattress where she'd been sleeping, searching for one of the two holes she'd previously torn at the corners. Two large nails and a hammer rested on her dusty windowsill. She poked one nail through the comforter's edge, and hammered it to the top of the window frame. She reached for the second nail. With determination, she swung the hammer. It failed to connect with the nail. Instead, it hit her thumb.

"Oow!" she yelled, dropping the hammer to the bare wood floor. The comforter now hung from only one nail, leaving the sun to continue pouring into the room. She performed a little Hurt Dance, hopping in an uneven circle. From her wall of rock-star posters, her icons leered at her calamity. She made a face at them and turned her back.

As the pain began to ebb, she trudged across the floor to her bathroom, where she reached the sink and turned on cold water to run over her hand. Looking up at the mirror, she couldn't help inspecting her recent piercing. *Still a little red, but the nose ring looks good. The rest of my face, not so much.* She stuck out her tongue at her reflection.

After whipping off her sleep-shirt, she turned on the water in her shower-tub and stepped in, holding herself away and wincing when the cold spray struck her. The water became tepid and she slid under.

As the warmth hit her body, self pity engulfed her spirit. She'd been perfectly in control just a few, short hours ago. Everything had been fine, until she met *him.*

Who is he? The nightmare began to seep back into her mind like water leaking through a crack. The rock poster, the nightmare, and the man she'd met backstage all seemed to combine in a confusion of anger and dismay.

Squeezing her eyes shut, she forced herself to visualize the *real* man: his black eyes intense, expressive . . . and kind, she realized. She visualized his strong fingers on the guitar . . . not pointing at her . . . and his quiet power. *So quiet he didn't even ask for my name, let alone my number.*

She knew she'd done everything right. And it hadn't made any difference. But men *always* responded to her. She didn't know why exactly, but she knew how to get a rise out of the opposite sex. In fact it was boring, how predictable their reactions were. That's how it had always been. But this guy hadn't responded at all.

As she rotated her back to the warm water, her thoughts turned to Kevin. *That whole thing went wrong, too. I got him a free pass—to a concert, not to putting his hands on me. He's always been so controllable. What happened?*

An awful exhaustion gripped her. *Angry at one guy cuz I can't reach him; angry at the other one cuz I can't keep him at a distance.* She watched the water circling the drain. *Just like my life.*

Kevin Ransom watched his favorite squirrel perform his morning ritual as angled sunlight filtered through the tall stand of pines behind his house. *Such an industrious little fellow. Seems like he spends the energy from all his snacking in the effort to get the snacks.*

His fat little body balanced perfectly on a branch. His front paws reached up and grasped the tiny berries just like he had little hands reaching into a Christmas cookie jar. Apparently planning his next move, the squirrel flicked his puffy tail rhythmically. Then suddenly he leapt to the next branch and clung to it like a tiny athlete on the uneven parallel bars, spinning once over the top before halting in mid-air, and coming to rest once again in perfect balance.

Kevin felt he was attending the pre-Olympic trials for

squirrels, cheering for his star athlete. This was the first time he'd felt okay since last night's concert.

He'd gone over the events again and again in his mind. Susan had invited him. She came to see him at work—with a real good sandwich, and a real short skirt. Going to the Doobie Brothers concert was her idea. She made it clear she wanted to go with him. She stood close enough to him that he could smell her cologne. She almost let him kiss her right then and there, but he didn't feel comfortable doing that kind of thing at Sawyer Construction. They'd gone to the concert and had a great time. Then he'd waited for her in his truck, just like she asked. *I didn't expect a big romantic thing, but I figured a kiss would be nice.*

He watched the squirrel leap onto a higher branch, inching farther and farther toward its narrowing end. The branch sagged low under the squirrel's weight, lowering him almost to the bird feeder Kevin had hung from the tree. Annoyed birds scolded the squirrel.

Kinda like my own situation. I got myself way too far out on a branch. But in my case, it snapped off and I'm still in free fall.

The squirrel chattered back at the birds. Kevin wished he could do the same with Susan, but he had no idea what to say. He could tell her he was confused, ask her what he'd done wrong.

He felt his jaw. *Still sore.* He couldn't believe she'd hauled off and punched him. *A slap would have been surprise enough. But a punch?* He was grateful she hadn't been able to see his face clearly in the truck. The humiliation and confusion he felt would have been written all over it. *Maybe it still is.*

Kevin regarded his busy companion. The squirrel was now

carefully retreating. Kevin sighed and stood. *Retreat seems like a real good idea.*

Meredith Jones slipped her silver BMW 328is into the stream of traffic on the 101 heading south out of San Francisco. Keeping her eyes on the road, she reached into the purse on her passenger seat, feeling for her cell phone.

She pressed the pre-programmed button that made the phone dial her sister and listened as Miranda's recorded voice announced she was either painting or was out and would be back soon.

"Hi, Mandy, it's me. Hey, I know this'll sound strange, but I've got a meeting in San Luis Obispo today, even though it's Sunday. These folks couldn't get together during the week. So, since I'll be close, I thought I'd stop by on my way back home. Won't be able to stay long, but at least I'll finally get to see your place and we can have a cup of tea. I could even take you out for dinner. I should be there around two p.m. Sorry for the short notice! See you then, Kiddo."

Miranda Jones sped down her hill, aiming her bike toward Main Street as golden rays of light slid over the hills of Milford-Haven.

If I scoot down Main, I can take Village Lane, cross the highway, and bike out toward the lighthouse. Then I can loop back up the far hill.

Back home, she had lots to do . . . unpacking from her trip, reviewing her painting journal to see which ideas she might want to develop into full-sized pieces, starting her double-assignment for PVNET, and going through her mail.

In fact, I opened a letter from my landlord, but then I must've gotten distracted when Shadow jumped up on the counter, because I don't know what it says. Time enough for all that tomorrow.

Today, aside from feeling the need for the exercise, she knew riding her bike would be the best way to begin processing recent events: her week in L.A. with its many adventures, and perhaps especially last night.

Following the show, Zack had apologized, saying he had to meet with the financial people, then get back to Santa Barbara. So as not to keep her waiting half the night, he'd ordered a limo to drive her home. *From a limousine to a bicycle. Well, my life sure isn't dull.*

The sights, sounds and feelings of the concert still lapped at her mind, each wave of recent memory bringing a fresh insight. *Never really understood how collaborative music is . . . the way the band members traded notes, synched to each other, poured out energy but then got it back from the audience. So different from painting . . . and yet, maybe more similar than I realize.*

The bike slowed as the reached the east end of Main Street, and she began pedaling past the shops and businesses, checking to see if any new establishment had opened since her last survey.

In fact, in October she'd noticed Shell Shock, a fantastic store that'd just opened. She'd become acquainted with the owner—named Shelly, of course—and painted the heart cockle for her. *Gorgeous shell. It's still sitting on my windowsill.*

Shelly had surprised Miranda by asking her—a brand new friend—to house-sit in early November. Though Shelly'd only been in town a few months, she'd bought a lovely sea-side home and furnished it with the same clever sense of style that permeated her shop. *I loved staying there . . . that living room that hovers at the edge of the ocean. It was almost like staying aboard a ship.*

As she approached, Miranda slowed, surprised to see Shelly herself come outside to hang a beautiful wind-chime just outside the front door.

"Morning, Miranda!" Shelly called.

Squeezing her hand brakes, Miranda pulled to a stop and dismounted. "Morning to you." She exchanged a brief hug with her friend. "You're here early."

"Early riser." Shelly smiled.

Miranda enjoyed the lilt of her friend's Australian accent and replied, "Me too."

"Thanks again for keeping my house so perfectly. You really didn't have to clean it from top to bottom."

"It was my pleasure. It's a *gorgeous* home." She watched as Shelly hung the array of cascading white disks, luminous in the morning sun, and heard them gently clanked in the breeze. Reflections from the flat shells played across the front wall and window, reminding her of the lens-like drops of water that'd caused a similar display in her studio. "Those are beautiful."

"These are called placuna," Shelly explained, pointing to the wind-chime. "Actually the shells come from a type of oyster called windowpane."

"They do sort of look like little round windows . . . or more like lenses."

"I have some more inside. Actually, I've been meaning to call you because this is the next shell I'd like to commission you to sketch. Can you come in for a moment?"

"Sure." Miranda leaned her bike just outside the open door and followed Shelly inside.

"First off, let me show you how the heart cockle sketch printed up on my fliers." She reached toward the stack on her front counter. "See? Ace job, truly. Loved your idea of making the heart cockle shell an ornament hanging from a tree branch."

"Well, I thought for the holidays. . . ."

"And it was very practical to give these to me as two separate drawings, so I can just use the heart cockle some other way if I need to."

Miranda read the flier. " 'Follow Your Heart to Shell Shock.' Great! Works well."

"I'll say," Shelly confirmed. "Business has doubled, and I don't think it's just because Christmas is coming up."

Miranda's mind had stayed with that notion of the "windowpane" shell. "You know," she began, "I just finished a little watercolor for my next postcard. It has a magnifying lens, and this circular shell reminds me of it."

"Oh!" Shelly exclaimed. "I like that . . . I mean, for my next flier, a person could be holding the shell as if it's a magnifier."

"I suppose so. Like they're looking at something?"

"Right, or looking *for* something. I think I've got it . . . the slogan could be 'Find Your Way to Shell Shock.' "

"Clever! Oh, my gosh. If you ever met my artist rep Zelda, the two of you would spontaneously combust."

Shelly burst out laughing. "Sounds like a winner!"

"Well, I want to get my bike ride done. So I'll see what I can come up with for your next sketch. But probably not till after the holidays, okay?"

"Absolutely. And Happy Christmas, if I don't see you."

Miranda smiled. "Merry Christmas to you too."

Miranda pushed herself through an excellent ride. When she arrived home panting and drenched with sweat, she parked her bike in the garage, marched herself directly to the laundry room and stripped off her soiled bike clothes. Even Shadow bounded out of the room a moment after she'd come to investigate Miranda's return, apparently wanting nothing to do with the smelly objects.

After a delicious hot shower, Miranda'd pulled on some comfortable cotton leggings and an oversized sweater. She'd given a treat to the insistent kitten. Now she stood in front of her refrigerator trying to decide what to make for lunch. *Nice crisp lettuce... a fresh tomato... a hunk of goat cheese. And I've got a ripe avocado.* When she placed the ingredients on her counter, she noticed the light on her answering machine was blinking and listened to the one message.

"Mer is coming for a visit, Kitty!" she exclaimed. "But once I eat this salad, there's practically no food left in the house ... but I'd rather *make* dinner for my sis, than eat out on her first visit."

How long will I have to be out shopping? Could be a while, since I might have to drive down to Morro Bay. Better leave her a note.

After quickly consuming her fresh salad, she dashed off a

scribbled missive, grabbed her fleece, purse and car keys, and headed for her Mustang.

Meredith Jones pulled her BMW Coupe to the curb in front of her sister's house, pleased her map had led her there so easily.

Pulling down her visor, she glanced at herself in the mirror, fluffed her hair, then stood and stretched. As she walked up to Miranda's door she saw a note attached.

"Hi, Mer! Come on in. Back soon."

Typical. Mandy doesn't lock up, and advertises the house is unprotected. She tried the door. Sure enough, it was open. *Something to be said for living in a small town.*

Meredith stepped over the threshold and pushed the door closed behind her. She glanced around the rustic artistry of her sister's space. Tossing her purse on the kitchen counter, she walked past it and glanced around the open area that served as both living and dining room.

There was something unpolished about Miranda's place that was surprising, given their upbringing: expanses of unpainted wood, ceilings undefined by crown moldings, lamps converted from simple pottery, earth tones and natural fabrics. *When we were roommates in San Francisco, of course I began to realize what different tastes we have. Still, with our blended place, it wasn't quite so obvious.*

The seating area caught her eye. First, she smiled to see the quilt draped over one of the two sofas. *So glad she's enjoying my housewarming gift. Those early landscapes of hers remind me of our childhood adventures exploring Mt. Tam and the "wilds" of Belvedere.*

The second thing she noticed in the living room was that on the floor in the "L" formed by the two chocolate-brown sofas, her sister had adapted an old-fashioned wooden toy box to serve as a coffee table. As though Miranda had lifted a chunk from the coastal forest bed, she'd painted the box in such detail it was utterly transformed. Bending down for a closer look, Meredith saw the brush-stroked pine needles looked so real she had to reach out to touch them. As her eye drifted to the box's corner she jumped when she saw a squirrel peeking out from behind an oversized pine cone, and laughed when she realized the little creature was painted into his surroundings.

Standing, she glanced around again. *No, Mother would never approve.* If their sophisticated, willful mother had her way, Miranda's heavy crockery dishes would be replaced with smooth china, antiques would replace the modern oak pieces, and even Miranda's own paintings would probably be moved aside in favor of classics from the family collection.

Yet Meredith could see her sister had begun to carve out something of her *own* here. *And maybe putting some physical distance between herself and our folks was the only way to do it.*

Suddenly thirsty, she went back to the kitchen and poured herself a glass of water from a counter-top decanter. Her gaze fell on an open piece of mail she couldn't help but see. *Dear Ms. Jones,* it began. She dropped her attention to the bottom of the letter, which was signed by a *Regis Ayres, Landlord.*

Hmm. Hope he's not raising the rent on her. Unable, now, to resist reading the note—and justifying the behavior as her older-sibling protectiveness kicked in—Meredith continued.

This is to inform you that we will be placing 29 Pine Ridge on the market shortly after the start of the new year. We hope to sell the property during the first quarter of 1997, and therefore cannot guarantee the new owners will honor your rental contract.

She put the letter back down on the counter. *Oh, dear, Mandy can't be happy about this! Well, they have to give her proper notice. Still . . . maybe I'll find out more about this building myself. Who knows? It might be a good investment.*

Meredith glanced at her watch. *No idea when she's due back. I may as well keep exploring.* She looked across the room to the studio's open door. Walking inside, she glimpsed a tiny painting she recognized as the original of the postcard she'd received in the mail. Tempted to further explore the inner sanctum of her artist-sister's work space, Meredith had just stepped into the room when the phone rang. Startled, and thinking it might be Mandy, she picked up the receiver.

"Hello?"

"Caught you in," said a deep, rich voice.

Playfully she replied, "Caught me in what?"

"In the mood, I hope," the voice shot back.

She laughed. "Definitely."

The man's breath seemed to hitch. "Sounds like I might get lucky."

Having too much fun to quit, Meredith quipped back, "Depends how far away you are. You know what they say about a woman's prerogative."

"To change her mind?" He groaned. "I'll be as quick as I can."

"I didn't say I wanted you to be *quick*." *Oh, my God, what am I doing? This is some friend of Mandy's! But I haven't had this much fun in months!*

When he spoke again she could have sworn she heard a

blush in his voice as he stammered, "I mean I'll *drive* fast. In fact, I'll leave now."

What if he really comes over here? "Oh," she hedged. "Where are you?"

"Home in Santa Barbara," he answered, "but not for long."

Two hours away, thank goodness. "Uh . . . oh, well, take your time!"

"The hell I will." His voice was husky now. "Damn. My other line is ringing. Hold on."

Meredith, you are completely insane. This must be the guy Mandy's dating! Unable to hear anything now but her own rising panic, she vacillated between hanging up and coming clean about her ruse.

"Sorry," he came back to the phone. "There's an emergency meeting. I can't get away after all. I'm sorry. *Really* sorry. I promise I'll make it up to you."

"Well, see that you do! I mean, really, it's okay." Meredith answered brightly. "I actually have to get going myself. See you sometime soon." She eased the phone down just as she heard her sister arriving. Mind racing, she steadied herself while she walked toward the entryway.

"Hey, Sis!" Miranda embraced her. "So good to see you!"

"You too, Kiddo." She hugged in return as a sudden pang made her realize how much she missed her sister. Standing back, she said approvingly, "You look great. So does your place."

"Thanks! I'll give you a tour later. Wait till I tell you about the concert!" Miranda enthused. "It was amazing. Zack was one of the organizers!"

So that's his name. Meredith helped her sister with grocery bags, then watched as she unloaded them and bustled around the kitchen, all the while bubbling about the Doobie Brothers concert and this new man in her life.

Unwilling to prick her sister's happy balloon, Meredith just smiled, listened and reassured herself. *Now that I've turned up the flame a little, they'll have even more fun next time they get together. After all, all I really did was play a little phone game.*

Miranda had decided to cook her "Neglected Chicken" dish for dinner: thighs and breasts, seasoned with fresh rosemary and dill, salt and pepper, were now roasting in the oven, along with two Idaho potatoes. She'd make a green salad just before they sat down to eat, before Mer had to start her drive back to San Francisco.

"Sure you don't want to stay the night and start the drive really early tomorrow morning?" Miranda asked.

"Tempting . . . but I better not. Have to get to the office early, and before that I have to change clothes and pick up some notes from home."

Miranda had enjoyed giving her big sister the grand tour, from bedroom to deck, and from living room to studio. She'd seemed pleased, if not totally thrilled. *But that's okay. That's just how she is . . . a cool assessor, unless something really lights her fire.*

While dinner cooked, they bundled up and sat on the deck sipping cups of Fortnum & Mason's Christmas tea, overlooking the view of which Miranda was so proud.

Then Meredith shared her own professional news. "You're not the only one who's started your own venture," she began.

"Oh, Mer! You did it? You went full time with Plan Perfect?!"

"Yup. You know I've already been working for my own clients. My boss has been very decent about it, allowing me the time. Anyway, last week he offered me an opportunity I really couldn't refuse: take one of the offices on their floor and hang out my own shingle full time."

"That's just fantastic!" Miranda gushed. "We should be opening champagne ... not that I'd have more than a sip ... but, I mean, to celebrate!"

"Your big reaction *is* a celebration. I really appreciate it." She lifted her tea, and they clanked their mugs together in lieu of champagne flutes.

"Hey, Sis, can you excuse me for a few minutes?" Miranda asked. "I need to make a call."

"Oh, sure. I think I'll go inside and take a little nap on your sofa, if that's okay."

"Good idea. Don't want you too tired for your long drive."

A moment later, Miranda dialed Zack from her bedroom phone. *I just have to thank him again after....*

"Hello?"

"Zack, it's Miranda."

"Oh, hey, sorry I—"

"The concert was ..."

"I'm so glad you could be there."

"... fantastic."

"I'm sorry I was so busy."

"I loved it. Loved every minute ... by minute ... by minute."

He laughed, getting her joke about the Doobies song.

"Thank you again *so* much," she continued. "Last night was absolutely amazing. I mean, seeing the Doobies on stage would've been extraordinary on its own. But to have been at rehearsal in L.A. first, so I knew them a little, knew their humor, their style of collaborating . . . anyway, I really loved it and just . . . just wanted to say thanks again. And the limo last night was a very glamorous touch."

"Oh, not at all. It'd been a long day and I just wanted to make sure you got home safely."

"So, any more concerts being planned?"

"Concerts? No, not for the moment. But I, uh, wanted to ask you something."

"Okay."

"I wondered if you'd like to come see my neck of the woods, maybe meet my dad."

Miranda felt a warmth in her chest. "Oh, I'd love to meet your family."

"Good. Well, it's just Dad. And, uh, I know it's a busy time of year, but why don't you come down to Santa Barbara next weekend?"

"I can't."

He paused, then said, "You . . . okay. Well, if you change your mind some time—"

"No, no, it's not that I don't want to come. Sorry, I'm leaving town . . . family obligation. But . . . I have another suggestion. After New Year's the gallery is having a small showing. You could come up here and bring your dad. That way I'll be on home ground. Far less intimidating for a first meeting."

"Listen, I'm not sure what's on the schedule around here. But I'll check, and I'll ask my dad too. Okay?"

"Yes, great."

"So . . . have a good trip, and happy holidays, okay?"

"Same to you."

"I'll talk to you soon."

"Soon," she said. "Bye."

She hung up the phone, and the image of their day together last fall hiking to the Cove popped into her mind. *He'd said he wanted me to do that painting for him, but he never followed through. So it seems our professional relationship isn't going anywhere. But maybe our personal one is.*

Zack Calvin now knew for certain that women really were the great enigma he'd always supposed them to be.

Today was a perfect case in point. Just when he'd concluded Miranda's shyness was one of her maddening—but primary— qualities, and that unless he wanted to upset her he'd have to avoid the kind of teasing and sparring he quite enjoyed . . . she'd revealed a completely different side. *Not only can the woman engage in a verbal fencing match when she wants to . . . she can go from zero to sixty in under ten seconds! Something only a very self-assured woman could do.*

Why had she suddenly shown this side during their earlier call? Whatever her reason, discovering this other side of Miranda made him more eager than ever to see her again. He did ponder, however, the wisdom of having impulsively invited her to Santa Barbara during the holidays, and was just as glad she wasn't available. He wouldn't have hesitated at all, were it not for Cynthia.

"Sinful Cyn"—the nickname she'd never quite outrun. She was a great party girl: gorgeous, sexy, more or less socially acceptable, and just naughty enough to keep him slightly off balance. Sometimes he even glimpsed their potential as a couple. The conquest was long since over, but she still had a knack for making things fun and usually knew how to make him look good in front of friends and competitors.

Whatever tension developed between them they solved in bed. Her body was flawless, and she begged, teased and taunted without saying a word. The sexual intensity was fun, and even addictive.

But lately, a different kind of intensity had crept into their relationship. The party had started as a game, and ended as a public humiliation. Even though Cynthia hadn't meant to hurt him, she'd made him feel vulnerable. *Am I bored? No, she's anything but boring. Uncomfortable? Yes. Is she getting too close? But I want closeness. Maybe just not with her.*

Maybe the easiest way to get the message across to Cynthia *was* to invite another woman to his home. She'd find out about it somehow, and it would send a signal.

I could take Miranda to the club ... Cynthia might even see us there. Talk about courting disaster! Why would I even be tempted to set up a scenario like that? Sure wouldn't be a gentle way to send Cyn a message. But then, he and Cynthia didn't seem to communicate with gentleness.

And speaking of signals ... she'd obviously been trying to send *him* a message by showing up at the concert with Rune. *But what, exactly?* He felt the irritation begin to crawl up his neck the moment he thought of it. Yet he *knew* there was really nothing to it. And if this was their only real means of communicating—by these manipulations—what did that say about their relationship ... and about who they were as people?

He liked Miranda, perhaps partly because he liked her

influence on him. She somehow made him feel better about himself. He enjoyed the new things she brought into his life . . . the art, the ecology . . . and the prospect of bringing new things into hers—things she'd never experienced. Perhaps he could change her world at least a little, introduce her to fine things for the first time. *She's designed for them . . . yet she lives an apparently simple life. All that could change.*

His thoughts came back to the potentially incendiary collision between Miranda and Cynthia. They could've met backstage at the concert—and didn't. They might've been about to meet in Santa Barbara—but wouldn't. His brain suddenly twisted the two women into an imaginary one: the refinement, grace and patience of Miranda with the heat, teasing and sensuality of Cynthia. *You're losing it, man. You've got enough trouble with the two women already in your life!*

Joseph Calvin took off his glasses, rubbed his eyes, and muted the ad now playing during the football game as the Washington Redskins battled the Dallas Cowboys. The temperature was in the forties today, and the fire James had made took the chill off the afternoon. Joseph poured himself another cup of coffee and pushed back in the comfortable leather sofa, enjoying his Sunday.

He still found his thoughts drifting back to last night's rock concert more often than he'd have imagined. In many ways he'd enjoyed the evening. But the whole thing had left him with a window into a Zack he didn't know. Even if he'd wanted to, he probably couldn't have connected with Zack. His son had been busy and the crowd boisterous. Thus he'd made up his mind to observe, and try to fathom what Zack had been up to.

That moment on stage when Zack and Rune Sierra helped the man stand up out of his wheelchair had been awkward at first, and then transcendent. He'd been moved by it, and he could tell Zelda had been intrigued.

His thoughts drifted to her. *Even though she always seems to be up to something . . . I don't really fault her for that. She wants to do well in life. If I complain about that I'll be the pot calling the kettle black. And I have to admit, her idea to get me to that concert was smart. She did me a good turn, even if she does have her reasons. Something else I have to admit . . . I feel more attracted every time I see her.*

They'd arrived back in Santa Barbara very late last night. He knew it would've been simple to invite himself in when he drove her home. Yet he didn't feel they were at that point. He smiled to himself. *I'm sure she'll let me know when we are.*

The knock on the door interrupted his musings. "Come in," he called. Zack opened the study door. "Hi, Son. I didn't know you were home."

"Yeah. Got a minute?"

"Of course. What's up?" Zack seemed relaxed today, though a little tired. *No surprise there. When should I tell him I was at the concert?*

"What's up," Zack continued, "is an invitation."

Joseph looked in his son's eyes. "From Cynthia? Or from the painter?"

Zack winced. "From Miranda, to go to Milford-Haven."

"Not during the week, I hope."

"Next weekend."

"Hair of the dog that bit you?"

"What?"

"No, nothing. It's an expression. You seem to be making these trips north a regular thing."

"Well, this time the invitation includes you."

"Me? You're kidding."

"She's having an art show. I know you like her work."

Joseph tried to assess his son's expression and found it hard to read. "You're not trying to tell me this will be a business trip for me, are you?"

"Well, you might find a painting you'd like to buy. But also . . . I'd like you to meet her."

Joseph paused. *He still doesn't know I was there at the concert last night, and saw him with Miranda. I caught a glimpse of Cynthia too, though I don't know if Zelda did.* "All right, Zack. I'd like that. But with the holidays, it's a crazy week. I'll have to check my schedule."

"True," Zack said. "Hope we can work it out. See you later, Dad."

Joseph watched as Zack closed the door behind him. *If we do head up there, it'll be a long drive up the coast to Milford-Haven . . . time enough for some very interesting conversations.*

Sally O'Mally washed her breakfast dishes and ran a sponge across her kitchen counter tops. *Land sakes, I always have so much to do on Sundays, I think I really do need a month of 'em.* She began mentally rattling off the list, which mostly had to do with the upcoming holidays.

Her top priority had been wrapping her gifts for Mama and

her aunt, and getting them in the mail last week. *So glad she's decided to spend Christmas with Aunt Ida Sue. Those two always get to larkin' with each other and have a grand time. Plus, Mama likes to visit with Aunt Ida's church people.*

What's my own Christmas gonna be like now? Jack and I had plans but unless I hear from that man, I surely ain't gonna call him. Not till I hear some kinda apology.

To avoid that subject, she dried her hands and walked into her cozy living room. The *Milford-Haven News* lay spread out on her coffee table. But that could wait till later. First, she wanted to decorate the tree Kevin had delivered for her last Thursday. He'd helped her string the lights, too—an easy job for him with his height and the long reach of his arms. *Promised him a special holiday lunch at the rest'r'nt in return. He'll let me know which day he wants it.*

Now she clicked on the colorful tree lights and walked toward her hall closet to pull out her box of Christmas ornaments. When she'd set it down next to her bare tree, she opened it, a smile lighting up the moment she saw the familiar treasures.

She started with the plain red-and-gold spheres that she always placed on the thicker, lower branches. Next she added the angels that Mama'd given her a few years earlier, each of them a relic from her own childhood. Her father's favorites had been "angels on the move," as he called them: one rode a bicycle, another a camel, still another a rocket ship. *That was Daddy's humor . . . always making sure we laughed about somethin' during the holidays.* Next came Mama's, and they all had different outfits: a tiny sweater, a swirling skirt, a white choir robe. *I know she made every one o' these with her own hands. She said it'd mean more to her to think o' them on my tree than it would to have them hangin' on hers.*

The tuneless song Sally often sang rose up, but this time she began humming carols, aware she was using the music to try to keep at bay her feelings about last night. A moment later, she knew her technique wasn't working.

I had such a wonderful time at the concert! The music was so fine, and it made the audience really happy. And I was so very proud of Tony, standing up like he did between those two friends, and makin' that speech. He like to brought the whole theatre to tears—good tears. And then afterwards, meetin' all those folks, the other vet'rans, their families, then the musicians.

She stood there replaying the moments again in her mind, honored he'd chosen to include her in such a special occasion. Then she thought about their drive home, the easy way they talked, the way he'd let her feed him that pie, how they'd shared their memories . . . well, *some* of their memories.

So ironic that Tony would come back into my life at just this moment . . . right when me and Jack had that argument and broke up. Well, if Jack hears I went off to a concert with another man, it'll jest serve him right.

Irritation . . . hurt . . . yes, those were in the mix of her feelings about Jack. *But those ain't the feelin's I'm tryin' to run away from.*

Hanging the little snowman ornament on the tree, she sighed. *I need me some Christmas music.* She moved across the room, then finger-walked through her small collection of albums and put one on her turntable. *I know folks are sayin' it's time to get cassettes, but I like the way the old vinyl kinda pops now and again. Makes it feel even more like home.*

To get things started, she chose the Kingston Trio's LP "Last Month of the Year"—a long-ago favorite record of her parents. But when the opening strains of "Bye Bye Thou Little Tiny Child" began, Sally felt tears well in her eyes.

Land sakes. This time next year'll be my baby's first Christmas! I can't hardly believe it! She grabbed a tissue from the box on the coffee table. *Well, Sally Girl, you better get to believin' it!*

What about the daddy? True, it was still possible Jack would change his mind. Any man who had such a strong reaction to the news of a child must have bigger emotions attached to fatherhood than he himself might realize.

Jack and me can't exactly avoid each other in a town the size of Milford-Haven. And I know he ain't about to give up eatin' my food, so I'm bound to see him at the rest'r'nt. How am I gonna feel about that? Don't know.

She flashed forward to an image of herself big-bellied and happy. *One thing's for sure, I'm gonna be proud of this baby, startin' right now. And if it turns out it's just me and her—or him—then we're gonna be fine.*

She looked down at her still slim figure and touched a hand to her flat stomach. As she did, her thoughts came back to Tony, and to the embrace they'd shared at the end of the night. *Lordie, that felt good. Well, of course it felt good to reconnect with such a good friend, someone from home.* Another memory wanted to assert itself. But she couldn't allow it. *Not now.*

She considered again her own circumstances including her

pregnancy, still such a new reality in her head and heart. It wouldn't be easy to have the child by herself. But she knew she could do it—have the baby and keep the rest of her life going too. Lots of women raised children on their own these days. *It's not the way I woulda planned. But if this is when the baby wants to come, then I gotta do my best.*

She took a deep breath as the needle on her record player popped during the scratchy pause between songs. Then some slapping bass notes began to sound through the room; as her foot started to tap, the cheerful, rousing male voices began their harmonies.

Some basic goodness seemed to swirl through the house as the music played, a cheerful, reassuring presence making itself known. She looked down and saw her feet angling toe-to-toe, then heel-to-heel, propelling her sideways in one direction, then the other. *Bet my people used to dance to music like this goin' way back . . . before they came over to Arkansas from Kentucky . . . maybe back in Ireland before that.*

She could almost hear the twang of the dulcimer her aunt Ida Sue used to play at family gatherings, with its Celtic tones. *Roots . . . that's what I want for me and for the baby.*

Rhythmic banjo chords began a-strumming on her record, and now Sally found herself time-stepping like she hadn't done since folk-dancing club back in high school. *Some o' these steps I learned, but some of 'em I just seem to know from the inside, born with the motions.*

A pang of homesickness seemed to zing along the guitar strings. Letting herself move through the timeless steps of the ancestral dance, she wondered suddenly if she'd done right to leave the farm and go so far afield.

Well . . . somethin' brought those people all the way across the ocean. They had big dreams . . . just like I have. I believe that hope in my heart's what brought me clear 'cross the country to California.

As if in confirmation, she now heard the lyrics repeating through the chorus. "Go Where I Send Thee," the Trio sang, and Sally began to hum along.

Chapter 21

from Samantha Hugo's Journal
written at the Lighthouse Tavern
Sunday morning

ichael Owen might have to start charging me rent, since I seem to show up at his restaurant almost every week to write in my journal. His place looks so festive now: by the entry, a tree decorated with white lights and white seashells—perfect for his seafood establishment, though I like it so much I might borrow the idea. And on his tables, fat white candles are surrounded with smaller shells and sprigs of pine.

I might've been tempted to make a reservation here for holiday dinner, if I hadn't already been invited by Lorraine to join her and her huge family. That'll be a raucous, fun time and I look forward to it. But for now, I'm loving the relative quiet and solitude—with only the sound of two workers way off in the kitchen.

I did promise Michael that in warmer weather I'll be back outside for these writing sessions. Meanwhile, something about this particular view of the coastline always inspires me. Besides, even though they don't actually open till dinnertime, they always offer me a great cup of coffee. Today I accepted, and it's kick-starting my rambling thoughts while it warms me up.

I seem to be swept up in the Milford-Haven Map idea that started with Miranda's latest postcard. Lorraine tells me the Town Council will entertain a proposal from Miranda's rep about a campaign called "Putting Milford-Haven On the Map" to bring in new business.

I have to admit it's clever. And—a little grudgingly—I have to give Zelda McIntyre credit for coming up with the idea. We do desperately need the tourism dollars, and this could catch on like nothing has before.

But what should be on our map? Should it be simple and include only the latest landmarks? Or should it be richly detailed and contain historical markers too?

I did my usual thing when an idea grabs me: start with research. That got me to my customary carrel in the library where I pored over several interesting texts, beginning with a history of cartography.

Babylonian agricultural maps on clay tablets date back to 2300 B.C. Polynesians mapped currents, winds and islands woven intricately into palm leaves. By Aristotle's time, around 350 B.C., the spherical earth was generally accepted, and Ptolemy was the first to project the spherical earth onto flat paper.

During the so-called Dark Ages, it seems Europe's progress occurred mostly in domestic matters—the practice of crop rotation being a prime example. But little is known about maps' evolution until the emergence of the Hereford Mappa Mundo of 1300 A.D. being typically church-centric with Jerusalem at the center.

During the next phase of the Europeans' zeal for exploration, the world itself seemed to expand, depicted not only in maps but also in navigation charts, which unto themselves came to be treated as national treasures. The first "Map of America" was created in 1508—after the exploration by Amerigo Vespucci—a gigantic document of twelve sheets. And until the fifteenth century print-ing didn't exist, so maps were precious objects, available only to those with wealth and power.

Reading a history of the world through maps would be a fascinating endeavor, and would show that in one way a map is a snapshot in time. But there are several other ways to think about maps too. Where a photo, for example, can't help but show every object in view of the photographer's lens, a map contains just what the cartographer needs to fulfill the particular purpose of the map and to fit its scale. So a map is, in fact, a subjective view of reality.

Also, though we seldom think about this any more, maps are actually written in code—filled with symbols like lines of varying widths, points and dots, patterns and colors—each of which is designed to convey information. Some of the colors are realistic, like green for mountain ranges and blue for ocean. But some are not: orange for a highway or blue for a country road. And because it's written in code, it needs to be deciphered.

So, by definition, a map is as much a matter of heart as it is of head—a way of connecting and interpreting data. The map-maker uses both logic and sense-memory to appeal to the code-reading ability of the user.

I'm wondering if mapping through time, from oldest to newest, or from farthest to closest, could be called head-mapping. In this way of thinking, you have to be externally focused, aware of others' trajectories, like the commander of a sub needs to steer clear of obstacles and know where his enemy is, or like a sperm whale needs to use his sonar to sound the depths for prey.

Then there's non-linear, internal, or heart-mapping. In this paradigm, the thought is that each drop of ocean water contains in itself everything the entire ocean contains. So emotionally, or spiritually, you stay in your own bubble, because it contains all. The idea even suggests that anything outside that bubble is an illusion, as in the Buddhist concept of "Maya." To put it succinctly, you're not in the universe, the universe is in you.

Maps are an intriguing combination of the inner and the outer. When Miranda paints one of her wild animals, she's giving her viewers an experience they wouldn't otherwise have—an intimate moment with an untamed beast that few of us get to enjoy. That experience takes place inside the mind of the viewer: an example of the external becoming internal.

But a map is a blend of art and science, and becomes a tool for the user, who takes artistic representations as a code he or she can use to move through the outer world, such that the internal becomes external.

Well, if the town itself is thinking about where it is on the map—be that map physical, political, economic, or sociological—I find it's made me think more about where I am on my own emotional map.

I sense I'm on some sort of trajectory the actual shape or destination of which isn't yet visible. Last time I wrote about this, all I knew was that it started not at some external linear point, but that it started centrally, internally, with the heart.

From that vantage point, it seemed at first as though I was at one end of the universe and that everything I was looking for was at the other: more linear thinking.

I blame that on our culture—our straight-line-oriented, goal-obsessed culture that admits of intuitive processes only peripherally. Actually I love the linear process, am committed to it in my work. It keeps me encouraged when it seems I'm making no progress implementing an important environmental policy, or when I'm dogging some scofflaw polluter.

But I'm developing a deep hankering to bring intuition into play in a more significant way, if not in my profession, then in my personal life.

To be honest, I'm not sure I've had a personal life for the last several years, except for my friendships with Lorraine, Miranda and a few other locals, plus the fleeting calls and e-mails with more distant friends. I'm shocked to realize how out of balance I am—all head and no heart. I'm thrilled, or relieved, that I started to address this last Fall.

This Winter I'm honing in on something else. Certainly some of it has to do with searching for my son. The most disturbing thing about trying to find my long-lost child is the fact that the search is bringing up memories.

I've been given so little to go on, so far. The records were destroyed—what poetic justice. It's too late, my soul cries! Somewhere in the deep recesses of my heart I always thought I'd find him one day, yet the daily barrage of life's minutiae has kept me from listening to what the heart knows, burying it with tiny procrastinations.

My mind tries to grapple with the news of this loss of data, and I am as infuriated as my mad scientists are when their computers crash. How could the records be destroyed? Where are your back-ups? In those pre-computer days, where were the vaults with carbon copies? Where are the nurses who remember? The administrators who knew everyone's name by heart? There must be someone. There must be some way. The identity of a person is not allowed to be squandered, misplaced and untagged like some forgotten key.

I go into "science-mode"—it is my defense, my grip on sanity. My scientist-mind grapples with fact, and with metaphor.

In my environmental work, I have a theory—and somehow I think it applies here. Scientists catalog the extinction of species, as though they, too, are so many misplaced identities whose very existence is being driven out of the universe. I have another idea.

It's not that I dispute the empirical evidence gathered by esteemed colleagues. Indeed, what they publish is indisputable. The number of species on the endangered list is more terrifying each year. World Wildlife Fund publishes a "top ten" list, and then, to add irony to the bitter news, a "runner up" list. U.S. Fish & Wildlife's lists are so long, they're sub-divided into multiple sub-lists, with an addendum as to how to petition for adding to the list.

One thousand of the black-footed ferret have been born in captivity, but only in a quarantine as extreme as an intensive care unit. Manatees are sensitive to human touch, love to play tricks, and have some of the best high-frequency hearing on the planet. What they don't hear are the low-frequency speed boats that kill them. 415 died in 1996; as I write this, 2,400 remain. Only one species of the manzanita plant exists, and it cannot self-replicate; it thus has earned the nickname "the living dead."

Dr. Edward O. Wilson at Harvard points out that while we tend to respond to the plight of the giant panda or the majestic gorilla, it is sometimes easier to ignore the plants and insects. But, as he says, "they cleanse the water, they create the soil, they generate the very air we breathe." He's so right. He also says that once a species dies, its genetic history dies with it, and the loss is permanent. I work at heeding his warning. Yet I sometimes dare to hope that the universe keeps secrets until we are chastened, and ready. Dan Christensen searched for "gold" in the Little Kern River of the High Sierra; he rediscovered the golden trout, long thought to be extinct.

Miranda paints sperm whales passionately, having seen them in their death throes far at sea. She sometimes cannot sleep at night, imagining she will have been one of the last humans to look into the eye of that vulnerable giant. Some species we seem to watch helplessly even as we edge them toward oblivion, like the great whale, swimming one final time over its watery horizon, never to sound the ocean depths again with its eerie song.

It's that song we cannot afford to lose, for it contains the history of the species in epic poem. NASA astrophysicist Laurance Doyle studies cetacean communication to be better prepared for interstellar messages. When Roger Payne floated month after month, attached to his probing microphone, listening to Humpback whales, he did a service for mankind the scope of which we have not even yet realized. He discerned the structure of the song itself, a long repeating sonnet-series, which regularly drops its first verse and adds a new final stanza. What messages are encoded there, waiting for us finally to understand?

My terror is: the message would be lost with the final

exhalation of the behemoth. And my theory is: the creature is never really gone. He disappears for a time—fades from the view of his enemy like the wise prey he has learned to become. He makes no sound, leaves no trace, until the hunter is convinced there is nothing left to hunt. But held in the secret vault of the universe is the essence that made the whale himself. Perhaps the scientists will one day explain this as tracings of DNA code; perhaps there will be some new technology to explain the obvious to the uninitiated. All I know is, the secret is not lost.

And so it must be with my boy. Perhaps fire consumed the offices where adoption records were kept so that inadequate mothers like me would be prevented from trying to interfere yet again with the life they so casually discarded. This does not mean the identity of that little soul is lost. It means it is being kept safe in God's secret vault. If so, like the scientists, I will have to discover the hidden code the cosmos has kept throughout my life and his, and perhaps make a bargain with the Unknown Forces to find him.

For now at least, there is virtually no external evidence. And yet the search expands and augments in spite of this, as though I were a detective who each day returns to her desk to find more clues anonymously delivered.

It's as though the search is as much inner as it is outer, and that is something I could not have predicted. With each inquiry, it is the inner doors that open, if not the outer, and I find myself in fascination and in horror with each opening. For the clues being delivered to me are my own memories.

I think of the boy, and I am catapulted into such vivid images of his birth that I can almost feel the pains. The face of my nurse floats over the edge of my bed as though she were comforting me still. I think of my pregnancy, and I am thrown back to my honeymoon with Jack, his gruff manner so charming to me then, his rough looks so enticing, his unpredictability so romantic.

For years now, I have had only one Jack Sawyer, and that has been quite enough. I never thought I'd have a nemesis, but when I moved to Milford-Haven, I found I inherited one as bonafide as that which took Captain Ahab to his famous watery grave.

Jack is the man who disagrees with my every admonition, who blocks my every vote in Town Council, who argues against every proposed change and flaunts his personal power over every regulation just for the sake of argument. My actual ideas never penetrate the thick crust he now wears like a custom suit of armor, nor do I feel the impact of his thoughts radiating outward as I once did. I think his basic charisma is still functioning, because I observe Jack's effect on others. But it no longer reaches me in any way but to irritate and frustrate.

Now, however, I seem to have two Jacks, and that may be one more than I can endure. Suddenly a Potential-Jack has appeared in my dreams—a future-perfect projection of the Jack that might have been. And even more disturbing than the dreams, is that even awake I've seen the ghostly appearance of this alter-ego—a deeply intelligent and sensitive man whom I glimpse as a creature who co-habits the body of my nemesis.

This Nemesis-Jack and I insult each other in a meeting and leave in anger and yet as I turn away, I glance back at him one more time, seeing a glimmer of compassion. We finish an argument and yet before I slam down the phone, I sense some unspoken understanding that would heal the moment.

I'm chagrined to say that Potential-Jack excites me almost as

much as Nemesis-Jack repulses me. Mercifully, the glimpses of P-J
are brief so far, and so fleeting I don't trust them. I assume this,
too, is just projection on my part, and not a true disclosing of the
soul of Sawyer.

And yet a great disclosing is occurring, and that is of my own
soul, the most difficult of all things to face. So this is the deal with
God, apparently—that if I want empirical evidence for finding my
lost son, I must be willing also to receive soul-evidence of all that
is lost within myself.

It's odd—perhaps this search is healing me in some unfore-
seen way. What am I looking for? I don't think it makes much
sense that I would begin this "search" within my own heart, then
discover I was at the furthest possible point from my goal. I think,
instead, that this is the beginning of awareness, and that the
moment I recognize something is missing, I've acknowledged a
gap that's actually been there for a long time, hiding in plain sight.

I believe gaps are an inherent part of universal design, and
that they have a specific function: they're here to allow for the
appearance of new possibilities. So what's in that space—or
what's about to be in that space—is what I'm looking for next,
and by definition I must already be close to it.

In this search I had been given only shreds of evidence. The
Chernaks tell me my son was adopted in California. Next the
original adoption agency tells me their records were destroyed.
This past week I called Deputy Delmar to see whether secondary
records might be kept by the state, and he said he may be able to
help me.

This doesn't tell me much. And yet it gives me hope. Perhaps
my son is not on some distant shore. Perhaps he is close. Where

is he? I feel myself asking this in the dark places of the soul. And deep voices seem to keep whispering—when the answer to the soul's desire seems furthest away, it is closer than you think.

If this is true, then I am—and have been—on a great journey. And when I put this idea in context with all this cartography, I can glimpse the map of my life like a satellite image over which I'm holding a magnifying glass, just like Miranda's painting. And not only am I on a journey; so is everyone—including my son. What's the starting point? I'd say it must be self-awareness. And what's the destination? I'd say a sense of home, of belonging, of being centered. Every true journey of the heart is the journey home.

So how do I map my journey? First, I have to become a good code reader—and I've made some progress, beginning to use both head and heart to read recurring symbols. But I think I also need to gain some spiritual altitude to really be able to see where I'm going. If so, I might need a psychological sextant—a navigational tool that can give me an accurate reading in this emotional twilight. At the moment I can see the horizon. But I'm not quite sure where my North Star is. Maybe that should be the subject of my meditations.

Ultimately, there will have to be an alignment of the outer and the inner, the head and the heart. It'll take both for me to find not only my son, but myself. Perhaps this is what we all need at this point in our collective journey.

It's as if we have two maps: the head lives on one, the heart on the other. But we've only been working from that first "head" map, and by now it's excellently rendered with fine detail.

It's the other "heart" map we need to consult now. It may appear indistinct and out of focus because it's a chart of desires and must be deciphered with the intuition. When we listen to the soul's desire, we find where the heart lives.

Cast of Characters

Joseph Calvin: mid-60s, 6'1, gray eyes, steel-gray hair, clean-shaven, lean, handsome; CEO of Santa Barbara's Calvin Oil; eligible widower; dates several women, including Christine Christian.

Zackery Calvin: mid-30s, 6'2, blue eyes, dark blond hair, handsome, lean, athletic; Vice President of Calvin Oil, works with his father; popular bachelor; dates Cynthia Radcliffe; becomes smitten with Miranda Jones.

Sojourner Carr: mid-30s, 5'9, brown eyes, brunette, attractive, mixed Italian and African American heritage; artful dresser, unique and savvy assistant to Rune at Sierra Promotions.

Nicole Champagne: mid-20s, 5'5, brown eyes, brunette, chic dresser; runs Milford-Haven's Finders Gallery; sells Miranda Jones's and other artists' work with skill; originally from Montreal, Quebec and speaks with a French-Canadian accent.

Stacey Chernak: late-40s, 5'6, blue eyes, blond hair, kind, submissive, speaks with a Swiss-German accent; married to abusive Wilhelm Chernak; works full time as Clarke Shipping secretary, and works part-time for Chernak Agency.

Wilhelm Chernak: mid-60s, 6', deep-set black eyes, silvered hair and beard, low resonant voice, a Swiss citizen who still carries an accent from his native Germany; capable of fierce and sudden anger; started the Chernak Agency, a service for locating adopted children; abuses his wife Stacey.

Christine Christian: early-40s, 5'6, aqua eyes, blond, vivacious, beautiful, intense; special investigative reporter for Satellite-News TV station KOST-SATV; lives in Santa Maria; frequent international traveler; dates Joseph Calvin.

Russell Clarke: early-60s, 6'3, coal black eyes, dazzling white teeth, dusky skin, deceptively strong, by turns charming and stern, adopted, has unknown mixed lineage; owner of Clarke Shipping; Stacey Chernak's employer; business associate of Joseph Calvin; commissions Jack Sawyer to build him Milford-Haven's most magnificent seaside mansion.

Tony Fiorentino: early-40s, 6'4, brown eyes, black hair, athletic wheelchair paraplegic, recipient of Veterans Assistance Award; lives in New York City but is moving to Milford-Haven; high school boyfriend of Sally O'Mally in Arkansas.

Kuyama Freeland: mid-70s, 5'7, pale gray eyes, long white hair down her back, strong and graceful, unadorned, Native American, a Chumash Elder.

Ralph Hargraves: late-70s, 6', blue eyes, gray hair, a face seamed with smile lines, pleasant disposition; a fixture in Milford-Haven, owner of Hargraves Hardware.

James Hughes: early-60s, 5'11, brown eyes, thinning gray hair, soft-spoken with a mid-Atlantic accent; the fiercely loyal butler at the Calvin estate, Calma.

Samantha Hugo: early-50s, 5'9, cognac-brown eyes, redhead, statuesque, sharp dresser; Director of Milford-Haven's Environmental Planning Commission; Miranda's friend; Jack Sawyer's former wife; a journal writer.

Deputy Delmar Johnson: early-30s, 6'2, brown eyes, black hair, handsome, muscular, African-American; with the San Luis Obispo County Sheriff's Department, assigned to the Special Problems Unit; originally from South Central Los Angeles.

Charles and Veronica "Very" Jones: late-50s, parents of Meredith and Miranda, elegant members of Bay Area elite society; long-ago friends to Joseph Calvin and his late wife.

Meredith Jones: late-20s, 5'8, teal eyes, medium-length brunet hair, beautiful, shapely, athletic; San Francisco financial advisor; Miranda's sister.

Miranda Jones: mid-20s, 5'9, green eyes, long brunet hair, beautiful, lean, athletic; fine artist specializing in watercolors, acrylics and murals; a staunch environmentalist whose paintings often depict endangered species; has escaped her wealthy Bay-Area family to create a new life in Milford-Haven.

Lorraine Larimer: mid-80s, head of the Town Council; known affectionately as the "crone" of Milford-Haven; known for her wisdom, tough-minded fairness.

Michelle "Shelly" Larrup: mid-40s, 5'6, hazel eyes, bobbed burgundy hair, well-toned dancer's body, flamboyant dresser; originally from Australia and speaks with the accent; owner of Shell Shock in Milford-Haven.

June Magliati: mid-40s, 5'2, brown eyes, dark brown curly hair, no-nonsense expression that goes well with her thick Brooklyn accent; Sally O'Mally's trusted friend and employee at the restaurant.

Mr. Man: age unknown, dark eyes and hair, medium height, medium build; one of reporter Chris Christian's anonymous sources.

Will Marks: mid-30s, 6', dark eyes and hair, athletic build; VP at Clarke Shipping; contact of Zack Calvin's at Calvin Oil.

Zelda McIntyre: early-50s, 5'1, violet eyes, wavy black hair, voluptuous, dramatic and striking; owner of private firm Artist Representations in Santa Barbara; Miranda's artist's rep; corporate art buyer; has designs on Joseph Calvin.

Mary Meeks: late-50s, 5'2, warm brown eyes, mousy brown hair perfectly coiffed, trim figure, conservative dresser; loyal secretary at Calvin Oil, remembers every detail of Calvin business.

"Notes"(Ken Casmalia): mid-30s, 5'9, black eyes, black hair past his shoulders, lean and long-muscled, handsome, Native American; a musician whose band often plays warm-up for the Doobies; an enigmatic man who hasn't revealed his name and listens more than he talks.

Sally O'Mally: late-30s, 5'3, blue eyes, blond curly hair, perfectly proportioned; owner of Sally's Restaurant; owner of Burn-It-Off; born and reared in Arkansas; Miranda's friend; dislikes Samantha; secretly involved with Jack Sawyer.

Burt Ostwald: age unknown, 6'2, dark eyes, close-cropped blond hair, quarter-sized mole on left cheek, burly; taciturn loner; freelance temporary-hire at Sawyer Construction.

Michael Owen: mid-40s, 5'9, blue eyes, black hair, slightly rotund; owner of Lighthouse Tavern.

Cynthia Radcliffe: early-30s, 5'8, amber-brown eyes, blond, shapely, gorgeous; passionate, petulant, persuasive; Santa Barbara social climber; Zackery Calvin's girlfriend.

Kevin Ransom: late-20s, 6'8, hazel eyes, sandy hair, strong jaw-line, lean, muscular; Foreman at Sawyer Construction; innocent, naive, kind; tuned in to animals; technologically adept; highly intuitive; has longings for Susan Winslow.

Jack Sawyer: mid-50s, 6', blue eyes, salt-and-pepper hair and mustache, barrel-chested, solidly muscular, ruggedly handsome; Milford-Haven contractor-builder; Samantha Hugo's former husband; secretly involved with Sally O'Mally.

Lucy Seecor: mid-30s, 5'6, black eyes, shiny black hair worn in a long braid; trim figure; photographic memory; manager of Rosencrantz Café.

Rune Sierra: mid-30s, 6', dark-brown eyes, black hair, muscular, handsome, Hispanic; President of Sierra Promotions, organizer of Doobie Brothers concert; heir to Max Petro Oil; Zack's longtime friend and rival.

Cornelius Smith: late-30s, 6'3, indigo-blue eyes, black hair, handsome, lean; grew up in Milford-Haven where his parents still live; a professional astronomer who works part time at NASA Ames and plans to build an observatory in Milford-Haven; a loner, an eccentric.

Susan Winslow: mid-20s, 5'4, black eyes, long black hair, rail-thin, attractive but sullen, Native American; Samantha's assistant at the EPC; avid rock-star fan; victim of traumatic childhood; feels trapped in Milford-Haven; defensive about her heritage; toys with Kevin.

Gladys Wilson: mid-50s, 5'9, heavyset, long-limbed, short black hair, African American; Director of Safe Haven; a former victim of domestic violence whose wisdom and compassion now helps other victims.

Milford-Haven Recipes

James Hughes's
Black & White Peppercorn Beef Tournedos
(As prepared by James at Calma)

Serves 4

Ingredients:

3-oz.	beef tenderloin steaks
1 t.	black peppercorns, ground
1 t.	white peppercorns, ground
4 oz.	heavy cream
3 oz.	Grand Marnier
2 oz.	mushrooms, sliced
2 oz.	cooking oil

Preparation:

Saute steaks in a large, well-oiled skillet, until browned. Remove from skillet and set aside. Add the black peppercorns, mushrooms and Grand Marnier. Be careful, the alcohol will ignite when exposed to open flames. Bring to a quick boil. Place two steaks on each of the four dinner plates. Pour black peppercorn-mushroom sauce over the steak on the left of each plate.

In another saucepan add the white peppercorns and heavy cream. Reduce cream until thick. Pour this sauce over the right filet on each plate.

*Provided by Marshelline Purl

Milford-Haven Recipes

Mrs. Smith's (Cornelius's Mom)
Star Anise Star Cookies
(As adapted after Cornelius's Star Party)
Pre-heat oven to 350°

Ingredients:

2 T.	Star anise pieces OR ground dried star anise
½ c.	sugar
pinch	salt
5 T.	unsalted butter
2 T.	Balsamic vinegar
¼ c.	all-purpose flour

Preparation:
1. Line 2 large baking sheets with parchment paper.
2. (If not already ground) grind whole star anise pods until fine in coffee/spice grinder.
3. In heavy saucepan bring anise, sugar, butter and vinegar to boil, then stir one minute.
4. Stir in flour and salt until mixture is smooth.
5. Cool dough in refrigerator.
6. Measure ½ t. sections of dough, roll into balls, flatten, then press star-shaped cookie cutter into dough ball, removing excess dough from edges.

Cooking:
7. Bake cookies ten minutes, or until golden.
8. Remove from oven, and place cookies (still on parchment sheets) onto racks or counter to cool.

*Adapted from Penzeys Spices
** Star Anise is a star-shaped fruit from a small evergreen native to China. When dried and ground, it becomes a spice with a light licorice flavor.

Return soon to . . .
Milford-Haven!

Coming in 2013

Mara Purl's
Why Hearts Keep Secrets

Book Three
in the exciting Milford-Haven saga

Reserve Your Copy Now!
Info@BellekeepBooks.com

Here's an excerpt from the
Prologue . . .

Prologue

Senior Deputy Delmar Johnson had a date with a ghost. No matter how many times he denied the absurd notion, some unmistakable presence seemed to haunt him. Nervously, he glanced at the empty chair across the table from where he sat in the restaurant. A shiver ran down his spine. *Does it matter if my date is no longer among the living?*

He shook his head as though to clear away the tendrils of an eerie dream and force his mind into its usual, methodical approach to his cases. Though broadcast journalist Christine Christian's body had never turned up, a gnawing intuition told him the missing woman would never be found alive.

He'd made special arrangements with the missing reporter's former television station to gain access to her most recent broadcast tapes. Whatever stories she'd been working on at the time might provide some clues to her disappearance. At the very least, he'd get a sense of who she was. He'd picked up the tapes himself from KOST-TV, and they had to be returned in a timely fashion. But not before he gave them a thorough viewing. *Tonight's the night.*

Technically, he shouldn't be racking up overtime on a Sunday, but when a case wouldn't let him alone, he often found the best time to work was into the wee hours, when phones didn't ring and colleagues didn't interrupt. He justified his marginal breach of protocol by reassuring himself he was up to speed on all his other cases.

About a recent reprimand, however, he couldn't let himself off the hook so easily. Under orders from his supervisor Detective Rogers, Delmar had interviewed Mr. Joseph Calvin three months earlier. Calvin had been a friend of Ms. Christian, eventually concerned about her unexplained absence. Del had conducted the interview at Calvin's estate in Santa Barbara, but then also met Calvin in Santa Maria, allowing him to enter the premises of Chris Christian's condo. This, apparently, had been deemed inappropriate. And though nothing official had been inserted in Del's personnel jacket, the verbal admonition still stung.

Perhaps to distract himself—or maybe just to give himself something pleasant to offset the sour residue of the professional slap—Del had decided to have an early dinner at the Lighthouse Tavern. He'd only heard about it since moving here, but had no firsthand experience.

There were *real* lighthouses on the Central Coast: Point Conception in Santa Barbara to the south, Point Sur near Monterey farther north; and between the two, the Piedras

Blancas light just north of Milford-Haven—the closest local lighthouse, now automated and inaccessible to visitors.

He'd been curious as to why Milford-Haven had only this pseudo-light... realistic enough to fool the eye, but without the powerful beam that would be visible from the sea. So, after a long morning run and a session at the gym down in Morro Bay, he'd gone home to shower, shave and dress in some pressed chinos and a chocolate blazer. Then, out of uniform for once, he'd driven to the Tavern to introduce himself.

As he'd pulled into the parking lot, he'd been unsure whether he'd find a tourist trap or a quaint coastal gem. As it turned out, he liked Michael Owen. The owner looked him straight in the eye when he talked, and seemed devoted to the culinary craft, sharing details of the special he was preparing for this evening's menu. Owen was also apparently a successful businessman, as his restaurant had the reputation of drawing both tourists and locals.

Sipping wine at the bar that offered a view into the kitchen, Del asked about the history of the building, wondering why what appeared to be a real lighthouse was not being used as such. According to the story Michael recounted, if Aberthol Sayer—an entrepreneur from Milford Haven, Wales in the 1880s—had succeeded with his ambitious plan, the American Milford-Haven would've had its *own* lighthouse.

Sayer had moved to California in 1975, the successful owner of a small shipping firm. Taking stock of developments on the Central Coast, he couldn't help but notice what a bustling export center the Piedras peninsula had become for the region. Convinced that Milford-Haven's smaller point of land slightly farther south posed a treacherous landing point for fishermen, Sayer had believed that by having its own light, the area could develop a profitable fishing industry. He'd thus gone to the trouble and expense of having a defunct lighthouse on the coast of Wales dismantled and transported on one of his ships across the Atlantic, then cross-country by rail from New York to California.

Certain he'd receive the appropriate commission from the U.S. Lighthouse Board, which had been established in 1852, he'd reassembled the structure at Milford-Haven. He even had his public relations slogan ready to use: "The first lighthouse to shine on two oceans." But because he failed to receive the requisite approval, he was never allowed to install a working Fresnel in the tower. He did install a lesser light . . . but nothing bright enough to "confuse navigation," as the Board had admonished.

It turned out Sayer's light *did* shine brightly enough to attract visitors from *land*. Some hundred-plus years later, another enterprising man named Michael Owen had purchased the property with its enticing structure and turned it into the Lighthouse Tavern.

Now, as he waited for his check after an excellent meal, Del took a final sip of coffee and pressed the napkin to his lips. He turned his gaze again toward the restaurant's window to marvel again at the view—a sweep of coastal scenery that would have few equals . . . all the more spectacular at close of day, with sunset painting vivid streaks across low-hanging clouds.

After paying his bill and thanking Michael again, Del stepped outside into the March evening. The sun had sunk into the water, the sky overhead just beginning to deepen to a

Prussian blue. *Nice the days aren't quite as short as they were a few weeks ago.*

The signs of early spring were everywhere on the Central Coast. Rains were no longer the steady pummelings of winter, but had shifted to blustery, intermittent storms. Tiny buds dotted the deciduous trees, and just yesterday he'd seen rows of huge iceplant flowers blooming along the beach at the Cove. Now a faint trace of jasmine hung in the air like the perfume of a woman who'd passed by and disappeared. *Ironic that in this season of renewal, the life of a young woman has almost certainly been cut short.*

Del's SUV rumbled to life and he made the short drive down Highway 1 to his workplace, glancing at darkening sky where he could just see storm clouds hanging offshore. He suspected they'd soon overtake the coast just as his own looming depression about the case seemed certain to swamp his mood.

He parked his truck and, before locking it, lifted out the box of borrowed tapes. After climbing the stairs to the front entrance and unlocking the double-glass doors he stepped into the darkened offices shared by the North Coast branch of the County Sheriff's Department and the California Department of Forestry. His footsteps rang into the quiet hallways until he stepped into the conference room and fired up the television and VCR. After loading the first cassette he squinted in the flickering illumination from the video screen, doing his best to read the button designations of the VCR remote control.

He was hoping no one from Forestry had the same idea any time tonight . . . to use the conference room. It'd been a matter of economic necessity, placing the San Luis Obispo County Sheriff's off-site offices in shared space. The new building lacked the charm of the old-California stucco municipal structures, but Del had settled in comfortably, and—thanks to his computer expertise—enjoyed being regarded as the technical hot-shot.

At the moment, he wasn't so sure he deserved the title. He squinted again at the VCR. Certain he'd finally discerned the difference between Fast Forward and Search, he pressed something, and the blue screen sprang to life with the rapidly talking figure of a blond woman standing in a playground. Horizontal lines of static stood still as the figure raced through her story and Del struggled to find the Stop button.

Rewinding the tape, he started it again by hitting Play, deciding to be more patient with the opening designations. White letters on a field of royal blue read:

KOST-TV NEWS FILE
KOST SUNDAY NEWS MAGAZINE
REPORTER: CHRIS CHRISTIAN
ARCHIVE NUMBER: 0395749:0CC889A
SUBJECT: ADOPTION [THREE-PART SERIES]
SEGMENT ONE:
"WILL THIS LOVE LAST?:
IF I ADOPT THIS BABY WILL SHE BE MINE FOREVER?"

A second or two after the writing faded, Chris Christian appeared. Del gulped air, the sight of her animated form causing his breath to come in sudden jerks. *Nice of you to show up for our date . . . even if you are a ghost.*

Del hit the pause button. *Get a grip, man. This is a case, not a personal relationship!*

He hit Play again, willing himself to catalog the details of her appearance. *Blond hair, tan blazer, white blouse, black slacks.* Her flawless on-camera makeup seemed out of place outdoors, but her professional appearance and calm demeanor inspired confidence, and she spoke with authority.

While the camera lens pulled back to reveal a playground Chris advanced, clasping her hands, looking down, then up at the camera, all the while introducing the topic of her show. If Del remembered his broadcast terminology, this would be what they called the Teaser.

"Adoption," said Chris in her news-voice. "It's one of the most consuming interests among Americans today." She stepped toward a swing and sat carefully in its leather strap. "Approximately three thousand five hundred children are adopted annually in the United States, with the trend rising more than 80 percent since 1990, the year November was named National Adoption Month. And the rules have changed."

Del hit the Pause button again. Ghostly light reflected onto the slatted blinds. The image of the reporter—crisp, animated, and *alive*—disturbed him. To give himself a few seconds' break he glanced at the pale gray walls offset by black trim and looked up at the unilluminated bulbs that stared back like glassy, unseeing eyes. He turned back to the TV, hit Play and watched the screen as the camera zoomed in on Chris's face.

"Adoption used to be a private and irrevocable matter. If you, as a parent, gave up your child for adoption, you knew you would never see that child again. You also knew it would be better for the child not to suffer the confusion of meeting a parent he or she had never known.

"Each state has its own laws regarding adoption and, as a

general rule, records were not legally sealed but were kept strictly confidential by a 'gentlemen's agreement'—which would now be considered an antiquated euphemism.

"While in most cases it's still difficult to find missing parents—or a long-lost child—recently developed websites mean that frustrating searches now take weeks or months, rather than years, and the Internet is brimming with information concerning all aspects of adoption. No matter how valuable adoptive parents may have been in the life of a child, as a nation, we seem consumed with uncovering our biological connections.

"Tonight we take you on the first of a three-part journey into the mysteries and emotional turmoil of adoption. If you adopt a child, will it truly be yours forever?"

After a brief pause, and a flash of white letters reading INSERT COMMERCIAL A, the program resumed. "A child of five is taken one day from the only home she's ever known," said Chris's voice-over. Del watched the screen as a wailing child held her arms out, yelling, "Mommy! Daddy!" while the adoptive parents stood paralyzed, tears streaming down their faces. On the far side of a police car, the couple—apparently birthparents—stood waiting to reclaim the child they'd given up several years earlier.

Three more three-minute reports followed, interviews with both sets of parents, interviews with Child Service professionals, and a wrap-up by Chris. Pressing Rewind, Del sat in the darkened room, deeply affected by the raw emotion he'd just witnessed. *Everyone in the story had rights; but no one seemed to have achieved a happy ending.*

Del realized he was getting drawn into the story, losing track of his own goal, which was to research the reporter. *Must mean she's doing a good job*, he acknowledged. Determined to keep an objective perspective, he hit Play and began the tape again from the beginning. This time it was details he was after—not details of the story, but of the journalist and her surroundings. *That playground . . . Miller Street Elementary in Santa Maria? I can check the photo file. Makes sense—shooting the footage close to home.*

As the segment played through, he looked at the background, pausing the tape intermittently to jot down notes or to see if he recognized the face of a passerby. *But nothing seems remarkable. I need to take an inning stretch.* He ejected the tape and held it in his hands for a moment. *Who else did I see on this tape, and not recognize? Was it someone hiding in plain site who wished you harm?*

Del peered out the window of the still-darkened room, watching starlight dance on the shallow coastal waters. The scene failed to make its usual impression, as his mind was filled with images from the videotapes.

His reaction to Chris Christian's series was intellectual, true. Her intelligence and insight were impressive. The depth and honesty of her reports revealed a great deal about the emotional landscape of the nation and the increasingly complex web of society.

But he was aware that another reaction gripped him too—something visceral. He couldn't seem to disentangle any one part of his response and all of it roiled together through his gut like an undigested mass. *This reporter was doing good work before she disappeared.* The realization made him more determined than ever to find her, discover her fate.

Thin though it was, he'd come up with one possible connection, and that was the name "Clarke" written more than once in her diary. He'd found it jotted on a page from several months earlier, unfortunately not in connection with anything else. No appointment was written, and the name didn't show up in other notes she'd kept on pending articles. More recently, he'd seen it again, this time circled several times, as though she'd been on the phone doodling or had realized something and decided to pursue it.

With its less-usual spelling, the name "Clarke" had been easy to find in the Central Coast directory. Clarke Shipping was located in Morro Bay. *Doesn't mean this is the right Clarke, but it's a place to start. I could head over there during my lunch hour.* Presumably few people would be at their desks. With any luck, he'd find a receptionist or secretary who might say something to him that might not be said with bosses looking on.

What trail was Chris following, and where did it lead her? Del knew from reviewing her work schedule that she was a "roving" reporter, often out of town for several days on a story. She'd also racked up plenty of overtime and had vacation days coming. These elements—plus the facts that no family members had filed a Missing Persons report and no body had turned up—conspired to keep her case sidelined. As a member of Special Problems Unit, Del had inherited the case. He was now sufficiently intrigued that he knew he wouldn't have had to be assigned this case; he'd have *asked* for it.

COLOPHON

This book is set in the Cambria font, released in 2004 by Microsoft, as a formal, solid font to be equally readable in print and on screens. It was designed by Jelle Bosma, Steve Matteson, and Robin Nicholas.

The name Cambria is the classical name for Wales, the Latin form of the Welsh name for Wales, *Cymru*. The etymology of *Cynru* is *combrog,* meaning "compatriot."

The California town of Cambria is named for its resemblance to the south-western coast of Wales, where the town of Milford Haven has existed since before ancient Roman times, and is mentioned in William Shakespeare's *Cymbeline.*

The dingbat is the Placuna shell, drawn by artist Mary Helsaple, and rendered graphically by cover designer Kevin Meyer. The placuna is a marine bivalve with a large, thin flat translucent shell, often found in Philippine, Malaysian and Indian coastal waters.

The placuna is also known as the windowpane oyster, and was chosen as the icon for this book because of its resemblance to a lens or magnifier.

LIGHTHOUSE

1931

Each of the *Milford-Haven Novels* features a real lighthouse. The Point Vicente lighthouse is a Southern California jewel, both for its visual beauty and as a life-saving aid to navigation through a treacherous stretch of coastline.

Located in Los Angeles, at the end of the Palos Verdes peninsula, the point of land was named in 1790 by explorer Captain George Vancouver in honor of Friar Vicente of the Mission Buenaventura. Following several maritime disasters, the U.S. Lighthouse Service commissioned the Point Vicente lighthouse in 1926.

The 67-foot high tower is perched on a cliff, resulting in a light source that, from its185 feet above sea level, can be seen 20 miles at sea. This is the brightest beacon in Southern California, with a 1000-watt bulb focused through a 5-foot Fresnel. The lens itself, crafted in Paris in 1886, shone for forty years in Alaska before being moved.

The lighthouse was manned by civilian lighthouse keepers until 1939, when the U.S. Coast Guard took over its maintenance and operation, automating it in 1973. In 1979 the lighthouse was added to the National Registry of Historic Sites. Its electronic sensors and automated controls still assist mariners today.

The Coast Guard Auxiliary now performs search and rescue duties, teaches boating safety classes, flies aircraft patrols and maintains a radio communications network.

Point Vicente is open to the public the second Saturday of each month and is well worth a visit. Junior Coast Guard trainees act as guides who will gladly escort you up to the very top of the lighthouse where both the operating Fresnel and a spectacular view of the coast are visible. To find out more of its rich history or to plan your trip, go to www.PalosVerdes.com/PVLight.

While the geographical and technical elements of this lighthouse are accurate in my series, since this novel is set in 1996, many new programs exist now that did not exist then.

Secret of the Shells

Special Messages about a Woman and Her Self, and about Discovering the Next Chapter . . . of Her Life

🐚 Shell 2: Where Your Heart Lives

- Do you have a deep sense of belonging where you live? Or do you often picture yourself living somewhere else? In choosing your present location, did you mostly consult a *logical* list (proximity to work; access to services; no stairs)? Or did you also consider how the location makes you *feel?*

- What would you do if your intuition told you to move? Would you dismiss this as "illogical"? Would you try asking yourself why you'd begun to have these feelings?

- There are many expressions that describe a journey using the word "heart." Examples are *the path with heart, follow your heart,* and *the way of the heart.* What do you think these mean? Where might they lead you?

- Imagine your life as a map drawn only with logic and intelligent planning. Draw this map with a starting point and important goals as specific destinations, using the most direct routes and the fewest detours. Make this map as well-engineered as you can.

- Now imagine your life as a map drawn only with feelings and desires. Draw this map (or paint it, or collage it) with its starting point at the center of the page, and with icons that represent major desires appearing in your imaginary landscape as hills and lakes, mountains and valleys, boulders and gardens. Make this map as beautiful as you can.

- Create a third map that includes elements from both your *head* map and your *heart* map. Include icons that represent past, present, and future events; people; desires and goals. Post this "Life Map" in a place where you can see regularly it. Re-map sections as you get new inspiration. Where are you on your map?

To discover more about the Secrets of the Shells
visit www.MaraPurl.com.
To join the author's blog
visit www.MaraPurl.WordPress.com.
Visit Mara's "Map Your Life" board on www.Pinterest.com.
To reach the author, by e-mail: MaraPurl@MaraPurl.com.
by mail: Mara Purl c/o Milford-Haven Enterprises
PO Box 7304-629
North Hollywood, CA 91603

Where the Heart Lives

Reading Group Topics for Discussion

1. Characters in this novel drive throughout southern California using every kind of road, from eight-lane freeways in Los Angeles, to the meanderings of coastal Highway 1, to Main Street in Milford-Haven. Is home for you a major city or a small town? Do you return home from road trips with a different perspective?

2. How does Samantha use her journal-writing? To a) gain perspective; b) track her research notes; c) allow her deeper thoughts to surface? How might you find your own journal writing useful?

3. What really happened to journalist Chris Christian? Is it her fault, or is she a heroine? Is Deputy Del Johnson doing a good job investigating her disappearance? Is Del accepted as a local? To what extent does his race influence public opinion of him?

4. Do relationships make us more complete? Or are we already complete, and we bring this quality to a relationship? Would you choose a life partner with your head or with your heart? Why?

5. Do you attend concerts? What do you think happens to people living in the world of popular music? What role does music play in your life? If you had a chance to go backstage, would you?

6. Why do people stay in abusive relationships? Is there an essential difference between emotional and physical abuse? Why does Stacey stay with Wilhelm?

7. Do you know family or friends who are Vietnam veterans? How are they treated today? Do their issues apply to other wars?

8. How are the ideas of maps and mapping expressed in this book? If you were to create an emotional "map" of your life, what would be the key landmarks? Where would the road be straight and easy? Where would it be winding and difficult?

9. In addition to being a writer, Mara Purl was also an actress on *Days of Our Lives*. As a performer, Mara worked from the point of view of her character. As a writer, does Mara drive her novels by plot or by characters?

10. Why is this book called *Where the Heart Lives?* Does this phrase apply primarily to Miranda's move to Milford-Haven? Or to Samantha's quest for her son? Or to Sally and her connection to her past and her move to California? How important is the "where" of your life . . . a) physically and b) spiritually?

To share or print these discussion points please visit:
http://www.BellekeepBooks.com

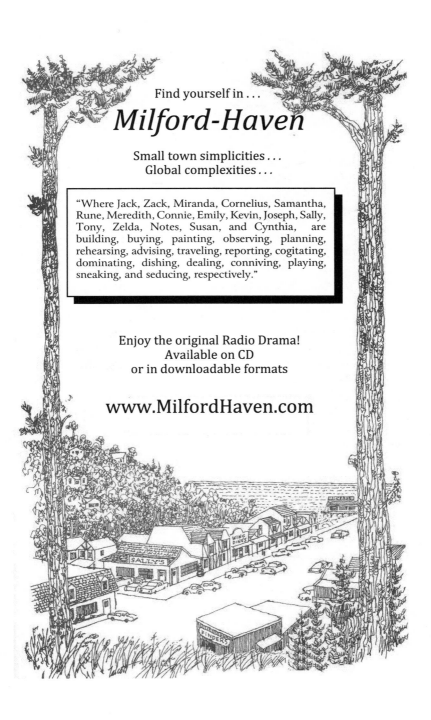

Find yourself in . . .

Milford-Haven

Small town simplicities . . .
Global complexities . . .

"Where Jack, Zack, Miranda, Cornelius, Samantha, Rune, Meredith, Connie, Emily, Kevin, Joseph, Sally, Tony, Zelda, Notes, Susan, and Cynthia, are building, buying, painting, observing, planning, rehearsing, advising, traveling, reporting, cogitating, dominating, dishing, dealing, conniving, playing, sneaking, and seducing, respectively."

Enjoy the original Radio Drama!
Available on CD
or in downloadable formats

www.MilfordHaven.com

Mara Purl, author of the best-selling and critically acclaimed *Milford-Haven Novels* and *Milford-Haven Stories*, pioneered small-town fiction for women.

Mara's beloved fictitious town has been delighting international audiences since 1992, when it first appeared as *Milford-Haven, U.S.A.©*— the first American radio drama ever licensed and broadcast by the BBC. The show reached an audience of 4.5 million listeners in the U.K. In the U.S., it was the 1994 Finalist for the New York Festivals World's Best Radio Programs.

What the Heart Knows (Book One) is an Amazon best-seller (ranked #5), won the Indie Excellence Award and was Finalist for the Book Of the Year Award. *When Hummers Dream* (Amazon best-selling prequel short story to Book One) was nominated for the Global E-Book award. In addition, early editions of Mara's novels have won fifteen finalist and gold literary awards.

Mara's other writing credits include plays, screenplays, scripts for *Guiding Light*, cover stories for *Rolling Stone*, staff writing with the *Financial Times (of London)*, and the Associated Press. She is the co-author (with Erin Gray) of *Act Right: A Manual for the On-Camera Actor*.

As an actress, Mara was "Darla Cook" on *Days Of Our Lives*. For the one-woman show *Mary Shelley: In Her Own Words*, which Mara performs and co-wrote (with Sydney Swire), she earned a Peak Award. She was named one of twelve Women of the Year by the Los Angeles County Commission for Women.

Mara is married to Dr. Larry Norfleet and lives in Los Angeles, and in Colorado Springs.

Visit her website at www.MaraPurl.com and subscribe to her blog at www.MaraPurl.WordPress.com. She welcomes e-mail from readers at MaraPurl@MaraPurl.com.